BEAUTIFULLY
MESSY

BEAUTIFULLY MESSY

a novel

NOELLE EVERLY

Cover design by: Raina Tinker

Cover image by: Jason Mavrommatis

Editing by: Kimberly Roberto

READER NOTE

Content Warning: This novel contains discussions of suicide and domestic violence (neither is shown on page). Explicit language and sexual content appear throughout. Chapter twenty-two includes a scene where sexual violence is threatened but not carried out. Readers sensitive to these topics should proceed with caution.

PROLOGUE

The tests sit on the counter, eight pink lines, merciless in their clarity.

I press the heel of my palm to my chest, trying to slow the panic gathering there, but my breath comes in short, shallow bursts. Too fast. Too tight. The bathroom feels smaller with each inhale. Cold tiles bite into my knees as I collapse, pressing my head between my knees to keep sobs from escaping. They rip free anyway. I should be excited. This should mark the beginning of everything I've dreamed of.

Instead, I feel the weight of a thousand choices collapsing onto my shoulders. I close my eyes, and I'm ten again, alone on Christmas morning with the same hollow ache spreading through my chest.

I stare at the presents under the perfect tree as the clock chimes eight. I've been up since five, but I'm not allowed to open anything until my parents come downstairs. That's my rule, not theirs. One of the only rules I cling to on the rare days when I can hope they'll see me: Christmas and my birthday.

They can't miss those... right?

Sunlight spills across the formal living room, catching on the golden ornaments arranged in the decorator's vision of "tasteful elegance." My handmade school ornaments don't match; they're banished to the little tree in my room.

Best kept out of sight, like me.

Madame Rousseau finds me still sitting in the same spot at nine, back stiff, fingers tracing invisible patterns on the rug, humming Christmas carols to myself.

"Ma petite." Her French accent wraps around me like one of the warm scarves she always wears. "Your parents were at the Hendersons' party late. They'll be down later. Shall we have some breakfast?"

"How much longer do you think?" I ask, twisting the end of my braid around my finger.

Something flashes across her face—a quick crease between her eyebrows, there and gone. "I cannot say, Sydney. A few hours. Maybe more..."

I nod because I know what that means. I'm ten, not stupid.

Her hand squeezes my shoulder. "Tu es une fille courageuse." You are a brave girl.

But I don't feel brave. I feel invisible.

"And brave girls," she says, "deserve a present they can open now." From behind her back, she produces a small box wrapped in bright, cheerful paper.

A tear escapes before I can stop it. I wipe it, turning toward the window so she doesn't see. Don't show anyone you care, my father always says.

"Merci, ma Nounou."

My fingers tremble as I peel back the wrapping. Inside is a copy of Little Women, the cover elegant, its pages waiting to be read. I press it to my chest. "I love it. May I start reading now?"

"Of course, ma chérie."

I curl into the window seat and disappear into the March family's Christmas. Their poverty doesn't matter. Their house is noisy and warm, full of sisters who fight, love, and dream big. I can almost smell the cinnamon and pine, see the fire dancing in the hearth. I imagine I'm right there, sitting among the sisters, listening to Marmee read the letter from their Father. I pull my knees to my chest. My throat does that tight, scratchy thing like I'm about to cry—but I won't. The clock chimes eleven, and I turn another page.

Grief has a way of looping back, stitching old pain into new moments. Steeling myself, I push up from the bathroom floor. I know what I have to do.

The only choice I have.

2009

She chose the gentle slope
over the uncertain climb, calling it wisdom.

one

CRISP WINTER AIR CUTS through the open car doors, sharp enough to make my breath visible in small puffs. I pull my coat tighter, the soft wool a barrier against more than the cold. I'm twenty-six, and this is my first real family Christmas.

The Wallis family cabin rises from the snow-covered forest. The large wooden house is far grander than the quaint retreat I'd imagined, though even from here I can tell it bears no resemblance to the cold McMansion of my childhood. Candles line every window; a wreath hangs against the wood with its bright, cheerful red ribbon. A plastic Santa with reindeer stands guard out front, faded from years of devoted service.

I might not know much about a family Christmas, but I'm a pro at faking my way through anything. Shoulders squared, smile plastered, one deep breath. I know how to play a role. Perform. The one thing my parents taught me well.

"Ready?" Mason squeezes my arm, giving me that smile—the one he believes is charming.

His over-styled blond hair gleams, Oxford perfectly pressed. Picture perfect as always. I had planned to break up with him. We'd never been serious. But then the invitation to spend Christmas with his family came.

How could I refuse?

Before we take two steps, a whirlwind of curls and energy comes flying out of the house. "Sorry if you're not a hugger, but I am," says the tiny force of nature, already wrapped around me.

"Jules, give her a second to breathe." Mason steps between us, as if he's uncomfortable with how easily his sister has claimed me.

"I'm fine, Mason." I hold up a hand to stop him, then lift an eyebrow at Jules, sensing a kindred spirit. "Are you always this friendly, or did someone spike your coffee?"

She laughs and loops her arm through mine. "Come on. Let's get you inside before you freeze to death, and I have to explain to my mom why the pretty one got hypothermia."

Inside is even more incredible. The home feels plucked from a Hallmark movie. Holly winds around the staircase railing, and mistletoe dangles from the ceiling. Floor-to-ceiling windows showcase the snowy mountain range beyond.

But it's the Christmas tree that stops me mid-step.

Towering in the center of the room, it glows with bright, colorful lights. Branches sag under the weight of homemade treasures: construction-paper snowflakes gone soft with age, hand-painted macaroni shaped into angels, grade-school projects preserved and displayed year after year.

Ornaments that most parents proudly treasure.

"Mom, Dad!" Jules shouts. "Mason and Sydney are here!"

A couple walks hand in hand from the kitchen, silver streaking through their blond hair. Gentle lines frame their eyes, softened by wide grins. A petite teenage girl follows.

"Syd, this is my mom, Margaret, and my dad, Gary," Mason says warmly. "You've met Jules already. And this youngster is Ivy."

Before I can decide if a handshake or friendly wave is appropriate, Margaret steps forward and pulls me into a warm embrace. "We're so glad you're here, Sydney. If there's anything special you do during the holidays, let us know. We'd love to include it."

Pretty sure my childhood holiday traditions aren't what she's hoping for.

"Your home is so lovely, Mrs. Wallis. Thank you for inviting me."

"Mrs. Wallis is my mother-in-law. Call me Margaret, and this is Gary. We're not big on formalities." She squeezes my arm and gives me a genuine, unfiltered smile.

Something tight in my chest begins to loosen as I take in their unguarded faces and the way this beautiful, lived-in home breathes with life. I spent a lifetime dreaming of what Christmas with a family could be, and this seems almost too good to believe. Tears threaten to spill, but I blink them away and settle onto the massive sectional with Mason and his sisters as Margaret outlines the holiday week: a Dickens Festival, hot cocoa bars, shopping in town, family dinners, Christmas movies, and skiing.

"Mom, can't you back off? I want to relax, not have every hour of every day planned out," Mason whines.

"Ouch, Mase." Jules punches him playfully in the shoulder. "Don't worry, Mom. We can leave him behind. It's more fun without him."

I wait for their reaction, for them to insist their son participate. Margaret's face tightens, and Gary rubs his hand over his jaw. But neither speaks.

"What do you think, Syd? You in?" Jules turns her inviting amber eyes on me.

"Hot cocoa and Dickens? I wouldn't miss it." I open my coat to reveal my ugly Christmas sweater. It was a risk, but Jules's boisterous laugh unknots my worry.

"I knew I'd like you." She lifts her pant leg to reveal a hideous Christmas sock. "Got a pair for you when Mason said you were coming." She reaches behind the couch and tosses them to me.

Ivy perches on the arm of the sofa. Home from her first semester of college, she looks ethereal in her bohemian dress and mane of wild curls. She watches me, quiet and cautious, wary of my judgment.

"You want these?" I hold up the socks.

She lifts the hem of her dress as Margaret does the same, exposing matching sets. Laughter ripples around the room as I pull the socks onto my feet.

I've got this. Everyone's laughing. Smiling. So far, so good.

Mason, true to his word, stays behind. As we bundle up in coats and scarves, he settles deeper into the sectional, remote in one hand, beer in the other. "Have fun with the tourist trap stuff," he calls as we head out. His family barely notices.

The village has been turned into a magical Dickens scene.

Actors dressed as characters from *A Christmas Carol* line the streets, greeting us and speaking in period-specific dialect, adding to the charm of the inviting town. Small mom-and-pop shops are decked for the holidays. Ebenezer Scrooge ladles hot chocolate to a growing crowd in the town square.

Jules and I peel away and find ourselves in the local bookshop, tucked between a candle store and a boutique. A miniature locomotive puffs around a winter wonderland in the front window. Santa's village is complete with tiny workshops and figurines. Elves no bigger than my thumb carry presents, while reindeer wait patiently beside a sleigh dusted with artificial snow. It's whimsical, ridiculous, and I absolutely love it.

"Do they set up this train every year?" I ask Jules, not bothering to hide my delight.

She crouches beside me. "They change the display yearly, but the train is always part of it. I've seen it go from a beachy Santa vibe to an epic gingerbread house village. Last year, it was *Madagascar*. Come on. Let me show you the rest."

Soft instrumental carols drift through the store, layered with the faint chug of the toy train and the gentle hum of conversation. I trail my fingers along the bookshelves, where sprigs of holly nestle between titles. Holiday books are prominently displayed, with quirky, handwritten staff picks beneath. The air smells of cloves, orange peel, and that magical blend of ink and paper.

This is my version of heaven.

Books line every inch, from the bright, open children's section to the darker, quieter shelves in the back. We reach the furthest corner of the shop with thrillers on one side, romances on the other. Jules and I turn, each drawn to our respective shelves.

"I'm glad to see you don't have the same aversion to books as my brother," Jules says.

"While I plan to be a boring corporate lawyer, I love nothing more than reading. I'm partial to thrillers. The darker the better."

"Ah, well, Miss Boring Corporate Lawyer, what's your take on romance novels?"

She thrusts an open book into my hands. After scanning a particularly steamy passage, I snap the book shut and laugh. "Damn, I need a cold shower. I always thought those books were all angst, bare-chested men, and busty ladies."

"Oh, girl, that was nothing. I'll introduce you to some of my favorites."

I open the book again. The scene where the heroine meets a stranger in a bar sparks a memory, and a small smile tugs at my lips.

Jules squints at me. "Okay, what was that look?"

"What look?" I flutter my lashes, feigning innocence.

"The I'm-remembering-something-deliciously-inappropriate smirk. Did my uptight brother actually do something scandalous?"

There's something disarming about Jules. Maybe it's the way she asks questions with the certainty that she'll love the answers, whatever they are. I find myself wanting to share rather than retreat.

"Well... Mason and I didn't exactly meet in the library."

She's practically bouncing on her toes. "Ohhh, do tell."

I look around to make sure others can't overhear. "It was at a bar near Capitol Hill." The memory pulls me back...

It was one of those swampy D.C. nights when the heat clings to your skin and even your bones feel damp. Rachel, another summer associate, dragged me to some sleek Capitol Hill hotspot after a brutal week. The place was packed with suits too expensive for interns, sipping cocktails priced to ensure exclusivity.

"Try to have fun," Rachel said. "Maybe smile and try not to scare every guy off."

I slid onto a stool, ordered a vodka soda, and pulled out my phone—my shield of choice—and began scrolling, internally noting what I still needed to finish up at home.

A man leaned in, a hint of whiskey on his breath. "Did that scowl come with the suit, or was it a separate purchase?"

I turned to see a guy with an expensive watch, rolled sleeves, and a smile born of never hearing the word no. I should have been annoyed, but the audacity made me smile.

"Let me guess... hedge fund?"

He laughed, unfazed. "Lawyer. Mason."

"Sydney. It's only 9. How'd you escape the office already?"

"So you're a first-year associate too?"

"No, summer associate, finishing my last year at Georgetown. I'm not looking to be picked up, so maybe shoot your shot elsewhere."

"Who said anything about picking you up? Maybe I just wanted to talk to the most beautiful woman in the room." He flashed a game-show-host grin, showing perfect white teeth.

I wish I could say my stomach fluttered or something, but mostly I noticed how put-together he was. I wanted to see if I could ruffle him.

"Did my resting bitch face not scare you off?"

"Not in the slightest." He leaned in closer. "Everyone else here looks desperate to be seen. You? You look like you'd rather disappear. It's refreshing."

I rolled my eyes, but he wasn't off-base either. Maybe there was more to him than his golden-boy energy?

"Sydney!" Jules snaps me back. "You totally spaced. What happened next?"

I blush. "Let's say one drink turned into three, and I ended up at his place."

"You slept with him on the first night? I love this. Mason always acts like such a Boy Scout."

"Hmmm. Maybe in some areas." I say, dry as toast. "But that night? He was all cocky-get-his-way Mason."

"So it started as a hookup?"

"We both said we weren't looking for anything serious. Just..."

"Sex?" Jules teases.

"But he called the next day, and the day after. And here we are, six months later."

"Meeting the family, decidedly more than a hookup. Did Mason at least warn you what you were walking into?"

She's so earnest, I can't resist answering. "Not really. He just said his family had a cabin and asked if I wanted to come since I didn't have other plans."

She looks at me thoughtfully, and asks, "And now that you've seen us in action?"

"Now I get why he wanted me to meet you all."

The Wallises are what I used to imagine when I was little, sitting alone by the Christmas tree. They're loud, messy, and affectionate; the kind of family people write novels about.

The kind I used to pretend was mine.

"Come on." Jules loops her arm through mine. "You have to try the hot chocolate, and I'll tell you all the delicious details about my boyfriend, Tom. He's on call today, but he'll be here tomorrow."

We easily find the others and enjoy the world's best hot chocolate. Everyone laughs when whipped cream clings to Gary's nose. Margaret smiles as Ivy lifts her camera to capture Jules and me walking arm-in-arm. With holiday music drifting through the air and laughter on our lips, I can't remember a more perfect afternoon.

The sun drifts behind the mountain, and everything softens, wrapping the streets in golden light. How much have I missed without having a family like the Wallises? And just how far am I willing to go so I don't lose it?

***

ONCE THE LAUGHTER FROM dinner fades and the others scatter, I remain in the kitchen with Margaret. She sifts flour into a wooden bowl, preparing pastry dough with practiced movements.

"Have you made cinnamon rolls before?" she asks, her voice warm with invitation.

"I'm afraid my baking skills don't go much further than a box of brownie mix." I look away, embarrassed by the contrast.

"Well, there's a first time for everything. Grab that apron, and I'll show you." Her smile deepens, softening the lines around her eyes. "My mother passed down this recipe."

As we mix and knead, the air fills with the scent of cinnamon and rising yeast. Margaret shares stories from when her kids were young. There's Ivy pulling pranks on her older siblings, squabbles over game pieces, a frosting disaster involving Jules and a dog.

Tiny details only a fully present mother would remember.

But it's Margaret's voice that transforms the space into something sacred. She reminds me of Marmee from *Little Women,* the mother I used to lie in bed dreaming was downstairs waiting for me.

Before I can stop them, memories slip past the careful walls I've spent years constructing. Dinners alone while my parents attended galas. Being trotted out: "Recite this poem in French. Curtsy prettily." Ice skating competitions where Madame Rousseau sat in the stands.

And the ache of their deaths. Those I don't touch.

Standing in this kitchen, steeped in decades of family love, I feel like an imposter, trespassing in someone else's story.

"Excuse me," I mumble, rushing away and hoping I can escape before any tears spill.

A hand catches my arm before I reach the stairs.

"Syd, why'd you rush out?" Mason's blue eyes search mine, but rather than concern, I see them narrow. His sharp tone can't hide his annoyance at my sudden departure from the conversation with his mom.

"I just... something got in my eye," I lie.

Mason doesn't know about my childhood. Some instinct says he wouldn't know what to do with the mess. He doesn't ask, so I don't share.

He accepts my answer, doesn't read into the hesitation, and nuzzles his mouth into the curve of my neck. "You know where you're standing?"

Mistletoe.

He kisses me, soft and sweet. "It means a lot to me that you came. I'm sorry I haven't been around much. I'm used to doing my own thing when I'm here."

Truth is, I hadn't even noticed his absence. Instead of admitting that, I say, "Your family is incredible."

"Yeah, they are. I was hoping this week might give us space to think about the future," he murmurs, and kisses me again. "I hope this is the first of many Christmases you spend with us."

It's pleasant, this slow kiss. Usually, kissing him is a means to an end, but this one lingers, like he can kiss me into believing what he's asking. Last week, even yesterday, hearing him talk about *our* future would have made me run for the mountains. Marriage and kids have never been on my radar. Something my childhood taught me only led to disappointment. But after spending a day surrounded by his family, a future with them included doesn't sound so bad.

"I might hold you to that," I say, even surprising myself.

He smiles, studying my face as he might red-line a contract.

"You should fix your makeup. Your mascara's smudged." His thumb brushes beneath my eye, the gesture affectionate. Until he adds, "First impressions matter, after all. You don't want to look like a mess in front of my mom."

The urge to bite back hits quickly, but I swallow it down as I was trained to do and trudge up the stairs. I should feel hurt, but it's nothing new to me. I'm used to remarks wrapped in concern, disguised as help. My parents specialized in that kind of affection.

Twisted as it sounds, part of me used to welcome it because in those moments, at least I knew they saw me.

This relationship with Mason isn't perfect, nor is it some grand romance. But I'm not searching for someone to sweep me into a fairytale or put stars in my eyes. My parents cured me of wanting such love. The kind that can crush you when it's gone.

Mason is a safe bet. Any lawyer would call him a solid deal. He's convenient, and honestly, someone I can live without. But this family? This family... changes everything.

2019

She tasted freedom on her tongue,
felt her heart remember its own song,
then the familiar gilded cage locked
and silenced her at the edge.

TWO

"UNCLE MASON, AUNT SYD is under the mistletoe!" Leo and Beck, Jules's six-year-old twins, come crashing by, all limbs and energy.

Mason either doesn't hear them over the roar of the football game or chooses not to.

No surprise there. Sweet mistletoe kisses are a thing of the past.

Ten Christmases in this cabin. A decade of laughter, of winter mornings spent drinking coffee with the scent of Margaret's baking wafting from the kitchen, snow piling high outside while the fire roars in the hearth. Noisy, family-filled holidays that I could only ever imagine as a child.

The familiar scene unfolds like a well-loved story.

Jules and Margaret stand side by side in the kitchen, laughter bubbling between the sizzle of butter and clang of pots. In the family room, the men huddle around the TV, Mason among them. His feet propped, eyes glued to the screen. The twins weave between them, more interested in snacks than football. Bell, the family's golden retriever, roams the chaos.

This is the holiday I used to dream about as a kid. And the reason why I'm still here.

"Oh, come on, Reynolds! Throw the ball!" Mason yells at the screen.

"Who's Reynolds?" Beck asks.

Without looking away from the game, Mason replies, "New quarterback for San Francisco."

"Uncle Mason, will you play Mario Kart with us later?" Leo looks up with hopeful eyes before tossing a small football to his brother.

Mason doesn't even shift. "I'm not into video games, guys. Why don't you sit and watch the game with us?"

But the twins are off, chasing the next adventure and leaving Mason and his dismissal behind.

My hand tightens around the banister as my eyes close and I breathe in the scents of rosemary and browning butter floating from the kitchen, willing them to settle the pit in my stomach.

This is fine. I'm *fine*.

"Syd?" Jules calls, and I open my eyes. She's watching me from the kitchen, jaw set tight. "You good?"

I take a deep breath. "Yep, I'm fine." The words come out automatically, a reflex I mastered as a little girl.

She studies me but doesn't press. "Mom and I were chatting about books. Have you read Jennifer Hartmann's *Still Beating*?"

"I haven't. Is it another of your gushy romances?"

"Hardly. It's right up your alley. A man abducts a woman and her sister's fiancé. Forces them to witness, honestly, the worst. But through it, they develop this intense bond. Fuck, it's so good. You have to read it."

Mason strolls in, catching the tail end of her description. He gives me a quick arm squeeze. His usual I've-got-this signal. "Why the hell would anyone want to read that? Sounds disgusting."

"Please, Mason, tell us what you think." Jules rolls her eyes.

His smug face and pompous, holier-than-thou tone grate on my last nerve. The words spill out before I can stop them. "You do realize that not everyone grows up in a fairy tale? Stories like that matter. They show what it means to crawl through hell and find something on the other side."

"If you want to see people suffer, watch the news."

I take a slow breath, trying not to bite, trying not to think about my hell, my childhood I crawled through. But Jules beats me to it.

"The book is ultimately a love story. Just not the neat kind where people fall in love and ride off into the sunset. Love can be complicated, overwhelming, and even show up at the worst possible time. It can happen with the entirely wrong person. It's not always sweet or safe. Sometimes it's messy and painful."

His blue eyes go distant for a beat as if considering Jules's words. Maybe we're about to have a real conversation. One with depth, for once.

"Is love code for sex in your novels?" His face lifts in triumph. "Anyway, I'm going to finish watching the game. Something real."

The momentary hope deflates, as it always does. Ten years together, and his emotional depth is still that of a puddle.

Right, why bother with a real conversation when a game is on?

I step back, catching myself on the counter as a wave of dizziness hits. Shaking it off, I turn to Margaret, who's been watching the back and forth with a furrow between her brows. "Do I have time for a quick run before dinner?"

"It's freezing outside," Mason interjects. "Why don't you run on the treadmill?"

Margaret studies me with unreadable eyes before speaking in her soft, lilting voice: "We've got at least an hour, Sydney. You'll be fine. Have a good run."

I don't wait for more opinions, least of all my husband's. In our bedroom, I strip off my sweater and jeans, trade them for thermal leggings, a long-sleeved shirt, and a thick jacket. Layer by layer, I shed the version of me that has to smile, to smooth things over. Out there, I can just be. A runner. Alone with breath and motion. I pop my phone in my Koala Clip and grab my headlamp.

Outside, the cold slaps me awake. My watch says fifteen degrees.

Perfect.

The night is clear and crisp, stinging the inside of my nose with each inhale. My feet find their cadence quickly, crunching over the road as the world narrows with each step. The burn in my quadriceps as I push up the first incline. The way the dying light filters through pine boughs, casting long shadows across untouched snow.

At the ridge overlooking the valley, I pause, hands on my hips, chest heaving from the climb. Below, the village glows. Above, stars blink into the black velvet sky.

This moment, alone with the mountains and sky, feels more intimate than anything Mason and I have ever shared. I had convinced myself, for a long while, that what we had was enough, and maybe it was then. I remember standing in that bathroom, rationalizing away how it's safer to settle. The family I wanted was within reach; all I had to do was grab hold of it. I didn't need an earth-shattering connection; all that led to was hurt and heartbreak. I mean, look at my mother.

But something's shifted.

Maybe it's age. Or perhaps it's the quiet, nagging realization that when it's Mason and me in D.C., the silence stretches. Far too reminiscent of my childhood home.

Or maybe it's realizing the word I always use to describe my life.

Fine.

The same word I used in childhood.

It's fine that Mom and Dad left for a trip without saying goodbye. Sending me to boarding school in France? Fine. Missing my birthday, fine.

Fine is the lie I wrapped around my loneliness like armor.

My stride lengthens as I find my rhythm, that floating sensation when running becomes flying. The one thing I haven't sacrificed or negotiated away.

The cabin comes into view. Candles line each window, and smoke curls from the chimney. The scene inside has probably changed little while I've been out. A picture of a life I thought I wanted.

I check my watch, just enough time to shower and reassemble my mask.

Tomorrow I'll run farther. Push harder. Find that edge where there's nothing but the burn in my lungs and the strength in my legs. Where I can outrun everything, including the gnawing awareness that maybe *fine* isn't what I want from life anymore.

***

WHEN DINNER WRAPS UP, my nephews bolt for their devices, thrilled to have free rein. Gary and Margaret settle on the sectional, queuing up a movie as they wait for Ivy and her boyfriend to arrive. Tom and Mason remain at the table, dissecting the earlier football game.

"Come on, let's escape to the deck." Jules grabs my hand.

The deck stretches the full length of the house, overlooking a forest dusted in snow. Mount Mansfield rises in the distance as moonlight reflects off crystallized treetops. The sky is unmoving, as if the world has gone still long enough to let something inside me unravel. No wind. No distractions. Only the quiet weight of something I haven't wanted to name pressing behind my ribs.

"You okay?" Jules asks, curling up in a throw blanket. A cozy interrogator ready to dig in. "And spare me the 'I'm *fine*' routine. You've been off since you walked through the door yesterday."

"It's just..."

The words snag somewhere between my chest and throat. Jules feels closer than family, but I've never told her the whole truth about Mason and me.

She leans forward. Her usual spark, bold and unfiltered, is softer now as if she senses what's sitting beneath the surface.

"Sometimes I... we're so different, Jules."

"You don't need to hold back, Syd. Talk to me."

"Do you really want to hear this? I don't want to make things uncomfortable. He's your brother, after all, and I'm only a sister by marriage." I let out a hollow, bitter laugh.

"Fuck him. You're my sister. Period. Talk."

Her amber eyes, the color of whiskey, flare to life. Like the drink itself, her gaze always loosens my tongue.

"In D.C., we're so busy it's easy to ignore the... disconnect. But here..." I pause, grasping for the right words. "Here, the country air clears away the fog, and I see everything clearly."

She looks at me in that way she has, reading between the lines of what I don't say. Her voice comes out soft, the tone you'd use not to frighten an animal. "Are you happy?"

The word *no* rises in my throat, immediate and unrelenting.

The truth I've spent a decade avoiding. Ten years of looking in the mirror, trying to convince myself that I'm fine. Ten years of watching Tom and Jules. Margaret and Gary. Seeing real intimacy, a connection that isn't easily explained, and it's a problem I didn't even realize I had until I saw it so plainly.

Something I told myself my life was better without.

A cold shudder rolls through my body. I'm thirty-six years old and sometimes as lonely as I was as a ten-year-old. But I can't answer her question because if I say it out loud, I'd have to do something about it.

Instead, I say, "You know our relationship is different from yours and Tom's."

She doesn't hesitate. "I might be an OB, but it doesn't take a therapist's license to see that."

I laugh dryly, tipping my head toward the stars. Once, I used to make wishes on them, believing the universe would save me. Now I know better. I watch, waiting for the next one to burn out.

A blast of cold air whips through the deck, cutting against any exposed skin. I gasp and move my chair closer to the flames. A storm is brewing.

"Fuck, that was cold." Jules wraps her blanket tighter. "Do you want to keep talking about this, or should I distract you with some gossip about the hot guy Ivy's bringing?"

"The latter, please." I swallow down my unease for another day.

"He's seriously hot. I'm talking Greek-god-meets-Roman-sculpture hot. And that's before he even speaks."

She collapses back in her chair, panting dramatically, fanning herself. Her strawberry-blonde hair glows against the firelight, the red catching flame.

"I do love looking at gorgeous men. Is this just another fling? She hasn't been serious about someone before."

"We met last month when I visited. Mason was there too. Didn't he mention it?" Jules asks as if this shouldn't be news. She shakes her head in disbelief. "James, her guy, he's an accomplished architect, very smart, around our age. And honestly?" She tilts her head, thoughtful. "He struck me as someone who enjoys a challenge. You should have seen him playing pool. Tom and Mason never stood a chance. I didn't get him and Ivy as a couple, but I guess it works."

The mention of pool brings me back to the only time in my life I knew happiness, those carefree years in Europe. While being sent away hurt, it also gave me freedom. I could travel, explore, and truly be myself without fear of disappointing anyone. The only time I get a glimmer of that feeling now is when I'm running or on the ice.

Bell's eager bark alerts us to the new arrivals.

Ivy bursts in, radiant. She wears a charcoal pencil skirt and cream cashmere sweater, a far cry from her usual fairy-girl aesthetic. Her hair is straightened and pinned into a sleek updo, as if she's auditioning for the role of perfect wife.

Behind her is a man. Ball cap pulled low, hands stuffed in his jeans pockets. He greets the others inside before following Ivy to the deck.

"Jules! Syd! It's been forever!" Ivy cries, pulling us into hugs.

He lingers a step behind, and when I finally face him, the first thing that hits me is his height. He's so damn tall. The kind of tall that makes you recalibrate the space around you. He removes his cap and runs a hand through dark hair. A tendril falls over his eyes.

"I'm James," he says, extending a hand.

"Sydney," I reply. The moment our hands touch, it's the same taut stillness I feel in the seconds before a starting gun. There's no movement, no sound, only a buzz beneath my skin that says: pay attention.

THree

What the hell was that?

I drop his hand, pulling mine to my chest and stumble into a chair. Mason and Tom join, easing into seats, and chatter fills the stark air.

"Ives, what's up with the clothes? Are you heading to the boardroom?" Jules enters interrogation mode.

"At some point, I had to get serious and think about the future." Ivy sits a little taller.

Her smile falters as she looks to James for backup, but he sits stiffly not listening. His eyes are cast toward the mountains. That grin is tucked away behind a pensive line set to his mouth, as if he were caught off guard by something.

"Hey, how's photography going?" I ask, jumping to save her from Jules's inquisition.

"I don't get out to shoot much anymore, with work and everything." She smooths down nonexistent flyaways. "It's a hobby. Growing up and everything."

"You're incredible, though. We could go hiking while you're here."

"I didn't bring my camera with me." Ivy's sparkle from a minute ago is replaced with a fake smile. The same kind of plastered-on look I use when someone asks about my marriage.

Mason rests one ankle across the other knee and jumps in to say, "I think it's admirable you're focused on your career, Ivy. Marketing's tough. You need every edge if you want to move up."

"Absolutely," Tom agrees, reaching over to grab Jules's hand. "But balance is important. Jules kicks ass at work and still makes time for what she loves. You'll never see her give up her reading time."

Jules leans in to whisper something in his ear. It's hard to make Tom blush, but his toffee-colored skin flushes a burgundy red. He leans back and winks at his wife. Even after fifteen years together, and two kids, they flirt with the giddy ease of first love.

"Well," Mason continues his lecture, ignoring Jules and Tom, "I think you need to get your master's. It's a shame you didn't do it directly after undergrad. It gets harder each year to go back."

"I'm looking into it, Mase. I've heard your thoughts on it. Extensively. And I've stopped focusing on my photography as you suggested to give more to work." Ivy sighs and looks over at James again. He's at least looking back at her this time, and she leans against his shoulder.

He doesn't say anything, doesn't reach out to touch her. Rather, his eyes cut to mine, but when he sees me watching, his gaze shoots to the mountains.

"Ivy, life is more than a series of responsibilities. You can have fun, have hobbies, and still keep those things that make you smile. Don't give up things you love," I say, offering a gentle smile.

While I might not have hope to cling to, she's too young for this kind of resignation or listening to her brother's misguided advice. Mason works fourteen-hour days and fills most evenings with networking events. Beyond watching sports, not much else holds his attention. Not exactly the epitome of work-life balance.

"Oh yes, Syd can tell you all about her fun hobbies. Reading. Running. Ice-skating. All sorts of thrills." Mason sips his whiskey, a shit-eating grin on his face. So pleased with how clever he is.

"And what do you do for fun, Mason?" a calm, deep voice asks.

Firelight flickers as James's voice comes out of nowhere. His face is pensive and serious as he studies Mason, clearly catching the sarcasm in my husband's words, and from the look in his eyes, he isn't impressed.

"You know," Mason replies, trying to keep it light, "guy stuff. Watching sports. Going out." He lifts a hand toward James for a high five.

James doesn't move.

Mason's smile fades, saving face by running his hand through his hair, playing off the dismissal. His eyes narrow to a glare that gives him away.

When I look at James, he doesn't look away. He returns my stare and gives the slightest nod. This time I'm the one who breaks, searching the mountainside.

"As much fun as this has been," Jules says, "who's up for a game? Monopoly?"

I'm quick to rise, eager to escape. "I'm always game to win."

Ivy bows out, claiming she wants to catch up with her mom. Mason, unsurprisingly, mumbles something about a basketball game and disappears. But James joins, jumping in next to me as we dig through the cabinet for the game.

"Prepare yourself," I say. "These two don't play Monopoly. They go to war."

Something sly curls on his lips. "I can handle some competition. Don't underestimate me. I play to win."

Oh fuck. That smirk. That's going to be a problem.

Mason and Ivy cross my mind, but I shove it aside. This is nothing. Harmless. A crush.

"Tom, get your hands off the money. I'm the banker," Jules says, slapping his hand away and whipping my attention back to the game board.

"Okay, because there are children present," Tom coughs dramatically and throws Jules a look. "We're going to draw game pieces from the bag. That way it's fair and no one fights over the coveted car." He holds out the little velvet pouch. "James, you pick first."

James dips in, his expression comically serious until he pulls out the car and grins, a dimple flashing crooked and unfair. "Hope you're ready to get your asses handed to you. I'm the king of Monopoly."

"I knew I liked you." Jules winks and picks her piece. "But don't you dare touch Park Place. It's mine."

The game escalates quickly. Within the hour, Tom's hoarding railroads, Jules has a death grip on Boardwalk and Park Place, while James and I methodically sweep up mid-tier properties. I haven't had this much fun in... a long time.

I need to roll a... "Six! Hell yes. Come here, baby, you are mine. Get ready to weep, everyone."

"You seem pretty confident, Sydney," James murmurs as he picks up the dice and passes them to Jules. "I play the long game, so you might want to settle in and get comfortable because I can go all night."

Jules chokes on her wine. "You did not say that."

Laughter erupts around the table. James smiles shyly, and my cheeks flush the color of my wine—Cabernet red—as I desperately try to shove the idea of "all night long" out of my head.

Jules surveys the board, glances up with a grin that promises trouble. "With that icebreaker, I think it's time to up the ante. Let James get to know us better."

"Please tell me you're not dragging out those damn questions." Tom groans theatrically, watching Jules take her turn and then he follows.

"Absolutely. If James is meeting the family, he needs the full Jules experience."

"That usually happens through normal conversation," Tom teases, shaking his head with a smile that's fully besotted.

"What questions?" James asks, picking up the dice and rolling.

"I'm so glad you asked," Jules says, sticking her tongue out at Tom. "Thirty-six questions designed by a psychologist to build intimacy. *The New York Times* wrote about it, claiming some people believe it helps you fall in love." She eyes James with mock severity. "That's not my objective, but they're great for getting to know people."

"Or... we could stick to Monopoly?" I offer, raising my brows.

"Where's the fun in that? Here's my pitch: every time someone lands on a property owned by another player, we answer a question."

"I'm game," James says with a boyish smile. "But I'm not up first. Sydney, it's your turn."

"Fine. I'll play," I mutter and roll the dice. Of course, I land on Jules's North Carolina Avenue. "Give me your worst."

Jules clears her throat and pulls up her phone. "Okay, Syd. *Given the choice of anyone in the world, whom would you want as a dinner guest?*"

"Off the top of my head, I would say Queen Elizabeth."

"Why her?" James asks.

I'm caught off guard by the question. He's asking for more information. Asking why.

"Think about everything she's lived through. Almost a century of incredible global change. Wars, world leaders, technological advances, not to mention the royal scandals. I think she'd have a fascinating, unfiltered view of the world."

James nods. "Strong pick. I'd go with Anthony Hopkins."

"Because of Hannibal Lecter? That's one of my favorite movies."

"Exactly. How do you even become that?"

"God," Jules groans. "Why can't people enjoy emotionally healthy characters? Syd is a glutton for morally gray men."

She winks, rolls, and lands safely. Tom does the same. James lands on Tom's railroad.

"Alright. Lay it on me," he says with a laugh, leaning back and bracing for impact.

Tom pulls on his reading glasses, taking a minute to inspect the list. "I'm going rogue and skipping ahead. *What would constitute a perfect day for you?*"

Before James can answer, Ivy breezes in and claims the spot beside him. "What are you guys up to?"

"Monopoly," Jules replies. "And some bonding questions. We asked James to describe his perfect day."

"Oh, mine's easy," Ivy chimes in without missing a beat. "Brunch at Café Luna, shopping on Newbury Street, and ending with wine on a rooftop bar overlooking the Harbor."

I glance at James, waiting, something in me wants to know whether his answer will be as superficial as Ivy's. He sits back, expression unreadable, then swallows hard and runs a hand through his hair.

"MOOOOOM!" one of the twins shouts from upstairs.

"Ugh, kids. Good night, y'all," Jules rises, half-waving her apologies.

Tom follows, saying, "I'm coming too, babe." He leans down to whisper something that makes her swat his hand with a laugh.

Ivy settles deeper against James. That flicker of heat in my chest? It twists.

"Well," I stand abruptly. "I guess that's my cue for bed. Good night."

And I leave without helping clean up the game or looking back. Twenty minutes later, when Mason comes out of the bathroom and slides into bed, his hands find my waist. The physical has never been our problem.

"Mase, hold on. I want us to do this question thing Jules shared. It's supposed to help couples connect."

"Syd," he pulls me closer, "I know how we can connect."

"Please."

"I'm tired. I thought we could fool around and go to sleep. We're married. That questionnaire is ridiculous."

"Okay, fine." I throw back the covers. "I'm not in the mood for sex. I'll go read in the sunroom if you're going to sleep."

Outside in the hall, I lean against the wall, clutching my book to my chest. The worst part isn't Mason's disinterest in the questions. It's how unsurprised I am. Intimacy has always been reserved for below the waist rather than sharing what truly matters. This has been our life for the past decade.

I know better than to even open that door. Let hope build that he'd want to talk. Hope is a luxury I stopped affording myself long ago. No expectations, no heartbreak.

Instead of the sunroom, I head downstairs. The house is still, quiet enough that my footsteps sound louder than they are. Moonlight streaks through in long, silvery lines.

From the kitchen, a golden light spills out. Someone else is there.

Four

"Hey, sorry to interrupt."

James sits at the island, hunched over a book. A tendril of dark hair hides his eyes until he looks up and smiles.

"It's okay. I don't mind, but don't judge my wine and tea combo. I couldn't decide if it was too late or too early, so I went with both."

"Rough night?"

"You could say that." He hesitates, weighing his words. "I... I tried to talk to Ivy about that list Jules mentioned and how her ideal day didn't exactly match mine. She blew it off."

"The Wallises, everyone but Jules, could win awards for shutting down conversations they don't want to have. Golden Globes for passive-aggressive conflict resolution." I laugh dryly, but I slap a hand to my mouth as if I could capture the words and shove them back in. Why the hell did I say that?

He tilts his head, studying me. "What about you? What led you down here?"

The irony isn't lost on me. I'm down here for similar reasons, but I can't tell him about Mason, about how my attempt at conversation was met with a grope and a sigh. That is way too much to admit out loud, not even something I'd tell Jules.

"Couldn't sleep. So, what is your perfect day if it doesn't match with Ivy's brunching and shopping?"

"""

"There are these lakes near where my mom lives, and I've always thought about taking a day to go out on a boat and enjoy the sun. Read, swim, a cooler filled with simple food and drinks."

I can see it, the lull of the boat, a sunny, hot day. Reading until sweat drenches you and jumping in to cool off. A soft sigh escapes as I smile and glance in his direction.

He clears his throat. "What about you? What's your ideal day?"

"First, how do you feel about brownies? Because the tea and wine aren't going to cut it." I quickly move to investigate the cupboards.

"I'm one-hundred percent pro-brownie."

I find a box mix in the cupboard. As I add the ingredients, I turn his question over.

"It's nothing glamorous. Nothing beats a sunrise run, then crawling back into bed with unlimited coffee and a book. Reading until it's time to cook something cozy, like lasagna and garlic bread."

Twenty minutes ago, Mason dismissed a simple question. And now, here's a man with his chin resting on his hands and his attention wrapped entirely around my words.

"Is Mason there, or are you enjoying this all on your own?"

"It's not his thing." I scrape the batter into the pan, ready to deflect. "Do you run?"

"Most mornings. I love being out with the sun rising while the rest of the world sleeps. It's when some of my best design ideas show up."

"I get that. Something about the rhythm quiets the noise." I tidy the ingredients as I softly say, "I normally run on my own, but I don't mind company. If you want to get a few miles in this week."

"I'd like that."

Instead of meeting my eyes, he's looking out the window—a tinge of red on his cheekbones.

We keep talking. He asks about my favorite places I've traveled, and I tell him about Chamonix in the French Alps. The mountain trails, a little café serving mulled wine where I'd sit and watch the alpenglow on Mont Blanc. "It was the first place I ever felt... peaceful. I could do what I wanted without worrying about what others thought."

My honesty surprises even me.

"Do you do that a lot? Think about what others want rather than what you want?"

"Hazards of being an only child." I give a half-hearted laugh and check the brownies. The look in his eyes says he sees right through my brushoff.

After a pause, he returns our conversation to travel. "I've always preferred small villages to cities. You get a better sense of people. I love nothing more than wandering a town with no destination or itinerary in mind."

The image of him wandering aimlessly brings a smile to my face.

When the brownies are done, he scoops vanilla and chocolate chip ice cream, and I slice the brownies. We work in tandem, conversation never faltering. I learn he went to MIT, which is why he's in Boston. I share about NYU and Georgetown.

"Okay, let's see if your brownies live up to the hype." He grins, taking a large spoonful.

The warm brownie and ice cream hit all the right notes, and I let out a soft, involuntary moan at my first bite. "God, that's good."

When I glance up, James is staring. His spoon suspended midair, eyes a shade darker. Instead of the vibrant green I've been watching all night, they've morphed into the furthest reaches of a forest. Deep. Dark. Inviting. The easy rhythm between us tilts. My skin prickles. Something tightens low in my stomach.

"Yeah, it is," he says, his voice rougher.

I blink, trying to clear the heat from my face. Shifting us back to neutral ground, I ask, "So... the lake near your mom's. Did you go there a lot as a kid?"

A pause follows. A slight tightening around his eyes. His voice comes out more guarded: "We moved there after... well, after we left my dad when I was thirteen."

I recognize his tone, the same one I use when people ask about my parents. Practiced casualness that masks what's jagged underneath. Rather than push or ask more questions, I take another bite of the brownie. I know how hard conversations about a less-than-pleasant childhood can be.

"These are good," he says after a beat.

"Hard to screw up a box mix. My baking specialty." I shrug, looking down at my feet.

"You sound like my mom. She'd buy a cake, come home announcing she'd baked."

"She sounds perfect."

"Don't get the wrong idea, though. I'd be an awful Italian son if I gave the impression she didn't cook. Her chicken parmesan is still my favorite meal. No matter how busy or tired she was, we always ate dinner together. One rule she wouldn't budge on."

"That sounds nice." I stand to rinse the dishes, needing some space, but I'm unable to stop asking, "So why haven't you had your perfect day on the lake?"

He tilts his head, considering. "I've gone out on it plenty. My best friend in high school had a lake house, but I guess my ideal day is more low-key. And... I haven't met someone who'd appreciate it."

"Ah, yeah, I get it." I flush and look down at the dishes. "Well, they say opposites attract. Maybe you can take Ivy shopping, then head out on a boat."

He stares at me for a second too long without saying anything. I feel him debating, lost in his head. What the hell is wrong with me? It's not like me to blurt out something without overthinking it.

Needing to fill the silence and change the mood, I say, "Sorry for interrupting your reading."

"I have no regrets. The book was about urban planning. Riveting stuff for midnight."

"Two kinds of ice cream and zoning ordinances? Wow, you're living dangerously."

He laughs—deep and real. And something in my stomach flips.

Settling next to me at the sink, he picks up a towel and begins drying dishes. "What can I say? I contain multitudes, but I draw the line at leaving dishes in the sink. My mother would feel it and call to scold me."

My arm brushes his, and I stumble back. Too quickly. My foot catches on the hem of my sleep pants. He reaches out to gently steady me.

"Pleasant dreams, Sydney."

And I definitely don't go to bed thinking about the way he said my name, slow and deliberate. Savoring each syllable as if he could taste it. Or the feel of his hand, warm and rough with calluses. Or the way his smile curves to tease that one dimple... which definitely doesn't make warmth spread like spilled honey.

***

"MARGARET, THIS LOOKS INCREDIBLE." I take in the breakfast spread. It looks straight out of a holiday magazine: flaky pastries, quiches, and carved fruit line the table in festive dishes. A poinsettia sits in the middle of it all.

"Thank you, Sydney." Margaret beams. "Thought we should do something special, since we're stuck inside. The town canceled the Dickens Festival."

A proper Vermont blizzard arrived overnight. Thick snow swirls in wild patterns, obscuring everything beyond the first line of trees.

"Snow is supposed to stop soon, and Bruce down the road thinks the plows will be through by noon," Gary says, pouring coffee. "Should we plan to ski then, take advantage of the fresh powder?"

James shifts uncomfortably at the mention of skiing. Ivy leans in to whisper, gesturing toward me.

"Syd, can James hang with you on the bunny slopes today? He isn't much of a skier, and I want to get in some runs."

Ivy and Mason exchange a look, like they've solved a minor logistical inconvenience. With us paired off, they don't have to feel bad about leaving.

"Of course."

"Sydney, did you make brownies?" Margaret asks, her tone light. "They look divine."

I force a smile, trying to keep from blushing. "Yeah. I couldn't sleep and wanted a midnight snack."

"Careful, Syd, with that fundraiser coming up, I don't want you feeling self-conscious in your dress." Mason leans over and kisses my temple. "Not the best time to go up a size."

The table goes silent.

Jules and Margaret gasp. James stiffens beside Ivy. Gary and Tom stare. Ivy stops chattering. I roll my eyes and keep eating my breakfast.

"Mason, apologize this minute," Gary admonishes. "I raised you better than that."

Mason glances around, shifting into his default defense. The smile that once disarmed me, I now recognize as a cover for the control he demands. His blue eyes can't hide the cold.

"I'm just looking out for you, Syd. You hate pictures when you're not at your best. You know, I think you're the most beautiful woman."

Sorry is not part of his vocabulary.

Breakfast continues in starts and sputters while everyone reels from Mason's interruption. The ease is gone. As is my leftover glow from the night before. I'm back in my reality.

After breakfast, I find myself alone in the kitchen with Margaret, loading the dishwasher.

"I'm sorry about Mason," she whispers. "He's always been... particular."

"It's okay. I'm fine." My automatic reply.

"No. It's not, Sydney. No one should be spoken to like that." Margaret stops me with a hand on mine. Her touch is gentle but firm. "When you walked in ten years ago, I watched you look around this cabin as if you'd never seen a Christmas tree before."

My throat tightens. "Never one that a designer didn't color-coordinate."

"The first time you helped me make cinnamon rolls, your hands shook. Like you were terrified of messing up."

"I was."

"But you've never gotten it wrong, Sydney. You're as much a part of this family as anyone born into it. I love you. Gary loves you. You're a daughter to us. Always."

I don't cry—I rarely do—but something inside me exhales.

The words land in that unguarded place she first unlocked ten years ago: a space where a little girl still lives, aching for words of encouragement and kindness from a parent. Words I've waited my whole life to hear.

***

"You don't have to babysit me. I can manage on my own," James says, stepping into his boots and giving me a guarded smile.

I look around to make sure no one is within earshot and lower my voice. "I don't enjoy skiing, so my plan involves coffee and reading."

"Now we're talking." He laughs, pulling on a forest green beanie.

Blinding sun bounces off the freshly fallen snow as we climb into the rental car. In the distance, people cut across the pristine landscape. Kids sled down a hill, and a couple glides on cross-country skis. Slowly, the world digs itself out.

James pulls his hat off his head and runs a hand through his hair. He opens his mouth, then shuts it. Before saying, "Why go through with this whole thing? Why not just stay back?"

"Skiing's the one thing Mason loves about coming up here. I don't want to ruin that for him. So I play along, pretend I'm more into it than I am. I've found little ways to enjoy it."

I keep my tone light, but I feel him listening harder than I want him to.

His brow furrows, and I pretend not to notice. Pretend he's not reading the spaces between my words, that he's not dissecting my marriage from an offhand comment about skiing.

"So you've adopted the Wallis motto of passive-aggressive avoidance?" he asks quietly.

I stare at him for a long beat, willing him to look away first. He doesn't. "I see you have a long way to go in understanding the concept."

He laughs dryly. "So, what's our plan?"

"The lodge is connected to the resort's hotel. I usually stake out a spot with coffee and a book. It's close enough to meet everyone when they finish skiing."

"I've got a book inside. I can grab it…"

"Nope." I cut him off. "You need something better than urban planning."

Instead of turning left toward the resort, I make a right and head into the village.

Seeing the bookstore through his eyes reminds me of my first trip with Jules. The train display is pure magic: tiny animals, gift-wrapped boxes, and miniature plates of food dot the snowy village.

James slows beside me, taking it all in. "Wow. This is incredible."

"It's one of my favorite bookstores." I step closer to admire the scene's details. "I always try to come here for a new book on Christmas Eve."

We wander through the aisles unhurried. The low hum of conversation and children narrating Santa's imminent arrival fills the silence. His eyes stay wide, his fingers tracing book covers. I look away quickly when he catches me watching.

"I can't believe we didn't talk about books last night," James says. "But I've got an idea. Let's pick a book for each other."

"Any rules? Because I'm not reading anything involving zoning codes."

"Ha-ha, funny lady. Fiction only. And no helping. Let's see how well we can guess what the other enjoys reading. We've got ten minutes. Go."

James rushes off, and I twirl around, the thrill of the game intoxicating.

This man is fascinating. There's something about him beyond good looks and being well-educated. Last night, when I asked him about the lake near his mom's house, there was more behind his deflection than a divorce; a pain I recognize.

I grab two new releases by authors I love and go with my gut instinct. He sees me waiting by the doorway and gives me a crooked smile, forcing me to bury my face in my scarf like a silly schoolgirl.

Five

THE RESORT IS A five-star hotel masquerading as a rustic mountain lodge, all the luxury amenities wrapped in carefully distressed wood and artfully placed antler chandeliers. A wooden trellis draped with flowing vines frames the entrance. Out back, panoramic mountain views stretch for miles, but I lead James to my favorite corner.

"This reminds me of the sunroom at the cabin," James says, admiring the tucked-away alcove where two dark green velvet couches frame a gas fireplace.

"I think that's why I love it. The sunroom's my favorite. It's where I go when I need a minute to myself." I look away, ignoring the way his nod seems to mean he understands. "Okay, before we do our little book exchange, what's the best novel you've read this year?"

James sinks into the couch across from me. Instead of manspreading, he leans thoughtfully forward, his elbows resting on his knees. "*Verity.*"

"You read *Verity*?"

"All the women in my office were talking about it," he says with an easy shrug, as if it's not the most outlandish thing I've heard all week. "So I wanted to see what the hype was about. Still not sure how I feel about it. It was dark as hell, but it seems like the point of writing a novel is to have it stick with a reader, and that book stayed with me."

"I love psychological thrillers," I say, relaxing onto my couch. "Something fascinates me about delving into the dark and twisty places most people hide. That book was truly disturbing. I still can't believe someone could think that up."

"What about something more charming? A Regency romance? I learned within five minutes of meeting Jules that she prefers a lighter read." He smiles, but it's soft. There's no teasing in his tone.

"Jules is very vocal about her reading preferences, but I was never the fairy tale type. And I don't need an English lord to give up his rakish ways and sweep me off to the countryside." I pause, but the rest spills out anyway. "Give me a dark, twisty tale full of uncomfortable truths any day. I don't believe in happily-ever-afters; just... doing your best with what life throws at you."

"Ah, but you know about rakish ways?" James teases.

I can't believe I told him my fucked-up view of the world. What is wrong with me? I recover and, with my cheekiest smile, I say, "A *well-read* woman is a dangerous thing."

After a beat, James smiles, looking... surprised. "So in one of your dark, twisty stories, would I be the first guy to get axed, or the mysterious stranger who causes all the trouble?"

"Can't say yet. But definitely not a brooding English aristocrat."

"Fair enough. Now, what do you have for me?" He leans forward, hand outstretched.

When he opens his and starts to laugh, I pull out his selection for me. The same two books I chose for him. A snort escapes before I can stop it—loud and completely unattractive. Heat floods my cheeks as I press my hand to my mouth.

What did my mother call that sound?

I was maybe six, playing in our backyard with my nanny while my mother worked under her umbrella, maintaining her careful distance from the sun. The neighbor's Labrador bounded into our perfectly manicured yard, tail wagging furiously as it ran straight for me. The dog's excitement was so pure that laughter bubbled up from somewhere deep inside me.

That's when the snort escaped for the first time.

My mother's voice cut through the air. "Sydney, that is the ugliest sound I've ever heard. Ladies do not make that noise."

The shame hit me, sharp and immediate. I learned it was best to swallow joy.

"I'm so sorry. That was…" I say, slowly dying from embarrassment.

Instead of looking horrified, his grin widens. "Now I know my goal for the week. To do something to make you laugh like that again."

I bury my face in my hands. To recover from the embarrassment. To hide the effect those words have on me. To let the embers of hope and warmth filling my insides die before I can allow myself to believe this is real. Once my mortification passes, I run my finger along the smooth hardcover, amazed at the coincidence in us choosing the same books for each other. And I say, "These are two of my favorite authors. I can't wait to dig into them. Maybe we should start a little book club?"

James smiles, nodding, but there's something beneath it. A pause. A softness. And I can't help but wonder if he feels it too. This quiet, impossible ease that shouldn't exist between two people who just met.

We read for a while in comfortable silence, cocooned in lamplight while a light snow falls outside. Even as I focus on the story, I'm keenly aware of him: the soft scent of his woodsy cologne mingling with our coffees, every page turn, every quiet huff when I imagine something delights him. When I finally permit myself to glance up over the top of my book, he's already looking at me. We quickly look away.

Guests hustle down the hall, chatting and laughing, carrying food back to their rooms. The smell of bacon hits me, greasy and overwhelming. The room tilts sideways. My throat tightens, mouth salivating the wrong way. Heat builds at the back of my neck. *Shit.* I bolt for the nearest bathroom, desperate not to lose my breakfast right there. I gag and heave, but nothing comes up.

James is leaning against the wall, waiting. "You okay? What was that?"

"I'm fine," I reply automatically. "My stomach feels off. I should head back. Don't worry about me, I can get an Uber and leave the car for you."

His jaw tightens, and he steps forward, raises his hand toward my cheek, but abruptly lowers it. "I'll drive you. Don't be ridiculous. Wait here, I'll grab our things."

I don't know what to make of him. It's like someone engineered him to be the anti-Mason. And now he's walking back to me with my purse slung over his shoulder, bookstore totes in one hand, as if it's the most natural thing in the world.

"Come on, let's get you home." His hand brushes the small of my back as he steers me outside, and I have to stop myself from leaning into him.

Once he's finished clucking around me and we're in the car, he blows a breath out of his cheeks and says, "You scared me. You went white as a sheet."

"I'm fine. Don't worry about me."

"Has this been happening?"

"A few times..." I regret the confession the moment it leaves my mouth.

"Maybe you should see a doctor or talk to Jules."

"It's nothing. Probably anxiety or something I ate isn't sitting well," I say, though a part of me is beginning to wonder. But I push that thought aside. It can't be that. "I'll be fine."

He doesn't argue but looks at me with weary eyes, not buying my explanation.

The cabin rests in hushed stillness. Beyond the glass, the mountains stand draped in white, breathtaking in their winter peace. My stomach churns, rough and unsettled, a turbulent force in this snow-globe world.

"I'm going to lie down."

He follows me upstairs, placing my things inside the bedroom. Before I can thank him, nausea sends me stumbling into the bathroom. The toilet seat smacks against the tank as I shove it up, and my stomach heaves, emptying itself in violent waves. After an eternity, I flush and rest my head against the wall, then look up to see James standing in the doorway wearing the most endearing expression of concern.

"Oh God, please go. You don't need to see this." I wave a weak hand, urging him away.

He disappears without a word, and I rest my head against the wall.

But minutes later, quiet footsteps return. James places a glass of water, a few crackers, and a bottle of Tylenol next to me. Grabbing a towel from the shelves, he spreads it on the floor, offering me somewhere warmer than the cold tiles. His eyes land on a scrunchie, lifting it in question.

My arms feel heavy, my head throbs. I nod, grateful.

Kneeling behind me, his fingers sift gently through my hair, untangling knots. He gathers it into a loose ponytail, his touch careful. I close my eyes and let myself absorb it. Forget this isn't mine. It's not something I can rely on.

"I'll try to reach Mason for you, but I'll be outside if you need anything."

"You don't have to do that." I can't bring myself to say, *'Don't bother. Mason won't hurry back.'* Even if that's my reality.

After a while, I rinse my face and brush my teeth. My body still aches, but my stomach has settled. I pull on leggings, an oversized sweater, and Christmas socks. The kind of comfort I can rely on.

I open the door and gawk. James sits in the hallway, phone in hand, Bell's head resting on his thigh.

He looks up. "You're still pale. Do you think it's a fever?"

The green of his eyes shifts with his concern, a kaleidoscope of sage and emerald that seems to hold entire landscapes.

"You've been sitting *here* the whole time?"

"This place is too fucking big. I wouldn't have heard if you needed anything from downstairs. Why do they call it a cabin?"

I smile without meaning to. It's such a sweet, silly thought. "I think it helps the family feel more salt of the earth, like this isn't a 6,000-square-foot estate. Rather a little ski cabin."

"I got in touch with Ivy. She said she'd let Mason know, but that was a while ago."

"It's fine. I can take care of myself." I gesture vaguely toward my room. "Sorry you had to see that."

He meets my eyes. "I know you can take care of yourself. But I'm here. Can I help?"

"I'm feeling better and going to throw on a movie."

"Want tea or anything?"

I ignore the question and take the stairs two at a time. I queue up a quiet film I've seen before. Two strangers share a perfect day before returning to their real lives.

It feels too close, but I hit play anyway.

Steam curls from the spicy ginger tea James places beside me. And somewhere between the soft dialogue and the warmth of his quiet care, my eyes grow heavy. I drift off, exhaustion pulling me under.

***

A DOOR SLAMS, CLATTERING through the quiet to jolt me awake. The Christmas tree glows in the darkened room, and I'm snuggled into a warm blanket I don't remember grabbing. Time has slipped away—an hour, maybe two. The sky is awash in shades of violet and charcoal.

Mason flips on the overhead lights and rushes over. "You okay? Can I get you anything?"

"I'm fine." I wave him off, rubbing my eyes to adjust to the harsh light. I don't need his faux-sympathy now. "An upset stomach, not a big deal."

Margaret appears behind him. She brushes her hand over my shoulder. "Let me know if you need anything, sweetheart." Pivoting toward the rest of the room, she asks, "Anyone have thoughts on dinner?"

"I made chicken noodle soup. Enough for everyone," James says, standing in the doorway to the kitchen. A checkered apron tied around his waist, wooden spoon in hand.

"Aren't you an angel?" Margaret beams and turns to Ivy. "He's a keeper."

Mason glances at James. "Thanks for helping, Syd. Glad you were there."

"Of course," he replies, looking away when Mason kisses my cheek.

As the others slip away to unload equipment and change, James walks over with a fresh cup of tea, placing it on the table beside me. The apron is no longer on, but it doesn't cause my body to react any less. Who knew a man in an apron could be so maddeningly irresistible?

"Did the nap help?"

"Reading, cooking, taking care of puking women—are you always this fucking nice?" I tease, though my tone is laced with a sharp edge. Defensive. A need to bury whatever it is he's drawing out of me.

"Are your expectations for men so low that holding your hair while you're puking makes me Prince Charming, Sydney?" His voice is low, cut with his own edge that makes my toes curl.

A hiccup of time passes. How long, who knows? My pulse trips, and heat stutters through my veins. This time, it has nothing to do with an upset stomach. His gaze doesn't flicker. Mine should look away, but I don't.

Not yet.

Until a throat clears and Tom walks into the room with a curious tilt to his head. "You guys have an interesting day?"

I head into the kitchen, leaving my tea and whatever that was behind. And because the universe has a cruel sense of humor, of course, his soup is perfect. It's exactly what my stomach needs. Simple and comforting.

"The soup is yummy, James," Ivy says, nudging his side with her elbow.

He looks up, dazed, returning from somewhere far away. "Thanks."

"Why don't you cook for me in Boston?" she asks, her tone hard to read.

"I thought you preferred going out." He shifts, glances at me, back to his soup.

"Speaking of going out, is anyone interested in hitting the tavern tonight?" Ivy surveys the room.

The table quiets. Margaret raises her brows, exchanges a look with Gary, but says nothing. I glance toward Mason, half-expecting him to offer to go with her. But he's lost in his phone.

"Feel free to go," James says, still not looking up. He stirs his soup with careful precision. "But I'd rather stay in on Christmas Eve."

What I wouldn't give to rewind to yesterday.

If I'd swallowed it down. Not opened up to Jules. Not let her ask that damn question: *Are you happy?* I could have kept up the well-practiced version of myself, going through the motions and grateful for this family above all else.

But that question led me to try. I asked Mason about the questionnaire. To connect. I put myself out there only to be met with the same old dismissal. And then *James* fucking arrived, riding in like some White Knight who reads, cooks, and takes care of you. Someone who instinctively understands what those questions were meant to do. A man who doesn't need a list.

Twenty-four hours of quiet moments replay like an old black and white movie, scenes from a life I'm not living—a glimpse through a doorway into another version of me, one who made different choices. I look up, and his eyes meet mine.

What if it's not too late?

"Ahh, Bell, get your nose off my lap!" Leo yells, yanking me back to the table and out of my head. A much safer place to be. "You can't have my dinner roll!"

The table erupts in laughter as the golden retriever's tail thumps eagerly, still watching for crumbs. Conversation shifts back to lighter things with the kids taking center stage, talking about Santa and last-minute wish lists.

Jules leans in, a look on her face that has me holding my breath. "You got sick a few times, and it passed?"

"Pretty much. Why?"

"Have you had this nausea at other times? Dizziness?"

"I've been dizzy, yeah. Nausea for a couple of weeks." My stomach drops to the floor as realization dawns. The thoughts I've been pushing down rush forward as the pattern crystallizes.

"When was your last period?"

"*What the fuck*, Jules?" I whisper-shout as water sprays from my mouth.

"Sorry, babe. But these are classic morning sickness symptoms. You should take a test. I'll run to the pharmacy if you want."

"No. Fuck. No." I stand, grabbing a napkin to blot the water from the table. Raising my voice to its normal level, I turn to the rest of the table. "Sorry, everyone. My stomach's not great again. I'm going to bed."

Upstairs, I yank out my phone, scrolling through my calendar. Trying to remember. What was happening the last time…?

Everything blurs. The room spins, fast and unrelenting.

We've talked about kids, but I'm still on the pill. I'm not even sure I want children. Mason's insistence that this is the next step has been a common argument over the past few years, as if this is just another item to check off his to-do list.

Looking at my calendar, one entry jumps out: a doctor's appointment after I'd fallen during a race and scraped my knees badly. He prescribed antibiotics and gave a warning that they might interfere with my birth control. And a few nights later—too much wine, numbing myself during another exhausting fundraiser. I didn't think about using backup protection. Didn't think at all.

Fuck. Fuck. *Fuck*.

I pull the covers over my head, slip in my earbuds, queue up some white noise, throw on an eye mask, and hope to lull myself to sleep and wake up from this nightmare.

SIX

My phone blasts the dark room out of its shadows. The remnants of the dream that startled me awake are hazy, edging into focus like a kaleidoscope.

A baby in my arms.

A warm hand on my shoulder.

A kiss that's slow and reverent.

His eyes are bright green, not blue.

And looking at me like I am his whole world.

My heart pounds, trying to escape my chest. But it's a dream, just a silly figment of my imagination. I shove the images down where I keep everything I can't face.

I lie there, staring at the ceiling, wanting to laugh and cry simultaneously. This is what hope gets me. The universe is crashing me back to reality. My hand gravitates to my stomach, drawn by instinct to what might lie within. The possibility that changes everything. The complication I never saw coming.

Slipping on my robe, I make my way to the sunroom. Beyond a wall of glass, snow-capped mountains rise against the sky, their peaks glistening in the moonlight. This is my favorite corner of the house.

With her green thumb and artistic eye, my mother-in-law has transformed the space into a lush oasis. Ferns, pothos, and monsteras spill from shelves and corners, their vibrant leaves creating the feeling of a secret garden. A cozy seating area with plush armchairs, a Chesterfield sofa, and a gas fireplace invites you to curl up with a book, disappear into the view, or escape for a moment of solitude.

I gaze out over the mountains as memories of Christmases here flood back.

Margaret's patience teaching me to bake, sharing stories about love and life. Hours of laughter with Jules, conversations that always made me smile and think. Watching the twins grow from tiny infants into opinionated, hilarious boys. Gary and Tom battling over snowman building while my nephews directed from the sidelines. Afternoons teaching my nephews how to ice skate.

My period has been late before—from stress, too much running, or simply not taking care of my body. It could be any of those things, and Jules could be wrong. Either way, there's nothing I can do about it today. It's Christmas, and nothing will be open—a charm of this little Vermont village.

I wrap myself in a chair and watch for hours as the moonlight dances across the peaks, until the sound of my nephews stirring begins to rouse the house. *Santa came.* Everyone but Mason and Ivy shows up. They both skip the early morning gift opening, choosing sleep over chaos. James is here, and somehow that doesn't surprise me.

Sinking into the sectional cushions, I get lost in the pleasure of seeing the twins' eyes wide with wonder at each new item unwrapped. James stands off to the side, his eyes analyzing the seating options. His Adam's apple bobs, and he gingerly makes his way to the open cushion on the sectional, which is next to me.

I fold my hands together and cross my legs, holding my body as still as possible. He seems equally affected by the proximity. His eyes stay on Beck and Leo until Bell walks over and rests her head on his knee. He exhales and pats the dog, finally looking at me.

"Are you feeling better?" he asks.

"Yeah, my stomach's fine," I say, hearing how sharp I sound.

What else can I say?

Actually, I'm a fucking mess. I had a dream where I'm pretty sure you were the leading man with me and my baby. Cool, right? We've known each other for forty-eight hours. Totally normal.

His hand pauses on Bell's head, and his jaw tightens. "Can I grab you a coffee?"

"No, it's okay. I'll get it later."

"It's a cup of coffee, Sydney. I'm heading that way anyway. How do you take it?"

"Well... okay." I glance away, flushed by how monumental the question feels. "Some oat milk. The color of a latte."

"So, a splash of coffee with oat milk. Got it."

My eyes, the traitorous things, can't help but follow him. Gray sweatpants hang loose over long, easy limbs. His old college sweatshirt faded and frayed at the cuffs. Even his tousled hair tells a story: no products, just a quick pass of his hand. Mason will show up in a crisp button-down, not a strand out of place, every inch of him composed to stay that way.

"Did I get it right?" James flushes, watching me examine the cup he's returned with.

"Yeah, you did."

After the presents are opened, the kids run off to test their new toys while the other adults drift off. But I stay rooted on the sectional, beside this man I can't seem to pull myself away from. He leans back, running a hand through his hair. I sit cross-legged, plenty of space between us, but when he leans forward and his eyes fix on me, my stomach flips.

"Tell me about young Sydney."

"There's not much to tell," I choke out.

"Come on, give me something. Were you serious? Funny in a self-deprecating way? Drive all the boys wild in high school?"

There's something about him that makes me want to open up. Reminds me of when I first met Jules, and she was able to pull truths from me that I normally lock away. Maybe it's how easy it's been to talk to him. Maybe it's how safe he feels.

What would I even say? That my presence was a burden to the people who should have loved me? That I learned not to rely on others because they never showed up for me? Or that I've always found it easier to keep people at arm's length—and that's why I married Mason, because he didn't ask questions. He let me pretend life before him never happened.

But here's James, asking me to share and giving me his full attention.

I take a deep breath and say, "I didn't have a good childhood. It's hard to talk about."

"Hey, I'm sorry. I get it. I don't like talking about my shit either. It's hard to talk about the things we try to bury."

I exhale, grateful for the way he doesn't press for the sordid details. "Exactly. It's like... if I don't talk about it, maybe I can pretend it never happened."

"But it happened," James says. "And it shaped you."

"You started reading the Riley Sager book yesterday, right?" I ask.

"Yeah. Are we starting our book club now?" He jokes, a smile tugging at the corners of his lips.

"Did you get to the part with the poem *Remember*?"

"Yeah I looked it up. *Better by far you should forget and smile / Than that you should remember and be sad.* But I don't know... choosing to forget feels like giving up. Maybe the hard stuff is what makes us who we are."

"That sounds nice in theory," I say carefully. "But what if some things are too heavy to carry around? What if remembering just keeps you stuck?"

"I guess that's the risk. Without remembering, how will you ever know if you've grown?"

Every instinct in me screams to reach for him. To fold into his chest and feel him tuck me under his arm. I want to ask what pain taught him to look at the world this way. Share why that poem doesn't even pertain to me since the person asking you to forget would have to love you first. To kiss the corner of his mouth and run my fingers through the lock of hair that falls across his forehead.

No, Sydney. He's not yours. Bad girl.

"What's the deal with you and Ivy?" I ask the question tumbling out of nowhere.

I plead temporary insanity.

He sputters into his coffee, glancing around to see if anyone is within earshot, then turns the full force of his gaze on me. "What's the deal with you and your husband? Because from what I've seen, he's kind of a dick. And you... You're not."

Heat rushes to my face, and I look out the window, pretending the cool mountain air can soothe the burn beneath my skin. I've spent so long making excuses for his behavior, explaining it away, that hearing someone else see it so clearly strips me of every defense.

"Ouch." I let out a shaky laugh and shift to break the tension, but our knees brush and I jump to my feet, dizzy from more than the movement. I grasp for something to steady myself.

His hand shoots out, gently holding my arm. "What was that? You just went white again."

"I'm getting a refill, just stood up too quickly. You want one?"

As I head to the kitchen, I fold away this conversation into the back of my mind like a fragile note I'll read later. I force my lips into an easy, soft smile, already knowing I'll unfold that note sooner than I should.

****

ONCE EVERYONE IS UP, Gary and Margaret hand out gifts. They always select something thoughtful. I peel back the paper on mine to find a deep red cashmere pashmina. Luxurious and soft, perfect for wrapping around my shoulders in the quiet mornings here.

"Thank you. It's beautiful."

"I know how often you curl up in the sunroom," Margaret says, her eyes crinkling with warmth. "Thought you might adore something to keep you cozy while you read."

Across the room, Ivy clutches a gift, tears in her eyes.

"I noticed you didn't have this lens in your gear," James explains. "I thought maybe the new focal length might inspire you to pick up your camera again. I haven't seen you use it."

"James, this is…" She's at a loss for words, staring down at the lens. "It's a lovely gift, but I'm no longer a photographer."

"Well, it's never too late to pick it back up." He squeezes her arm and picks up the sweater she gave him. "Thank you for this. It's great."

His eyes briefly meet mine across the room before turning back to her.

A reminder of where my attention should be.

I hand Mason a slim box with a faint smile. He opens it, revealing a simple black Casio watch. "I read that the cold drains Apple Watches, and I know you time your ski runs."

He nods and slips it on his wrist.

I lift the flap on the envelope he hands me. A gift card.

"Figured you could get books or whatever. I didn't want to pick out the wrong thing." Mason kisses my cheek.

"It's great. Thanks." My mouth twitches into what I hope passes for a smile. "Does anyone need more coffee?"

I grip the carafe tighter, as if the warmth might anchor me, help me lock another thing away.

Jules follows me into the kitchen and finds me staring down into my mug. "Wanna go axe-throwing?" she asks, bumping her hip against mine. "What was in the card?"

I hand her the envelope, and Jules's smile fades. We've had this fight many times. It's no secret where I believe books should be bought. "Take it. At least you can load up your Kindle."

Her eyes soften, though the concern doesn't leave them. "Have you gotten sick again?"

She hasn't forgotten what she implied last night, and neither have I. But I can't go there. Not yet. I want to live in denial until I have no other option. Until hard evidence is presented to me.

"Wanna go ice skating? The resort rink is open today, and we've got time. The boys would love it."

"Oh, look at you, thinking you can throw me off your scent." She smirks. "I see exactly what you're doing. But sure, I'm game. Let's round up the troops."

Jules claps her hands together the second her feet leave the kitchen, a general gathering her cadets. "Alright, fam. We've decided ice skating is on the agenda for this afternoon. Who's in?"

"Ugh, you know how I feel about ice skating," Mason groans. "I'm not going, that's your thing, Syd. I hate it. If I'm going to be cold, I'm going skiing."

I roll my eyes and catch James looking, something knowing in his expression. He remembers what I said yesterday. Mason has never returned the favor of pretending for me.

"I'm going to pass," Ivy chirps. "I need to catch up on some work."

"I haven't skated in years, but it can't be that hard, right?" James laughs. "I'm game."

So it ends up being Jules, Tom, Leo, Beck, James, and me piling into their SUV. Jules takes the wheel, sunglasses on despite the gray sky, radiating the chaotic good energy she brings everywhere.

"Mom, put on 'We Will Rock You'! We've got to get pumped for this!" Leo shouts from the back seat.

"Nah, dude. We need something else. Get ready to shake your tail feathers. Syd, you ready?"

It hits—the beat, the strut, the unmistakable riff. Kesha blares through the speakers with her not-so-kid-friendly anthem about not needing anyone, especially a man, to validate your worth. Tom rolls his eyes but throws his hands in the air and grooves to the tune, laughing at his wife, clearly convinced she's the best part of the whole ride. You don't soften Jules. You roll with her.

Jules drums the steering wheel, singing along off-key. The bass shakes the car, the boys wave their arms with exaggerated attitude, and James smiles. A full, carefree smile, the kind that says he doesn't give a damn how he looks. He grooves as well as a 6'3" man in an SUV possibly can.

As we pile out at the rink, she catches me by the elbow, pulling me aside while the men race Beck and Leo towards the skate rental.

Jules grins. "Thought you could use a reminder."

"A reminder of what, exactly?"

"That you, my darling, are a badass."

"Yeah, yeah. Thanks for the pep talk."

"Syd, don't do that." Her voice lowers. "Sometimes the universe throws you something so ridiculously obvious to make sure you're paying attention to what you actually need." She lets it hang there before her grin returns, and she loops her arm through mine.

"God, I love you."

"Obviously," Jules says. "Now let's go humiliate some men on skates."

With the thump of Kesha still in my bones, I decide to let it all go, at least for now. When I'm on the ice, everything else fades. It's always been that way. The ice was my first refuge, the one joy I didn't have to ration or question. The only thing from childhood that felt unapologetically mine.

James steps onto the rink, a man at war with gravity. Arms flailing, he grips the wall with both hands, his face twisted in fierce concentration.

"Okay," he mutters. "I've got this. It's walking. On knives. With no friction. No big deal."

"You good there, Bambi?" I skate backward in front of him, biting back a smile.

"If I fall and die, call my mom and tell her I went out bravely."

"Bravely?" I laugh. "You're clinging to that wall like it's a life raft."

He wobbles dramatically, nearly taking out Leo, who zips by with the finesse of a miniature Olympian. "Okay, wow. That kid is fast. Shouldn't there be speed limits out here?"

I move closer. "Want me to get you a skating cart?"

James eyes me with mock horror. "I couldn't live down that level of humiliation."

"You know the thing about bikes? Same deal. You'll fall on your ass a time or two. Start with small steps. Get a feel for the skates."

He cautiously pushes off the wall. His legs wobble, but he stays upright. "Okay, okay. This is going well. My dignity's still intact."

"For now," I smirk. "We'll see how you do with turning."

"Nope. Straight lines only. I'm a one-way train. No curves, no brakes, and no style."

I laugh, and he looks at me. That seeing-you gaze he has. The one that slips past my walls and makes me feel unmoored.

"At least you're smiling," he says, a flush creeping up his cheeks. "My humiliation makes it worth it. Not a snort, but I'll take it."

Can he ever say the wrong thing?

I stay beside him, feeling protective of this gangly, uncertain version of him. I'll skate off once he's steadier.

"Aunt Syd, show me a spin!" Leo does a dramatic hockey stop at our feet.

"Not right now, I'm trying to keep James vertical."

"No, no. I want to see this," James says, edging back toward the wall. "Come on, Sydney. Show off a little."

"She's so good," Beck jumps in. "She can do a bunch of tricks on the ice."

"Okay, okay." Heat blooms in my cheeks. But instead of downplaying it, I remember Jules's words. "Let me warm up first."

I skate off, building speed. With each glide, I push harder, falling into the rhythm. The sharp scrape of blades. The wind against my face. The way my body remembers what to do. I lean into a turn, gather speed, center myself, and spin. Arms lifted, one reaching behind me, the other forward. I twist into shapes my body hasn't made in years until I'm breathless and shaking.

My hair is a tangled mess under my hat. My cheeks are flushed. My lungs are burning. A smile is wide and unfiltered.

Behind me, Beck and Leo erupt in cheers, their little fists pumping the air.

James exhales, the sound caught somewhere between his throat and stomach. "Wow. That was amazing."

"Ah, it's nothing a few thousand hours of skating lessons won't teach you."

He shakes his head, seeing through the brush-off. "No, that was something else. That woman? She owned her space." He takes a few tentative steps forward, lowers his voice so the boys can't hear. "A motherfucking woman who takes what she wants."

The smirk tugging at his lips as he calls back the anthem from the car sends a rush of tingles through me. A wild, unhinged wave of possibility takes hold. I skate until my feet touch back down to earth.

I spend the next hour teaching the boys a basic spin while the man on the sidelines watches my every move. By the time we leave the rink, my cheeks are flushed from the cold, my muscles pleasantly sore. And for the first time in a long while, the smile on my face doesn't feel borrowed.

James holds the car door open, his eyes catching mine for a beat too long. Something in my chest tightens. Whatever it is, it steals the breath right out of me.

"You looked really free and happy out there."

If only I could stay in that feeling.

seven

Flames leap against the dark, lambent on flushed cheeks, half-empty wine glasses, and my teacup. Laughter flows easily, softened by good food and wine. But the glow from this afternoon has faded. Whatever glimpse of freedom I found earlier is tucked away again, buried beneath the layers of obligation and expectation, under the weight of tomorrow's test. I curl deeper into my chair, wrapping my arms around my legs, sealing in whatever warmth remains.

"I love all the questions it raises," Ivy muses, picking up the thread of conversation about the movie I put on the other day and its sequel. "Can you imagine? Meeting someone, falling in love over the course of a single day, and reconnecting years later, after life has completely changed?"

Tom leans back, resting a hand on Jules's thigh. "It's a question of soulmates, right? Are they real, or something we convince ourselves of?"

Jules sighs dramatically and drapes herself across his lap. "You know you're it for me, baby. Forever and always." She leans in and kisses him as though the rest of us aren't sitting here. When she finally comes up for air, she picks up right where she left off. "But it does make you think. What happens if you meet 'the one who got away' again, and you've already built a whole life?"

Silence falls as we all sit with the question, suspended in the winter air.

"People aren't stagnant. If the person you choose doesn't grow with you... That's when the questions start forming." James stares into the flames, shadows dancing across the planes of his handsome face. "Do you stay where it's comfortable? Or do you take a chance?"

He leans back, all casual ease, but his eyes find mine.

Jules rests her glass on her knee. "You're right. That movie only works because neither of them is happy. If they were, there wouldn't be anything to tempt them. No what-ifs to chase."

"Exactly." James nods. "I think connection is like music. You don't always know why a song stays with you or strikes something deep, but when it does, it's as if you've touched something larger than yourself."

The fire crackles. The cold bites, challenging me to hear him. Hear her.

Mason looks up from his phone. "Are we still talking about this? This soulmate stuff is Hollywood nonsense. Relationships are about making smart choices, not some mystical connection."

Ivy leans in to nuzzle James. "I don't know about mystical connections and soulmates, but I'm *really* into this guy and the orgasms he gives me."

"Oh, Jesus," Mason groans, shaking his head. "No one wants to hear about your orgasms."

Laughter erupts around the fire, as if the night itself is in on the joke. Everyone's caught up in Mason's response, everyone except me and the man whose gaze finds mine through the flames.

He looks away, a swift, guilty movement. The flush creeping up his neck turns his honeyed skin a deep crimson. He looks... apologetic? As if the thought of me picturing them together unsettles him. I tug my shawl tighter around my shoulders, hoping the soft fabric might somehow shield me from the unwelcome pang twisting in my stomach.

"Orgasms and soulmates are entirely different questions." Tom clicks his tongue to stop the giggling nonsense. "The real question James asked was about that deeper connection when you and someone just click. How do you work as a partnership, and does it endure as you grow older?"

"Exactly." James recovers with a casual tone. "People evolve. Sometimes what someone once thought was right turns out to be all wrong. To continue the music metaphor: one day, a soulful R&B track catches your ear, and suddenly your love for country doesn't feel so steadfast anymore."

His eyes sweep to mine again, just for a second. But it's enough.

I suck in a deep breath as the anger—a slow burn from the last few days, months, and years—rises unbidden. Fuck him, his knowing smirk, and bullshit metaphors.

"That's ridiculous. There's not some music god strumming a guitar and saying, 'Let's switch things up today.' We have free will. We decide what music we enjoy. Who we connect with." My voice is steadier than I feel.

Laughter ripples. But James doesn't flinch.

"Who are you trying to convince, Sydney? Us... or yourself?" He leans back, ankle crossed over opposite knee, eyes full of challenge. "Can you say you've never felt a connection you couldn't explain? Something that defied logic or reason?"

My breath stalls somewhere in my chest, and I grip my tea with white-knuckled fingers.

Mason pauses swiping across his phone. His eyes lift in a long, slow analysis. But he says nothing.

I keep my face neutral, take a slow sip of tea, and let the moment hang while buying time. "Well, I once felt an inexplicable connection to a pint of mint chocolate chip ice cream after a particularly bad day. Does that count as transcendent, or just pathetically basic?"

Jules chuckles. "Oh man, I was waiting for this. You're both too stubborn to back down. We needed someone, besides me, to keep Syd on her toes."

I force a smile and play along, pretending his words mean nothing. I sink deeper into my chair, tugging the shawl tighter, grateful for the firelight. Because I can feel it. The mask I wear is slipping. And I need to fix it. Fast.

Mason leans in, whiskey on his breath. "Let's go upstairs."

His hand slides up my inner thigh, a touch that leaves no room for misinterpretation. Maybe I can lose myself in the one part of our relationship that works. Let the physical drown out everything else. Drown *him* out.

"Sure."

But as we leave, I can't help myself.

I glance back one last time.

James watches with a stern furrow to his brows.

***

MASON CLOSES THE DOOR behind us, the soft click echoing through the quiet. He steps closer, thumbs grazing over my cheekbones. "You're so beautiful."

When his lips meet mine, I savor the taste of whiskey on his tongue, the feel of his soft hands against my skin. His arms, warm and familiar, circle my waist, pulling me closer as he moves us toward the bed.

There's no music in this, just rhythm. Motions I know well. I surrender to the feeling, the knowledge he'll bring me pleasure as his lips move to my jaw, my neck, nip at my ear.

"What do you think of James?" he asks, watching me as I try to keep my breath even and face blank. The way he's studying me makes it clear he's trying to piece something together. Needing to distract him, I unzip his jeans and reach inside, wrapping my fingers around him. He hurriedly pulls down my leggings and slips his fingers between my legs. A moan escapes before I can swallow it.

"Shhh, or I'll have to stop. And you still haven't answered my question."

"He's fine. We've hung out some. Ivy's infatuated," I add, hoping it's enough to satisfy whatever suspicion is brewing.

"I've noticed him checking you out. He can't keep his eyes off you." He pulls back, his free hand caressing my cheek. "I know I'm not good with deep conversations, and I don't always say the right thing. But I do love you, Syd."

How convenient. Suddenly, he's self-aware.

His mouth returns to my throat, his hands strip away my shirt and bra. He murmurs, "How can I blame him for looking at you? You're the most beautiful thing I've ever seen."

Maybe I should feel guilty, but my mind slips sideways into forbidden territory. Mason's hands may be on my body, yet my imagination overlays them with different ones. Rougher. Calloused from graphite pencils and blueprints.

How would James touch me? Would he be assertive, taking what he wants with quiet confidence? Or slow? Would he tease me until I'm shaking, pleading for more?

I let myself linger in the fantasy a breath too long, until Mason pulls me back to reality. I flinch as pain flares on my chest where Mason's teeth graze too hard.

"Mase, they're feeling sensitive."

"Oh," he chuckles against my skin. "I guess it's about time. It's been a while since you mentioned your period."

A cold wave crashes over me, but Mason doesn't notice. He's focused on chasing his own release, lost in the rhythm as he pushes inside me, oblivious to the way my body has gone still. The climax that had been building? Dismantled in an instant, like a match tossed in a snowbank.

Mason shudders between my legs, then presses a quick kiss to my lips before rolling to his side and falling asleep.

I stare at the ceiling, his arm heavy across my abdomen, wondering if there's a *Guinness World Record* for "Most Inconvenient Time to Discover a Pregnancy."

If there is, I'm surely in the running for gold.

Because in the morning, I'm taking a pregnancy test. And there won't be room for fantasies. No space for reckless indulgence in the way James looks at me, or in the quiet connection simmering between us.

If only I were Kesha, and I could take what I wanted.

But I'm me. And a baby changes everything.

EIGHT

Sleep never comes. I give up at five and start firing off emails to my paralegal while drinking as much coffee as I can to distract myself from the growing anxiety. I watch the sun crest the horizon. A new day is here.

I slide into my sneakers by the door and throw on a final layer. Footsteps from the kitchen catch my attention, and I look up to find James draining a cup of coffee, dressed for a run.

He takes in the form-fitting Lycra and freezes. His stare is heavy and blatant, lingering long enough to warm my whole body. Then Bell walks through the foyer, nails tapping hard against the floor, and he tears his eyes away, leaning down to lace up his sneakers.

"Mind if I tag along? I promise I'm much more capable on my feet without skates," he says without looking up.

I pause for a second, debating whether inviting him is a good idea. Seriously, I'm running to buy pregnancy tests. But knowing something is dumb and not doing it are two different things. What's the harm in a few easy miles together?

"I'm running into the village to grab something from the convenience store. You can come if you're up for six or seven hilly miles. But don't expect me to slow down for you." I wink and head out the door before I can flirt any further.

As we set off down the driveway toward the main road into town, the crisp mountain air fills my lungs. Being outside, surrounded by the quiet beauty of the forest and the sting of the cold, steadies my mind. We run in easy silence, our strides naturally in sync, until I decide to break it. I need to set some boundaries, especially after his bullshit last night.

"Okay, convince me you're not a fuckboy stringing Ivy along. I saw you checking out my ass. That didn't feel brotherly."

A flush stains his cheeks, and my resolve stutters.

"How do I convince you I'm a good guy? Twenty questions."

"Twenty questions? What is this, a teenage sleepover?"

James lets out a low chuckle. "Humor me, Sydney. Twenty questions. Completely honest answers. No deflecting, no half-truths. You ask, I answer. Then I ask, and you answer. Deal?"

Torn between curiosity and self-preservation, I stall. But there's something in his expression, a vulnerability beneath the charm, that has me nodding.

"Fine. But I go first," I say. "What's the number one thing on your bucket list?"

"Hmm, I haven't really thought about a bucket list. I'm thirty-six, not exactly in the last throes of life. But there are a few things. I want to run all six major marathons. And I want to climb Kilimanjaro."

"Have you run any of the majors yet? I've crossed New York City and Boston off my list."

"So you weren't kidding about not slowing down for me? I've run Boston and London. Running Chicago this year." He pauses, considering, and asks, "Were you Homecoming Queen in high school?"

"What kind of question is that?" I scoff, but feel the heat creep into my cheeks. "My school didn't even have homecoming. And I wouldn't have gotten it anyway. I was too quiet and weird for anyone to appreciate. Favorite color?"

"We're diving deep. It's green. Are you a flowers-and-chocolate person, or do you prefer adventure?"

"One hundred percent, I'd choose an adventure. No matter if it's just a run or something bigger like hopping in the car for a spontaneous road trip, I'd prefer those any day over a bouquet. What's your longest relationship?"

His eyes gleam golden green in the soft morning light. They crinkle at the edges as he smirks.

"What? It's part of my fuckboy research. I need to know if Ivy's dating a player. You're not exactly a young man."

"Six years. It ended last year, but honestly? I should have ended it way sooner." He pulls his beanie off his head and runs a hand through his hair before pulling it down again, never losing his stride. "I'm not a player. I... just have this bad habit of holding onto relationships longer than I should." He pauses. "I'm not scared of marriage. Just haven't found the right person."

"Is that why you're dating Ivy? Looking for your forever person?" My breath hitches as I force the words out.

"Nope. It's my turn." He lets out a sharp exhale through puffed cheeks. "What made you decide on corporate law?"

"My parents were both lawyers. Their parents before them. You know, the whole carry-the-torch, family tradition thing. Corporate felt less personal. Companies, buying other companies, are far less messy than dealing with people and their problems."

James stays quiet for a few minutes. Our sneakers scuff the pavement, the only sound apart from a winter bird's cry slicing through the silence.

Then, softly, "You said *were*, not *are*. Have your parents passed away?"

"They died during my senior year of high school."

The memories crash in: my dad's car accident, and before I could even fly home, the call from my mother's assistant telling me she was gone, too. The deep, dark hole that's never left since those fateful calls opens again.

"What's your biggest regret?" slips out before I can stop it.

James doesn't flinch. His footfalls don't falter. "That I didn't step in sooner to stop my dad from hitting my mom."

His honesty stops me cold. I stand in the middle of the road. Tears well in my eyes, and I fight to keep them in. *Well, fuck.* I was... ignored. He had to live with *that*. James keeps his eyes on me, steady and unflinching, waiting to see my reaction.

"Wow. Okay." I clear my throat, trying to steady myself. "Hard truths it is. Do you... want to talk about it?"

"Nah. Not right now. Come on, let's keep going."

We let the silence wrap around us, turning over the weight of his words.

This man—his care, his understanding, the quiet way he's moved through the past few days—it all makes sense. What kind of boy must he have been, so scared, and still brave enough to try to protect his mom?

"My turn." He clears his throat. "What's something you've never told Mason?"

Yesterday, when we sat beside each other and gave the barest hints of these hurts, I wanted so badly to lean into him, into the way he listens. And he didn't just listen, he got it. Now I know why.

I inhale deeply, filling my lungs with the bitter air, and instead of deflecting, I see how it feels to speak the truth. "I've never told him the full extent of the neglect I experienced growing up. No one ever hit me, but... I've never admitted how crushingly lonely I was."

His gaze sharpens, but he doesn't rush to fill the silence with empty reassurances. Instead, he asks, "What do you mean?"

"My parents didn't have room for me in their lives. Nannies raised me until I went off to school. And I know how privileged it sounds to complain about not getting enough time with Mommy and Daddy. I was nothing more than a trophy. Something brought out during dinner parties to charm their friends, tucked away again the moment I became inconvenient. Honestly, my life didn't change much after they died."

He stays quiet, giving me space, letting me decide whether to go on.

The path curves around a stand of pines. Instead of heading toward town, I follow the trail, and we come to a covered bridge. Icicles hang from the eaves, scattering prisms of light around the entrance.

"I love this place." I slow to a stop at the bridge's entrance.

James steps forward, his eyes widening as he takes in the structure. "This is incredible." He moves closer to examine the joinery. "These builders understood how forces work together. They knew that in certain configurations, pressure actually strengthens the connection rather than weakens it."

I place my hand on the beam, feeling the grain of the wood, the strength that's held for generations.

"How old is it?" he asks.

"Built in 1875, according to the plaque."

"A hundred and fifty years, and it's still standing." He pulls off his mitten to run a hand along the beam. "This isn't just construction. It's *art*. A testament to what people can create when they build with purpose. To make something that lasts, that connects one place to another."

Standing here on this bridge, there's nowhere else I'd rather be. Not at the law firm. Not back at the cabin. Not running alone on some distant trail. Just standing here, listening to this man talk about a bridge like a prayer I'd long forgotten how to say.

This is what Jules's question was about and what I've been reaching for all these months. There is no need to pretend or search. Because it's written in every glance, every conversation turned confession, every instinct that urges me to share more. It's a connection that exists without even trying.

My stomach turns, and I catch myself against the bridge. Oh yeah. The purpose of the run.

The jarring reality of what I have to do rushes back. I close my eyes, pushing it down to the abyss. But it hovers right there, on the tip of my tongue, behind the tears threatening to spill. It won't be tucked away, as if my body is saying, 'Be brave and ask for what you want.'

"Sydney?"

"The pharmacy is a few minutes ahead." I take off without looking back.

James stays a few paces behind as we continue into town, giving me the space I need.

My hands won't stop shaking, and the flickering fluorescent lights in the pharmacy, straight out of a horror movie, don't help. My trembling fingers grab what I need. The boxes go into the bathroom trash; the tests are buried deep in my coat pocket.

The sun makes an appearance when I step outside, and I stretch my face toward the soft, warm light. My eyes flutter closed, absorbing it the way a plant gathers energy. When I find James, he's leaning against the building, looking at me in a way that makes me feel naked, like he's reading every thought racing through my mind.

A scream wants to break free. But instead, I say, "Race you back!"

I don't wait for a response. My shoes kick up snow, pulse pounding with something that has nothing to do with the cold.

At first, I hear nothing but my own breath and footfalls against the packed road. Then, although faint at first, there's the steady sound of him chasing after me. He doesn't pull even; instead, he stays a few strides behind. Close enough to feel his presence, far enough to give me space, understanding the doors we opened and my need to gain some distance. Maybe he needs it too.

Laughter rises in my throat as I push harder, feeling the thrill of the moment. I'm flying. Free. Having fun. No second-guessing or hesitating. It's how I felt on the ice yesterday. For these few stolen miles, nothing else exists as we charge up the road in this unnecessary but entirely wonderful race.

As we near the cabin's snowy drive, I hear his breathing deepen, feel his effort to close the final distance. I call over my shoulder, "Nice try, bud. You're not catching me today."

But as I turn, my foot catches on a patch of ice hidden beneath the snow. I lose my balance, my body sliding backward. Before I hit the ground, strong arms wrap around me, pulling me into a solid, unyielding chest.

"I've got you."

His breath falls into rhythm with mine, fog curling in the frosty air between us. He leans in, mint and warmth brushing my neck, and a different kind of shiver runs through me.

My mind goes blank, and I stand there in his arms.

Breathing. Pretending. Wishing.

I feel the pull of his breath as he inhales, then the soft warmth as he releases it against my skin. My hands tighten on his jacket, and he responds by pulling me in even closer.

"Good catch." I push away, chest heaving to suck in air.

How do I train my body to understand how inappropriate this reaction is? What was that conditioning study I learned about in undergrad psych? Pavlovian something?

My feet pound the final stretch up the icy driveway, desperate to escape. I grip the rough wooden railing on the porch and allow myself one look back at James, standing where I left him.

The elegant slope of his nose tilted toward the sky. His hand is running through his hair. His profile is painted in a beam of sunlight.

What could happen—

If these tests are negative—

If my options are wide open—

I learned long ago not to count on hope, and I don't stop until I'm inside the bathroom door locked behind me.

With trembling fingers, I pull out the pregnancy tests—several, to be sure. Before I can talk myself out of it, I unwrap them, use them one by one, and line them on the counter to develop before stepping into the shower. Hot water cascades over my skin, scalding and soothing all at once, but it does nothing to stop me from spiraling.

The absurdity of it all crashes into me, fierce and unrelenting. Who invites another man along to buy pregnancy tests? Who plays stupid games and spills truths to someone you just met, when you can't even bring yourself to tell your closest friend?

My father's voice echoes: "Sydney, you are an Allistair. Act as such."

Despite the hot water, my body never warms. I don't dare close my eyes because I know whose handsome face I'd see. The timer buzzes. All I have to do is open the door and see the results.

Breathe in. Breathe out.

Steam curls as I step out of the shower and grab a towel, my eyes zeroing in on the eight undeniable pink lines.

The tests sit on the counter. Merciless in their clarity.

Pregnant.

The word echoes, deafening in the silence.

I press the heel of my palm to my chest, trying to slow the panic gathering there, but my breath comes in short, shallow bursts. Too fast. Too tight. The bathroom feels smaller with each inhale. Cold tiles bite into my knees as I collapse, pressing my head between my knees to keep sobs from escaping. They rip free anyway. I should be excited. This should mark the beginning of everything I've ever wanted.

Instead, I feel the weight of a thousand choices collapsing onto my shoulders.

What is expected of me.

What it means for the future.

I close my eyes, and I'm ten again, alone on Christmas morning with the same hollow ache spreading through my chest. The same Christmas, Madame Rousseau gave me *Little Women*. I can still feel the relief of opening that book and slipping into the March family's world. The same sense of belonging I felt during my first Christmas with the Wallises.

"Syd?" Mason calls with a sharp knock.

I swallow my sobs, cutting them off before they can slide under the door. I inhale sharply and hold it, not trusting whatever sound might escape.

This has to be my future. The man on the other side of this door. The man I chose ten years ago. For this baby, I can do what my parents never did: choose the child over myself.

This baby will know they are loved unconditionally.

They'll never sit by a Christmas tree alone, pretending a family from a novel is their own.

"Syd?" Mason knocks again.

"I need a minute." I wipe away my tears and reach for that place in me where I've always hidden my needs, shoved down every inconvenient truth. This time, my body accepts the offering, letting me breathe without a crushing weight on my chest. Slipping into sweatpants and a tank, I steady my breath.

I can do this. I've lived my entire childhood swallowing my desires.

For this baby, I can do it again.

When I open the door and bring my shaking hands forward to reveal the test I'm holding, Mason's eyes widen.

"Is this what I think it is?"

"Yep," I say with a tentative smile.

He steps closer, resting a hand on my stomach. "I'm gonna be a dad?" There's awe in his voice and disbelief in his eyes, like he's found certainty where I feel nothing but adrift.

Silent tears fall down my cheeks.

"Hey, hey." Mason pulls back, his thumb brushing a tear from my cheek. "What's wrong? Aren't you excited?"

"I'm overwhelmed. I... we hadn't planned it."

I don't tell him the rest. A childhood of love, stability, and every wish fulfilled left him no concept of what toxic, selfish parents can do to a child. And it isn't lost on me that the one person who might understand these fears isn't the man standing here.

"You're not alone, Syd. We're in it together."

I say nothing, only wrap my arms a little tighter around him, and squeeze my eyes shut, trying to believe his words. But James's face outside the pharmacy flashes behind my lids, and I cry harder.

"How about we tell everyone at dinner tonight?" Mason says, brushing away a tear.

No. Not in front of him.

I sniffle and say, "Can we hold off until we confirm with the doctor?"

"Sure. Whatever you want."

When he pulls me close, I let myself sink into the warmth of his arms, into the illusion of certainty he offers.

NINE

Fresh snow blankets the ground, muffling the world in a hush. The sky stretches silver and soft. I breathe deep, letting the brutal cold settle in my lungs, hoping it might dull the ache in my chest.

Bell bounds through the snow beside me, her joy untouched by the slow collapse of my world. Out here, I can breathe—escape Mason's hovering, the tests buried under tissues in the trash, and the decisions already made for me.

I need a moment.

Just one moment to breathe.

Cry in solitude before I piece myself back together.

I sink into the snow, bury my face in my hands, and let it out.

There's no one here to judge, no one to witness the wreckage. I grieve for the girl always left behind, who never knew the meaning of family. For the woman who wanted it so desperately, she married the wrong man to get it. For this baby, I already want more than anything. I know I could choose not to have it, but this is my chance to finally have what I've wanted all my life: a family of my own.

And mostly, I cry for what this all means—the hope I hardly dared to feel.

Footsteps crunch up the drive, shattering the fragile stillness. I don't need to look up. I know his stride. When I finally lift my head, concern marks every line of James's face. He takes in the sight of me kneeling in the snow, tears frozen on my cheeks.

Grasping for a shred of bravado, I force a smile. "Fancy meeting you here."

"What's wrong?" He's next to me in two quick strides.

"I'm fine. Just thinking."

"Hey, I can be your friend. I'm a pretty good listener."

"No. It's nothing... I can't talk about it with you."

James exhales, tipping his head toward the sky. Beads of sweat trail down his cheek. His breath is still ragged from his run. "Did you talk to a doctor today, or did Jules give you some insight into what's going on?"

Bracing against something colder than the night air, I hug my arms around myself. "Yeah, something like that. But I don't want to talk about it."

"Why not?" James takes a step closer, his body blocking the wind, creating a pocket of stillness around us. His scent, cedar and something distinctly him, wraps around me in this cocoon.

My lips purse as I exhale, the fog of my breath mingling with his. "Because...I don't think I can handle any more truths with you."

He lets out a low chuckle, the sound reverberating through me. Under the soft glow of the moon, I glimpse the ghost of another life. One where we met at a different time, in a different place. Where I wasn't who I am now. But this isn't a fairytale with an easy ending. The tests in the bathroom trash have already written our tragedy. There's no world where I can keep the Wallises and explore whatever this is with him. I'd lose everything. So I do what I've always done. I perform.

"You've passed the test. I'll tell Ivy you're a keeper."

My smile stays fixed, wide and polished. I ignore the bitter taste the words leave in my mouth and the twist in my gut when I see the disbelief on his face.

"That's it? That's what you think this is?" he scoffs.

I tilt my head back and let snowflakes kiss my skin. They fall and melt, disguising the tears threatening to spill. With gentle fingers, he brushes away a flake and cradles my chin, guiding my eyes to meet his.

"Can you honestly tell me you don't feel this between us?"

We stare at each other, unmoving, the weight of his question orbiting like a comet through the dark.

"I'm not an option, James. Go to Ivy, or move on from her. But leave me out of it."

His silence stretches, but I don't dare fill the space.

"Sydney, what are you not telling me? What happened? I know this can't all be in my head."

My hand drifts to my stomach before I can stop it. I drop it quickly, but his eyes follow, narrowing. "Nothing that changes anything. I'm going inside to my husband. That's the end of it."

He doesn't move.

"Bell, come." I keep my steps steady as I climb the stairs, back straight. I can feel James watching, dissecting me. But I don't look back.

As I reach the door, his voice cuts through the stillness.

"The way you look at me doesn't match what you're saying, Sydney."

For a heartbeat, I freeze. His words strip away all my defenses, leave me bare, as my fingers tighten around the doorknob. But I don't turn back. I step inside and close the door, sealing whatever this is behind it.

***

BREAKFAST IS SUBDUED, DEVOID of the usual soft hum of conversation. Everyone is lost in their own world. Some read newspapers, others check emails, or scroll on their phones. I keep my eyes on my plate, pretending not to feel the green eyes watching from across the table.

"Mom, Dad, Syd and I have one last Christmas gift for you." Mason squeezes my hand and pulls a shiny, wrapped box from behind his back.

No. No. No.

He was supposed to wait. We agreed. I should've known he wouldn't.

Did he dig the test out of the trash?

A sour burn creeps up my throat, but I clamp it down, eyes rooted to the wood grain. James watches, his gaze leaving a trail I can't mistake. But I don't dare look back.

Margaret takes her time unwrapping it, her fingers delicate with anticipation. When she finally sees what's inside, her scream fills the room. Gary leans over, spots the test, and together they rush us, pulling us into a suffocating embrace.

At least my tears can be mistaken for happy ones.

"Mom, Dad, what is it? What's in the box?" Ivy practically vibrates in her seat.

Before I can even breathe, Mason blurts it out. "We're having a baby!"

The room erupts—laughter, cheers, voices overlapping. Margaret dabs her eyes, already planning nursery themes and baby showers. Gary claps Mason on the back, brimming with pride. Tom raises an imaginary glass.

"Oh my gosh, this is amazing!" Ivy gushes. "You're going to be so gorgeous pregnant. It's so unfair. You'll have this perfect little bump while I'll look like an Oompa Loompa."

"Will the baby come out of Aunt Syd's belly button?" Leo asks, lifting his shirt and poking his as if he's conducting a scientific study.

Beck rolls his eyes with all the superiority of a worldly six-year-old. "No, dummy. The doctor uses scissors. That's why moms have that line on their stomachs."

"Boys!" Jules cuts in. "Clearly, I need to explain better what I *actually* do all day. But anatomy lessons later, okay?"

Tom winks over the twins' heads. "It's time to discuss the birds and the bees."

I try to laugh, but the sound doesn't land. The voices blur. The room grows too warm, too small. A cold sweat beads on my forehead as I stand frozen.

James stands outside the circle, hands shoved into his pockets, eyes downcast. When he finally looks up, I see it—surprise, hurt, something else I can't (or won't) name. He swallows, hides it all behind a tight smile and dulled eyes.

"Congrats to you both." His voice is hollow, devoid of any emotion.

"Thanks, man. We're thrilled. We found out yesterday." Mason beams, pressing a kiss to my cheek. He's oblivious to the way I go still, to how I slip further into silence.

I see it: the moment James pieces it all together. The nausea at the resort. The stop at the pharmacy. Our conversation in the snow. His Adam's apple bobs and he looks away, focusing somewhere above everyone's heads.

Jules squeezes my hand, pulling me away from Mason. Her eyes hold mine, seeing the truth behind my smile, the tremor in my hand betraying what I'm holding in. Two people see through my performance, and neither is my husband. I look from her to James as I stand, frozen like a deer caught in sudden light.

"Excuse me. I need a minute." And I flee.

"Poor Syd," Jules calls after me. "Morning sickness is no joke!"

Laughter drifts from downstairs, muffled but inescapable. I curl deeper into the corner of the sunroom, wrapping a blanket tightly around myself. Here, I can breathe. Ari Lennox plays through the speakers, her voice filling the empty spaces inside me, weaving lyrics of love and longing, of brokenness and never-weres. Maybe I'm a masochist, letting the words sink in, refusing to turn them off.

"Thought I'd find you here," Jules says, stepping in with two mugs of tea. Her curls are piled into a messy bun, her ugly Christmas sweater doing its best to soften the tension.

We sit in silence, breathing with the music. Until she leans forward and says, "I was going to ask if you're okay, but that feels like bullshit."

I huff a soft laugh. "Yeah. It kind of is." I pause before meeting her eyes. "*Fuck*, Jules."

"I know, babe." She pulls me into her arms and lets me cry.

Even though she's smaller, she holds me like a wall, fierce and unwavering.

"Syd, when I asked you the other night if you were happy, it wasn't a question. I see you. I see the distance between you and Mason. How much you've changed. And from experience?" She stops, gathering the words to say: "Babies don't fix what's broken in relationships."

"How can I be a mother when I feel so lost?"

"Do you know who I see when I look at you?" She asks, brushing tears from my cheeks. "I see a woman who survived a shitty childhood. Who clawed her way out of a frozen house. Who wasn't carved from stone like her parents. Who loves *hard*."

Her words wreck me, my tears falling freely. I wish I could see that version of me, too.

Maybe Jules sees who I could be. Maybe she's holding up a mirror to my potential, not my reality. The question is whether I'm brave enough to become that woman, or if I'll keep hiding behind fear.

"Do you ever get lonely?" I whisper, because it feels wrong to say out loud.

"All the time," she admits without hesitation. "Even with a good man. Even surrounded by love. Because no one can fill you up...but you. I had to learn that the hard way too, babe."

"I don't think I've ever wanted something just for myself."

"Syd, the woman I saw ice skating, she was alive and free. When was the last time Mason made you feel the way you looked out there? When was the last time he even tried?"

I stare into my cold tea, unable to answer. We both already know the truth.

She disconnects my music from the speaker and throws on "Good as Hell" by Lizzo.

"Maybe it's time you let yourself *live*." She shimmies toward me. "But until you're ready to claim what you want, we're dancing this shit out."

"I don't think this is..."

But she's already pulling me to my feet as the beat pulses through the room. My resistance lasts about three seconds before I let go, a little.

She twirls me until the room becomes streaks of color and light. We dance until sweat dampens our shirts, until a genuine smile spreads across my face. Until I almost believe in the strength Jules swears I have.

All that's left is to bury the pieces of this week so deep that someday I can lie to myself and pretend he never mattered, that this beautiful week was never supposed to be anything more.

From the window, I watch Bell bounding toward the forest. She pauses at the tree line, ears perked, tail wagging, suspended in a moment of possibility. My heart seizes at the glimmer in her eyes.

What's out there? What if she keeps going?

But she turns back, trotting toward the house with her tail wagging.

2020

The bird with a chick to protect
forgets how to trust the wind,
choosing the withering branch
over the storm that might teach them both to soar.

Ten

EXHAUSTION SEEPS INTO MY bones.

My arms burn under the weight of the diaper bag, my exhaustion just as heavy as the thousand necessities I'm carrying to keep a tiny human alive. Each inch I take from the car through the front door is a reminder of the load I carry. Mason, Anna nestled in his arms like a prop for a family portrait, strides ahead.

"You're here!" Margaret rushes forward, arms already outstretched, reaching for the baby. Gary swoops in to take the gear from me. Relief hits the moment I step into the warmth of my in-laws' house, into their quiet care. For the next week, their help will be freely given. No need to beg. No need to plead.

Two people giving without expectation.

Looking at the little bundle wrapped in her grandmother's arms, I can't help but think back to the first moment I saw Anna. All the fears I'd carried about motherhood, about becoming my mother, dissolved in an instant: I knew I'd do anything to keep her safe. Give her everything I could.

She became my focus. My salvation. Any hope I'd had that Anna might bridge the divide between Mason and me vanished during the long months that followed.

A year of pregnancy and childbirth, set against the backdrop of a global pandemic, stripped us bare. With COVID raging and nowhere to hide, we were trapped in the same space, again and again. What had once been easy to ignore became impossible to miss.

Especially now, as I meet the green eyes I've spent countless nights dreaming about.

James stands by the window, silhouetted against the pale winter light, a steaming mug cradled in his hands, wearing worn jeans and a hoodie. His gaze drops, moving over me slowly. I know what he's seeing—the way my body has changed since Anna, how my clothes fit differently now. From the way his jaw tightens, he's not unaffected. The moment stretches long enough to pulse through me, everywhere.

"James, come meet Anna." Ivy's voice calls, and I finally tear my eyes away from him. She's watching, a hint of something flashing in her stark blue eyes.

The family hasn't gotten together since last Christmas. COVID forced Tom and Jules to withdraw for a while, focusing on their patients and the mechanics of being doctors while caring for the boys when their school closed. I begged Mason to leave D.C., retreat here during the worst of lockdown. He wouldn't hear of leaving the city, as if our proximity would magically make it reopen. We stayed, with only silence and the news filling the space. Margaret and Gary visited after Anna was born, but they'd sequestered themselves for weeks beforehand to ensure they weren't sick upon meeting her. Ivy didn't come, but that isn't surprising.

"Is Anna a family name?" James asks.

"Annabelle. After my grandmother," Mason beams. His smile for the audience never falters, though he slept through the 2 AM and 5 AM feedings last night. And the night before. And every night since Anna was born.

"I see," James says, and something in his tone makes me glance up. He's smiling. Sly. "Annabelle. Not Anna *Karenina*?"

A smile escapes before I can stop it.

That's why ultimately I gave in. People think *Anna Karenina* is tragic. But to me, she's brave. A woman who refused to play by the rules. Who wanted more. Who refused to settle.

Everything I could want for my daughter.

But I can't say any of that. And I can't think about the warmth pooling in my chest at how quickly he caught the reference.

Instead, I pivot: "How has COVID affected your projects?"

"Like everything else, we were delayed. But one of my favorites finally broke ground. I helped design a new music hall along the harbor." He pauses and takes a sip from his mug. "The goal is to create a state-of-the-art amphitheater where artists of every genre can play without fighting the acoustics of a massive stadium."

"Even country artists?" I quip, remembering our debate last winter.

"The real test will be pouring some smoky R&B through the space." His voice drops on those words, and for a moment, I'm back at that fire pit, the moon shining bright, words loaded with meaning.

And I make the utterly unforgivable mistake of looking at him.

That smile.

That *devastating* smile that hits like a memory and makes my insides twist.

Jules appears from nowhere, throwing her arms around me. "Who are you kidding? You love R&B. Why are you pretending to listen to country?"

"Okay, okay," I laugh, trying to play it off. But the heat flaring up my neck gives me away. "Maybe I have a secret love for R&B."

"I knew it." James chuckles, eyes dancing. "Any other secrets you want to share, Sydney?"

I half-hide in my oversized turtleneck, hands tucked deep into the sleeves as if that might stop the heat blooming in my chest. Anna's small coo draws my attention. A welcome reminder of what matters now, of the tiny person who depends on me entirely. I feel the tight, thin rubber band gripping my wrist. Angling my body away from the others, I pull it hard. Once. Twice. Three times. The sharp sting grounds me. Calls me back. Snaps me back to my reality.

Mason's seen it. I know he has. I've done it right in front of him, but if he's wondered what I'm doing, he hasn't asked. He looks past it as he looks past me.

"Syd, it's honestly *unfair* how good you look already." Ivy's hand lands on my arm.

"Ah, thanks."

There's a hint of something behind her smile, looking a little too forced. Is that sarcasm? Or just guilt playing tricks on me?

Not that I care about bouncing back. But it's hard not to compare myself to *her*. She doesn't have dark circles under her eyes or stretch marks across her stomach. Today, in her cigarette pants and silk blouse, she looks effortlessly put together, while I have spit-up and dried milk on my sweater.

Fuck. It's going to be a long week.

Her voice dips to a conspiratorial whisper, loud enough for those nearest to hear, and says, "Damn, your boobs are out of this world."

Heat flashes up my neck, pooling in my cheeks. I don't have to look up to know both men heard her. I can feel it. One of them is absolutely staring while the other is doing everything he can to look anywhere else.

"Well... nursing will do that."

"Guess that's one thing I can't complain about," Mason snickers, like he's landed the joke of the century. He bumps his elbow against James. "Perks of fatherhood, right?"

James says nothing. I'm not even sure he's breathing.

"Well, *this* has been fun. Come on, let's get some coffee." Jules wraps her arm around mine. "You've earned yours spiked."

"I'm going for a run." James jumps at the escape. He's already halfway up the stairs before anyone responds.

I let Jules pull me into the kitchen, away from the awkwardness. This cabin has always been a refuge, where laughter echoes and fires burn low into the night, while snow blankets the world in something soft and safe. The first place I truly belonged.

But now? Everything feels... off.

"You look tired." Jules, not known for subtlety, gets right to the point.

"Yeah, I know. I'm sore, still leaking from everywhere, and haven't slept in months."

"Has anything gotten better with him?" She watches me, reading between every breath.

At first, Mason was in awe of our daughter. I remember the way he'd trace her fingers and listen to the tiny sounds she made in her sleep. But reality set in, and with each passing day, Mason pulled further away.

He wanted the version of parenthood that can be posted, filtered, admired.

Not the one that required patience, persistence, and selflessness.

"We're here this week. Let us help you." She fills my mug with coffee, then asks, "Want some Bailey's?"

But Margaret enters with a crying Anna, gently bouncing her in her arms. "I think she might be hungry. Mason said to find you. Do you have any bottles so we can help with feedings?"

"I'll pump when I can." I wince, already feeling the telltale letdown as I take Anna.

"Come on, feed her on the sectional, and we can keep catching up." Jules snatches my mug, already on the move.

Anna's tiny fists flail against my chest. Even in her rage, she's all softness and certainty. The one thing in my life that feels entirely, unquestionably right. We settle into the chair and she calms immediately. My sweater falls gracefully around us, hiding my breasts.

"It feels so good to have everyone here," Margaret says, squeezing Jules's arm. "I was worried it might not happen."

"Mom, I wouldn't have missed this for anything. Not even a pandemic." Jules pulls her mom into a hug. "The house looks incredible."

Margaret has always decorated beautifully, but this year she's gone all out. Holly hangs over every doorway. The windows glow. A Christmas tree nearly touches the ceiling. Her signature simmer pot of cinnamon, cloves, and orange rinds fills every room. The scent is at once comforting, and I finally feel my shoulders relax. I sink into the chair, closing my eyes and resting while Anna nurses. Their chatter a soft backdrop of gossip and news.

Twenty minutes pass in this comfortable haze before I hear Gary's voice from the entryway. "Sydney, I found the crib we used for the twins and set it up in your room. Want me to put the pack-and-play in the sunroom?"

"That'd be perfect. Thank you."

"Mom, have you seen—" Mason's voice cuts off mid-sentence. "What are you doing? You can't do that in the middle of the family room."

It takes me a second to catch on. He means breastfeeding, *the horror*.

"That's not appropriate." He gestures with two fingers, sharp as an accusation, toward Anna on my chest.

"Mason, *chill*," Jules snaps. "She's feeding your daughter."

Margaret remains carefully composed. Gary disappears.

"No, seriously. Don't feed her out in the open." Mason's face reddens. "You're... you're all exposed. Please go upstairs to feed her."

The request hangs in the air.

A year ago, I might've said okay. Six months ago, I might've reached for a blanket.

But today?

"Actually," I say, meeting his gaze, "I'll feed our daughter wherever I choose." I shift Anna gently against my shoulder. "But she's done eating."

I stand, adjusting my sweater with calm precision. "I'm going for a run. Margaret, would you mind watching the monitor? I'll bring it down before I leave."

Margaret nods, a little too quickly. Jules offers a small, satisfied smile. One that says *finally*. And Mason? He doesn't have a word to say. A muscle in his jaw twitches and he follows me upstairs, gearing up for round two.

But I have something else in mind.

"I don't appreciate being spoken to like that in front of my parents," Mason mutters, unzipping his bag while I lay a sleeping Anna in her crib.

"I'm sorry, Mase." I turn and lift my top over my head, letting the moment unfurl as my breasts spill from the nursing bra, full and tender. Making sure he's watching, I slide out of my jeans, revealing lacy boy shorts. Sitting on the edge of the bed, I part my legs and lean back on my hands, presenting the body he once couldn't get enough of. "Can I make it up to you?"

He looks me over, but instead of desire, all I see are the same dull, bored eyes I've been seeing for months, since my pregnancy started to show and my body changed. Grabbing his clothes, he disappears into the closet.

I change fast, not looking in the mirror.

And that's been the biggest shift over the past year. No matter how distant Mason and I have always been, he wanted me. That desire was the tether; the thing that made it bearable.

But now? I'm invisible.

That shift—quiet at first, now loud and unmistakable—has turned the space between us into a chasm. Something I can't smooth over or deny. And because we don't *talk* about things in our marriage, it festers, grows in the silence and stretches wider with every passing month.

***

AFTER DINNER, MARGARET WHISKS Anna away, giving me a rare moment to enjoy uninterrupted adult time. I settle beside Jules and the others out on the back deck, the fire pit crackling behind a curtain of sparks and smoke. The air is crisp, the kind that bites your nose but feels oddly comforting. Conversation flows easily, a rhythm of familiar banter and easy laughter.

Jules and Tom fall into their usual game of one-upmanship. Their version of foreplay.

"You won't believe what happened during a delivery last week…" Jules begins, launching into a wild tale of medical chaos that sounds more like *Grey's Anatomy* than anything from a real hospital.

Tom counters with an equally absurd story, eyes sparkling, trying to out-charm her.

Being surrounded by adults is a reprieve. But I'm quieter than usual, unsure how to slip in when my world revolves around nap windows, cluster feeds, and baby-wearing hacks.

Ivy snuggles beside James, draping her legs across his lap. He sits stiffly, hands clenched into loose fists instead of resting on her.

Our eyes meet for a fraction of a second.

Barely anything.

But it's enough.

Because I see it. The same look he gave me earlier, out on the snowy road.

I'd been burning through a run, lungs aching, muscles tightening, chasing the cold for relief from everything: Mason's rejection, my own exhaustion, the heat James stirs by existing. Each step cut loose something knotted inside me. Each breath gave me space.

Rounding a bend, I nearly slammed into a body coming from the opposite direction.

The dry, smoky whisper of bergamot and cedar hit me first.

James.

His hands gripped my shoulders, steadying me. He was damp with sweat, breath steaming in the cold, beanie pulled low.

"You good?" His chest heaved with the question.

"Just needed some air," I said, stepping out of his reach.

"You and me both."

The moment stretched between us longer than it should have. Until he turned left. I turned right. But the heat lingered.

Now, by the fire, I tip my head toward the stars, inhale the sharp scent of smoke and snow, and sit between two worlds. The man to my right, who will never understand what it is to look at the night sky and *wish*—and the man across the fire, who ignites something impossible to ignore.

"Syd?" Ivy's voice cuts through the haze. "How long is your maternity leave? When are you heading back to the firm?"

Jules and I share a look; only she knows how much my old ambitions don't fit anymore. I want something slower. A life with time in it. A balance between my career and life. One that was always skewed toward work before.

"I have two more months left of leave," I pause and decide to open the window into my mind and see how Mason reacts. "But honestly, I don't know if I'll go back in the same capacity. I'm not interested in sixteen-hour days or chasing the partner track anymore."

Mason's smile falters for half a second, then he barks out a laugh. "Leave? More like a paid vacation if you ask me."

The word he's been rolling his eyes at for months. He's never outright said it, but I think he expected me to take a few weeks, hire a nanny, and be back to the grind. Because no matter how much he said he wanted a baby, he didn't want it to shift my priorities.

A quiet, bitter fire sparks in my chest. I think of the night feeds, the sleep deprivation, the cracked nipples and crying jags. The endless effort I give to Anna. And he dares to call it a *vacation*.

Jules straightens her spine, ready to go to war.

But it's James who speaks first.

"That's one hell of a vacation," he says coolly. "No sleep. Constant caregiving. I wonder when Club Med will start offering that package?"

He leans forward, elbows on knees, eyes fixed on Mason. I hear the challenge in his voice. They stare at each other for a beat before Mason leans back and shrugs.

"I wouldn't go *that* far. There's way too much shit involved for it to be an actual vacation. But come on, I've seen our Netflix queue. It can't be all bad."

"What the fuck, Mason?" Jules snaps. "Are you seriously this much of a dick?"

James scoffs and walks away. Ivy sits there wide-eyed watching.

"I get it's not a luxury vacation," Mason says with a dismissive wave. "But babies sleep too. And when you've got nothing else to do all day, how hard can it be?"

The words land with stinging force.

My vision blurs, but I blink hard, forcing the tears back. He won't see me cry. Eyes are on me, waiting for my reaction. I give them nothing.

"I think I've had enough. Goodnight, everyone."

My voice is steady, more than I feel. Back straight, steps measured, dignity clutched tight.

Eleven

ANNA NURSES PEACEFULLY IN my arms, her tiny fingers curling against my skin, a balm to the sting of Mason's careless words as we nestle into a corner of the sunroom. I trace each tiny finger, memorizing every detail. The delicate knuckles, the tender creases—each part of her changing so quickly, I can barely capture these moments.

There was a time I couldn't imagine stepping away from my career.

I'd never planned to take the full six months my firm offered. But the moment I looked into Anna's eyes, everything shifted. I knew taking leave was career suicide, but for the first time, I didn't care. My priorities realigned, and I know how lucky I am.

The trust fund my parents left, their one kindness, means I have economic freedom and a choice to go back or not, and decide what fits my new goals.

A tree glows in the corner, its twinkling lights casting gentle shadows. The scent of pine lingers, wrapping around me as Tinashe's velvet-drenched Christmas album unfurls into the hush. Music sways through the room and I let it carry me, stirring what's been humming beneath the surface since we arrived.

The creaky floorboard in the hallway groans.

I freeze.

"Sorry," James whispers. "I couldn't sleep. Heard the music... thought I'd find you here."

"This is one of my favorite Christmas albums. I only play it at night; not exactly the cheery carols people expect from holiday music."

"Is it okay if I join you?"

I hesitate, not because I don't want him to, but because I do. More than I should.

"Yes. Please."

He sinks into the chair across from me. Eyes closed, he lets the music move through him. Tinashe's voice is low and aching, each note suspended in the air.

When his eyes open to find me already looking at him, the dimple I've tried not to think about for months deepens. James's gaze sweeps down for the briefest second. My bare legs are tucked beneath me, my sleep shirt undone enough for Anna to nurse. He finds the freckles on my collarbone. He swallows hard, and every inch of me tightens.

The desire, the restraint, the thread pulled so tight between us that one tug would snap it.

Don't you feel this?

I've tried to smother every thought, convinced myself time and distance had warped it all, turned it into something it never was. Told myself it was exhaustion. Loneliness. A fleeting moment spun into fantasy.

But the way he's looking at me now?

I know the truth.

It was never nothing. Whatever sparked between us last year hasn't faded.

Anna stirs against me, her tiny mouth still working in her sleep—and the duality of this moment, my child at my breast while my heart pounds for a man who isn't her father, feels like the most honest metaphor for my life.

He opens his mouth, ready to say something—

Footsteps thump down the hall.

James straightens, sinking back into the chair instead of crossing a line he couldn't uncross.

I glance at the rubber band on my wrist. Wanting something doesn't mean I can have it. I pull. Hard.

The snap makes me wince, but I welcome it. I need it.

"Hey." His voice cuts through the pain. "What was that? The rubber band… why would you do that?"

I don't meet his eyes. "It's nothing. Just something I do to remind myself of my responsibilities."

He moves without a word and kneels beside my chair. His thumb skims over the welt, back and forth. A shiver shoots up my arm from that single point of contact.

James clears his throat. "I'm gonna grab a drink."

As soon as he's gone, I lay a sleeping Anna in her pack-and-play and snatch my phone from the table, fingers moving frantically to change the music. By the time James walks back in, I want to pretend whatever passed between us was only in my head.

"Wine?" he asks, returning with a glass in one hand, a large cup of water in the other, and an ice pack. *Damn him.* He sets the glasses on the side table, runs his thumb along the welt again, then places the ice pack on top, his eyes holding a softness that threatens to pull me under.

"Thanks," I manage, the word catching in my throat.

Taylor Swift plays now. One of my favorites, a quiet, acoustic, stripped-down album. More to do with relationships ending than night conversations full of innuendo. I wrap my free arm around my knees, but I leave the ice pack in place. He did go to the trouble, after all.

"I love this album," James confesses. "One of the best things to come out of the pandemic. I'm secure enough to admit I'm a Swiftie."

"If that's true, what's your favorite song?"

It comes out half-teasing, half-daring; like I'm hoping he'll name one of the overplayed radio hits and prove he's not as thoughtful or sincere as he comes across.

He smiles. Slow. *Knowing.* "That's tough. She's the one artist I'd most want to headline the amphitheater. Imagine her, a piano, and a guitar."

"I'd be the first to buy tickets," I let out a wistful sigh.

"You'll be the first person I call if it ever happens." He leans forward, nothing playful in his tone.

I tilt my head, skeptical, keeping us in the safe zone. "Ahhh, but you still need to prove you're a real Swiftie. I need a song. And not one of the chart-toppers."

His mouth twitches, and he reaches for his phone, disconnecting mine from the speaker.

Taylor's voice spills into the room, breathless, impossibly vulnerable. The slow, hypnotic beat winds its way through the quiet. The lyrics seep in, their meaning impossible to ignore, singing of that fragile shift where attraction becomes something deeper. Something *Delicate*. Something real.

The seconds stretch endlessly, each one sinking deeper, reaching through walls I thought were impenetrable.

When I finally meet his steady green eyes, he asks, "Does that work?"

I take a slow breath, swallow it all down. "Tell me more about the amphitheater."

And so, we talk.

For *hours*.

While Anna snores. While the fire crackles low. While the world falls away.

It's the kind of conversation that feels like slipping into a favorite sweater. There's no posturing, no need to perform. Laughter comes without hesitation, stories tumble out freely, and that rare ease that comes when someone... gets you.

"Have I ever told you how I discovered I'm allergic to cats?" James asks, and I see the mischief in his eyes.

"I'm guessing it's not a severe allergy based on your grin?"

"I was fifteen, desperately trying to impress this girl. Sarah Mitchell. She was way out of my league, but somehow I'd convinced her to let me come over and study." He runs a hand through his hair, grinning. "Her family had this massive Persian cat named Duchess. Pure white, fluffy as a cloud, and, according to Sarah, 'the sweetest thing in the world'."

"Hmm. Sweetest thing. I can already tell where this is going."

"So I'm sitting next to her trying to be charming, when Duchess jumps up, purring and rubbing against me. Sarah's practically melting, saying Duchess never likes anyone, that this means I'm 'special'." He shakes his head. "I'm thinking I've hit the jackpot."

"But?"

"I start sneezing, my eyes watering. I realize I'm having some kind of allergic reaction, but I can't push the cat away because Sarah thinks this is true love." His voice rises, animated. "So I'm sitting there, eyes streaming, trying to breathe through my nose, when Duchess decides my lap is the perfect place for a nap."

I'm laughing so hard I have to wipe a tear from the corner of my eye. "Oh no."

"Oh yes. And that's when I discovered this 'sweet' cat had razors for claws. Every time I tried to shift, she dug in deeper. I was being held hostage by a furry dictator while slowly suffocating. I'm sure the red eyes looked great on me in my pursuit of the girl."

"How long did this go on?"

"Twenty minutes! Twenty minutes of torture while Sarah's going on about calculus, and I'm dying. Finally, I couldn't take it anymore. I sneezed so hard that Duchess went flying off my lap, landed on the coffee table, and knocked over some antique vase."

"No!"

Lost in the moment, I don't hear the approaching footsteps.

"Aren't you two cozy?" Ivy stands in the doorway, scanning our faces. "Who's this Duchess?" She crosses the room, eyes darting between us before settling next to James. One hand drapes casually around his neck.

"I couldn't sleep. Sydney was kind enough to let me hang out. I was telling some silly story from high school." He shifts, gaining some space between their bodies.

"Wow, I didn't realize how late it was." I'm already gathering Anna's sleeping form into my arms. "I should get some sleep before she wakes again. Goodnight."

As I walk away, Ivy whispers, "Will you come to bed?"

Jealousy rises, sharp and metallic in my throat. Impossible to swallow. I bite the inside of my cheek, trying to drown out the burning images, burning questions. *Will he follow her? Will he touch her the way he stroked my wrist?*

Entering our dark bedroom, I place Anna in her crib, my fingers trailing across her soft cheek. So utterly dependent on me for everything—including the choices I make. I can't get this wrong. Can't let my whims overshadow the most important thing: keeping her safe and loved.

Mason stirs as I slide into bed. "I'm sorry about earlier, Syd."

"I know. It's okay. We're both tired."

It's not okay, and it wasn't fatigue. But every nerve in me buzzes with restless, aching need. I press against him, searching for something to ground me, to dull the burn James left behind. He's still more asleep than awake. I reach down, rubbing my hand along the front of Mason's sleep pants. I stroke him back and forth, waking his desire as I unbutton my sleep shirt and bring his hand to my breast.

"What are you doing?" he asks, slowly awakening.

"Mase, I'm healed. The doctor gave us the okay months ago. I need you. Please."

He wakes enough to take charge of his hands. His touch remains tentative, as if he's unsure or worried I might leak.

"I won't break," I growl, desperate.

His eyes widen, and something clicks. His grip tightens. I gasp.

"Are you sure, Syd? I don't want to hurt you."

"Yes. God, yes."

Finally, Mason flips us over, pinning me beneath him. His hands roam, relearning the planes of my body. I will him on; will this to fill what I need. His lips trace a slow path down my collarbone, and I let myself sink into it. The memory of how it used to be. The safety in rhythm. The knowing that together our bodies will find pleasure.

He grips my wrists, bringing them over my head. His thumb brushes over my skin and he slows, pausing on the welt. "What's this?" He asks, kissing my shoulder.

"It's nothing. I forgot it was there."

And I'm no longer here.

I'm back in the sunroom with James's eyes on me, his fingers rubbing that same welt, looking at me like this body, reshaped by motherhood, is something to revere. Not beautiful in spite of the changes, but because of them. Every curve, every softness: honored. Wanted.

I pull Mason closer, clinging to him, desperate now. Trying to anchor myself in the familiarity of his body, of this life we've built.

As if I can force myself back into this moment, into this marriage, by sheer will alone.

TWELVE

My eyes blink open, the harsh morning sun clearing away the shadows of last night.

I stretch my body for a long, luxurious moment—only to feel the ache between my legs, a sharp reminder of everything I tried to chase in the dark. My wrist still bears a faint red welt, tender to the touch.

That damn rubber band has never once stopped my mind from drifting to James, just like crawling into Mason's arms didn't erase the memory of James's fingers brushing my skin.

Pavlovian training, my ass. I hurl it across the room.

When Anna and I finally make our way toward the sounds of the family in the kitchen, I pause at the bottom of the stairs. Mason sits at the table, a newspaper spread wide, chatting easily with his parents. The scent of Margaret's early morning baking drifts through the air, mingling with the soft hum of "Silent Night" playing from the speaker. My nephews, game devices in hand, are locked in silent competition.

Gary stands and kisses Margaret's cheek. "Can I get you some more coffee, love?"

"Thank you, sweetheart. I'll take another."

After all these years, it's not a performance. It's just love. Worn, comfortable, sure.

"Good morning, sleepyhead." Mason glances up and notices Anna and me. He stands briefly to kiss her cheek, and offers me a small, sly smile. "You look... rested."

His voice is light, teasing. And for a second, I catch a glimpse of the man I married: the one who used to run out for bagels after my morning runs, who programmed the coffee pot every night, who, that first night we met, read my desire to be invisible and met it with acceptance.

I take in his easy grin, the casual warmth. Maybe last night meant something. Maybe, even if it's not everything, it's enough. I almost convince myself of that lie until James walks up from the basement.

He's in gray sweatpants, a sweat-dampened tee clinging to his chest and trim waist, hair swept back from his forehead. I track the length of him before I force myself to stop. Too late. He catches me, a slow smirk curving his mouth.

"Morning," James says, casual and unbothered.

Anna turns her head, her big eyes tracking his movement. She smiles. A wide, toothless grin, the kind she's only started giving out. He stops to tickle her belly, eliciting a soft giggle. His arm brushes mine, barely a touch, as he reaches for a coffee mug. I step back too fast, sloshing my coffee dangerously close to the rim.

"Careful." His hand steadies me before pulling away.

The kitchen feels smaller. Too warm. His scent, fresh sweat, and that woodsy cologne, cut through the cinnamon and baking pies. I glance down, automatically reaching for the rubber band. Damn it.

"Good workout?" Mason asks, joining us near the coffee pot.

"Didn't sleep great. I needed to burn some steam." James takes a sip, eyes darting toward me.

I look away, burying the blush that rises too easily, as I take in them standing side by side.

They keep talking about workout and training plans, falling into safe territory, while I force myself to breathe. To look normal. I reach for something solid to say, instead of standing here like a fumbling teenager.

"Did you run Chicago? I haven't been paying attention to whether races were on or canceled."

James lifts an eyebrow, surprised I remembered. "Another casualty of COVID. Hopefully, it will happen this coming fall. Want to run it with me, get your next star?"

"Not sure I'll be ready for a marathon by then. I don't want to push too fast and end up injured."

"We bought you that treadmill. It only takes a little prioritizing." Mason's voice takes on that condescending tone that grates every last nerve.

"Sometimes sleep is a priority. Especially if Anna's had a rough night."

"If running was a priority, you'd find the time." He shrugs. "It's not like you've got a ton going on right now."

James, though, is having none of it. "Right. Because growing, birthing, and keeping a human alive—that's totally low effort."

His sarcasm is thick enough that even Anna probably hears it.

Mason doesn't say another word. He drains his coffee, announces he's heading to the gym, and walks out without a glance back. James watches him go, jaw clenched.

A silent scream builds in my chest, clawing at my ribs. I want to break something. To watch it shatter and join everything else I've spent months trying to hold together.

But I don't.

I raise my coffee to my lips and swallow down the bitterness.

"Sydney," Margaret's gentle voice calls out. "Can I take Anna? We'll play and I'll put her down for her nap."

"Thank you. That would be great."

Breathe. Smile. Don't crack.

"The Dickens Festival is this afternoon. Will you join us, or is it too much, even with masks?" She asks, taking Anna in her arms, pausing to blow a raspberry on her stomach.

"As much as I'd love to go, I think it's safer if we skip this year."

Another sting to add. Not missing something I love, but knowing it won't even occur to Mason to stay with Anna. A simple, thoughtful gesture that would cost him nothing and mean everything.

"James, is the guest room okay?" Margaret asks.

He nods, flushing. "Yeah, it's great. Thank you."

"I don't want to make you uncomfortable, but you know it's fine if you stay in Ivy's room. We're all adults here." She disappears, her words echoing in her wake.

I turn to the sink full of dishes. Anything to silence the quiet chaos left behind from Mason. From Margaret.

James grabs a dish towel and steps beside me, falling into sync. Wash, dry, put away. The rhythm is oddly steadying.

"You okay?" he asks after a round of drying mugs.

"I'm fine."

He tilts his head, studying me with that unnerving ability to peel back layers I've spent years stitching in place. Layers no one is supposed to see.

I snap, sharper than I mean to. "Will you please stop doing that? I can't have you looking at me like that."

His brows lift with that maddeningly smug expression. "Like what?"

My pulse trips. Because this man is making it impossible to keep lying to myself.

His voice drops. "You know, there's a thin ring of gold around your irises. When you're flustered, it's like it catches fire. You keep yourself so locked down, but that, Sydney... you can't control."

"Stop saying my name like that."

"Like what, Sydney?" He lets each syllable roll off his tongue. His eyes pin me in place, and when he bites his lower lip, the smugness sharpens into something darker.

My careful control shatters. And the truth slips out.

"Like... you're undressing me."

His eyes drop to my mouth. He breathes in, slow and deep, and I feel it everywhere. I lean forward as his towering body bends. One more inch and—

"Good morning!" Ivy says breezily as she enters the kitchen.

I jerk back, spinning toward the sink. My cheeks blaze as I grab an already-clean plate and start scrubbing desperately. I pray Ivy doesn't notice.

Doesn't see. But the chemistry is so potent it could set a high school science lab ablaze by sheer proximity alone; I don't know how she can't.

James stands frozen, blinking like someone turned on a spotlight. He clears his throat and says, "We're finishing up the dishes."

"What are you guys chatting about? Looked intense." Ivy leans against the island, tone casual.

A high-pitched laugh escapes, quick as the lie tumbling out of my mouth. "Just debating a book we both read."

Her head tilts. "What book? Maybe I'll read it too."

"A thriller, dark and twisty," James offers. "Probably not your thing."

"But maybe it could be, if I gave it a shot."

"*Lock Every Door*," he says without hesitating.

One of the books we picked for each other, and my heart skips a beat.

I stare at him for half a second before I blurt out, "I'm actually heading to the gym."

And force my feet to move as my pulse hammers in my throat. Still tasting the heat of him, feeling that reckless second where I thought he might kiss me. Knowing how badly I wanted it.

One more second.

That's all it would have taken to blow up my life and turn this careful dance of glances and loaded conversations into something that would shatter everything. My marriage. Anna's world. The thought terrifies me as much as how badly I wanted it to happen.

Running has always been my escape, the way I outrun what I don't want to feel. But pregnancy changed my body, and now, running has to be paired with weightlifting. So I have to hope that throwing some heavy weights around can absorb this crushing ache.

Each squat, I push against the confines of my life. Each lunge fights against the pull threatening to disrupt everything, pushups to maintain my control.

I catch my reflection in the gym's mirrored wall and force myself to look. See beyond the things I've been conditioned to critique. My body might be rounder, but it carried Anna safely into the world. My stomach is softer, my hips wider, my skin marked by change. But my arms are stronger from holding her close through sleepless nights. My legs are steady from hours of bouncing her to sleep.

Different. Not broken.

Every inch of this new skin is a testament to motherhood. To love. To sacrifice.

From the corner of my eye, I see Mason watching me through the mirror. He steps off the treadmill, sweat gleaming on his skin. He moves with the ease of someone who's never questioned his own worth.

He steps behind me, aligning our reflections as his hand settles on my stomach. The touch is light, absent-minded. I almost believe it's reverent.

Leaning close, his breath warm against my ear, he says, "Don't worry, babe, you'll lose this pouch in no time."

I freeze. Muscles coiled. My breath catches. I meet his eyes in the mirror, searching for awareness. But his expression is earnest, as though he handed me a gift.

"What?"

Mason frowns. "I meant...you'll be back in shape before you know it. Keep putting in the work."

My hand instinctively tugs at the hem of my tank. With a cold stare, I say, "Thanks for the encouragement, honey. I think I'm done for today."

"Hey, come on," he calls out as the door slams in my wake.

I escape to a scalding hot shower.

This isn't even surprising. His blind spots aren't new. They're old bruises. Familiar ones. He's never had to think twice about his body. Never wondered if he's too much, or not enough. A man with money, access, endless praise. His confidence came prepackaged. He has no concept of what it means to internalize every unspoken judgment until it shapes you.

The bathroom door opens.

"Syd, look... I didn't mean it like that. I didn't think you'd take it that sensitively."

Of course, he didn't. And I know exactly what he's saying: *I'm* the problem. My reaction is the issue, not his words. For years, I've swallowed these casual cruelties, smoothed them over, made everything easier for him. But I'm done making myself small to keep him comfortable.

"I'm not being sensitive, and I'm not worried about getting my body back. Every new curve, every mark—I wear them with fucking honor. They're not something I want erased."

Mason stares as if this conversation has veered wildly off-script. "I didn't mean… I know running matters to you. That's why we bought the treadmill."

"Fuck the treadmill." My heart pounds as if I've sprinted up a mountain. "Running has never been about calories or looking a certain way. It's about freedom. Pushing myself. Feeling strong. How do you not know that?"

Silence stretches as we both take in everything left hanging in that question.

Anna whimpers. Crackling through the baby monitor, breaking our stares. When she latches on, the tug at my nipple is sharp, a reminder that this, here, is where I'm needed—in the role where I can't afford ambiguity, and the nudge I need to soften and lower my expectations, once again.

Mason stands in the doorway, shifting on his feet.

"Are you not attracted to me anymore?" I ask.

He blinks, caught off guard by my directness, staying rooted in place.

"This is me now. I might not be the same woman you married, but I'm still here. Still your wife. Still a woman. I need you to *want* this version of me."

Mason closes the distance and lowers himself to his knees, a soft smile on his lips. "I'm such an asshole. You're so beautiful, Syd. Please forgive me."

I search his face for any sign that his words are more than just an empty script. For any hint of the fire I saw from James. He tucks his face into my neck as though he knows it will show the lie.

A lone bird perches on a nearby pine tree, its head tilting, listening to something in the wind. A calling that only it can hear. Its wings flutter, hesitating for a heartbeat, before lifting off and flying away.

No second-guessing. No turning back.

THIRTEEN

The cabin walls feel smaller with each passing hour.

I'm trapped with a newborn, unable to go out with COVID rampant. Anna is too young to be vaccinated. Outside, the sun bathes the mountain in gold, promising a freedom beyond my reach. Inside, I'm frozen.

Laughter and voices drift up as the house stirs around us. Sounds of the family returning from the festival.

"Hey, you." Jules stands in the doorway of the sunroom, where Anna and I have been playing.

"How was it?"

"Cute as always, a little weird with masks. What's up? You've got that deep-in-thought look again." Jules sinks onto the carpet, tickling Anna's belly.

I choose my words carefully. "Can I ask you something… personal?"

"Of course. What's going on?"

"After you had the boys… did things change between you and Tom? Physically, I mean?"

She studies me, her amber eyes softening in the pause.

"I know you don't want to hear about your brother's sex life, but… something has shifted between us." I clench my shaking hands. "He barely touches me, and when he does, it's after I've practically begged."

"Tom and I had a readjustment period. Your body changes. Your priorities shift. You're exhausted. It takes time to find your way back to each other. But the difference is...we talked about it. We showed up for each other. Even when it was hard."

I swallow. And say it: "It's more than the sex, Jules."

"I know that, babe. Are you ready to finish the conversation we started last year?" She holds my eyes with a strength I wish I could find. "I'm here for you whenever you're ready."

But she's not done, and the wicked glint in her eye says she's about to go full Jules on me.

"Luckily, this isn't the seventeenth century. You don't need Mason for orgasms. That's what vibrators are for." She smirks and grabs my phone, switching off the soft nursery rhymes. "And you don't need him to feel good in your body. You can claim that all on your own."

A beat drops. Beyoncé's sensual voice booms through the speakers.

Jules pulls me up, eyes glittering, "Come on, Syd. Channel your inner goddess. Walk out of here knowing you're a bad bitch with a fine ass."

"Fuck it." I accept the dare, throw my arms in the air, and let my body move. Awkward at first, self-conscious.

Each sultry lyric pushes something loose inside me. I start to sway, letting the music lead. The rhythm builds, and I follow, hips rolling, shoulders rocking, something waking up inside me.

I catch a glimpse of myself in the window's reflection, the way I move, the way I own the space. There's allure in it. Grace. Power. For someone who's spent so long feeling unseen, it's revolutionary to truly see myself.

I don't need anyone else to see it.

I see it. I feel it.

Jules scoops up Anna and twirls her, laughing, while I keep dancing, this rhythm meant for no one but myself.

Beyoncé becomes my anthem. I grind. I shake. I reclaim. Every beat sinks in a little deeper, filling me up, so when the song ends, I'll carry this feeling with me.

This proof that I don't need permission to feel good in my own skin. A *Partition* between the past and future.

This liberation? It's mine.

Jules glances over my shoulder, and I don't have to turn to know. I *feel* him. That almost physical sensation of his gaze brushing the base of my neck, trailing heat down my spine.

James leans against the doorframe, ten feet away, and my skin tightens in response. Our eyes meet. A look similar to the one in the kitchen flashes across his face. Undeniable. Scorching hot. Before he looks away, down at the woman beside him, Ivy.

Jules calls out, "Want to join our dance party? The more the merrier. Syd is showing off her moves."

Ivy hesitates, glancing at James but his eyes are closed. She moves into the room with slow, seductive choreography. James doesn't follow. When his eyes open, they go straight to me.

And I'm too aware of myself.

The flush on my cheeks. The thin sheen of sweat on my skin. The rise and fall of my chest, too quick, too shallow. Every sway of my hips becomes a prayer.

Jules leans close, her voice a low, calm force. "And maybe someday soon, you'll tell me why James is looking at you like he's trying not to drown."

She spins me, forcing me to face him.

His eyes are heavy-lidded, and I'm mesmerized by the rhythm of his breathing. A small hollow forms at the base of his throat with each inhale, vanishing as he exhales. I count that gentle rise and fall four times when—

"Yes, ladies!" Ivy bumps her hip against mine.

I reach for my phone, swallowing down the heat on my cheeks, switching the music back to lullabies as I take Anna from Jules. My lips press to her head as I inhale the sweet scent of baby soap and dried milk. "Now this is more our speed."

Jules gives me a knowing look. I will my face to cool because whatever she is trying to decipher, I'm not sure I'm hiding it well. She turns to Ivy, "Come on. Mom asked us to help her with dinner."

As their footsteps fade down the hallway, the hush that settles in the sunroom is anything but calm. It crackles—electric, alive with everything simmering underneath. I meet his eyes again, and every inch between us feels too loud.

James steps toward me, humming along to the faint lullaby. Each step he takes is measured. His hand hovers near my shoulder, close enough that I feel the heat of it, trembling with the effort not to touch me. He sets a small bag on the chair and steps back. His hand presses lightly to his heart in a quiet, devastating gesture that steals mine.

"That was the sexiest thing I've ever seen."

And he leaves.

I stand there, my breath caught somewhere between my head and my stomach. Swallowing hard, I reach for the bag. My fingers brush the hard edges of a book cover before I pull it free. A new release I haven't read yet, but have been dying to get my hands on.

Tucked between the pages is a folded note.

Thought of you when I saw this.

Wanted to make sure you got your Christmas Eve book.

-J

I close my eyes, willing my heart to slow. "Shh, shh," I murmur to Anna, though she's already fast asleep.

***

AFTER DINNER, WITH ANNA and the older kids in bed, I bundle up and leash Bell for an evening walk under the moonlight. I need the cold air, the quiet. Something to ground me before I can sit on the back deck with the others, another performance of being "fine."

"Jules, will you keep an eye on Anna?" I hand her the monitor before slipping away, avoiding the eyes of everyone else.

Bell and I meander down the snowy trail behind the house, the path winding deeper into the trees. The evergreens stand tall, their snow-crusted limbs bending under the weight of winter. Wind whips through the branches, swirling flakes into the air, biting at my exposed skin. The moon burns bright enough to light my way.

Suddenly, the sharp crunch of snow—

A twig snaps—

The night splits open with sound—

I snatch up a fallen branch, raising it like a weapon.

"I'm sorry! I didn't mean to sneak up on you." A deep voice cuts through the dark. One I'd recognize anywhere.

James steps into view, his hands raised in surrender.

I toss the branch aside. "In my years of running, it doesn't take much to put me on high alert. I'm conditioned to be ready for anything."

He exhales. "Fuck. I hate that." A pause, before he asks, "Can I join you?"

"If you want," I say, starting toward where the path divides.

We walk in silence, weaving through the trees, stepping carefully over fallen limbs, avoiding hidden divots in the snow-blanketed ground. The night is still, broken only by the wind's low whistle, a distant owl, and Bell's occasional bark.

Our shoulders brush—once, twice. As if by instinct, we drift closer and just as quickly, we remember we can't.

"Did you write a letter to Santa this year?" He asks, clever amusement warming his face.

"Of course. Didn't you?"

"Naturally. Though I'm not sure how the big guy feels about fulfilling the wishes of a grown man."

"And what exactly did you ask for?"

He pauses dramatically until I can't help but smile. "Peace on earth. End of world hunger. And... new running sneakers."

"Ah, so the basics."

"Exactly." He nudges me lightly with his elbow. "What about you? What does Sydney Wallis put on her Christmas list?"

"Sleep. Long, uninterrupted sleep," I sigh, staring at the night sky.

"Now that's a solid wish. If I could give you that, I would."

Night enfolds us, stars scattered through the naked branches. How long has it been since I stood under the stars with someone who's made me laugh? Who's asked about my wishes? We walk in silence for a while, lost in our heads. The charge in the air grows with each quiet step. Like each step is willing truths to spill.

"What's your favorite Christmas memory?" I ask, aiming for something safe.

He falls quiet, his breath fogging in slow, visible puffs, eyes cast forward.

"The year I got my first set of professional drawing pencils and a sketchbook. My mom gave me the drawing stuff. It wasn't a lot, but it was just her and me sitting around a tree and drinking hot cocoa. It was the first Christmas we spent without my father."

"I've seen you sketching around the house. Is it for work, or do you still do it for fun?"

He studies my face, deciding how honest to be.

"Both," he says at last. "I hand-draw all my building concepts. It's how I start every design. But lately... I've been sketching for myself again."

I hesitate, my pulse stuttering, because I know the next question. I know what I want to ask. And the way he's looking at me, already waiting for it, makes it worse. I look away and search the night sky.

"What about you? Favorite Christmas memory?" he asks, rubbing the back of his neck.

My mind flashes through a thousand fragments: ornate trees in cavernous, silent houses; gifts from my nanny; parents who didn't show; Europe in winter—train rides alone, hotel-room dinners, pool halls smelling of second chances and regret. Instead of getting lost in those memories, Anna's face and her milk-drunk sighs come to mind. The warmth of her tiny fingers curling around mine, the way her entire body softens in sleep when she knows I'm near.

"I... I don't have great memories from Christmases with my parents. But I think... this one will be my favorite. And every one after. I want Anna to have the kind of Christmas mornings I never did—to come down the stairs, knowing I'll be there, waiting with the biggest smile, blasting cheesy Christmas songs while she rips open presents even at 5 AM."

We keep walking, the sound of our footsteps muffled by fresh snow. The conversation lingers, mirroring the space we pretend to keep.

"You're a good mom." He bumps my shoulder, this time on purpose.

It's a simple phrase. One mothers hear all the time. But coming from him, it lands differently, because he doesn't just see me as Anna's mother. He sees me. The woman beneath all of it, with sharp edges, soft centers, and all the damn feelings I try to lock away.

"Is your wrist better?" he asks. "I noticed the rubber band wasn't on it."

There's a gentleness in his voice, but the question is anything but casual. He's not asking about my wrist, he's asking what it means. Why did I take it off?

"Yeah. My wrist is fine."

"Sydney..." His voice drops, dangerous truth hovering at the edge of his words, his hand soft against my elbow.

Voices drift from the back deck: Tom, Jules, Ivy, Mason. Laughing. Waiting. Margaret and Gary sleep unaware of the tremors shaking the cabin's walls. And Anna. The one person I can't let down.

I cut him off. "I think you should go up that way. I'll go up the back stairs."

The moment the words leave my mouth, I hear what they betray. It's an admission, plain and simple. That there's something between us worth concealing. That no matter how innocent the walk was... it wasn't innocent at all.

James stops walking and stares at me until he exhales a harsh puff of air. "Yeah. I'll go around and wait a few minutes before heading out to the deck."

His eyes hold mine a moment longer as he pulls off his beanie and runs his hand through his hair. He tilts his head, listening to the voices, and walks off into the trees. I tip my head back and slide my mask back into place. Pretend I'm not returning from anything more than a walk in the woods.

Jules spots me first. "She's still out."

"Thank you. Any wine open?"

"Here you go, love." Mason hands me a glass, offering it as if this simple gesture could erase this morning's sting. "How was your walk?"

"Fine."

His smile falters when I don't return it. I sink beside Jules, gripping my glass, trying to calm the storm inside.

"Hey, handsome. Where'd you escape to?" Ivy calls as James steps onto the deck.

"Ah, just relaxing for a bit."

I keep my eyes on the flames, pulsing in the dark, a heartbeat too loud to ignore, matching my own.

God, if this were lust, it would be simple. Lust is easy, fleeting, physical. A spark you can burn through and walk away from. But this? This is something else entirely. It's as silent and delicate as a web, spun tighter with every stolen moment.

A Pussycat Dolls song, sultry and provocative, cuts through the night. Jules stands in the center, hair blazing, hips already swaying.

"Come on, you sexy goddess." Jules grabs my hands. "Time for a repeat performance."

I hesitate, glancing toward Mason, rigid, hand gripping his glass. The ease from before is gone. Is he reacting to James? Or me? Did he notice our coincidental return? But tonight, I refuse to shrink beneath his disapproval. With a defiant lift of my chin, I surrender to the music and dance. Ivy hops in.

We become a tangle of limbs and laughter, casting aside inhibitions. My movements grow deliberate, sensual. My hands glide down my curves, tracing each dip as my knees bend and hips roll with confidence. I channel long-forgotten music videos and hazy college nights.

Am I doing this for myself? To see the look on James's face? To make Mason see me?

Maybe all of the above.

The three of us dance wild under the stars, and I let myself get lost in the freedom.

Until Mason steps forward.

He grabs my wrist. Not hard enough to hurt, but with enough force to make it clear it's not a caress. His fingers press against my skin as he pulls me away.

"Syd, sit down and act like a mother."

The words are quiet but laced with a sharpness that cuts through the evening air. I pull back, but his fingers dig deeper. Ivy lingers farther down the deck, back turned—too far to hear or unwilling to face what's unfolding behind her—while everyone else's attention zeroes in on his hand gripping my wrist. Something dark passes over James's face. Concern, yes, but also something primal, making him look ready to strike.

My pulse pounds in my ears, shame flooding my cheeks. I force a smile, brittle and defiant, and yank my hand free. I spin back and let the music reclaim me.

Tom pulls Mason aside. From their hushed, heated exchange, it's clear Tom isn't backing down.

"Fuck him." Jules forces me to look at her.

Tears sting behind my eyes, but I blink them back. All he sees is me dancing, my smile wide and brazen. My body moves to the beat, a performance of boldness I don't truly feel. Until at last I hear him walk inside and slam the door, and I can breathe again.

With Mason's departure, the air shifts. Jules switches to a new song as Tom and James join. They twirl us around, taking turns with dips and spins. Easy and light. James keeps his distance, spinning Jules and Ivy while Tom takes my hand.

He wraps an arm around me. "I've been biting my tongue for too long. He might be Jules's brother, but you deserve much better."

"You're a good man, Tom. Thank you for loving Jules as you do."

"We're not as rare as you think." His eyes sweep over my shoulder to James, spinning Jules until she's doubled over with laughter. I follow his gaze and swallow hard.

"I think it's time I head upstairs."

"Hold up, Syd. Want me to walk upstairs with you?"

"I'll be fine." I squeeze his hand as Jules clicks off the music.

We stand in an awkward circle, and I keep my eyes fixed on my feet.

"Should we put on a movie?" Ivy suggests filling the silence.

"Not tonight, Ives." Jules cuts her off. "I think it's time to call it a night."

"Did I miss something?" Ivy's voice softens, as if she's only now realizing the tension.

"No, it's nothing. Goodnight." I slip away before anyone can respond.

Relief washes over me as I enter our empty room. I press the door closed, unable to shake his grip on my wrist, the sharpness of his words. Hot tears spill down my cheeks as I breathe through the sting in my nose.

Is this what I want Anna to see?

A man grabbing you when he disapproves of how you're acting? Directing your body like it belongs to him? I imagine Anna years from now, letting someone treat her this way because she grew up thinking it was normal. The thought makes me physically ill.

I wipe away my tears and draw in a shaky breath, letting my mind go where it shouldn't.

To a man who offers something else entirely.

A world where James is beside me. Where I lean into his touch instead of pulling away. Nights swaying together in the dark, our bodies moving in quiet harmony. Mornings wrapped in blankets and books, Anna between us. The scent of coffee and his cologne mingling as he makes breakfast while I feed her.

But that's false hope, gone in the blink of an eye.

One man touched my elbow so softly it ached; another grabbed my wrist hard enough to leave faint red marks. Try as I might, neither sensation fades. I wrap my arms around my ribs, absorbing the pain the only way I know—curling inward, willing it down into the abyss where it won't hurt as much.

Fourteen

"Aunt Syd, come look at the pile of presents Santa left for us!" Beck squeals.

The boys dive into presents. Another Christmas morning, and the world keeps moving.

The deck and my wrist are now just memories pressing on the edges of my sanity this morning. The numbness I crave, the way I survived my parents, won't come. Instead, my mind frays, my body a tangle of nerves. Mason never came to our room last night, the only bright note. Jules and Tom keep a measured eye on me. James stands off to the side, gaze flicking to my wrist, lips set in a stern line.

It isn't long before he approaches with two steaming mugs and hands me one.

"Thank you." It isn't enough, but that's all I have, all that can come out.

Jules, across the room, catches the whole interaction. Tom whispers something that makes her smirk. I've never been so thankful to hear the monitor come to life, and I'm on my feet, escaping.

With snow falling outside and laughter ringing as wrapping paper flies, I settle into an armchair by the fire to nurse. Anna is so beautiful it makes my chest ache. I run a finger along her cheek, that pert button nose, and impossibly smooth skin. How do I keep her wrapped in this bubble and the pains of the world outside her grasp? A mother's job is to protect her child, no matter the cost.

Anna's eyes grow heavy as she nurses, her grip on my finger loosening. By the time she's finished, the wrapping paper frenzy downstairs has mellowed into conversation.

"I know we usually do adult gifts later, but I wanted you to have this now." Margaret approaches with a small box.

"That's so sweet. Would you hold Anna so I can open it?"

"With pleasure."

I hold my breath, unwrapping the thick paper, to reveal a small, square jewelry box. Inside lies a gold bracelet, a slim, polished plate engraved with my name.

"Motherhood changes so much," Margaret says, meeting my eyes. "I want you to remember you are more than a mom."

Air leaves my lungs. My fingers close around the cool metal, tracing the delicate script of my name.

"Thank you." I wrap my arms around Margaret, resting my head on her shoulder, Anna tucked between us. A second later, another set of arms wraps around us. Jules.

Three mothers, holding one another. Women who understand the silent burdens, unseen struggles, the ache and beauty wrapped in a simple bracelet.

"Come with me." Jules steps back, wipes my tears, and pulls me into the cold. She lights the fire pit, tosses me a blanket, and fixes me with her unyielding gaze.

"What's going on with Mason? Why is he being such a dick? What was that last night?"

"I wish I knew." I search through the windows for Anna, still wrapped in the warmth of her grandmother's arms.

"Don't do that. Don't deflect this time." Jules says, her voice sharper now. "He grabbed your wrist. *Hard.*"

"I... fuck, Jules. I wish I could say it's adjusting to fatherhood, but it's not. We haven't been good in so long."

The admission spills out, something inside my chest unhooking. My shoulders fall, breath easing for the first time in months.

Jules doesn't blink. She meets my confession and demands even more honesty.

"Syd, we've been circling this conversation for over a year. The question isn't what's wrong, it's—are you ready to stop pretending you're fine?"

"Fine has been my whole life. I don't even know what more than *fine* feels like."

"What do you mean?"

Wetness slips down my cheek before I even realize a tear has escaped my eye. Instead of answering, I ask a question of my own.

"What if our hearts can only hold so much love? Maybe there's only so much space to fill. Maybe that's why my parents never had room for me?"

"Fuck that, Syd," she snaps, grabbing my hand in both of hers. "Look at Tom and me. Look at my parents. You didn't deserve your childhood, and you sure as hell don't deserve Mason's bullshit now." She sucks in a breath, but she isn't finished. "You love Anna more than anything. You love me. Love is not finite. It expands and grows as you do. The people who believe there's a limited amount of love in the world are either too scared or too selfish."

We both know which one I am.

I wipe my eyes with the back of my hand and take a shaky breath. Jules waits, letting the silence stretch. My wedding band glints in the sunlight, weighing a thousand pounds.

Jules shifts, something electric sparking in her gaze.

"I find it interesting James brought you coffee this morning, like he's done it a hundred times before."

"It's just a cup of coffee, Jules."

She crosses her arms. "Mm-hmm. He left almost immediately after you gave me the monitor last night and came onto the deck two minutes after you got back from your walk."

I look away, but she doesn't stop.

"You think I haven't noticed? The way he watches you, like the rest of the room disappears? Or how you light up around him? I don't even think you realize it." She softens, reaching for my hand. "I'm not judging. Is there something going on?"

Most people would keep their distance. No one wants to get caught in this web, especially when it involves siblings, but Jules walks into the fire and holds up a mirror. It shouldn't surprise me that she's already noticed what I haven't dared to admit. Her loyalty is fierce to those she loves. She'll be just as blunt with Ivy.

Before Jules can press further, the door swings open. Ivy stands in the doorframe, a broad smile lighting her face. "Mind if I join?"

"Of course," Jules says smoothly, her eyes never leaving mine. "We were talking about relationships."

"Perfect, I could use some advice." Ivy drops onto a chair, gearing up for some girl talk.

I turn to stare out at the mountains, willing my eyes to dry and searching for an escape.

"How did you guys know Tom and Mason were *the ones*?" Ivy asks, her words landing like a detonation.

Jules shifts beside me. "Is this about James? I thought you two were just hanging out again after... some time apart?"

Time apart—

I didn't realize they hadn't been together since last year. Did he break up with her? Her with him? Questions I never once thought to investigate about how last Christmas affected him now flood through me. Unanswered. Unaskable.

"I mean... yeah, we did just recently reconnect. We're taking it slow, *really* slow, but I know he wants kids and a family. I've overheard him talking with his mom."

Jules tilts her head. "I knew Tom was the one when I got sick and he tried to make me soup. It was awful, truly inedible. But even in my fever haze, I could see how hard he was trying. I spat it all over the blanket, and he laughed. We're friends first. The physical part was always there, but friendship is what holds us. He doesn't flinch at the mess. He never makes me feel like I need to be easier to love."

"Or when you throw things at him," I add dryly.

"Hey, that shoe incident was an accident! The game board, though..." She shrugs, grinning, before giving Ivy her attention. "But seriously, is James your friend?"

Ivy shifts, an uncomfortable fidget. "He's... so mature. Different from anyone I've dated. And even though we don't share a lot of the same interests, I don't think that's a dealbreaker."

"No one knows what goes on inside a relationship." Jules nods slowly, taking her time to process. "But does he make you feel special? Like he'd wake up every morning and make your coffee exactly the way you prefer and be happy to do it for the rest of his life?"

Her eyes find mine on that last line, and the air catches in my chest.

"But, Syd, that's not how it is with you and Mason, right? You're not all over each other or doing a lot together. How did you know?" Ivy's big blue eyes gleam in the bright morning sun.

"Oh, I'm the wrong person to ask. My marriage advice would be like getting fitness tips from someone on life support," I say, laughing it off as a joke.

The silence that follows is heavier than I intended. Glancing toward the mountains, I watch the wind rustle through the trees. For a moment, I envy it. I long to move without hesitation, without fear, toward something.

I meet her soft, questioning eyes. "I married Mason for a million reasons. But love wasn't one of them. I don't think my relationship is one you should try to emulate."

Ivy stills, her brows furrow. She's quiet for a long moment before her voice comes out smaller than before. "What do you mean?"

"I was young and lonely. I knew the career I wanted, but I didn't have a family to share it with." I pause, weighing my words. "Mason seemed a logical choice. But I didn't realize what that meant. The little things Jules was talking about—connection and friendship—they're important and hard to build if they aren't part of your foundation."

We all sit there, sisters and sisters-in-law, in a rare moment of honesty.

Until Ivy finally asks, "So why are you still married?"

My stomach twists and I look off, staring at the mountains once again. Some truths are harder than others. Especially when the consequences reach far beyond me. I rub the slight red welt still sitting on my wrist. A rubber band. A caress. A grab. How much it has gone through in seventy-two hours.

Jules touches Ivy's arm. "If I'm being honest, if you have to ask whether someone's forever... *that's* your answer. Because when it's right, it isn't a question."

Her eyes meet mine, meaning unmistakable. She's not only talking to Ivy.

The door swings open again. Leo and Beck spill onto the deck, followed by a silent Tom and James. The three of us women exchange glances, still reeling from the confessions shared.

"Mom, we're going sledding. You want to come?" The twins jump on Jules. "What about you, Aunt Syd? Aunt Ivy?"

"I don't know if you can handle me on the hills." I laugh, grateful for the distraction.

Ivy breaks out of her reverie, the confusion on her face replaced with a soft smile. "Thanks for the invite, guys. But I'm going to stay behind. James, maybe we could spend some time together?"

"Sorry. I promised the boys I'd go."

His eyes find mine as he takes a seat across the fire pit. It lasts only a second, but the look is unmistakable. I might be sitting here in leggings and a Christmas sweater, but I've never felt more seen. More wanted.

When he said my name last night under the moonlight and touched my elbow, I knew what he wanted to ask. And there's no denying it. I feel it, every goddamn beat of it. And maybe that's the scariest part.

"Can we talk later?" Ivy curls a hand around his jaw, pulling his mouth to meet hers.

The breath leaves my lungs in one sharp exhale. I stand quickly, my chair skittering backward, and cross the deck with shaking legs, unable to watch his lips touch hers and still pretend none of this matters.

FIFTEEN

AN HOUR LATER, I'M trudging up a snow-covered hill, dragging a blue plastic sled behind me.

Tom stops halfway up, packing snow, building a ramp, taking directions from the twins on width and height. Jules hauls a basket filled with blankets, hot chocolate, and marshmallows. James walks beside me, pulling more sleds. Anna is with her grandparents. Margaret practically pushed me out the door, pressing my jacket into my hands and assuring me Anna would be fine. Mason and Ivy stayed behind, catching up on work.

The sky is that impossibly crisp blue you get after a fresh snowfall, the sun so bright it bounces off the hill in glittering sheets. The elementary school below sits quietly, its silence a reminder that the world is paused for the holiday. Families dot the slope at careful distances, waving across the white expanse while navigating both COVID precautions and the chaotic trajectories of flying children.

"When was the last time you went sledding?" James asks.

"The boys try to get us out every year. I think we missed it last year... with everything." I stop. It's the first time either of us has acknowledged how last year ended. I take a slow, centering breath before teasing, "I hope your sledding skills are better than your skating."

James tugs my hat down over my eyes before he says, "We had this perfect hill behind our house growing up. My mom would wrap me in so many layers I could barely bend, then send me flying down it for hours."

"Your mom sounds lovely."

"She is. But she swore I shaved years off her life."

"Leo and Beck are fearless. Wait until you see them hit that jump Tom is building."

We reach the top of the hill, where Jules is already setting up with military precision, laying out a waterproof blanket and unpacking supplies, pretending not to watch our approach.

"Aunt Syd! Watch this!" Leo calls, positioning his sled at the crest.

With a triumphant cry, he launches himself over the jump Tom built. Beck follows seconds later, veering off course and wiping out in a glorious explosion of snow.

He pops up immediately, shouting, "Awesome! Did you see that?"

"Boys," Jules mutters fondly. "Only creatures who celebrate pain."

"I don't know," James says, eyes glinting with mischief. "That looked pretty fun to me."

"Don't tell me you're one of those adults who reverts to a nine-year-old the second it snows."

"Guilty as charged." He positions his sled at the edge. "Race you down?"

"You're on."

Jules catches my eye with a look I pointedly ignore.

We line up our sleds side by side, the boys counting down with exaggerated enthusiasm. At "Go," we push off, speeding down the pristine hillside. The cold air whips past, stinging my cheeks, but all I can focus on is James beside me and how his laugh carries over the snow.

He hits the jump, catching impressive air before landing smoothly. I'm not so lucky. My trajectory is off, and I hit the edge of the jump, sending my sled into a wild spin before tipping over. I tumble into a snowbank, snow flying up around me.

Before I can even catch my breath, James is there, kneeling beside me. "You good?"

"Show-off," I mutter, brushing snow from my face.

"Jealous of my sledding dominance?"

"As if." I scoop a handful of snow and fling it toward him, but he catches my wrist as gently as he did that night in the sunroom.

For a heartbeat, we stare at each other, our faces inches apart.

His eyes, in the bright morning light, shine as green as summer leaves, searching mine with a look so endearing that when I open my mouth, I laugh so hard I snort. The loud, horribly unattractive sound that escapes only when I'm genuinely, truly happy.

"I've been wondering how I could hear that sound again." James smiles, brushing snow off my face.

With my free hand, I grab a handful of snow and shove it down the back of his jacket.

He jumps up, pulling his layers away from his body. "You'd better run, or I can't say what I might do in response." Mirth shines in his eyes.

We spend the next hour racing down the hill in various combinations—sometimes competing against each other, sometimes with the boys, once with Jules insisting on riding toboggan-style with all of us piled onto one large sled, resulting in a spectacular crash that leaves us all rolling in the snow with laughter.

As the morning wears on, the boys' energy flags. We gather around Jules's blanket, passing the thermos of hot chocolate.

"Best day ever," Leo announces solemnly, his cheeks rosy from cold and excitement.

"Seconded." James raises his cup in a mock toast.

Jules checks her watch. "As much as I wish we could stay, Grandma needs help with dinner."

Begrudgingly, we pack up. With the boys running ahead with Tom, Jules falls in beside me, while James stays behind, rummaging in his backpack.

"Are we still pretending nothing is going on between you two?"

My head jerks up. "Jules—"

"Don't Jules me." She holds up her hands. "I'm saying what I see. I've never once seen you look at my brother the way you spent the last hour looking at James."

"You need to get your eyes checked."

She studies me for a long moment. "Okay, Syd. Keep lying if you need to. But this was one of the only times all week you looked like *you*. Not the tired mom version, but *Sydney Wallis*, the woman I know. The one who glows like she's lit from the inside. You want to know the other time? The sunroom. Dancing."

She squeezes my arm gently before jogging ahead to catch up with Tom and the boys.

I trudge alone to the cars, holding tight to the warmth still burning in my chest. James comes up beside me and hands me a small bag.

"It's for Anna. I saw it yesterday and thought of her."

My heart twists as I take the small package. Nestled inside is the softest little ladybug, its hazel eyes lined with thin golden rings.

"The eyes," I whisper, not realizing the words had escaped.

"Same color as hers." He pauses. "Exactly like yours."

Warmth floods my cheeks, and I can't help but wonder if my eyes are flashing now, the way he described yesterday.

"Why are you giving this to me here?" I finally tear my eyes from the toy.

"Thought it might be best to share when... others weren't around."

There's so much more I want to say. So much I can't. A fat tear rolls down my cheek. And this is exactly what Jules was talking about. The glow. It's happening now, spreading through me like light in a place that's been dark for too long.

I simply say, "Thank you."

***

ANNA'S CRIES HIT ME as soon as we step into the cabin.

"I don't know what's wrong," Margaret says, looking frazzled, swaying back and forth with my screaming daughter. "She started and won't stop."

I take Anna, immediately feeling her body relax against mine. Her cries soften to hiccups as I bounce her gently, rubbing circles on her back. But I hear fingers flying across a keyboard at the kitchen island, the sound rhythmic and unbothered. When I peek through the doorway, it's Mason. Earbuds in. Absorbed in whatever he's writing.

"Did you ask Mason to help?"

Margaret's pause is longer than it should be. "He said he couldn't be interrupted."

"How long was she crying?" I ask, my voice tight.

"Twenty minutes, maybe more. I tried everything. A bottle, diaper, walking around the cabin." Margaret sinks into the sectional. "I'm sorry, Sydney."

"You have nothing to apologize for."

Anna's breathing finally evens out against my shoulder, her tiny fist curling around a strand of my hair.

"She just needed her mama." Margaret looks relieved.

Beneath the tenuous calm, I'm caught between the warmth of the sledding adventure, the ladybug tucked in my bag, and the growing fury I feel at Mason typing away.

He finally pulls his earbuds out when he sees me glowering from the doorway. "Do you need something?"

"No, Mason. I don't need a damn thing from you. Though our daughter needed some comfort, something you might have been able to offer."

"Don't start with me, my mother was handling it. Anna was crying. It's what babies do."

"Do you hear yourself? I thought you wanted to be a dad. It's like your life hasn't shifted at all with Anna around."

"Oh no. It's shifted. I have a wife who's decided she no longer wants a career. Most of the time, she can't even get out of sweats before dinner. And still hasn't lost her baby weight."

"Fuck you."

I storm past the dining room and frozen expressions on Jules, Tom, and James's faces. They heard everything.

"Jesus Christ. I can't just pretend I didn't hear him say that." Jules says as I take the stairs as fast as possible.

Shame burns hot in my cheeks, not because of what I said, but because they witnessed how little he cares. I don't stop until we're in our room.

After laying Anna in her crib, I grab the ladybug from my bag. My fingers tremble as I clutch it to my chest and stare out into the mountains.

The door opens.

"Where'd that come from?" Mason gestures to the ladybug.

I ignore his question and go about putting away Anna's things.

"Syd, what was that downstairs? Jules just reamed me out."

"I'm tired, Mason. I'm tired of doing this on my own. The ninety minutes I went sledding today were the most time I've had away from Anna in four months. I've counted how many minutes you've spent with her since we got here. Want to take a guess?"

"My parents are around. They love helping take care of her." He shrugs like that explanation should satisfy me.

"Twenty-three minutes," I say flatly. "That includes carrying her in when we arrived. And it's not just this week I'm talking about. You do not help. Ever."

"You're on maternity leave." He states it like a legal fact. "That's what you signed up for. If it's too much, let's hire a nanny and get our lives back."

The air whooshes from my lungs. Rage flares, quick and hot. I fight to keep my voice down so I don't wake Anna, but what I want is to scream, to let every buried hurt rise and detonate.

"When I found out I was pregnant, you told me you'd be with me every step of the way. And you disappeared. I don't want a nanny to raise our daughter. I want us to be there for her. Both of us." My voice shakes. "But you do what you want, when you want. I'm assuming you're going skiing tomorrow."

His expression doesn't change, the same glazed look as someone half-listening to a podcast he can't skip. "Of course I am. I always go the day after Christmas. Don't make this a big thing. It's one day."

He presses a hand to my cheek. Once, that gesture might have soothed me. Now, it curdles.

The bathroom door shuts behind him, final as a verdict.

Tears fall, no matter how much I try to blink them back. The floor beneath me feels as fragile as a frozen lake at midnight, the surface glassy and beautiful beneath me, cracks spreading with each step. Am I walking toward solid ground or straight into the cold below?

sixteen

Anna, usually a placid baby, joins my quiet symphony of despair, her cries echoing through the room in solidarity. She's inconsolable. Each wail is a cruel reminder of how I feel.

Somewhere in the fog of exhaustion and frustration, Mason's voice cuts through. "Can you take her downstairs? I need rest if I'm going to hit the slopes tomorrow."

The urge to smother him with a pillow is overwhelming.

Instead, I scoop Anna into my arms and retreat to the sunroom. My footsteps are soft against the hardwood floor, a lullaby of motion as I bounce and sing until my voice cracks with exhaustion. Hours blur into a cycle of soothing and nursing, trying to comfort her while holding myself together. As dawn paints the sky in soft streaks of gray and lavender, Anna succumbs to sleep. Her warmth is a fragile comfort in this hollow space. Exhaustion claims me, and I drift into a restless slumber in the armchair.

It doesn't last. A clatter in the hallway jars me awake. I blink, disoriented, as muffled voices and shuffling feet move through the house.

James appears in the doorway, wearing sleek army-green ski pants and a fitted midnight-blue base layer that clings to his chest. I must look as wrecked as I feel, because whatever he sees makes something flicker across his expression. Pain? Pity? I offer a weak smile and a thumbs-up, silently telling him to let us be. He nods and slips away, leaving me to stare off into the cold landscape, hoping sleep will return.

Coffee wafts through the air as the house falls silent.

A floorboard groans.

James stands in the doorway again, this time in old jeans and a soft sweater, a steaming mug in one hand and a tray in the other.

"Figured you could use some caffeine."

"Weren't you going skiing with everyone?"

"Changed my mind." He pauses. "Honestly, you looked like you had a rough night. I thought... maybe I could help."

"You stayed to help me?"

"If you'll let me. I can hold Anna while you get some real sleep in an actual bed."

"I can't ask you to do that. I'll drink a pot of coffee and be fine."

"Nope. I'm not taking no for an answer. I saw bottles in the fridge. She needs milk, a clean diaper, and arms to hold her. I've got that covered."

He leans in and lifts Anna from me. His touch is gentle and sure, his chest a warm haven for my sleeping child. "I can't give you a full night's sleep like you asked Santa for, but I can give you this."

I watch him. The way he holds Anna. The way he remembers that stupid little joke from our walk in the woods. The tenderness in his eyes as he looks at me.

"Are you sure?" I blink hard, trying not to cry from the relief, from the offer.

He nods without hesitation.

"Diapers and clothes are in the bag downstairs by the front door. Warm the bottles. And seriously, if anything feels off, wake me."

I turn away before I can fall any further and collapse face-first onto my mattress. The image of James cradling Anna loops in my mind, a lullaby I don't want to shut off. Soothing, impossible, and precisely what I need to sleep. It brings back the dream I had the night I first suspected I was pregnant. Green eyes full of something I didn't yet know I needed.

***

I STRETCH, MY MUSCLES protesting the sudden movement, and blink at the unfamiliar light filtering through the bedroom window. The house is silent, eerily so. A glance at the clock sends a jolt through me.

Five hours! I slept for *five* hours!

Panic lurches me upright, guilt slamming into my ribcage. I rush to brush my teeth, throw on a clean sweater with shaking hands, and bolt downstairs, adrenaline thudding in my veins. I meant to nap for an hour, at most two. Long enough to take the edge off, wash away the dark circles, and feel human again. But now, James has been alone with Anna too long, and the shame of that burrows deep.

The sight I'm greeted with steals my breath. James lies sprawled on the sectional, Anna curled on his chest like she was made to be there. One fist rests beneath her chin, the other curled around his thumb.

Oh, my ovaries.

The intimacy of it punches straight through me. He's *with* her. No phone. No half-attention. His arms curve around her, natural and effortless.

I stand there, rooted, breathing through the ache of *wanting* something so badly it hurts.

Eventually, I turn toward the kitchen, clinging to the ritual of coffee like an anchor. The low hiss and gurgle of the machine doesn't break the spell. Even here in the kitchen, I *feel* them. The sense that something sacred unfolded while I wasn't looking, and I almost missed it.

God, I want him. I want him for myself. I want him for Anna.

But I know this feeling. A pit in the bottom of my stomach when something matters too much. The voice that whispers:

This will never last.

Take the safer option.

Leave before you're left.

I'm staring into my cup of coffee, repeating over and over in my head how this is a fairy tale, a hope I can't believe in, as footsteps thud across the floor. James steps into the kitchen. Anna is tucked in his arms, her head resting on his shoulder, one tiny fist clutching his sweater. His eyes find me, and that familiar lopsided smile spreads across his face. My heart clenches, despite every warning I'm giving myself.

"Hey, you. Feeling better?"

There's no frustration in his voice, no resentment for the hours spent caring for my daughter.

"I can't thank you enough." I reach for Anna. "I feel so much better. Are you guys okay?"

"Of course. She's a dream, just took a little singing and dancing. She seems partial to Maxwell, by the way. Once she had her bottle, she was out." He rubs the back of his neck with a sheepish grin. "I might've fallen asleep, too."

I can't look at him, not when it would be so easy to picture this as something more than it is. I turn away, open the fridge, and search for dinner ingredients.

"Pretty sure I saw everything we need to make chili." James peers over my shoulder, breath warm on my neck. "There's crusty bread on the counter. Want to tag team it?"

"Let's do it." My voice squeaks, and I gain distance from him, from the pull. Settling Anna into her bouncy seat on the floor so she can watch us, I queue up a Maxwell album, one I've always loved to fill the quiet with something softer than my thoughts.

"I see why Anna knows this album by heart," James says with a grin.

"Careful with the teasing. I will head straight to the pet rescue and come back with Dutchess 2.0."

"Ruthless." His deep laugh fills the room.

We move around the kitchen in tandem. Chopping. Laughing. Sliding past one another with familiar ease. The conversation meanders, winding around us, sharing old stories from college meals, bad road trips, and songs tied to nights we barely remember. Little things that don't matter, but neither of us holds back from sharing.

When Anna fusses, he confidently walks over and picks her up, swaying as he sings along. Instead of looking away, guarding my heart from further intrusion, I ask, "How are you so good with babies?"

"After we left my father, we moved near my mom's family. My aunt is much younger, and she had kids while I was in high school. I got roped into a lot of babysitting." Anna's hands reach out to honk his nose. They both laugh.

"Is that why you don't go home for the holidays? Because she has family nearby?" I keep pushing around the sautéing onions, not daring to look at them standing together, framed in the light sneaking past the windows.

"We left on January 10th." He pauses, rubs his neck, then says, "I always go home after New Year's to be with her."

Something deep and quiet passes between us. Neither of us looks away this time. Only someone who knows what this means would understand. His eyes soften and I imagine mine look equally affected.

"I usually go home for the holidays. But last year my mom and a friend went on a cruise, and I had no interest in being the third wheel, so I came here instead." He pauses, voice dropping and changing the air. "I'm glad I'm here now."

His words wrap around me like a slow exhale, curling into every space I thought I'd sealed shut.

Anna fusses again, giving me an excuse I'm grateful for. "She needs to eat."

I settle on the sectional while James stays in the kitchen tending the chili, and let my head fall back, trying to pull myself together, to lock away everything he's bringing out.

The music shifts. Maxwell is gone. Tinashe's lush voice flows like a confession.

He walks toward us, a glass of water in hand. His green eyes study me, memorizing this version of me. A woman completely undone and trying to hold her heart steady.

Not just looking.

Seeing.

I don't know what to do with it. I've never had someone look at me as if I'm the sun and make me laugh like it's his favorite sound. And it terrifies me more than Mason's silence ever could because indifference is safe. You can't lose what was never given.

But James is offering something real. Something solid. Steady hands. An open heart. The unbearable hope that I could have this. I could *keep* it.

What happens when he sees the truth? When the shine wears off and all that's left is a thirty-seven-year-old woman with enough baggage to fill this cabin?

"Sydney, can I get you anything else?"

"No, I'm fine."

His face falls, but he doesn't ask where the warmth went. He simply sets the glass down and walks away.

I sit nursing Anna, watching him walk back into the kitchen to finish making dinner, and something shifts inside me. This is about the kind of mother I want to be, the kind of world I want Anna to live in. I want her to know that love is steady, not conditional. That tenderness isn't a trick. That absence isn't something you excuse with a smile.

Everything I never had as a child.

But what if we start to expect James? What if she gets used to his presence—his steadiness, his goodness—and he leaves? I can't bear the thought of her learning heartbreak through me, through someone I bring into her life.

Mason may not give us the home I imagined, but at least his absence is predictable. It's a safer bet than inviting a love that could vanish, shattering her nascent trust.

I can't risk falling for someone who might give us everything, only to disappear.

With Anna napping in her crib, I find James at the stove stirring chili, relaxed and steady in a way that ignites my indignance.

"Can you stop the act?" The words snap out of me.

James turns, eyes narrowing, reading everything I'm trying to hide.

"No more glasses of water. No more of this album. Stop being so damn considerate."

Hurt flashes, then something sharper. He isn't going to stand there and let me yell. "Why? Because your dickhead husband is too selfish to see you need help?"

"No. You don't get to swoop in and play the hero. What's happening between Mason and me is none of your business. I can take care of myself. I always have." I cross my arms, posture automatic. Defensive, like it might keep me from unraveling. "I don't need your pity. And I sure as hell don't need your regret for giving up your vacation to babysit me and my kid."

"You think I *regret* today?" His nostrils flare, frustration blazing across his face. "There are only two things I regret from this week. You want to hear them?"

"Sure. Whatever."

"One," he says, his voice so low it ripples down my spine. "I've met the most incredible woman... and I can't have her. She's brilliant, funny. We talk for hours, and it's easy. And she's so goddamn sexy I can't think straight." He swallows hard. "I've thought about her every single day for the past year. And it's so bad, Sydney, I have to take multiple showers a day to jerk off, just so I can look at her without losing my goddamn mind."

His words strike like flint.

My body sparks to life before my mind can catch up. Something tightens low and insistent, pulse hammering against my ribs. The image of him in the shower, wanting me. *Fuck.*

"Two," he says, stepping forward, closing the space, "I watched her husband grab her, and I did nothing. Every part of me wanted to put him through a wall. But I didn't, because I knew she wouldn't want that. She wouldn't want me to fight her battles."

He pauses, voice softening. "Even though she deserves someone who would."

I inhale sharply, but it's not enough. His words crash over me. I try to stand my ground while the tide pulls harder.

"Actually, make that three. She's married to a jackass, and I'm dating her sister-in-law instead of her."

We're standing inches apart, but it might as well be an ocean. The heat from his body radiates across the small space, making it hard to breathe, hard to think clearly.

"Why are you with Ivy?"

His jaw clenches, but he doesn't flinch. "I know this makes me a fucking asshole. How wrong it is that I'm with her when I can't stop thinking about you." His voice drops, rough and broken. "When I imagine a life with you."

The truth is brutal and blinding in its clarity.

I want to tell him he makes me believe I could be more. That freedom isn't something I chase on long runs or under frozen lights. That life doesn't have to hurt. That being chosen by him is both the most intoxicating and terrifying thing I can imagine. I open my mouth to say something. The words form and die as the front door bursts open. Laughter floods in, boots thudding on hardwood, voices rising in cheerful chaos.

I force my legs to move and slip into the living room, past the noise, past the almost of it all. The practiced, gleaming smile appears as I drop my shoulders, pitch my voice higher and become who they expect.

"Hey guys! How was skiing?"

Jules clocks me instantly. Her eyes dart to the kitchen. Something sharp shifts in her gaze—a tilt of her head, a narrowing of her mouth—and I follow her line of sight. James stands where I left him, eyes locked on me, jaw set, every inch of him taut.

"Do you need some time to finish the conversation we clearly interrupted?" She lowers her voice, her eyes skating across the others, as if she's devising a distraction.

I feel it—all of it—burning through me. Every word he said. Every one I didn't. I stand frozen, fists clenched, agreeable Sydney fracturing.

Mason steps in, blocking my view of the kitchen. He reaches for my hand, his touch light enough to look loving. "I'm sorry about yesterday, and for leaving the way I did today. Let's go home in the morning and have a quiet New Year's Eve."

I swallow my laugh as a lifetime of possibilities flashes in a heartbeat.

With Mason, I know what to expect. I can handle his disregard and cutting words. It requires low expectations, a steady dulling of self. I can do that. I've done it for thirty-seven years. I know how to shelter Anna from it.

But James?

What he offers is something else entirely. Something alive. Unpredictable. Messy and beautiful. It terrifies me because it demands that I believe in a world where love is freely given and won't be pulled away.

"Syd." Mason squeezes my hand.

"Yes. I think we should go home." I swallow hard.

***

SLEEP WON'T COME.

I know I shouldn't leave the room. Shouldn't check if he's still awake. But knowing isn't the same as listening.

Barefoot, I slip into the hallway, my feet silent against the wood floors. Oversized sweatpants hang loose on my hips. My bare face feels exposed, hair pulled back in a messy bun. Nothing to hide behind. Inside, I feel just as unguarded.

But I don't stop, not until I reach the sunroom.

He's sprawled on the sofa, a book open in his hands. His eyes stay fixed on the pages; he doesn't look when I step into the room.

"I never thanked you for the book. I haven't started it yet, but... It's one I've wanted to read."

"You're welcome."

His voice is clipped. No glance. No inflection. The twitch of a muscle in his jaw is all I get.

I sink into the chair, unsure why I'm here or what I want to say. The tick of the distant hallway clock and the sharp rustle of pages are the only sounds breaking the silence.

Without a glance or preamble, he begins. "You asked me earlier why I'm with Ivy. I'm with her because she doesn't make my blood boil. She's kind. Sweet. Easy to be with. She doesn't make me feel all of this—anger, frustration, jealousy." His eyes finally rise from the page, landing on me like a blow.

A sharp, humorless laugh escapes me. "She sounds perfect."

"I want a family, Sydney. I want kids. I'm thirty-seven years old."

"So, what... are you threatening me? If I don't burn my entire life to the ground and chase some *maybe* with you, you'll marry her?"

He sucks in a breath before his voice comes out softer, more measured. "Will you tell me what you were about to say before everyone walked in?"

Ignoring his question and my hammering pulse, I say flatly, "Easy isn't the same thing as right. Sadly, I figured that out too late."

"Tell me if this is all in my fucking head. Look me in the eyes and tell me you don't want me. That you don't feel the same way."

I try to say it, but the words won't come out. Instead, I hiss, "Can't you find someone else sweet and nice who'll give you perfect babies—so I don't have to fucking watch it."

His eyes snap to mine, hearing the truth buried in those words.

Some lies are too much, even for me.

My fingers curl into fists, nails biting into my palms. I pause at the doorway, waiting to see if he'll say more. His mouth stays pressed in a thin line.

"Goodbye, James. We're leaving early in the morning."

Tears, held back, fall in silent streams as I sweep into our dark room. Mason snores on. Anna's eyelids flutter as I wrap her in my arms, pulling her to my chest. Her hands fold together as if in tiny prayer.

I watch the steady rise and fall of her breath, committing this moment to memory: the peace of her, soft dark hair beginning to grow, the perfect bow of her lips as she dreams. Each delicate inhale reminds me how completely dependent she is on the choices I make.

My love for her is so absolute that it stirs the memory of a different kind of love—one I buried long ago:

Mother sits on my father's lap. I hear a commotion and come to the top of the stairs as they stumble inside from their party. Hiding behind a potted plant, I watch. It's the first time I've seen them all day.

She leans down and kisses my father, long and slow. "I couldn't live if you ever left me."

"You'll never have to worry about that, love." He cradles her chin. "What if we go away for a long weekend? Paris or Turks?"

My mother sighs. "It's Sydney's birthday on Sunday."

"Bah. She's so young. She won't even notice. We'll tell Madame Rousseau to do something special." My father kisses my mother again. "Anyway, she needs to learn that some loves are more important than others. She'll eventually leave us. But you and I are forever."

Oh, how tragically right my mother was.

When other girls had their parents cheer after skating competitions, I smiled and found my nanny. When classmates had parents visit during boarding school weekends, I buried myself in books and ran through nearby towns. I learned how to fill the quiet with motion, how to protect the softest parts of myself, to build walls that kept their absence from breaking me.

It wasn't until the call from my mother's assistant that everything crumbled. Not even twenty-four hours after hearing my father died in a car accident, I learned my mother was gone too. By choice.

All the walls I'd spent years building shattered. Because the truth was, I did love them. Despite their distance and neglect, I still clung to the foolish hope that someday they might see me, might want to love me in return.

But my mother's choice made everything clear: I wasn't enough to make her want to stay. I had never been enough for either of them.

I trace a feather-light finger along Anna's cheek and whisper, "I'll always be here for you. No matter what."

But even as I make the promise, the parallel haunts me. My mother chose passionate, destructive love over her child. I'm choosing the opposite.

As sleep tugs at me, a quiet voice rises from somewhere deep inside:

What if the home Anna deserves... isn't the one we're walking back into?

2021

Love sits on her chest like a bird waiting in the wind,
singing its truth to her daughter's sleeping face.
What if she breaks the only thing worth saving?

seventeen

You know what's hard to swallow?

Knowing what it's like to have someone help you, care for you, see you. Then losing it. Going back to loneliness. Constantly having to take care of yourself with no one to lean on.

It never occurred to me that I wouldn't be able to slip back into the mask of indifference I'd worn for thirty-eight years. That James had dug his way so deep into my heart, it would be impossible to ignore everything I was missing.

Now I know something better exists. And I can't pretend I'm fine anymore.

I stare at the cabin, shadows gliding through the windows. Outside, the wind whips off the mountains, rattling the evergreen branches. The midday sun bounces off the snow-dusted peaks, scattering diamonds of light across a washed-out blue sky.

It's been three hundred and seventy days since I ran from his confessions.

When I left, a small, foolish part of me expected to fall back into life with Mason. I thought time and distance might mend the widening rift between us. But as days bled into weeks, weeks into months, the void never changed. Margaret and Gary flew down regularly to spend weekends with us, and I soaked up Margaret's presence, yet it never closed the ache in my heart.

And no matter how hard I try, the old numbness I used to rely on for survival won't surface.

Cold wind lashes my face as Anna buries hers against my chest. Snowflakes kiss my cheeks, melt against my lashes. I let myself feel it all and summon the courage to step inside because I know who will be there.

James.

The man who has haunted every quiet hour of the night. The reason I haven't slept in weeks, every restless hour leading up to this trip filled with thoughts of him.

This past summer, when the family got together for the Fourth at the cabin, he didn't come. A work conflict, supposedly. Ivy, though, glowed. She couldn't stop gushing about their romantic vacation to the south of France: beaches, tiny villages, and romantic dinners all painting a picture of a deepening connection. I walked away when she started giving Jules the sordid details. Jules watched me closely every time Ivy brought him up, but she never asked more about what happened that day last winter.

No matter how hard I've tried to bury the ache, seeing him again feels like standing at the edge of a cliff, waiting for a gust of wind strong enough to finally push me over.

The door swings shut behind me, and my steps falter.

The first person I see is him.

His gaze meets mine, sweeps over me from head to toe. The air crackles. I bite my lip, waiting for his dimple, for a smile, any sign. But his mouth hardens, the corners turn down. He gives a slight shake of his head and turns away. He dismisses me as if I'm nothing and places his hand at the small of Ivy's back.

And Ivy—she's glowing. Her fingers flutter as she raises her hand. A sparkle on her finger catches the light.

A goddamn diamond ring.

He fucking proposed.

My lungs forget how to function. My brain stutters, stunned by the realization, even as the room erupts around me. Ivy's delighted laugh rings out as she extends her hand for everyone to admire.

A small, involuntary sound escapes me as I try to suck in air.

Everyone turns. The laughter stops. All eyes land on me.

"Sydney? Are you alright?" Margaret's gentle voice breaks through my haze.

I force a smile onto my face, praying it appears genuine. "Of course, something caught in my throat. Congratulations. That's... that's wonderful news."

Even as I say it, a hollowness spreads beneath my ribs where something vital used to be.

I glance at James, helplessly drawn to him like a moth too dumb to know better. Our eyes meet for the briefest of seconds. While his face remains carefully composed, indifferent even, his eyes tell another story. Sadness flashes before he looks away, out the windows.

But maybe it's only my desperation reflected at me.

Jules wraps an arm around my back and leans her head on my shoulder. Her solid strength keeps me upright. I stand there staring at him, at Ivy, until my eyes sting with tears.

"I need to change Anna."

Once safely upstairs, hidden in the quiet sanctuary of our room, I hold Anna close, pressing my lips against her soft curls. I flip the lock on the door, sealing myself away from the world and Mason.

Great, gasping sobs shudder through me, filling the room, filtering out to the bright sky. Anna looks up, her small hand brushing my cheek.

"It's okay. I'm okay, Bug."

Every day since I made the choice I did last year, I've wondered if it was the right one. Every time I swallowed a retort to one of Mason's sharp comments. Every time he asked me to put on a pretty dress and play the role of the perfect D.C. wife. Every time I said staying was what was best for Anna. Every night I dreamed of something else.

And now, James has made his choice too.

***

I TAKE MY TIME dressing for dinner.

Because now my despair is wrapped in anger—simmering low and sharp, waiting for a target. And tonight, I know exactly where to aim. Standing before the mirror, I smooth my hands over the short black skirt hugging my hips and the oversized sweater that drapes just so. Knee-high boots complete the look.

The moment my boots hit the stairs, I feel *him* watching. A pull as strong as gravity. I don't falter or show an ounce of emotion. My chin stays high, smile wide, and eyes crisp as the thick line of eyeliner.

Reaching for Mason, I let my hand trail along his arm, resting it lightly on his leg. If he's surprised by the sudden intimacy, he doesn't let it show. His eyes stay on his phone, thumb continuing to scroll.

I smile—soft and practiced—as I greet everyone, deliberately avoiding James, who sits beside Ivy, her hand absentmindedly stroking the back of his neck. But I feel his attention like a touch, tracking my every move. When I finally let myself acknowledge him with a curt hello, his eyes drop to his plate, and he shrugs Ivy's hand off his neck.

My hand drifts higher on Mason's thigh, pressing a kiss to his cheek. His eyes finally lift from his phone. Leaning in, he asks, "Is that skirt appropriate for dinner?"

I close my eyes, summoning every last reserve I have, and let the performance continue.

Ivy is deep in conversation with Margaret, but her gaze drifts to the ring. She lifts her hand, caught in its shine. I know they're talking about the wedding. James stares at his plate, his fork pushing food around without actually eating. Ivy places a hand on his arm, trying to draw him back in. He mumbles a reply I can't hear.

Whatever it is, he's not the excited fiancé you'd expect to find, and—horrible as it is—that makes me smile.

"Syd." Jules watches me, one brow arched. "You're setting the bar pretty high for casual cabin dinners."

"Oh, this old thing?"

The words fall out light and playful, part of the character I've slipped into tonight: the glowing, unbothered wife, a woman so thoroughly satisfied in her marriage, she couldn't possibly be coveting her sister-in-law's fiancé.

"What's that old saying? Pride goes before the fall?" Jules leans back, eyes narrowing.

A hush falls as the others watch with rapt attention, trying to decode what she means. Heat prickles at the back of my neck, but I hold my smile.

"Actually, Jules, you're the one who said I didn't need anyone else to make me feel good." My smile sharpens. "And I feel so damn good right now."

She scoffs and whispers something to Tom.

Mason leans in, his voice intimate yet loud enough for the others to hear. "You do look beautiful tonight, Syd. Should we blow off dinner and head upstairs?"

A chair scrapes against the hardwood.

I glance up in time to see James rise abruptly and disappear into the kitchen without a word. Satisfaction twists through me. So. He's not as indifferent as he pretends.

As dinner winds down, Margaret offers to put Anna to bed, her eyes shining with the kind of tenderness only a grandmother can give. "Let me have some time with this little one. You young people go enjoy yourselves."

Anna giggles and smooshes her face against Margaret's neck. Bell comes to check for food.

Gary perks up, pushing back from the table. "Have you guys checked out the new pool table in the basement? Got it delivered last month."

"Mom, okay if we go up and play our Switches?" Leo glances between his brother and Jules. At breakneck speed, the boys take off, not giving her a chance to reconsider.

That leaves Jules, Tom, Mason, Ivy, James, and me drifting toward the basement.

The space has been transformed. A sleek bar is tucked into the corner, and pendant lights glow over the emerald felt of the new pool table. A high-top table and stools sit near the bar, inviting and casual. My mother-in-law's touch is everywhere. Pillows are tossed artfully over the leather couches, thick blankets folded across chairs, bold abstract art warming the space.

The guys gravitate to the pool table while Jules, Ivy, and I circle the bar. I close my eyes and try to let my simmering rage settle enough to catch up with Jules and keep her from digging beneath my mask.

"What are you reading these days?" I ask.

"I started a new series. It involves a dominatrix, a priest, a book editor, and a retired French spy," Jules says, winding a strawberry blonde curl around her finger. She twirls it absentmindedly before flashing a sly smile.

"So your standard beach read?"

Jules's grin widens. "I mean, it's erotica. But it's *high-brow* erotica."

"Oh, the best kind," Ivy jumps in. "Where you feel morally compromised *and* somehow smarter by page three hundred."

"Do I want to know how the priest fits into the story?" I lean against the bar, resisting the urge to look at the man bending over the pool table wearing jeans that hug his legs in a way that should be illegal. "Wait, don't tell me. He's the submissive?"

"I won't spoil it. But let's say he spends a lot of time wrestling with his... inner conflict."

"Inner conflict is such a tasteful way to say *horny guilt*." Ivy retorts.

And I'm so caught off guard by her joke, a rogue snort erupts—loud, feral, and utterly undignified.

The kind that sends your drink flying and rings throughout the room.

The kind that causes every head to turn and gape at you.

"I've never heard that noise come out of you before, Syd." Jules raises her glass. "But I like it."

My face burns tomato red, and because I'm not sufficiently embarrassed, I glance at the pool table. Mason looks horrified. Tom grins. James just stares, eyes wide as he lifts his beer and swallows hard.

But damn him and his utterly lovely words: *Now I know my goal for the week. To make you laugh like that again.* My anger flares, and I look away.

"Are you serious about reading a book like that?" Ivy's voice drops, her cheeks flushing. Her earlier bravado evaporates. "I mean, I guess I thought you were joking about it. Doesn't it make you feel... I don't know... like you're doing something you shouldn't?"

"My dear." Jules sets down her glass with deliberate care. "I'm ordering you this series right now. There's nothing wrong with reading erotica. Or sometimes, grabbing your vibrator after a particularly good scene." Jules's cackle carries across the room. "And Tom certainly doesn't mind."

"What's happening over there, ladies?" Tom calls. "I'm just over here watching James give us a thorough smackdown."

Mason's voice carries. "Come on, James, at least give us a fighting chance."

"I am. I'm using my non-dominant hand." The crack of the cue ball echoes.

"Brutal, man," Tom laughs.

"That's what happens when you get soft, Mason," James adds, chalking his cue. "Too much time behind a desk, not enough life."

"Some of us have real jobs."

"Real jobs?" James straightens, eyebrow raised. "I wasn't aware architecture was fake."

I catch myself before I smile. I always appreciate his ability to put Mason in his place. But I won't give him the satisfaction of seeing me affected. I won't let him see me watching.

But Jules has no such limits. "Oh good, nothing says 'family bonding' like a dick-measuring contest over a pool table. Should we get popcorn for this testosterone parade?"

"I don't know what has gotten into them," Ivy laughs, soft and delicate. She smooths the ivory silk blouse, tucked into the waist of her tailored slacks, pausing as her ring catches in the light. A tightness sets at the corners of her lips.

"Good question. Any thoughts, Syd?" Jules asks innocently.

I glare before pivoting. "Ivy, did you bring your camera? I was hoping you might take some pictures of Anna?"

"No, I don't do that anymore."

The shift is jarring. Ivy's voice turns clipped as she looks off toward the moon-filled night. The woman who was giggling about erotica has vanished completely, as if she looked down at a script and remembered that laughter and photography no longer fit this version of herself.

"So, Ives," Jules says, swirling her wine, "what's the engagement story? We haven't gotten the full romance yet."

Ivy stretches her hand out under the lights, and I take a long sip of wine, the acid burning all the way down. My skin itches. I need to move. To *do* something. To remind myself I'm not some delicate thing wilting on the sidelines.

Because I don't have to listen to this story.

I drain the rest of my glass, set it down with a neat little clink, and stride toward the pool table. I know what I'm about to do, but can't stop myself.

"All right, boys," I say, flashing a grin. "I've got the winner."

Mason raises a brow, Tom chuckles. And James... He leans against the wall, confident and relaxed, beer in hand, arms folded, one ankle crossed lazily over the other. His head tilts, taking me in.

"Worried about getting your asses handed to you by a girl?" I flutter my eyelashes.

"We wouldn't dream of underestimating you, Sydney." James lifts an eyebrow, that maddening smirk tugging at his mouth.

A wave of heat crashes through me. My name in that voice, wrapped in low rumble and pure challenge, slides under my skin. I bite my lower lip, trying to suppress the way my body responds.

"James wiped the floor with us. Are you sure you want to take him on?" Mason asks, his tone tinged with curiosity.

"Don't worry, babe. I can handle him."

Taking my place at the table, I feel their eyes on me. Assessing. Appraising. None of them knows the kinds of bars I used to haunt on weekends away from boarding school. Escaping the brats I was forced to smile at all week, I found solace in dimly lit dive bars across Europe. My first glimpse of freedom, making that choice and leaving the curated life of boarding school for one with real people.

It led to the nights in college and the beginning of law school, where I found another kind of comfort in those same bars.

The sharp crack of the break echoes with a clean, satisfying sound. I sink the first ball with a no-nonsense shot, and surprise moves through the group. I examine the options, lazily move around the table, casual but deliberate, closing the distance with James.

I tell myself it's strategy, but I know better.

With my eyes on the felt, I ask in a tone low enough only he can hear: "The real question is...can you handle me?"

He keeps chalking his cue, rhythmic circling, never stopping or faltering. I wouldn't even know he heard me, until his voice like gravel says, "I would fucking love to try."

The roughness in his voice sends electricity straight down my spine, and I have to grip the felt to keep steady. He moves to the other side of the table, studying his options. Studying me. His gaze holds mine for the first time all day, unflinching when I stare back. I stand, cue in hand, feet planted. Not shrinking under the intensity. I know how damn good I look tonight. With his back to the others, his eyes never leave me, even when he bends to take his next shot. One he badly misses.

A speaker on the bar flares to life and I look away, surveying the room. Jules casually sips her drink, and when the slow, smooth chords of "Tennessee Whiskey" kick in, her knowing smirk says it all. The song isn't random.

Lining up my next shot, my heart pounds in rhythm with the slow beat of the song. James doesn't move. But I still feel his eyes on me—a slow, deliberate drag while the lyrics weave between us. My eyes shut for a second, letting the words settle. Lyrics about finding love as salvation. Something that steadies you after a life of heartache.

But I'm still angry, and my game isn't over.

"Jules," I call, "turn it up. I'm really into country music these days."

Glancing up, I smile. A smile that cuts. His gaze goes lethal, knowing exactly what I mean. That stupid fire pit conversation about music and connection, way back when this whole mess began. I turn back to the table, breathing through the searing cocktail of jealousy simmering in my chest.

"Syd, where'd you learn to play like that?" Mason cuts through it all.

They are all watching, tracking our every step. Mason and Ivy observe with sharp awareness while Jules and Tom play amused spectators. I hope they're only seeing the pool.

"High school" is all he gets and I sink my next shot.

James plays with a quiet intensity, every movement intentional. It suits him. A game of patience. Control.

But neither of us speaks, as though last year's pain has left us unable to bridge into even pretend friendship. The air hums with everything. The words he gave me, the ones I didn't return, are now wrapped in a proposal to another woman. But there's no quick victory. Just two people who won't let go, each move stretching out what neither wants to finish—missing shots, sinking scratch after scratch. Anything to keep the closeness alive, even if it's cloaked in silence.

When we're down to the last two balls, we stand side by side. Close enough that I feel his heat, and hear the slow rise and fall of his breath. I line up my shot, hands steady, heart not.

"Don't miss, Sydney." He draws out my name the way he always does. Testing me. Waiting for a spark of something. A flash of gold in my eyes.

My body responds instantly, but I don't let it show.

The ball sinks into the pocket with a clean, final sound. And because I can, because I want to—I drop into a slow, mocking curtsey.

A queen, claiming her victory.

I walk away, not bothering to meet his eyes again. Triumph in every step. When I reach my husband, I slide my hand around his waist and press a kiss to his neck. Lingering. Calculated. His fingers skim the back of my thigh, tracing circles under my skirt.

A soft whimper escapes me.

A sharp crack follows.

The room goes still.

James stands rigid, staring at the broken bottle at his feet.

Ivy startles, her ring catching the light as her hand flies to her chest. Her eyes are wide with surprise. If she questions what happened, she doesn't let it show. "Be careful, babe! Need help cleaning it up?"

Crouching to gather the shards, he mumbles an excuse and disappears up the stairs. As his footsteps recede, petty satisfaction curls through me. I smirk, ruthless and unrepentant. Let him carry the same gut-wrenching ache that's been eating me alive since I walked into the house and saw that ring on her finger.

"Wow, this floor is hard. We should warn Mom and Dad that a bottle slipping out of someone's hand can break," Jules laughs, her eyes cutting to mine. "Maybe they can add some area rugs."

Tom chuckles before saying, "Totally. I think a blue one would look nice."

I step out of Mason's reach and sip my drink. His eyes move from me to the spot where the bottle hit the floor. His smile falters, and he rubs a hand along his jaw, analyzing me in a way that feels uncomfortable. I take another sip.

"So, Ivy," Jules says, yanking the spotlight back. "I don't think everyone heard the full story. James proposed completely out of the blue this morning, as you were about to drive up here?"

Her glance at me is sharp, warning me not to leave.

"Yeah!" Ivy beams, tucking a piece of hair behind her ear. "We'd talked about it, casually. But when I stopped by his condo this morning, he was standing outside with the ring. He didn't even say anything. Just handed me the box like... like it didn't need words. Like we were already on the same page." She laughs, dreamily. "It was totally swoon-worthy."

Jules tilts her head, lips twitching. "Totally swoon-worthy."

Ivy doesn't hear it. She's already diving into wedding talk, rattling off plans lost in the fantasy.

He proposed this morning? Standing outside his condo with a ring?

My mind spins, trying to reconcile this story with the man I know. The man who remembers my coffee order. Who finds the perfect books. Who holds my baby with complete focus. That man doesn't do things without thought. Or feeling.

This wasn't a grand gesture. It was a calculated decision. A shield. A line drawn in the sand by someone trying to prove something or protect himself.

"Good night, everyone. I'm wiped," I say, already making for the stairs. I pray Mason doesn't follow; I've used up all my acting skills for one night.

Staring at the ceiling, my eyelids finally begin to drift shut. For the first time in weeks, sleep pulls at me. Because somewhere deep down, beneath the chaos and the lies and the pain... I don't believe this is over.

EIGHTEEN

THE BAREST SLIVER OF moonlight ghosts through the windows, shrouding the sunroom in pre-dawn shadows and hiding the book my foot strikes, sending it skidding across the floor.

"Shit," I whisper.

A lump on the couch jolts upright. I jump, the sweater I'm still wearing from last night billowing out from the motion. James runs a hand through his tousled hair, eyes still clouded with sleep. A soft blanket is tucked around his waist. I smooth my hair into something more presentable than when I crawled out of bed to a babbling Anna.

"God, I'm so sorry."

"It's okay," he mumbles, rubbing the sleep from his eyes. "I was reading and must have dozed off."

"I'll leave. Sorry again." I look away.

"Please don't go." His voice cracks, betraying what we've both been holding in since yesterday.

In the quiet shadows of the sunroom, sheltered from prying eyes, everything between us feels simpler. We don't have to measure our words or glance over our shoulders. Here we don't have to pretend. In this early morning, tucked away in this beautiful space, we exhale enough to let go of the hurt and tension—if only for a moment.

With a flip of the switch, Christmas tree lights flicker to life. Anna drinks her milk while James and I slip into conversation about work and running, sharing our latest reads, the races we have coming up. Just our easy, natural connection when we forget the rules and limitations that should exist. He selects a Sade album, her silken voice floating through the shadows, a low hum beneath our words.

When Anna finishes, we slide to the rug with her toys. James follows, dropping onto the floor as Anna moves between us. She climbs on to James's lap, stopping for a moment to put her hands on each side of his face and just looking at him. She smiles, then walks off, heading toward her toys.

"I was telling my mom about you the other day," he says, nudging my shoulder.

Surprised he'd mention me, I realize I don't know about her life now, or what happened after she left her husband all those years ago.

"She was worried about a woman in a dangerous situation. Concerned she wouldn't get proper legal help."

I wrap my hand around his without thinking about it—without weighing whether it's right or wrong. The contact jolts me, but I don't pull away. Talking about these deep wounds is hard, and I want him to know I'm here; that I understand.

"Is she in Boston?" I ask.

He pauses, staring down at our joined hands as if surprised to find them there. Then he turns our palms over, interlacing his fingers with mine, exhaling long and slow. "After we left my father, we moved to western New York, where she grew up. She still lives outside Rochester."

"I'm licensed to practice in New York. I took both the D.C. and New York bar exams because I wasn't sure where I wanted to stay after graduating. I don't practice family law, but I might be able to help."

"I'd love that. Cases like this take their toll on her, and I want to wipe away her guilt and fear over what happened when I was younger."

"Let me give you my number so she can call me." I release his hand, and he passes me his phone.

He laughs when he sees how I saved my name: *Dutchess Fan*.

"It's only fair I get to name myself something too." He holds his hand out, and I relent mostly because I want to see what he does.

He hands back my phone with a grin as mischievous as a high school prankster's. I look down to read: *Skating Stud*. I laugh so hard my stomach aches.

"Where'd you actually learn to play pool?" He bumps my shoulder, trying to steer us to safer ground, not knowing what he's asking.

My deflection last night wasn't only because Mason asked a question twelve years too late. It's the hurt wrapped in those memories; the hurt that might never go away, the hurt I'd rather not feel. Even though James never judges, telling him about boarding school means revealing the whole truth.

True to form, I deflect. "When you spend your teenage years at boarding school with more freedom and money than oversight, you pick up a few useful skills."

"You were at boarding school?"

"Yeah." I pause, gathering courage. "Nannies raised me until I was thirteen, then my parents sent me to school in France."

James doesn't push, reading my unease. "Aha, so you learned how to hustle in shady European bars?"

A grin takes over his face, eyes glittering, and I feel it down to my toes. The dangerous current, the one always just there below the surface, zaps to life.

"Among other useful skills," I say, wetting my lips.

His gaze snags there. Breathing becomes hard. Heat pools as I take him in. His worn college T-shirt stretches across broad shoulders, muscular arms taut beneath the fabric, sweatpants bunched around thighs carved from endless miles of running.

"Are we going to talk about how we left things last year?" He asks, a tilt to his head, daring me to lie or deflect.

"Not necessary, right? You're engaged. Future's set."

I say it like it's nothing and haven't spent the past year replaying every word, every glance, every single moment I walked away from—or the last twenty-four hours spiraling.

"Don't." He catches my hand, his grip firm. "I'm so tired of the games."

I look at our hands, at how easily mine fits in his. His fingers are rough, calloused. Not just the hands of a man who designs buildings, but one who builds them.

Someone who knows how to shape something from nothing.

Part of me wants to fight and yell at him for proposing. For simply existing. But the woman worn thin wants to stop pretending that he hasn't wrapped himself around my heart, burrowed so deep I can't extract him without breaking something essential. That woman wants to stop lying.

"I'm scared," I say it aloud, never breaking contact.

"Of what?" he asks.

"Of...this."

We stare. Breathe. My truth is finally out. Then, he drops my hand, crossing the room to close the French doors. When he kneels in front of me, his eyes are steady, but his hands tremble. "Why are you scared?"

"Because I shouldn't feel this way. I have Anna to think about. You're with Ivy. We met a decade too late." The reasons spill out, excuses I've clung to like a prayer.

"Love isn't always neat and convenient, Sydney. We don't have to fear this if we both choose it."

I look away, finding Anna as she toddles over and plops down, her chubby fingers brushing my arm. She looks up with such pure, unwavering love.

"Love destroyed my mother."

James stays silent, giving me the space to say what I've never spoken aloud.

"My parents didn't have room in their lives for me. That's why they sent me away." I pause, steadying myself to get the words out. "During my senior year, my dad died in a car crash. My mom called me... completely distraught. Inconsolable. I...I couldn't get a flight home until the next morning, but before I boarded, my mom's assistant called. She was found lying in bed with an empty bottle of pills, holding a picture of my dad."

The tears I usually try to hold back flow, and my shoulders shake with the force of them. James doesn't try to stop them or pull me close. He simply holds my hand, a steady anchor as I finally let myself feel the weight of it all.

"There was no note, no missed call on my phone. No indication she thought of me at all in those final moments." Sobs punctuate the words between gasping breaths. "She would rather have died than live without him. I...I wasn't enough. I was never enough."

James exhales and cups my face, gently wiping my tears with his thumbs.

"You're not her. The way you love Anna, anyone can see that. Nothing will come between that. Nothing." His hands stay on my face, holding me there. "And you are enough. You are enough. Just as you are."

I lean back, examining every plane across his face: the slope of his nose, his full lips, the stubble he hasn't shaved in days. The man who's shown me a glimpse of another future. One I have to be willing to put my trust in and believe the rug won't be pulled out from under me.

"I know this isn't simple, that I can't just ask you on a date. But Sydney, what we have is real. I've never been more sure of anything in my life."

"Why did you ask Ivy to marry you?"

He looks away, pausing as he searches for the right words. His fingers thread ours together, a soft stroke on my pulse point. The sun peeks over the mountains. Spreading rays of yellow across the soft carpet. We've been here for hours. Christmas morning must have started as my nephews rarely sleep past sunrise brimming with excitement. Within these walls, we've missed what else has been happening in the cabin.

"When you left last year, after I told you everything and you said nothing, I was so fucking angry. And I thought... if I tried hard enough, I could forget you." He draws in a shaky breath. "And I did try. I'd been thinking of proposing for weeks. But every time I tried, I couldn't do it, couldn't bring myself to say the words." He pauses, running a hand through his hair. "Standing on my steps, knowing I was about to see you with *him* again, I thought if I did it, maybe I wouldn't fall apart when I saw you."

A humorless laugh escapes him. "But I couldn't even get the words out. I know how much of an ass this makes me. But sometimes... sometimes we make choices out of fear. Out of the desperate need to avoid pain."

Understanding his words doesn't make this easier or change how much I stand to lose if this falls apart. I lift Anna, and she wraps her body around me, hiding behind the security of her warm little body.

"It's not that simple. I can't walk away from this family when they're the only ones who've ever shown up for me." I force myself to speak the truth that terrifies me most. "Maybe you'll tire of me the second I say yes. Maybe this is about the chase. Wanting what you can't have. And I'll be left in the wreckage alone, again."

Color drains from his tan face as he holds himself rigid, fighting his immediate reaction.

I don't wait for his response. I'm out the door when I hear "Sydney, wait." By the time I reach my room, Mason's gone, and the sobs come in silent, shaking waves. I brush a curl from Anna's forehead and find the small, worn ladybug tucked in her crib. It has become her most treasured possession. So much so that the nickname *Bug* is now woven into our day-to-day, spoken with love and a constant reminder of him.

With her settled and playing safely, I step into a searing shower. Maybe this isn't even about him. Maybe it's about me admitting I can't let things go on like this anymore. I have agency. I'm not stuck in this life if I give myself permission to believe in a different future—to let go of the idea that staying is what's best for Anna and that leaving means I'm selfish. That losing the family is not the worst thing.

I take my time getting ready. Christmas may have started but I need these minutes. I smooth foundation over my skin, each brush stroke a layer of armor. Concealer hides the shadows under my eyes. Powder blurs the turmoil. A hint of blush fakes vitality I don't feel.

When I reach for lip gloss, a defiant ruby shade falls into my hands.

It's not soft or delicate.

It's bold. A statement.

Just not one I know the meaning of yet.

Nineteen

I DESCEND THE STAIRS, shoulders squared, game face on.

The floor beneath the tree has transformed into a sea of colorful paper, ribbons, and boxes in various stages of destruction. Everyone is gathered. Mason sits perched on the edge of the sectional, dressed in a pressed Oxford and slacks as if Christmas morning calls for business casual. His eyes find mine immediately.

"Merry Christmas. Did you fall asleep in the sunroom?" he asks, patting the spot beside him. He examines me more closely than he has in a long time. "That lipstick is a bit much for Christmas morning, don't you think?"

My red lips curl into a forced smile, and I sit, careful to leave space. "Merry Christmas. And no. I think it's exactly right." I ignore his question about where I've been.

Anna wriggles in my arms, impatient to be free, and bolts the second I loosen my grip. She heads straight for Bell, the benevolent guardian among the wrapping paper, climbing her like a personal jungle gym. The dog thumps her tail in lazy approval, and I slide down to the floor, needing to be where the air feels easier to breathe.

Ivy leans against James, her hand resting possessively on his thigh, the diamond catching the light every time she moves. James shifts—subtle, but telling—never reaching for her.

Instead, his gaze finds me. It rakes over the curve of my cheek, the sharp red on my lips, the ugly Christmas sweater that should be ridiculous, but under his gaze, feels sinful. His eyes trace me like a memory, as though he's tucking it away for later. My pulse thunders, and I'm grateful I'm already sitting, because my knees feel weak.

The questions hang between us. The accusation I threw. The confessions we shared.

My hands clasp together on my lap as I struggle to arrange my features into something resembling a cheerful Christmas morning greeting. Try to pretend my world hasn't been altered in the early hours by the man not bothering to hide watching me. Pretty sure I'm failing.

"So… are we still into country music today?" Jules whispers, sliding onto the floor beside me.

"I have no idea what you're talking about."

"Oh, please," she scoffs. "I saw the pool game. I know that meant something."

I shift, checking who is paying attention. James tilts his head, his attention split between Ivy's chatter and my whispered conversation with Jules. Mason, thankfully, swipes at his phone, distracted as always.

"Jules," I warn, under my breath.

"Relax." Her tone softens; the teasing slips, revealing her sincerity. "We don't have to talk about it here. But we *will*. We're going to have a long, honest conversation about everything."

"Can you drop this? Please."

She lifts her hands in mock surrender. "If you're trying to convince anyone nothing is going on, you might want to stop looking at him like he's the last cookie on the plate. Eventually, it won't only be me noticing."

My cheeks burn. She's not wrong. I look again despite myself.

He's already waiting, meeting my gaze. The man who saw me broken and raw this morning and didn't flinch. There's no caution in his eyes now. I'm met with the same unwavering intensity that's unraveled me more times than I can count. My heart stirs, wild and untamed, recognizing where it wants to land.

"Syd." Mason touches my forearm. "I have something for you."

My stomach sinks. We hadn't discussed gifts, and I don't want one...here.

He pulls a small box from his pocket. "It's nothing big, but... I saw it in a little shop when I ran into town yesterday. Thought you might like it."

Inside the velvet box rests a gold necklace. A pendant—the letter *M*—glints mockingly. I look down at the bracelet Margaret gave me last year, the one with my name carved on it as a reminder that I'm still me beneath the layers of motherhood and obligations. The one I've worn everyday since.

This... is the opposite.

"Is the letter M for mom?"

"Or Mason." He smiles. "Here, let me."

He leans down to grab the necklace, gently moving my hair toward my shoulder and kissing the back of my neck. I flinch as tiny little spiders spread across my skin but he doesn't notice. When I look up under my lashes, James watches. His jaw is clenched, fists tightening at his sides, before directing his gaze out the window.

"I didn't get you anything."

"It's okay. I didn't expect anything."

The necklace feels heavy against my skin, a collar I never asked for. I look over my shoulder to thank him, but Mason's not looking at me. He's watching James staring out the window. A hard set to his eyes willing James to turn. To see.

It hits me like a physical blow.

He hasn't been blind after all. This isn't a lovingly selected gift or a peace offering. It's a message. How long has he been watching? How many glances has he catalogued? How many moments has he filed away as evidence?

Anna walks over, arms raised. "Pan'kes?"

"Yeah, Bug. Let's go help Grandma make pancakes."

Jules jumps up, snaking her arm through mine. "What a nice necklace."

"Please, not right now," I plead.

But as I move toward the kitchen, the necklace tightens with every breath. I catch my reflection in the window. My red lips stare back. The pendant gleams against my skin.

I press my fingers to it.

Wrap them tight. And pull.

***

ANNA SETTLES FOR A nap, and I seize the quiet. I grab my laptop to check a few emails for work, then plan to escape into a book—a little solitude in the sunroom before dinner. My hand settles on the grain as voices float through the opening. I hesitate and snatch my hand to my chest.

Mason. And Ivy.

I shouldn't listen, shouldn't invade their privacy. But I don't move, not when I hear my name mentioned.

"How are things with you and Syd?" Ivy's voice is light, but there's an edge beneath the words; a question she's not asking.

Mason sighs. "We're fine. Why do you ask?"

"She's been off lately. Last year, this past summer. Last night. She hasn't seemed like herself."

A long pause—the kind that tightens your stomach before the answer even comes.

"Do you have a point, Ivy?"

"Did James and Sydney look... tense during their pool game?" She stops and takes a breath, I can hear from outside the door, before continuing. "They weren't even talking. It was like they were locked in a silent feud."

My stomach drops and I press a hand to my mouth to keep from gasping aloud.

"Are you implying something?"

"No... I don't know. He's been off since yesterday. Quiet. Not excited about the engagement."

"It's been one day. Maybe he's dealing with that. You know, losing his freedom, being tied to one person. Would he propose if he didn't want to marry you?"

There's a scoff. "That's the thing. He didn't ask. He handed me the box. And he kind of looked like he wanted to throw up."

The vulnerability in Ivy's voice is unmistakable. The same uncertainty I remember from her college years, when she'd cry about boys who didn't deserve her tears. Except now I'm the reason, not the comfort.

"Mase, I've walked in on them talking a few times. And it felt like I was interrupting something."

Silence. A heavy kind.

"Stay out of my marriage," Mason seethes.

"Have you noticed any shifts? Like one minute, Sydney's staring out the window, a million miles away, and the next, it's like you're the life raft keeping her afloat." A soft, sad sniffle follows. "Ever since we left last Christmas, James has been all over the place, quiet one minute, irritable the next, then suddenly acting like he can't stand to be alone. I chalked it up to... I don't know what... but now, I'm not sure."

"Maybe you should take that up with your fiancé. I'm trying to work now. Do you need anything else?"

"I came to you because something feels off. But sure, go ahead and make me feel stupid. That's easier than admitting something might be wrong."

I hear her shift in her chair. Silence follows.

Warm breath hits my neck—cedar and bergamot, I know who it is before he asks, "Who are we eavesdropping on?"

"Shhh," I hiss, backing away from the door. I make my way down the long hall, and take the steps two at a time to get as far away as quickly as I can. I don't stop till I'm in the basement. James follows at a more leisurely pace, a few steps behind. "Why are you following me?"

"I want to know what made you all flushed and furious." He grins, settling on the leather couch with a large sketchbook in hand. "Where's your necklace?"

"I took it off," I snap. "Didn't suit me. It was Mason and Ivy in the sunroom. They were talking about us."

"What exactly did they say?"

"She's read more into the times she's interrupted us. That you didn't even propose, you just handed her a box, that our pool game felt like something more."

He doesn't flinch. "And?"

I stare at him—at his calm, his certainty. It makes me want to throw a shoe at him. I understand how Jules feels with Tom's ever-present calmness and support.

"Sydney," he says, quieter now, more serious, "I think we both know the answers to her questions. The real one is yours. Will you ever trust me?"

I swallow hard.

"I'm still here," he continues. "I've tried to move on, tried to convince myself I'm better off without this. Without you. Hell, I've thought about ending it with Ivy, so I wouldn't have to see you again. But when I imagined never seeing you again... that hurt worse. So here I am."

He leans forward, eyes never leaving mine. "Hoping you'll finally see that I'm not going to disappear when your claws come out. I like them. I like you, especially when you let me see the fire you hide from everyone else. I'm waiting for the day when your eyes flash gold, and you don't look away."

I sink into the nearest chair, breath dying in my throat. My shoulders sag under the weight of all I've been carrying. I stare at the ceiling, letting his words settle into the cracks in my walls and thread into the crevices of my heart.

"What happened with my mom... with my parents. It really fucked with my head."

He nods, steady and sure. "I know. That's why I'm still here, why I'll keep showing up."

The certainty in his voice makes something quake deep inside me. Hope. The thing I haven't let myself believe in since I found out my mother had taken her own life.

Without another word, he opens the sketchbook and pencil scratches across the page. Rather than pushing anymore and demanding I make a decision right this second, he accepts that I need to move at my own pace. He chooses to stay close. Show up. And somehow, that might be the most romantic thing anyone has ever done.

I open my laptop and bury myself in legal contracts and client briefs; the endless paperwork between companies fighting for more money and control. The space is quiet with just our tools and even breathing, working our respective trades. When my last email is sent, the soft click of my laptop closing startles James. He flushes, realizing I'm watching.

"What are you working on?" I ask, tilting my head to the side.

"Nothing." He snaps the sketchbook closed, hesitates, fingers grazing the edge. "Actually... here. You can look. I usually sketch the buildings I'm working on. But lately..."

My hands shake as I hold the still-warm linen cover and open to the first page. It's me, lying on a couch, reading. The ski lodge—the first day we spent together. The next page is me too, standing outside, looking up at the sky as snow falls, before I told him I wasn't an option.

Page after page. Moments from the last few years, each one a confession he couldn't say out loud.

The last is incomplete: the beginnings of me sitting here, one hand beneath my chin, brow furrowed in concentration, laptop on my legs. He started drawing this moment while I was sitting across from him, trying to keep my heart from skipping out of my chest.

Years of being *seen*—a record of something I've longed to believe but never dared trust.

"You drew *me*," I say aloud.

"Yeah, I did."

When I lift my eyes, tears blur the room's edges, but I don't hide them. I don't blink them back or stop him from seeing how undone I am. My fingers graze the curve of the page, as if to test its reality. I've replayed these memories over and over. But he didn't just remember, he made them permanent.

He made *me* permanent.

Heavy footsteps on the stairs jolt me back to reality. I slide the sketchbook beneath my laptop and wipe the corners of my eyes. Mason stops at the bottom step. He pauses, taking in the scene: the flush in my cheeks and James leaning forward, body angled toward mine. Ivy has interrupted us before. But Mason?

This is the first time he's stepped into the charged hum of something too heavy to be casual.

He clears his throat. "Anna still napping?"

"Yeah. She'll be up soon." My voice comes out calm, unaffected—despite my world being flipped inside out.

"What happened to your necklace?" Mason's eyes land on the bare space at my throat.

"The chain broke. I'll have to get it fixed." I meet his eyes and don't look away.

"I see." His tone is even, but the silence that follows is thick.

"I was catching up on some work. You heading to the gym?"

"Interesting. Seems counterintuitive to work on vacation, especially after scaling back so much."

"I do what is needed."

"Good to know your *priorities* are in order." The words land hard. His eyes flick from me to James. "Ivy was looking for you. Better go find your fiancée."

Neither man moves—hard blue eyes locked on fierce green. They hold until Mason breaks. His footsteps echo, each one louder than the last, until the gym door slams behind him.

The reverberation fades and I ask, "What are you thinking?"

"You want the truth?" He asks, but the words spill out before I can answer. "I look at you, and it feels like I can't breathe. I want you so badly it scrambles my thoughts, makes it impossible to focus when you're near." He draws in a shaky breath, his always-steady shoulders dipping under the weight. "It destroys me every time I see you vanish behind his eyes, like you're folding yourself away to survive."

He closes the distance between us in two quiet steps and sinks to his knees. His warm, calloused palms cradle my face in trembling hands.

"You have all the power here," he whispers, his voice barely brushing my skin. I smell the coffee on his breath, the cedar in his cologne. "I'm on my knees, asking you to trust me."

Something shifts in my chest.

A wall begins to crumble.

A long-locked door creaks open.

His hands fall away, leaving ghost prints of warmth on my skin. He grabs his sketchbook in one swift motion and walks upstairs. I remain frozen, the echo of his touch still burning on my face.

TWENTY

CHRISTMAS DINNER IS AN epic spread. Prime rib takes center stage, with sides spilling across the table. If you can keep your pants buttoned after, it's a Christmas miracle.

Leo and Beck have vanished, hypnotized by their new video games, and the rest of us gather in the living room, sprawled across the sectional in post-dinner contentment. A silly Christmas movie plays while conversation drifts in soft waves. Anna climbs from lap to lap, babbling and giggling, showing off toys.

Mason sits apart. One leg is crossed, phone in hand, eyes glued to the screen. He's been silent since the basement. His eyes travel to my collarbone every few minutes, teeth clenching each time he finds it bare. His barely contained animosity is oddly freeing.

I don't have to pretend and let my mind wander.

You have all the power here.

I've felt powerless for so long, and James has handed me everything. His heart, his future, his vulnerability—and he trusts me not to destroy them. It wasn't a plea or seduction. It was a vow.

Night settles over the mountains, streaks of moonlight stealing across the dimly lit room. The sky stretches wide and obsidian, every star a tiny, defiant truth. Constellations I used to wish on as a girl before I knew better. Before I knew the sky never promised anything but presence.

Every risk. Every choice is up to us.

"Sydney, how has work been?" Margaret asks, her tone warm. "I haven't heard you say much about it."

"Things are good. Same as the last time you were visiting. We're still remote, so if our sitter needs anything, I'm right there."

Margaret nods approvingly, but before she can respond, Mason interjects. "Mom, don't buy this martyr act. She's basically working part-time now compared to the hours she used to put in. It's a joke."

He laughs alone. The room sits in silence.

And the worst part?

He thinks I'll take it, that I'll absorb the blow with grace, the way I used to. The way I was trained. I see it in the smug set of his jaw, the way his eyes lift like he just won a case in court.

I sip my wine, letting the bitterness settle on my tongue, waiting for the fire in my chest to cool before I speak. The old me would've let it pass, smoothed it over with a laugh or deflection. But I'm not that woman anymore. Not since Anna. Not since James showed me true respect.

The bold, unapologetic woman I've been clawing my way back to—she's here now.

"You're right." My voice is clear enough to carry across the room. "I've cut back my hours since having Anna. My priorities have changed. I love being a mom, and I have zero interest in making partner or losing myself in that grind again. I don't need *that* to feel fulfilled anymore."

"Such a waste of your law degree," Mason scoffs, shaking his head.

I refuse to flinch. I look at Jules. At James. Their eyes burn with fury, and I let it steady me. Let it remind me I'm not alone.

"Mason, what is wrong with you?" Tom snaps. "Do you hear yourself?"

But I don't need saving.

"It's okay, Tom." I flash a wide, wicked smile. "Mason's made it clear that showing up has never been his thing."

The morning's holiday cheer vanishes without a trace. Jules and Tom exchange a look. Gary studies the ceiling, and Margaret turns to Anna. James scans my face with complete, undiluted attention. Ivy's unease is impossible to miss. Mason stiffens, color rushing to his face.

I smile wider. Let the silence stretch.

Sorry, Mason. I'm no longer your polite punching bag in pearls. If you want to pick a fight in front of your family, don't expect me to play nice.

Margaret clears her throat, her discomfort obvious. "Well, it's wonderful that you're finding a balance that works for you, Sydney."

"It really is." I pause, waiting to see if she's going to turn to Mason. Instead, she tickles Anna.

"That's so inspiring, Syd," Ivy says, a broad smile on her face. "I've been thinking a lot about balance lately. James and I have talked about me scaling back at the firm once we're married. You know, focusing more on…other things."

James coughs. "Have we?"

"Once we're married, kids and a house follow." She looks around the room. "I mean, that's what marriage is about, right? Building something together?"

"It's important for couples to be on the same page about those things," Margaret offers diplomatically.

"Until a baby comes, you don't realize your spouse might want a completely different future." Mason's eyes gleam blue as a frosted lake. "But trying for a baby is certainly fun."

"Don't be crude." Margaret chides him.

James's eyes find mine across the room. This time, I didn't fold away or hide behind Mason trying to tear me down. But instead of pride in my strength, all I see is a man dying inside, forced to watch from the sidelines, absorbing the awkwardness as best he can while pretending to be nothing more than Ivy's fiancé.

"If you'll excuse me, Anna needs to go to bed."

Once Anna's settled in her crib, I see the text I was expecting.

Sydney, this is Vera Navarro, James's mom. He mentioned you're willing to talk. Please call me when you have a chance. Even today is fine.

I lock myself in the bathroom and dial. Talking to a woman helping others escape bad situations is the perfect ending to this day.

She answers on the second ring, her voice warm and instantly calming. Our conversation flows with the ease of old friends, while she fills me in on a woman who recently found refuge in her shelter. I slip into work mode, taking notes, asking questions, and outlining next steps. This is something I know how to do, even if my day to day involves more paper pushing than people helping.

"I'll pass along your number," Vera says. "I think she'll be ready soon."

In the background, I hear movement. A deep male voice says something I can't make out. Vera hushes him gently. "I'm on the phone."

"Sounds like you're needed. I won't keep you."

She chuckles. "Oh, you're not getting rid of me that easily. That's Darrell. He can wait. I can't let the infamous Sydney off the phone so soon."

I blink. James talks about me? More than just mentioning I could help? But it's the name Darrell that sticks. There's something in the way she says it. Something soft. Curious, I venture, "Darrell is...?"

"My partner," she says, without hesitation. "James told me he shared some of my history with you. So no need to tiptoe around it."

I hadn't expected her to be so direct, and dozens of questions surged forward.

How did she learn to trust again? To open up? How did she bring a new man into her child's life after so much uncertainty and pain? Wasn't she scared the past would just repeat itself?

As if reading my thoughts, she continues, her voice softer, more reflective. "Coming out of that marriage... It wasn't easy. I stayed too long. I knew it. The way it ended..."

She exhales, then continues. "It took a long time, but when I met Darrell, I knew he was different. Opening up again wasn't easy. Letting someone in after all that damage might have taken more courage than actually leaving my husband. But I had a choice. I didn't have to stay stuck in the pain. I could stop just surviving and start really living. The hard part was realizing the power had been mine all along. I only had to choose it."

The line crackles, as if urging me to lean in and hear what she's offering.

"What made Darrell different?" The question slips out before I can stop it.

"Darrell never needed me to be anything but who I was. He didn't try to fix it. He just stayed and let me carry what I needed to."

Her words slice right through every guarded part of my soul. Tears follow.

"I'm sorry, Vera, I have to go. Anna is fussing," I lie, barely getting the words out.

"Sydney," she says, warmth threading every syllable. "Call me anytime, for any reason."

I run a hand over my face, breath shaky, as I perch on the edge of the bathtub.

Our pasts aren't the same. But for the first time, someone *gets* it. The fear of letting someone in. The guilt that trails every thought. The endless calculus.

I see it now. How I've been living in the shadow of my parents' wounds, always bracing for the next blow. Is this how I want to keep living? Guarded, afraid, already grieving the loss of a love I've never even allowed myself to have?

No. I want more than survival.

I want a life that *moves* me.

Jules once said the universe sometimes hands you a truth so obvious it splits you wide open. So clear you can't hide from it anymore. And Vera's truth is screaming at me, impossible to ignore.

TWENTY-ONE

I WAKE BEFORE THE sun, pulled out of sleep by a restlessness I can't shake.

The world is hushed, bathed in the soft hues of pre-dawn with shades of blue and lavender bleeding into each other. Cold air sharpens my senses as I run, each footfall crunching against the snow-packed road.

The family is planning to ski today. Anna and I are on our own, unless a certain green-eyed man decides not to go.

Can I let myself have a day with him if he stays behind? The thought of uninterrupted hours—after the sunroom, the sketchbook, and Vera's conversation—makes my heart race with more anticipation than fear.

What happens without the buffer of family?

As I near the driveway, a shrill voice slices through the stillness, stopping me in my tracks. I slip toward the edge of the woods, not wanting to interrupt.

"What do you mean you're not coming skiing?" Ivy's voice is sharp with disbelief.

James, ever calm but firm, replies, "I don't enjoy skiing. I've mentioned this before. You're welcome to go. I'll hang here and read."

"But..." She cuts herself off, unable to say what's on her mind. She knows I'm not going. "Okay, love. You can make it up to me and sleep in my room tonight." Her hands slide up to his face as she pulls him down. "No more sleeping in the guest room, it's silly. We're engaged."

Instead of looking away, I watch her rise on her toes and kiss him. His hands stay at his sides, letting the quick press of lips pass.

"Have fun," he says, and starts up the porch stairs.

"James," she calls out. When he stops, mid-step, she hesitates. Almost like she regrets calling after him. Then she says, "Is everything okay?"

"Can we enjoy the holiday and talk about all of this stuff later?" He runs a hand through his hair, trying to tame the mess, the guilt.

"Sure." Her back is to me, but I imagine her face matches the resigned tone to her voice. "I'll see you tonight." She drops her head and drags her boots through the snow, kicking at it as she walks toward the back.

He stands there staring off into the distance without moving a muscle. It's too far for me to see his face, but I can imagine the tight set of his jaw, guilt warring in his chest. His clipped tone and closed-off demeanor I just witnessed are so far from the man he is with me.

Conversations and relationships take two people, and Ivy has played her part. It takes two people to build a relationship on half-truths. And I get it. I really do. Sometimes not knowing feels easier than facing what it might mean.

Guilt gnaws my insides as I slink back, leaning against a tree. I've known Ivy since she was eighteen. But I can't keep twisting myself around her choices.

Maybe all these splinters, all these fissures, come from the fact that we're living double lives: the one in our heads, full of desires and dreams, and the one we're living out loud. For me, it's always been this way.

What would happen if those lives aligned?

If my actual life reflected what I have only dared to imagine?

Today might give me a glimpse, because he's staying. The cold air can't compete with the heat growing in my chest.

I move through the rhythm of our morning routine: diaper, clothes, milk, each step familiar and grounding. A soft contrast to the buzz of anticipation thrumming beneath my skin.

Mason offers a curt good morning, his eyes briefly darting to my bare neck before he disappears for his beloved day of skiing. He leaves without a glance back, still nursing his wounded pride.

With the house empty, I take my time getting dressed. I want to feel like myself. Not a tired mom, but the confident Sydney who at twenty-five would walk into a dark pool den and challenge any guy to a game. The woman who survived her teenage years in France.

Sans peur. Without fear.

I pull on jeans, the soft denim hugging my curves. An oversized sweater, the color of a winter sky at dusk, slips off one shoulder, exposing a sliver of skin. It's not a drastic departure from my usual look, but it's also a quiet declaration. I'm not dressed for a day of toddler play.

The house is silent, except for a clink of a coffee mug hitting granite.

James sits at the kitchen counter, coffee clasped between his fidgeting fingers. His navy Henley strains just enough across his chest and arms to make me forget how to breathe, freezing me in the doorway.

His eyes soak me in, roaming from the top of my head to the curve of my exposed shoulder, down the length of my body. He draws a steadying breath and tips back on the stool.

"Hungry?" he asks, casual, as if this is just another morning.

Anna bounces in my arms, babbling, reaching for her chair. James is already there, setting down a plate with tiny, perfectly cut pieces.

Without a word, he pours coffee into a mug, adds the oat milk, and slides it toward me with that damn lopsided grin. "Here you go."

I wrap my fingers around the warm ceramic. There is no one here to stop us, to make us not look at each other, only guilt and conscience. All I hear is the pounding of my heart. "Thank you."

"Would you have any interest in going to the bookshop today?" he asks, as we sit on each side of Anna. We sip our coffees while she spreads pancake and syrup around her tray, as much landing there as in her mouth. Bell waits eagerly for her offerings.

"I was thinking of taking Anna. I didn't get there on Christmas Eve and need my annual fix." I laugh and take another sip.

He nods, pleased, and moves through the kitchen, grabbing a bowl, berries, yogurt, and granola before setting it in front of me.

"I know you ran this morning. You need to eat."

"How did you know that's my breakfast?"

A finger skims the bare skin of my shoulder, the light touch sliding down my spine and pooling deep in my stomach.

"I pay attention, Sydney."

He scoops Anna from her chair. "Come on, Bug. Let's go play with Bell while your mama eats her breakfast." He carries her airplane-style, her giggles trailing behind them.

And as I eat, bite after bite, I watch them on the floor. James, fully engaged, making silly faces, catching her in his arms. His laugh carries. A rich, unfiltered sound that wraps around the room and settles somewhere I've tried to protect.

The flutter in my chest?

It's a full-blown woodpecker now pounding at every wall I've built, every doubt I've fed, demanding louder and louder: *Lady, when are you going to wake up?*

***

THE BOOKSHOP IS A haven of quiet corners and overflowing shelves. The train table is its own wonderland with Mickey and Minnie waving from boxcars, Pluto guarding a tiny present. Anna giggles and stands in awe. It's a memory I'll cherish forever.

We browse for hours, starting in the toddler section, reminiscing about our childhood favorites, pulling out book after book.

"Do you think *Where the Wild Things Are* is too much?" he asks, scanning the back.

God, it's so damn cute—his quiet contemplation of it. And I have to stop myself from imagining all these little decisions that I now handle on my own. What if I could *share* them? To have a partner who cares enough to read the back of a child's book.

"Nah. Who doesn't want a pack of monsters treating you like a king?"

"Well, a queen in your honor." He pokes Anna's belly, and she collapses in giggles.

As we wander toward the fiction section, Anna tucks her hand inside his, further disorienting me. This is the same shop where our story began, the same day I suspected I was pregnant with Anna. Now my daughter's hand holds his as she looks up, amazed he's still there. She is so pure and fearless in her acceptance of him spending the day with us.

Deeper into the stacks, lush foliage winds the shelves, and soft fairy lights transform the bookstore into something enchanted.

I choose a safer topic than what I'm feeling. "What's your favorite book?"

His brow furrows, that quiet, contemplative look that always makes my pulse stutter. "*Dune*. It's not about the politics or power dynamics for me, even if they are fascinating. It's about surviving against the odds. Becoming stronger not in spite of the hell you go through, but because of it."

"Do you think I'd like it?"

"You'd get it. You like dark and twisty stories—ones that don't hand you easy answers. *Dune* is messy. Brutal. Beautiful."

Survival. I know a thing or two about that. So does he. The thought catches in my chest until his hand brushes mine, pulling me out of my head.

"Should we pick books out for each other again?" A shy grin tugs at his lips. That stupid, beautiful dimple I've imagined under my thumb too many nights taunts me.

"Our tastes might've changed." My fingers twitch at my side, aching to reach for him. But my words hide the truth; those books are still on my shelf at home, well-read and treasured.

"Is that the case?" A small gasp escapes as his fingers cradle my chin. "It's still one of my favorite days."

His eyes drop to my mouth.

My breath stalls. My heart trips.

And without thinking, I reach up, tracing the dimple I've dreamed of. He leans into my touch like he's starving for it, a low groan vibrating from his chest. The sound unspools something tight inside me, and I clench my thighs against the building ache. In my heeled boots, there's not much distance between his lips and mine. A slight tilt of his head, a small lift of my chin, is all it'd take to close the final inches. His fingers slide down my neck, along my naked shoulder, settling in the small of my back, drawing me closer.

"Mama." A tiny tug on my sweater and I come crashing back to earth.

I laugh, breathless, and step out of his reach. Thank God. Not sure my hormones or willpower could take much more.

"You've got impeccable timing, kiddo." James huffs a laugh. "Should we check out and head back?"

***

Anna fades fast, her eyelids drooping the minute lunch is over, despite protesting she's not tired. James promises he'll play after a rest, and she finally relaxes enough to lie down in bed. Once she's asleep, I sneak off to the sunroom with *Dune* in hand.

Peppermint wafts through the room as James sets a steaming mug of tea beside me before stretching out on the couch with his own book. Bell pads in behind him, circling once before curling up on the rug between us.

For the next few hours, we read in contented silence, occasionally pausing to share a particularly moving passage. We could have been doing this forever. I catch him peeking at me over his book, disbelief written across his face. All I can do is smile and snuggle deeper into the warmth.

When Anna wakes, still warm and dozy from sleep, we fall into step in the kitchen making spaghetti, Anna's current favorite. James chops while I stir, our rhythm natural while Anna and Bell play at our feet. The last dregs of sunlight filter through in honey-colored bands.

But my damn mind won't stay in the moment.

It feels so normal. So good. Too good—surely I'm tempting the universe, inviting it to be taken away. I can already feel it slipping. This pocket of time that isn't built to last.

James sets down the knife and turns to me. His hands cradle my face, tilting my gaze to meet his. "I can hear the wheels turning in your head," he says. "Would it help if I kissed you? Something to distract you from all that worrying?"

His eyes drop to my lips. And for a second, I don't think he'll wait for an answer.

I stumble back a step, far enough to draw air. My body's already reacting, caught up in the idea of his mouth on mine.

"Oh no, no. That won't be necessary."

He chuckles—a low, rich sound, like thunder rolling through me. "Today wasn't a game. I was trying to show you what life could be like with us. A normal day. The mess, the quiet, the in-between parts. That I'd be there for it. All of it."

A pause to let the words settle.

Give them a second to seep through my crumbling walls.

"I meant what I said last year. And what I said yesterday. Every word. It's true today, and it'll still be true tomorrow. I don't know what the future holds, but this? It isn't fleeting. And I'm not going anywhere. I'm not asking you to turn your world upside down over some passing fling, Sydney."

He brings my palm to his lips, pressing his nose to its center, a warm tickle against my skin. His stubble grazes my wrist, my forearm, the bare slope of my shoulder. When he reaches the hollow beneath my ear, he pauses... then inhales deeply.

A moan escapes before I can stop it.

I push him away, not because I want to, but because I *have* to. My body trembles with need, every cell screaming for him—his mouth, his weight, the scrape of his rough hands on my skin. But I'm clinging to the thinnest thread of control. I close my eyes and try to tether myself to something, *anything*, that isn't the way he feels.

"I'm here," he whispers as his lips brush my ear. "I'm here. Waiting. When you're ready."

And right when I'm at the edge, the front doors burst open. The spell shatters.

Our day is over.

James sweeps Anna into his arms as she charges him, tossing her into the air with a carefree laugh before catching her against his chest.

Over his shoulder, he winks at me. And I swear, my heart flips like it's caught midair too.

TWENTY-TWO

THE SKIERS SHED THEIR gear as James helps me set the table. We move around each other with the ease of muscle memory, fluid and instinctive. When I stumble over the dog, James catches my elbow.

A touch so soft, imperceptible, I have to look to believe it's there.

I glance up, not bothering to resist. His eyes are warm and soft, so full of yearning. Is this what I look like when I'm looking at him? Because there is no hesitation, no hiding his feelings in that look.

His fingers tighten, sending heat straight through me, reigniting what's been simmering since his nose touched my palm and traced its way up to my neck. His cologne fills my lungs, and I step closer. He dips his head, his gaze dropping to my mouth. My chin lifts—

"Hmm... can I help set the table?" Mason clears his throat and strides toward us.

I jerk away. "Nope, all good. I stumbled. James saved your mom's favorite dishes."

"Is that so?" Mason stands, hands on his hips, eyes cold as a frozen lake.

What did he see? He's watching us like he caught that moment. And how could he not? James stands rigid, hands shoved in his jeans pockets, meeting Mason's stare head-on. I take a deep breath and continue setting the table.

Anna tosses a ball, and Bell launches after it. Paws thud across the wide oak planks before she skids into the door, snatches the ball, and trots it back to a cackling Anna.

Laughter from upstairs, chaos downstairs, unspoken truths everywhere.

Just your average family holiday.

"Anna, don't do that in the house," Mason snaps. "How many times do I have to tell you? We don't throw balls in the house."

She looks up with tears collecting in the corners of her eyes, gaze moving from Mason to me to James. Sticking her thumb in her mouth, she slowly walks over to James and lifts her free hand in the air. My breath dies in my chest as I watch her choose him. James picks her up and disappears into the kitchen, his voice a gentle murmur.

Mason seethes, seeing her choice for what it is.

"Do you have to speak to her that way?" I set the final dish on the table. "She's one."

"Should I let her do whatever she wants? She takes after her mother that way."

He doesn't wait for my response; he just huffs off toward the liquor cart.

I stand there waiting for surprise or hurt to hit me. But at this point, why would I feel either? The comment should sting. Instead, it barely registers. And I follow the sound of James and Anna now laughing in the kitchen. They sit on the floor, Bell curled beside them. James stacks measuring cups into a tower while Anna babbles happily, tears already forgotten.

"Thank you," I say.

He looks up, eyes soft. "When I said I was here. I meant it. For both of you."

The sound of chairs scraping and family conversation reaches our temporary sanctuary. There's a dinner to serve and a table full of family waiting. Anna knocks over the tower of cups and claps delightedly. The sound makes me smile, but it also reminds me that we can't hide in this kitchen forever.

"Come on, Bug," I lift Anna. "Let's go eat."

"How was skiing today?" I ask as we all take our seats and begin passing the dishes, clearly unable to handle the awkward tension hanging from the rafters.

"It was good. Beautiful day on the snow," Ivy replies. "I'm more interested in hearing about your day. Did you guys hang out?"

"I needed a book, so I tagged along to the bookstore," James says, shrugging in a way that doesn't quite achieve the nonchalance he's aiming for.

Anna leans against Bell, soft as a marshmallow. "Un J!" She waves a toy in one hand, beaming at James with the kind of adoration reserved for someone who hung the stars.

"Bell makes a good pillow, huh?" he says with a deep chuckle that fills the room.

Without meaning to, I smile. Anna speaks ten words, and today she added his name. The bond between them, so easy and natural, tugs hard at the truth I've been fighting for too long. I want more of these days. More laughter around a table we call our own. The fears I've clung to—of what this might mean for me and Anna—are beginning to quiet. Telling me it's not leaving that should worry me. It's staying.

A firm grip tightens on my thigh. Mason's fingers dig into my skin. A warning I should probably heed. My head pounds. I'm so fucking tired of this show. I push his hand off and keep my breath even.

"James, you up for Fortnite later?" Beck asks.

"Yeah. Once I'm back from my run, I'll find you guys."

He plays video games with them? It hits harder than it should. There's no ego. No hesitation. It's not a performance or something he's doing to impress me. It's just him. Warm, caring, involved.

And somehow, that feels more intimate than anything else that's happened today.

"Jules, that book series you ordered for me arrived. I read the first few pages. It might be best left for reading after dark." Ivy smirks, leaning into James to whisper something only he can hear. His eyes dart to mine, and his cheeks flush. I choke back the bile rising in my throat.

"Honestly, it's a great story. About way more than just the...sex." Leo and Beck snicker and Jules waves a hand to hush them. She leans forward, resting her elbows on the table, and says, "A large part of it is about people not communicating with each other and opening up about what they truly want. Who wants who. Who loves who."

Her eyes sweep across the table. Challenge on full display.

"Anna, time for bed. Say goodnight," I say, needing out now. From this table. From them all.

"I'll come with you," Mason says, collecting Anna into his arms.

Oh, hell.

He never does bedtime. If he shows up at all, it's a quick kiss on her forehead before disappearing into his home office. And I have no idea what to make that tonight of all nights, he shows up.

My eyes meet James as I leave the table. If he senses my apprehension, he doesn't show it, but I feel his gaze tracking me up the stairs. I keep my hands steady and focus on the routine. Anna and I have mastered it: bath, milk, diaper, PJs.

Mason strokes Anna's back, his voice soft as he sings her a lullaby. He tickles her tummy, pulling a delighted giggle that echoes. It's a scene of domestic bliss that doesn't match our reality. A year ago, I would've given anything for this—for his presence, his effort. But now, clumsy and calculated, I want no part of it.

"Sweet dreams, Bug." I kiss her forehead before slipping into the shower.

The glass door hisses open, cold air rushing in.

Mason steps in as if it's normal. Maybe once it wouldn't have turned my stomach, but now I turn my face into the stream, letting it hide the stiff set of my shoulders and the dread tightening in my chest.

"How was your day today?" he asks, tone hard to read.

"Good. Like I said. I took Anna to the bookstore."

He leans closer, mouth brushing my ear. "Did James go with you?"

"Yeah. But you already know that." I turn to face him. If he wants this fight, let's have it. "Don't pretend you care, Mason. You've made it clear Anna and I are not your priorities."

"You don't think I care. Oh, I care." His hands tighten around my hips, pulling me flush against his body. "Do you think I don't see it? The way he looks at you."

Pushing out of his grip, I leave the shower and wrap myself in a towel. I see no trace of desire in his eyes. All I see is pride, a wounded ego. The jealous rage of a man who feels his claim is threatened. He isn't looking at me as a lover—he's looking at me as a possession.

"If you don't like what's happening, look in the mirror. I've tried for years to make this work, and all you've given me are snide remarks and groping hands. Sex won't fix this."

I don't wait for a reply. I dress quickly, heart hammering, and slip downstairs, needing air. Space. Anything.

Fuzzy boots. Blanket. Back deck.

It's quiet, a kind of eerie stillness where sounds carry. I see movement through the windows. He's following me. Mason doesn't chase; he avoids. Fear grips my insides. I hold my breath. The door swings open. I stumble back a few steps, my lower back hitting the railing.

"Do you need a reminder of who you're married to?" His voice is sharp, eyes wild. "Are you trying to make me jealous? That skirt the other night. The thing in the dining room before dinner. Whatever *that* was yesterday in the basement..."

He stops inches from me. He's not particularly tall, only an inch or two taller than me, but he looms. Trying to intimidate me. Make me cower.

"Mason—"

He cuts me off, yanking me hard against him. "You want me to fuck you? Right here? Let him watch me bend you over the railing?" He spins me fast. His chest presses against my back. "Because he's always watching you. And I think you like it."

Dread coils down my spine as panic sets in. His nose ghosts over my neck as he presses harder against my body.

"Mase, this isn't you," I whisper, finally finding words—and my balance to either kick or drive an elbow if I have to. Because Mason has crossed plenty of lines, but he's never touched me when I didn't want it. And no way in hell is that happening.

For a moment, his breath—hot and ragged—ghosts across my neck, his fingers digging into my skin. He sucks in a long, shaky breath and his hold loosens.

First one finger, then another, until his hand falls away completely. He steps back as though space might absolve him.

"I'm so sorry. I don't know what came over me." His voice is soft now, almost fragile. A careful smile spreads across his face as he cradles my cheek, all traces of anger tucked neatly away. "The thought of losing you...The idea makes me so angry. I'm going to catch up on some work so I can spend the next few days with you and Anna."

He turns and disappears inside while I stay frozen, releasing a slow, shaky breath as my body trembles.

The woods call to me. How many times have I stared at those trees and wished I could escape into them? Now I don't hesitate. I force my feet to move and don't stop until the trees swallow me whole. Only here, surrounded by silence and space, can I finally breathe. The sobs I've been holding back break free. The woods wrap tighter, offering silence, safety, and all the time I need.

When the tears finally stop, when my breathing steadies, the thoughts I've been avoiding creep in.

What happens tomorrow? Next week?

Mason has never touched me in anger, but tonight he crossed a line I never imagined he would. If he can do that once, what's stopping him from doing it again? Am I safe? Is Anna? Do I need to keep my distance from James—to make sure Mason has no motive to escalate, to go further?

Today may have been the happiest I've felt in a long time, but what's happening between James and me doesn't exist in a vacuum. There's a messy web of relationships caught between us. Tonight was a warning. A glimpse at how badly this could all fall apart.

But it was also something else: a preview of what happens when I stop playing by Mason's rules. When I stop shrinking myself to fit the box he's built for me.

I sit there long after the cold has numbed my limbs. Remembering the bookstore, the kitchen, the sunroom—the warmth that promised a better future.

And the truth of my marriage: it's no longer only about happiness.

TWenTy-THRee

Waking up to a storm would have been fitting after the night I had.

But the morning dawns clear, crystalline blue, ice glittering on the trees. Mount Mansfield stands tall, its snow-covered peak gleaming in cruel perfection. Even with flames crackling in the hearth, the cold seeps into my bones. Around me, the house hums with life. The family bustles through breakfast, voices overlapping, silverware clinking, laughter floating despite last night's darkness.

"Syd." Margaret's voice pulls me back. "You're white as a ghost, sweetheart. Are you sick?"

"I didn't sleep well," I say softly, not looking up from my plate.

Mason's eyes bore into me. I feel them without looking up.

"We fought last night," he says with a theatrical shrug, still wearing yesterday's wrinkled clothes. "I was a bit of an ass."

James sets his coffee mug down sharply, his face is a mask of fury, and the force of it knocks the breath from my lungs. A choked sound rises in my throat as the weight of it all—last night, yesterday—crashes into me. He doesn't know what happened, but his gaze cuts straight through me. He sees it was more than just a fight.

Jules clasps my hand. I sit frozen, coffee untouched. Her grip tightens as she feels me trembling. "What happened?"

I shake my head, eyes fixed on my untouched plate. I can't speak it. Tears threaten, and I blink them back.

Breathe in. Breathe out. Get through breakfast.

"Son, there's a saying: happy wife, happy life. I find groveling works wonders when I've pissed off your mother." Gary chuckles, leaning across the table to kiss Margaret's cheek.

Jules straightens and claps once. "Okay, family. We're going ice skating. We need some fun today, and I'm not taking no for an answer."

"Ugh, you know I hate skating," Mason groans.

"When you're in the doghouse," Margaret scolds lightly, "a little effort goes a long way. We all know how much Sydney loves it."

"Don't worry, Uncle Mason," Beck pipes up. "You can't possibly be worse than James. He was terrible last time."

"Har, har." James rolls his eyes, but there's warmth in his smile. "I've been taking lessons, so watch out. I'm basically a threat to the NHL now."

I do the unforgivable and glance up. Our eyes lock. *He took lessons.*

"Syd, will you hold my hand? Help keep me upright?" Mason cuts in with that smile, the one that once got him what he wanted. Now it just looks smarmy.

"They have carts. Come on, Bug, let's get bundled up."

"Okay, Mom and Ivy, you're with me, Syd, and Anna," Jules announces, already clearing plates. "Boys, find your own way."

"This is great. James, we can scope out the ballroom at the resort. Might be perfect for the reception." Ivy fluffs her hair with perfectly manicured nails.

She glances at me and smiles. A reminder that, skating lessons, soft looks, and earth-shattering words aside, *he's still hers.*

***

THE CAR IS BARELY out of the driveway when Jules snatches the Bluetooth.

"Sorry, Syd, but mom jams aren't cutting it today. We need something to unleash our inner ice queens."

I lift a brow. "You mean like Elsa?"

"Please. Elsa wishes she had this energy."

A beat later, Doja Cat's "Boss Bitch" blasts through the speakers, bass thumping hard enough to rattle the glove compartment. Jules cranks the volume, tosses her curls, and dances in her seat with wild abandon.

"Woooooo!" Anna squeals from her car seat. Her little arms wave in sync with Jules, a miniature mirror of her aunt. Margaret rolls her eyes but laughs.

"Isn't this song too much for Anna?" Ivy glances up from her phone, her brows lifting with disapproval.

Jules spins dramatically. "Oh, sorry. I left my Stepford Wives playlist in the trunk. Make sure to spend some time with your new books today. Might help pull the stick out of your ass."

I bite back a laugh, because honestly? I miss the old Ivy. The Ivy who snuck wine into movies, who cannonballed into the resort pool in a designer dress, who *laughed* with us.

This watered-down version is a far cry from the woman she was just a few short years ago.

Outside, snowflakes swirl through the morning light as we head toward the rink, Doja Cat still unapologetically raging through the speakers. I forget about Mason—about what happened, about the choices in front of me. For these few minutes, I'm just a woman in a car with her daughter, her best friend, and music turned up loud enough to drown out everything else.

Until we park and there he is, a dark cloud hanging at the edge of the lot: Mason.

"Hi, Bug," he says warmly as we exit the car. "I thought we could all skate together." His eyes dart to mine, gauging my reaction.

"Sorry, Mase. Go get your skates on. I need to talk to Syd." Jules sticks a hand up to stop him from coming any closer.

He looks at me, hoping I'll run interference. I let Jules pull me away with a defiant lift to my chin. His head drops, shoulders sag, maybe realizing last night isn't going to blow over.

Jules's voice turns uncharacteristically gentle. "I don't know what happened, but you don't have to pretend you're fine with me."

"I don't want to talk about it, Jules. When I'm ready, I will." I inhale. Exhale. Repeat. "Let's just skate. Get Anna on the ice for the first time."

"I'm here for you. One hundred percent in your corner, you know that, right?"

"Do you mean that? Like no matter what?" I ask, holding my breath. This answer is suddenly the most important answer to all my questions.

"Yes. No matter what."

I wrap my arm around her and feel a bit of tension release. "Now let's go bring our Elsa energy to the ice."

The skating rink stretches before us, an expanse of white nestled in front of the lodge. Children dart across the ice, their laughter carrying in the cold air. Families glide hand in hand, leaving silvery trails in their wake. Festive music blares out of speakers.

Once we're all on the ice, the group naturally spreads out.

Tom and Jules race ahead with the twins, shouting out challenges to each other. Margaret and Gary move at a leisurely pace, hand in hand. Mason clings to the railing, his skates slipping as he tries to find his footing. Ivy glides gracefully near James, who now moves across the ice with ease.

I can't help but watch him. He took lessons. My heart constricts as I take him in. His long legs graceful on the ice, the dark green beanie that I've always loved—a beacon I keep seeking.

"Mama." Anna's soft voice pulls me back to her and her little mittened hand clutching mine.

"You ready?"

Her little legs wobble above the tiny double-bladed skates strapped over her boots. Her cheeks are pink with excitement, eyes wide as saucers as she takes in the glistening rink.

I take a cautious step onto the ice, crouch down so I'm eye level with her, and pull her gently forward. She lets out a squeal—half fear, half delight.

"You're doing it," I whisper, more to myself than to her.

We make a slow, careful loop. Her hand grips mine. Her smile never wavers. "Mama. Fun."

"Yes, baby. I love ice skating. But it's okay if you don't. I'll never force you."

On our next pass, Mason notices me watching, and he lets out a short laugh. "Guess it's been a while since I've skated." He tries to sound casual, but the tension in his shoulders gives him away. His movements are stiff and careful, trying to control something he can't.

"Want me to grab you a skating cart?" I ask, teasing.

"No. Definitely not. I'll be fine. It can't be that different from skiing."

I nod, but the moment doesn't pass easily. Mason can't stand being off-kilter. I hold my breath, almost waiting for his next move.

"Aunt Syd, can you show us a jump?" Leo and Beck skate over. "Please!"

"Well..." I look around to see if anyone is available to hold Anna's hand. James skates toward us, steady and sure. Ivy sits on the bench, face now in her phone.

"Un J!" she squeals, wobbling from the quick movement before I stabilize her.

I glance at Mason and see his jaw tighten. He heard her. His gaze lands on James's approaching figure, his posture shifting instantly. His back straightens, arms crossed in front of his chest, like he's leaning casually against the side rather than gripping for help.

"Syd," he calls out. "I could use your help. You're the expert here." He extends his hand toward me, his smile tight.

"Boys, why don't you show off? I'll take my turn later." I can't resist turning to James. It might be the dumbest thing with Mason fifteen feet away, but what's he going to do with the entire family here? I drop my voice low. "Bambi, you've improved."

"Someone once told me all it takes is a few skating lessons." He winks, gliding to a smooth stop in front of us. "Wanna take a lap with me, Bug?" Anna slips her hand into his secure grasp.

"Syd," Mason snaps. "You coming?"

I skate toward him and see his outstretched hand, waiting expectantly.

"No, Mason. I'm not," My voice stays even, calm. My eyes lock on his. "You can't expect me to flip a switch and pretend last night didn't happen. Get a cart if you need something to hold on to."

His face hardens, but I don't stay for his reaction. All he can do is watch as I push off and leave him behind.

I want to skate toward James and Anna, but I know I can't. Not yet. Instead, I gather speed and skate for myself. For the girl who found freedom on the ice. For the woman fighting to claim it again.

The ice beneath me feels solid, certain.

"Come on, Aunt Syd! Do a jump!" The boys cheer.

"You know it's been a while, right?" I laugh, shaking my head.

"Come on!"

The ice calls to something deep in me—the part that remembers joy without fear. Freedom. Fun for the sake of it. Those tiny moments I carved for myself as a little girl, a teen alone in a foreign country.

I pick up speed, cold air slicing my cheeks: swizzles, long glides, muscle memory returning in waves. I pull out moves from routines I learned as a girl. I remember how to line up, the instinct to launch myself off the ice. I start with a single axel and land it smoothly. I take a lap, center my breath, and line up backward, lifting my back foot and pushing off with my right leg. My skates cross, my eyes stay up, and the ice welcomes me back: a double axel.

Claps and cheers burst through my haze.

"Aunt Syd, that was awesome! You're so cool!" Leo shouts while his brother throws his hands in the air.

"Mama!" Anna's little voice carries.

From the corner of my eye, I glance to where Mason was, but he's gone. His absence doesn't surprise me; he only ever shows up for appearances, never for the parts that matter.

"Thank you, thank you. I'll be here all week!" I throw my arms in the air and take a bow.

"Will you show us some new moves?" Beck skates forward. He glides into the spin we worked on the last time we were here.

"Anna, are you okay hanging out with Uncle J?" I ask my daughter. I know it's not even a question worth asking as she gazes up at him.

"I've got her. Go have fun," James says. He keeps Anna's hand clasped tightly in his as they take another slow lap, her giggles trailing, cutting through the cold like sunlight.

I spend the next thirty minutes skating between the boys and Anna. The rest of the family is outside the rink, sipping warm drinks. Ivy stormed off after James declined to check out the ballroom with her. Mason is still nowhere to be seen.

James skates up with Anna in his arms. "I think she's wiped. You want some hot chocolate, Bug?"

"P'ease!"

Looking between them, I can't help myself. I smile. Wide and free. Somehow over the last hour, I went from pretending to actually being okay. And as my smile grows, last night softens and becomes less important.

Because I'm pretty sure my future is standing right here.

"Sydney," Margaret calls out. "You were marvelous out there."

I cough, hoping my red cheeks look flushed from the skating. "Thank you. It's been a while since I've skated like that."

"I've seen you skate plenty, but I've never seen you do a jump. What's it called?" She smiles, all motherly affection.

"It's a double axel. I don't know if I ever told you I skated competitively until I was thirteen." Margaret leans against the wall, listening attentively. "I moved and lost my coach, so I gave it up. I wasn't good enough for the national team or anything."

"How lucky are you guys?" She says, turning to Leo and Beck. "Your aunt looked like an Olympian out there. She has to be able to help with your hockey skating."

Anna's giggles draw my attention. James extends his arms, supporting her as she stretches out like a bird, gliding toward the hot chocolate stand. Her laughter bubbles up, pure and uninhibited.

My eyes track them until I remember myself. Margaret is watching me. She looks away, but not before I catch a flash of something crossing her face. Whatever it is, she tucks it away and smiles broadly.

A hand brushes my arm—Mason. A massive bouquet of expensive flowers in one hand, down on one knee. Performance-ready.

"Syd, I'm so sorry for how I behaved last night. Can you forgive me?"

I look from his face to the people behind him. His parents' expectant smiles. Jules's pinched frown. James's unhidden frustration. Tom discreetly moves the boys away. Mason's saccharine smile says he thinks this grand gesture can erase last night—or the years I've put up with him. I'm supposed to be a good little wife and say, *it's okay.*

He doesn't even realize I don't want cut flowers. Never have. There's something so perverse about giving someone a bouquet—something that will die in a week—as a symbol of love. He doesn't know that staying, skating with us, would've meant more than a thousand roses.

But it doesn't matter. It's too little. Far too late.

Because the damage isn't from last night.

I see it clearly now: Mason hasn't changed. He's still the man I married.

The difference... is me.

I've changed.

"We should head back," I say and look beyond Mason to his parents.

Margaret and Gary look away. That's all it takes. Years of believing I'd found a real family, gone. They won't protect me. Not from their own son. I mistook their warmth and easy affection for the kind of family bond that shows up even when it's hard. Their silence tells me more than their words of affection ever did.

I leave Mason standing there with his flowers, daring him to react.

TWENTY-FOUR

For the first time in forever, I do something for myself.

I schedule a makeover. Not out of vanity, but out of necessity. A quiet reclaiming of the woman buried beneath the labels of wife and mother. My hair has been long my entire life, the kind of femininity men such as Mason expect—soft, compliant, easy to wrap around their fingers. And today, I'm ready for something new.

The stylist chops it short, giving me a layered bob that settles sharp at my chin. The weight that lifts is both literal and symbolic, shrugging off a version of myself I've worn too long. I shake it out and catch my reflection in the mirror. I look... like me. The *real* me.

Mason barely blinks when he sees me. "What did you do?"

His voice is all shock. Not *Wow, that looks great,* or *I love it.* Just accusation.

"It's a haircut," I say calmly, reaching for Anna and heading upstairs to pack for her overnight with his parents.

Tonight is New Year's Eve, and my in-laws have generously offered to take Anna and my nephews to the resort, giving the rest of us some rare adult time to celebrate—or as Margaret put it, "remember what it's like to let loose."

Margaret isn't clueless. She's a mother who *notices.*

She watched the aftermath of skating and my refusal to accept Mason's flowers and apology. We maintain the distance of polite strangers. Ivy and James speak in short, terse exchanges. Ivy has moved full force into wedding planning, ignoring James's request to wait until after the holidays. Jules and Tom exchange whispers with the eagerness of tennis spectators.

This offer isn't just to let loose. It's a message: *Get your shit together.*

My dress for tonight is a masterpiece of black silk. From the front, it's elegant in its simplicity. But the back is something else entirely: a plunging V that bares my spine, dipping above the curve of my ass. Paired with my new haircut, it's bolder than anything I've worn in years.

Tonight, I feel powerful.

Tonight, I take up space.

"Syd? Are you ready? People are arriving." Mason calls from the bedroom.

"Just a sec." With one last glance in the mirror, I smooth the edges of the dress and take a deep steading breath.

Mason's jaw drops as he takes in the sight of me. "Wow. You look... incredible."

"Thanks," I reply, a playful smile curving my lips, meant more as a shield than a welcome.

We've politely danced around each other since the ice rink, neither addressing the deck incident nor abandoned flowers. It's standard Wallis family strategy. Don't rock the boat. Don't address the elephant in the room.

But tonight, I'm playing with fire.

As we descend the stairs, eyes fall on me. Jules, ever the supportive friend, whistles her appreciation. Ivy, her expression a blend of disapproval and fascination, purses her lips but says nothing. She's wearing a demure sheath dress. Conservative, boring. Safe.

"Damn, girl." Jules walks over to get a closer look.

"Thanks. You look pretty good yourself." I touch her curls, taking in the vibrant red dress.

A small crowd gathers in the family room. Mason and Ivy, ever the social animals, have taken advantage of their parents' offer and invited friends to join us.

But my eyes are searching for one person.

James stands by the fireplace with a glass of champagne in hand. His gaze meets mine, and the rest becomes white noise, the way everything disappears when you find your rhythm on a long run. He's breathtaking in a dark gray tailored suit. His hair, normally a wild overgrowth of curls, is pushed back and tamed. His face is... clean-shaven. He's always worn trimmed stubble, a line drawn between him and the world.

But tonight, it's gone. He's changed, too.

"You ready, Syd?" Jules asks, her eyes saying more than her words.

"Yep, I'm ready."

Ivy and Mason are too caught up entertaining their friends, graciously fluttering from guest to guest rather than keeping a close eye on us. It leaves James, Jules, Tom, and me to our own devices. And we take full advantage, slipping into our familiar foursome in a quiet corner.

"That's an awfully nice dress." Jules leans in close, whispering near my ear.

"Thanks. It felt right when I saw it at the boutique in town."

"Ah. So it's new." She grins, a devilish glint in her eyes, as she turns her attention to the two men across the table. Tom and James are deep in conversation, easy in each other's company. "This is nice. The four of us. They have a serious bromance brewing."

I nod absently, pretending to listen while trying to hide how distracted I am. But I feel him before I look up, the caress of his eyes like a physical one.

A smirk plays on his lips as our eyes meet. The heat in his gaze sears through every layer of clothing between us. He bites his bottom lip, and heat pools between my thighs, leaving me aching and squeezing my knees together.

I barely register Jules still talking, "...his rugged good looks. Massive hands..."

"What?" I sputter, snapping back into focus.

"Just checking if you were paying attention, because the way you and James are eye-fucking each other? I think it's time we have that honest conversation."

I try to school my expression, to smother the flush creeping up my neck. That constant hum that lives under my skin whenever he's near.

"You two are into each other. It's been obvious for years."

"We're friends." I drop my gaze, watching the bubbles rise in my champagne.

Jules chortles, loud and unfiltered. "Oh, please." She leans in, dropping her voice low. "I have *friends*, Syd—and not one of them looks at me like they're dying to memorize the shape of my mouth, or as if touching my hand might actually ruin them. That's not friendship."

She grabs my hand, dragging me deeper into the corner. "Tell me the truth. I know you well enough to know this isn't just physical. Are you in love with him?"

I shake my head. I can't answer that.

Jules exhales, her grip on my hand tightening. "Do you remember that time in the sunroom, right after your pregnancy was announced? You asked me if I was ever lonely, and you said something like, *I've never let myself want something just for me.*" She holds my hands, refusing to let me look away. "I haven't forgotten that. And you know what? I've seen you more alive and more broken in these last few years than I ever did in the previous ten. This thing with James? It's not nothing because it's bringing you out. The real you."

I squeeze my eyes shut, willing the tears not to fall.

"Syd, people get divorced. Kids adjust. Life goes on." She tugs on my hand again, forcing me to look at her. "And everyone else? They'll survive. So don't push aside your needs and wants because you're worried about all of them. You are too important to waste away in this half-life."

My heart kicks up. He stares at me, lips parting as his gaze trails down my body before returning to my face. Something dangerous burns in the depths of his stare. The same look I've been catching since that morning in the sunroom. It's a look that tells me everything.

He loves me.

I blink, unable to breathe as all my desires and wants crash against me. I... I love him too.

Jules has slipped away in my stunned silence. She takes control of the speaker, and the shift in music is so seamless I don't register it at first. The first few notes sweep through the room, bold and confident, the kind of song that makes you want to move without thinking. It's not background music; it's the kind that demands attention, that makes you feel powerful in your own skin. The bass slams straight through my ribcage, a thrum I feel low in my stomach, in my pulse, everywhere, my body brimming with excitement and trepidation. Jules's smug face suggests she knows exactly what she's doing.

Exactly why she chose this song as the lyrics kick in. To *Make Me Feel*. It's saying everything I'm not. Each lyric lands sharp and dangerous, a dare I can't unhear.

And it's working.

Jules moves first, pulling me onto the makeshift dance floor. The music pulses between us. We're not the only ones dancing to the infectious beat.

I should stop. Walk away. Shut this down.

But I don't.

Just like I shouldn't look.

But I do.

James watches with dark eyes, posture tense and focused, as my hips sway and knees bend. He leans forward, elbows on his knees, never breaking eye contact as if the music is a language only the two of us can hear.

Jules's hand clasps mine, and she spins me once before pulling me close, her stomach to my back. "Should I ask Tom and James to join us? They both look eager. Very eager."

My body tenses with anticipation at the mere idea of dancing with him. Her lips curl into a wicked smile. She laughs, loud and satisfied, pleased to have finally drawn a reaction out of me after all these years.

I don't even try to recover. Because for the first time since I was a girl wishing on stars, I'm letting myself hope. While I want him—God, do I want to know what his hands feel like on my body—more than that, I want him waiting for me each day after work, waking beside me each morning, and growing so ridiculously old and wrinkled together that we'll look back on this night and think, *damn, we were so lucky*.

Hope, the thing I've spent years protecting myself from, floods through me.

But Jules isn't the only one watching.

Mason, mid-conversation, shifts his gaze between us, his grip tightening around his drink. His eyes darken to that deep midnight blue I remember from the deck, storming with anger. Ivy's eyes settle on James, something calculating in her expression as she watches his focus on me.

I look away, calming my breath. In. Hold. Out. And when I look back at James, his eyes are still on me. Something fierce and wholly mine breathes free.

Jules tugs me close and says, "You know why I love romance novels? It's not for the smut." She laughs. "Well, it's partially for the smut. But really? It's because they prove that even in the midst of life, love still finds a way in."

She pauses, her chaos temporarily quieted.

"Life's full of pain. Some of it is crushing, like what you've been through. And some comes from the mundane daily grind of being an adult. But we don't have to live in fear of it. We can feel all of it, the highs and lows, and know we're truly living." Her voice grows fierce. "Stop letting the past dim your light, Syd. Life's too short for what-ifs. It's time to burn it all down."

***

BEFORE THE CLOCK STRIKES midnight, Mason finds me.

He's had enough to drink to be emboldened and curls a possessive arm around me. "Why don't you dance with me that way?"

"Mason, we can't pretend we're fine because you've had a few drinks."

"You went through a lot of effort if you weren't looking for my attention."

"I cut my hair for myself. I'm wearing this dress because I like how it makes me feel. This is for me. It's not for your approval."

His lips curve, but not quite to a smile. "Funny, it seems like you were trying to look nice for someone."

The countdown begins before I can get away.

Ten.

He moves closer, his palm trailing down my exposed back.

Nine.

His fingers press, trying to pull me against him.

Eight.

Seven.

Dread coils deep in my stomach.

Six.

Five.

The noise swells around us, the room's energy electric. All I feel is what he's expecting.

Four.

Three.

Two.

The room erupts as the ball drops, voices rising in celebration. Mason's hands tighten. His mouth crashes into mine. His lips taste of champagne and control. I choke on the memory of the deck. The revulsion is instant and total. I pull back, breaking the kiss, and throw myself toward the nearest people—Jules, Tom, anyone but him. Searching. But I don't see the man I'm looking for. Ivy stands with her friends, laughing, nowhere near James when midnight struck.

I slip outside onto the back deck in desperate need of fresh air. Cold air whips around me, the scent of pine and distant smoke riding the breeze as I take a deep, steadying breath, gathering my strength for the next steps forward.

"Having a good New Year's?" His deep voice comes out of the shadows. He's leaning against the side of the house near the stairs, already out here. "Wanna come over here, away from all those windows?"

I smile and close the distance. James settles a blanket over my shoulders, his hand resting on my elbow as he leads me down the stairs, away from prying eyes.

"I heard you talked to my mom."

"Yeah, we had a great conversation. I loved her. I'm going to help."

I don't tell him the rest. How Vera's words burrowed beneath my ribs and haven't let go since.

"You took my breath away tonight." His voice is silk against my neck. "I love the haircut. Any reason you decided to do it?"

I exhale slowly, my fingers tracing the sharp, smooth line of his jaw. That lopsided grin spreads across his face. Without thinking, I let my fingertip press gently into his dimple.

"Any reason you shaved?" I counter, my touch featherlight, tracing the warmth of his skin.

His eyes find mine. Dark, hungry, and so damn soft. "Felt like it was time."

I suck in a breath. "Me too."

"I don't want to push you, but tonight is about new beginnings." James captures my hands, interlacing our fingers. "Sydney, let me be your family. You, me, and Anna."

His grip tightens around my fingers. "I'm in love with you." He lifts our clasped hands and presses his lips to the back of my hand. "Please. Trust me. I'm yours."

I stare into his eyes, and I feel it: certainty. I know what I want. I can take his hand and walk away from a life that has been more about surviving than living. I don't have to fear it if we both choose it. And he's shown me repeatedly that he's choosing me.

Leaning my head against his chest, I breathe in his cologne, warm spice and something I could live inside forever. I feel his heartbeat against my body and give myself a moment to find the words.

But as I open my mouth—

"Syd, you out here?"

Mason.

Ice floods my veins. I jerk back instinctively.

Mason catching us would be catastrophic. The memory of his hands on the deck, the way he grabbed me, flashes through my mind. What would he do if he caught us?

Panic grips my insides.

I turn toward the stairs, toward Mason. But before I reach the top, I glance back and my eyes lock with James's—a silent plea written in the depths of his. I don't have time for words. But I hope he sees it in my face.

Yes.

I hope my desperation is as clear as his.

"What are you doing out here?" Mason asks, his eyes sweeping the deck.

"Needed some fresh air."

Mason scans my face, searching for the lie. His golden hair, combed over and frozen with product, defies gravity and weather alike. It stays rigidly in place, matching the scowl on his lips, even as a strong gust rolls off the mountains. I brush past him, stepping into the cabin's warmth. Conversation and clinking glasses wash over me as I pretend my feet are on the ground rather than floating from the almost-confession Mason interrupted.

When James finally slips back inside a few minutes later, Mason's head snaps toward the door. For a split second, confusion flickers—then realization strikes. His eyes cut to me, sharp and damning, the truth snapping into place without a word spoken. James slips past everyone, not seeming to notice us. Gone is the charming host, replaced by something dark and vicious. Mason clamps a hand around mine, the grip punishing, and he yanks me toward the stairs.

The bedroom door slams shut behind us. His hands are on me instantly, pulling at the hem of my dress, his breath jagged.

Using all my strength, I push his hands away. "Mason…" The truth scorches my tongue, but I can't let it out, not like this. Instead, I lie. "I have my period. The cramps are brutal."

He stills, his face hardening. "Funny how your cramps didn't stop you from putting on a show with Jules."

With an indignant turn, he disappears out the door.

I stand there, stunned, my skin still crawling from his rough hands. I wait for the anger, the sting, the shame, but it doesn't come. Echoes of the party hum through the house, laughter and music drifting under the door. Inside this room, I finally let myself breathe, James's words playing on a loop through my mind.

"Let me be your family. You, me, Anna."

The plea in his voice. The way his lips brushed against my hand, fingers tightening around mine, clinging to hope itself. And the way "yes" was on the verge of leaving my lips.

TWENTY-FIVE

THE HOUSE IS STILL, wrapped in the hush of a late morning after a long night.

But inside me, everything churns. I need time to think without eyes on me. I lace up my running shoes and step into the cold. The winter air slices through me, shocking me fully awake. The cold strips away the noise and the fear.

With every mile, the fog in my head lifts. A plan begins to take shape.

I've spent too long shrinking myself. There is no more vacillating between staying or leaving. It's time to build a life that's mine and step out of the shadow of my mother's suicide. It's time I demand what I deserve. I can be as brave as my daughter and be fearless in what I choose.

I step inside with a long, exacting breath, ready for the truth to come out. Tell Mason I'm done. Let go of my life-raft Wallises. And tell James yes.

Until I look up—and a sharp gasp catches in my throat.

Ivy is straddling James on the sectional. Her hands tangled in his hair, her body flush against his. She devours him with reckless abandon, lips moving over his with desperate hunger.

And he lets her.

He doesn't push her away; instead, his hands clench the cushions. Her body moves against him, a slow grind, lost in a world where no one else exists.

Except I exist.

I stand there. Watching. Unable to look away.

A low moan escapes Ivy as she shifts against him, deepening the kiss—and something inside me twists so violently I'm shocked to find I'm still standing.

I should move. Say something. Let them know I'm here.

Before I can, the door behind me swings open. Footsteps. Laughter. The sound of my in-laws and the kids returning from their night at the hotel.

Ivy pulls away, grinning when she sees me. She wipes a hand across her lips and straightens her clothes, drawing out the moment and letting it sink into my bones.

James goes rigid. His face, God. The color drains from his skin. His eyes meet mine, and everything about him crumbles. We stand there looking at each other in mutual devastation.

Everything he said. Everything I wanted to say. It's just gone.

And Ivy. Ivy kisses his cheek. He flinches and steps away. Her smile never falters.

"Ewww, why are you guys kissing like that?" Beck wrinkles his nose while Leo giggles behind his hand.

Gary clears his throat. "Glad to see last night's party worked its magic."

Margaret pinches him. Her eyes dart to me and then to Ivy and James.

"Sorry about that," Ivy chirps. "We got a little... carried away." And she glides off toward the kitchen like she didn't set fire to the last thing I believed in.

James meets my eyes once again, stopping next to me, but I look away, and he slams the front door behind him.

My stomach lurches, nausea rising fast. But on the outside, I stay calm. I think about chasing after him and unleashing the pain churning inside.

"Sydney." Margaret runs her hand down my arm.

I reach for Anna, pulling her into my arms, pressing my face into her curls, inhaling her sweet scent. She babbles something against my shoulder, and I hug her close, willing the tears forming in my eyes not to fall. There is no way I'll give Ivy the satisfaction of seeing that.

"You guys have a good night? I'm going to get cleaned up. Come on, Bug." I kick off my sneakers and climb the stairs, holding it together until I reach the empty bedroom. Only then do I set Anna down on the floor and let the pain crash over me.

How could he do this? Did he think I was choosing Mason when I walked away?

I was about to tell him I loved him, that I wanted him to be my family too. I touched him, gave him every indication I was ready.

Was this a game to him?

How could I have been so stupid?

Believed him so completely?

I cannot, will not, throw away everything for a man who whispered he loved me, who said he wanted to be my family, and couldn't even wait a day before letting Ivy climb into his lap as if it had all been in my head.

It's as I suspected: I'm not enough. At some point, he'd turn out like everyone else—tiring of me. Leaving me. It shouldn't surprise me.

I will not let myself break for something that was never mine.

***

THE REST OF THE day drifts by in a haze of hollow conversations, a fake smile glued to my face. I move on autopilot, my walls rebuilt and reinforced, thick as ice over a winter pond.

I maintain it constantly, relentlessly. Ignore every attempt James makes to meet my eyes. Ignore Ivy's smug parade as she floats around the house, spouting wedding ideas and honeymoon itineraries. Margaret and Jules are unwilling spectators to a horror show they never meant to sign up for.

But I won't hide and cry. That can wait until I'm alone in D.C. It will not happen while I'm under the same roof as them.

Where's Mason in all this? I have no idea. And I honestly don't care.

Keeping my chin high and my gaze distant, I play unaffected.

Jules, though, won't let it go and drags me to the sunroom. "Syd, will you talk to me?" She pleads, gripping my hands. "Last night, you looked like a woman in love. And now? It's like you've been body-snatched with a robot."

I say nothing. Because if I speak, the ice will crack. And if the ice cracks, I fall through. That thin layer is the only thing keeping me upright, keeping me from collapsing into bed with a bottle of wine and sad Taylor Swift on repeat. Except today I need fuck-you Taylor. A full glitter bodysuit, red lip, and middle finger to the world.

That's the version of me that can survive right now.

"Whatever happened, talk to him. That's what people in love do. They show up. They mess up. They talk. You don't throw it all away over a misunderstanding. Not when it's real. Not when it matters."

"Jules, this isn't one of your romance stories. Some of us live in the real world, where life is full of people who disappoint more often than they show up. And to survive, we don't run into that pain."

She watches me closely, waiting for more, but I have nothing left to give. I blink hard, pushing back the tears pooling at the corners of my eyes.

"I was clearly mistaken. And honestly? It's a crush. A stupid, silly crush. It didn't mean anything."

A cough from the doorway cuts through the air. It's him.

My heart stutters against my ribs before I can stop it. I turn away, inhaling slowly, summoning every last shard of anger I have left, bracing myself as my chest heaves, trying to pull in air.

Jules looks at me once more and grabs my hand. "I'll be right outside. Just *talk* to him."

She crosses the room, her footsteps light against the floor, and murmurs something to him that I can't hear. He steps inside. The lock clicks, sealing us in to talk free from interruption. His footsteps are cautious. I keep my eyes locked on the mountains. Behind me, I feel his heat radiating from a few steps away, close enough to set my skin on edge.

"Sydney, will you please look at me?"

When I don't respond, when I don't turn around, he begins talking.

"When you walked away last night, I didn't know what it meant. Part of me thought that was my answer. I told you I loved you. I wanted to be your family. Then he called out, and you bolted." His voice cracks at the words.

I swallow hard against the bile in my throat. My worry over Mason finding us. Memories from the deck and his words press into the cracks of my fury.

Maybe it wasn't as clear as I thought.

Maybe in the dark, he didn't see the plea in my eyes.

The silent choice I was trying to make.

"Ivy found me sitting in the family room this morning. I was waiting for you... Hoping to run together. Hoping for clarity. Her litany of complaints and questions was endless. Why was I being so distant? Why wouldn't I talk about the wedding? Why wouldn't I touch her? Why wouldn't I share her bed? She wouldn't let it go."

He circles to stand before me, blocking my view of the mountains, forcing me to look at him and see the devastation in every line of his face. He pauses and steadies himself for the part that will wound us both.

"I hate hurting people, especially women. Growing up watching my father's cruelty, I swore I'd never be the one to inflict pain. I tend to let relationships dissolve naturally and keep it cordial. I couldn't bring myself to tell her we were done so abruptly. So I was trying to brush off her questions, but also not provoke."

I hear the pain behind the admission. How much he carries from his childhood. How lasting that kind of trauma is. I *know* how deep the effects run.

"Mason walked by. Smug. Gloating. And he said, 'You know, if you guys are fighting, I'd skip right ahead to the makeup sex part.' And I fucking snapped. The idea of him touching you. I saw him leading you up the stairs last night..."

James closes his eyes as the memory sears him. His fists clench at his sides, knuckles white, before he forces them to unclench and takes a breath.

Tentatively, he reaches out to graze my jaw with his fingertips.

"All I could think was that you chose him. That you wanted him, and I had lost you." He's not hiding anything—remorse, love, anguish shadow every feature. "And when she kissed me, I let it happen because I was jealous. And angry.

And I wanted it to be you. You begging me, pleading with me. Needing me as much as I need you."

His hands cradle my face. "It's always been you."

I hear his desperation, but Ivy's moan rings in my ears. Any hesitation over hanging on to my anger dissipates like mist rising off the mountainside. There one moment, vanished the next.

"That's a funny way of showing it, shoving your tongue down her throat. I don't even know what to believe. This week was..." I bite my lip to stop myself. I can't finish those thoughts. Because if I say it, the ice will crack and I'll feel everything. "It doesn't matter, James."

"Don't say that. Don't shut down like this. Yell at me. Fight me. Show me something." His eyes blaze with something beyond sorrow and grief. They burn, and he wants me to burn right back. "I know this is messy and complicated. I'm so fucking sorry about this morning." A tear slips from the corner of his eye. "I'm sorry I let my insecurities get the better of me. I'm sorry I let her kiss me. I love you. Today, tomorrow, always."

"No, James. I've suffered enough disappointment for one lifetime. I can't take any more. I can't keep waiting for the next shoe to drop." I force myself to meet his eyes. Steeling my expression, I will my eyes to match the coldness of my words. "Marry Ivy."

His face falls, matching the deep, aching sorrow that mirrors my own as if he's finally accepting that right now there's no chance I'll hear what he's saying.

And I feel my heart, the one I've tried to wrap in ice, splitting in two.

We stand there, suspended in a war with no winners.

I know I should listen. *Hear* what he's saying. How this morning makes no sense, how it doesn't match the man I know. But I can't hear anything over the pounding of my own fear.

The voice that whispers:

You're not enough.

Love like this always disappears.

Some people deserve love. But you're not one of them.

"Sydney, please. Don't pretend this doesn't matter." He swallows, brings his hand back to my face, and caresses a rogue tear that escaped before I could blink it back. "I made a mistake. One in this whole fucking mess. And it's like you're working so hard to prove I'm not worth the risk."

The riot inside me is deafening. But I keep my chin high, my breath steady. I won't let him see how close I am to breaking.

He draws in a slow, pained breath, and with one final glance, he leaves.

The door slides shut, and my knees give out. I sink to the floor, hands trembling as I press them to my face. I suck in breath after breath to keep sobs from escaping.

Am I trying to prove myself right? That he'll be like everyone else and leave?
Possibly.

Because chasing a love that could destroy me the way it did my mother? That's not brave. That's lighting a match and standing in the fire.

2022

The bird learns to trust its wings
not for where they'll carry her,
but for the sky that was always her birthright.

TWENTY-SIX

EVERY YEAR, I WALK back in here, and every year, I question my sanity.

Tonight I'm walking into a party honoring my sister-in-law's upcoming marriage to the man I've spent the past year trying, and failing, to forget. The man I still dream of and ache for.

I haven't responded to a single text message James has sent. Every day, first thing in the morning and late at night, they arrive. I never fail to read them—dissecting his every thought, reading far too much into what he doesn't say.

The only time I can bear his name, the only thread I allow myself to hold, is when I speak with his mother. Vera and I have grown close this year through my volunteer work at the shelter. Anna and I have spent countless weekends at her house, finding comfort in her warmth, the stillness of her quiet country road, and the endless running trails beyond her back door.

After long days at the shelter, Vera pours wine and shares stories about James. Embarrassing tales of his childhood mischief, teenage drama, and college disasters. The little things that made him, that led him to be the man he became. She never mentions Ivy, never brings up the engagement, never says how he's doing now. Only the boy he was. The son she still fiercely loves. And somehow, that makes it bearable.

We gloss over my marriage and never discuss Mason. I never tell her about the dream that was crushed on New Year's. About how I relive those moments every day. More often than not, under dark skies filled with stars or when the sun crests the horizon on quiet roads where I'm fully alone, I wonder if I made a mistake.

Otherwise, I pretend everything is fine and move through my days with laser focus, pretending I'm not a walking shadow—because I miss him so much it physically pains me.

Mason and I broached the subject of what happened on the deck once. I told him if he ever touched me again like that, I was done. But we're still technically together. Still married. I couldn't bring myself to face the fallout and lose the Wallises when I was already carrying so much loss, even if they aren't the perfect family I had placed on a pedestal all these years. They're still the only one I have.

Ivy and James's wedding is set for December 28. Tonight is the bachelorette party. The men arrive tomorrow for the holidays, then comes the grand finale—the joyous wedding. *Yay.*

I've stayed as far removed as possible from everything leading up to this. I've skipped every shopping trip and family get-together. Ignored the concern in Margaret's voice every time she paused, as if she were about to raise the subject of why I've shut down since last New Year's.

But tonight, I can't miss.

The cabin is cloaked in silence as I gingerly step inside. Pine and cloves mingle in the air. Holly and lights sparkle throughout. The place I once loved now wraps its talons around me, assaulting me with memories and images of last year. But it's not only those memories haunting me. My disastrous phone call with Jules from a few weeks ago rises to the forefront of my mind.

Our first real fight.

"Sydney, will you listen to me? Do you know he hasn't participated in a single decision for this wedding? He nods, goes along with whatever Ivy wants. He's so clearly heartbroken. A shell of himself. Ivy knows something is wrong. But she's steamrolling toward the altar and won't listen to reason. I don't know what's going on with her, but it's like she's decided being Mrs. James Navarro is the only thing that matters."

"Jules, just support her. Don't worry about me. I'll be there, with a smile on my face."

She exhaled so hard I could practically hear her pacing on the other end of the line.

"This isn't even about you and James. Or you and Mason. It's about you. Why are you doing this to yourself? Staying with Mason like some penance for a crime you didn't commit?"

I said nothing. Sealed my lips tight so no sound escaped.

Her voice softened, while her words hit, sharp and unrelenting.

"I've thought about why he's going through with the wedding. Why he's not backing out. And I think I finally get it. It's how he keeps a connection with you."

My lungs stopped working. A sharp gasp broke through.

"If he ends it with Ivy, there's no reason to see you. You'll vanish into your world, he'll disappear into his, and you'll both spend the rest of your lives pretending you aren't miserable."

"Fuck off, Jules. I don't need this from you."

"No, Syd. You do need to hear this. Because it's not too late. You have to stop letting fear run your life, stop letting your past trap you. Choose yourself."

I closed my eyes, feeling the sting behind them, willing the walls to slam back into place.

"I've got to go." And I hung up.

We haven't spoken since. I'm utterly alone walking into tonight. I close my eyes, roll my shoulders back, and lift my chin. Take the final step. Grab a glass of some sickly-sweet, pink concoction to hide the tremor in my hands.

The basement is a pink paradise—soft, romantic, and unmistakably Ivy. Bouquets of peonies spill from every corner, their delicate fragrance blending with the warm vanilla of flickering candles.

Everything is beautiful.

Everything is perfect.

Everything feels suffocating.

I tug at the hem of my deep burgundy dress, its thick wool hugging my body in a way that feels both comforting and armored. Paired with nude tights and sky-high stilettos, it's a deliberate contrast to the lacy pastels and glittering fabrics worn by the other women.

A quiet rebellion against the pretense of my attending.

I needed something that made me seem put-together. To not let Ivy see the wreckage beneath.

Jules stands at the center of the room, backlit like the ringleader of some elegant circus. When our eyes meet, a wicked grin plays at her lips as she brandishes a handwritten list. "Alright, ladies. Time for a game I call: Ivy's Wedding Hangover! I asked James all these questions earlier, so no fibbing, Ivy."

The room erupts, and Ivy, already flushed from cosmos and attention, claps excitedly. She glows, eyes glittering at every mention of James. She touches her engagement ring absentmindedly, in awe that this is her life.

It starts light, harmless.

"How did they meet?" *In the elevator at their office building.*

"How does he take his coffee?" *Black.*

"What's his favorite color?" *Green.*

Ivy nails every answer, giggling like a schoolgirl. Until the questions shift.

The surface-level trivia fades, and the questions begin probing deeper. His hopes and dreams, the moments from the past that have shaped him, things that make him... *him*.

Ivy's smile falters. Her eyes shift with uncertainty. She laughs it off and takes a sip of her drink.

But I see it. The moment she realizes she doesn't know the answers.

She's marrying him, and yet, she doesn't know.

But I do.

A reluctant smile tugs at my lips because these aren't hard questions, not for me.

"What musician is James most looking forward to seeing in the amphitheater he designed?"

Ivy straightens, confidence snapping back into place. "U2!"

"Taylor Swift." I scoff, letting the answer slip out in a whisper, barely audible.

"Drink up, Ives." Jules clinks her glass against Ivy's. "It's Taylor Swift."

Ivy's cheeks flush, but she waves it off.

"Where does James want to travel most in the world?" Jules keeps asking, keeps pushing.

"Africa?" Ivy ventures.

"Not good enough. It's a big continent. Be specific."

I breathe out, soft as a snowflake landing. "Climb Kilimanjaro."

Jules watches me, a hint of trouble glinting behind her lashes as she delivers the correct answer. The one I didn't have to hesitate to find.

It's like she's forcing me to see this. Hear it. She planned this whole game for this moment. For me. For Ivy. A cruel airing—for Ivy to see how wrong they are for each other, and for me to finally admit everything I've denied this past year.

"Dear, don't you think this is enough?" Margaret's voice breaks the tension. Jules stares at her sister, as if willing her to concede and bow out.

Ivy fluffs her hair, smiles wider. "It's all good, Mom. Just a harmless game."

The look on Margaret's face suggests otherwise.

Jules doesn't wait—she fires off the next question, her voice all innocence and sugar. "What's James's favorite book?"

"Oh, that's easy! *The Alchemist*." Ivy lights up in triumph.

I groan but keep myself under control. "*Dune*" is the correct answer. Jules smirks like she's developed a sixth sense for things I mumble under my breath. She gives Ivy the correct response and turns her smile directly to me as if she's daring me to break.

"What is James's favorite comfort meal? The one his mom made for him growing up?"

Ivy shifts uncomfortably as all eyes in the room land on her. "Lasagna?"

Something inside me snaps.

"Drink up, Ivy." My voice is loud and clear. "It's her Chicken Parmesan."

The room stills.

A long pause follows.

The kind that comes after a bomb goes off.

The friends who know me as Ivy's sister-in-law look puzzled. The extended family eyes me wearily. Margaret wraps her arms around herself and looks off into the night sky. Jules watches with quiet satisfaction. Ivy's eyes, usually clear and kind, hold the fury of a nor'easter.

"Sorry, it's nothing," I laugh half-heartedly and will my face not to flush. The lie comes out easily: "Just a little trivia Vera mentioned when we were working. Now *I* drink for interrupting the game!"

I force a smile, playing it off, pretending this wasn't a shot fired in the dark.

But Ivy's eyes don't leave me. She's studying me, dissecting every word, knowing my outburst wasn't a joke at all. The three of us know that what we've ignored and lied about is finally out in the open.

This game was never a bachelorette party pastime.

It's become a dangerous, unspoken test. One I fail.

But the party goes on. Ivy's friends ask about gifts.

A fist closes in the pit of my stomach as I sink deeper into my chair. I've been to enough wedding showers and bachelorette parties to know what's coming: the sheer lace, the satin nightgowns, the gag gifts designed to make everyone blush. The entire spectacle makes me want to tear through the room, like a toddler on a sugar high, raving and uncontrolled. Instead, I try to go to a happy place in my head, drowning out the inevitable.

Jules, ever the commander of chaos, takes charge, handing Ivy gifts—until only one box and gift bag remain. The box shimmers, wrapped in silver paper, and the small bag comes from the book shop in town.

"This one's from me and Syd," Jules says, a dangerous grin directed to me.

My heart slams against my ribs and I want to throttle her.

Ivy lifts a nightgown from the tissue paper, sheer black lace, impossibly delicate, undeniably provocative. A collective gasp swirls through the room, followed by squeals of delight.

I dig my nails into my palms, pressing hard enough to leave marks. The crescent moons they carve into my skin feel earned. Necessary. My stomach knots so violently I lock my jaw.

From the bag, she pulls out *The Kama Sutra*.

Laughter explodes. Everything inside me twists.

"Oh, my dear sisters, this slip is gorgeous," she purrs, her eyes sharp as ice. "Maybe I'll give James a little sneak peek." She draws out each word like a carefully placed dagger, then goes in for the kill: "Though James and I don't need any help from this book."

Teasing whistles and high-pitched giggles follow.

I smile, or what I imagine passes for a smile. "Cheers to that."

After the presents are unwrapped and the games have run their course, the rest of the guests depart. Margaret goes to bed without a word to me or Jules. Ivy and a few close friends retreat to her bedroom for a sleepover, leaving Jules and me to tackle the aftermath. We still haven't talked, politely staying out of each other's orbit.

I don't know what to say.

Our phone call, her antics tonight—they're chipping away at all my defenses.

It's taken me a long time to realize it wasn't the kiss that caused me to shut down last year. It was me, doing the same thing I've always done when things get too big or out of control: isolate and withdraw. The same way I did as a kid. As a teenager. After my parents' deaths.

I've never learned how to cope otherwise.

I scrub at a wine stain on the counter, lost in thought, when I feel a soft touch on my arm.

Jules is there, her face open, searching. "Hey, I'm sorry."

The words undo me. I wrap my arms around her and whisper, "I've missed you."

Because without her, my life has shrunk into a monotonous loop—work, home, Anna. Anna is the only light in my days. Somehow, over the course of my relationship with Mason, my choices have narrowed and my village shrank until my whole world revolved entirely around my husband and his family. Between juggling motherhood and trying to stay afloat professionally, I haven't had time or the energy to build the kind of mom-friend group everyone swears by.

But Jules? She won't let me hide or sweep what happened tonight under the rug.

"Syd, you've spent your whole life trying to scrub away the damage your asshole parents left behind. Like if you work hard enough, it'll all just disappear. But living isn't about forgetting. It's about healing. Accepting that there aren't always explanations for the way people behave." She pauses. "And believing that you had no part in their choices. I love you. And I want to see you happy. I honestly don't care if that is with James or without him. But you can't keep living like this."

"What if I'm too late?"

"What's the worst that can happen? He says no? Because even by asking him, you're making a choice. Acknowledging that you deserve better. That Anna deserves better." She pulls back and wipes the tears from the corners of my eyes. "If you love him, you need to say something. For yourself. For him. For Ivy and Mason. You all deserve better."

"I hear you. I... need to think, and we can talk more tomorrow. Now go to bed. I'll finish the dishes."

"I love my brother and sister, but you're my person. Forever. You can't get rid of me." She holds me in a fierce hug that betrays just how much strength lives in her small body. "Regret is a hard way to live. When you look back on your life, is that what you want to remember?"

Her head tilts, examining me before tapping my phone. "Good night, love. Maybe you should read those texts you pretend I don't know about."

I grip the edge of the counter and stare at her retreating figure. I try to recall all the reasons. The obstacles. The pain. But James's lopsided smile is the first thing that comes to mind. And I pick up my phone to read through a year's worth of his daily thoughts.

twenty-seven

Wind howls against the windows; the soft crackle of dying embers in the fireplace is punctuated by the steady click-clack of my heels against the wood grain as I pace the kitchen. Every message is another crack.

Skating Stud: Coffee shop was out of oat milk. I can't stop adding it. Who knew it was so much better than black coffee?

Skating Stud: Sometimes I think buildings are easier to understand than people.

Skating Stud: Ran over a covered bridge this morning. Do you still think certain pressures can make things stronger?

Skating Stud: It's been raining for days. Just finished The Paris Apartment. Have you read it?

Skating Stud: Mom called. She mentioned you were visiting the shelter. Said you've been running a lot. I hope you're taking care of yourself.

Hundreds of messages like this. Never asking for forgiveness or explaining away what happened that morning. Just little thoughts reminding me he's still trying to show up. To prove he's still there. Waiting.

I hop up onto the counter, my legs dangling, and fill the quiet kitchen with a song I listen to when I can't outrun the longing. When the hurt creeps out, no matter how deep I try to bury it, when I want to stop pretending.

The last message came this morning.

Skating Stud: *Another night with no sleep. Just watched the moon. Wondered if you saw it too.*

The opening beat pulses through the speakers, low and sultry, and I shut my eyes, letting myself feel it all. His words echo: *"I wanted it to be you. Begging me. Pleading me. Needing me as much as I need you."* Rihanna's voice follows—unyielding, unapologetic—about wanting and being wanted, about a woman who knows her worth and refuses to apologize for her desires.

Then the side door blows open. James steps inside, like an apparition in the desert.

He's in a suit, tie loose. His hair is tousled from repeatedly running his hands through it. A few gray strands show at his temples, new lines near his eyes. His jaw is dusted with week-old stubble.

He says nothing. Neither do I.

The memories hover as ghosts in the room, pressing in around us, but I meet his stare. His gaze burns a path along my skin, cataloging the changes in me, taking in every detail. A sharp intake of breath escapes my lips under his scrutiny. His pupils darken, a primal reaction he can't hide.

"Want a drink?" I ask, my voice lower, huskier than normal.

"Sure." He sets his bag down with a quiet thud, never looking away.

My heels land with a sharp tap as I move to pour him a glass, giving myself a minute to think, to breathe, to process. I wasn't ready for this. I wasn't prepared to see him alone, with only the hush of the house and no distractions or interruptions.

A year ago, I told him no. Said this was too much.

Is that the truth, though? When you've spent a lifetime of lying and suppressing, separating what you really want from what you believe is possible, how do you even know?

Our fingers brush as I hand him the glass. That charge, the energy that has always burned white-hot and electric between us, zings at that smallest touch. His nostrils flare, but I snatch my hand away and climb back onto the counter.

The smoldering voice sings of need barely veiled. It settles over us, a whispered confession neither of us is ready to say aloud. Three years of yearning and wanting. Never touching.

James doesn't speak. He moves, closing the space until he's in front of me. In that pause, so much passes across his face: hurt, uncertainty, desire. They war for dominance.

But I feel the pull of him like gravity, a force greater than my resistance, stronger than the walls I've built—and part my legs, a silent invitation for him to close the remaining space. He steps between them without hesitation. The heat radiating from his body is tangible, pressing against me, surrounding me.

My hem rides higher with every inch he claims.

Without tights, there would be little left to the imagination.

But tonight, I'm fresh out of fucks to give, and I don't move away.

Instead, I take a slow sip of wine, letting the smooth, rich flavor coat my tongue, feeling it trickle down my throat. It does nothing to cool what's building.

Two large, warm palms settle on my upper thighs, and a shudder rolls through me. My thighs flex against his hips, and he groans, feeling my muscles beg him to pull me closer. Our eyes never leave each other, as though we're daring the other to blink. To pull back.

It's always been our rhythm, one step forward, two steps back, this constant, aching dance that neither of us knows how to resist.

Then, the softest touch—a single, whispered stroke along the curve of my thigh. So soft it might not have happened if not for the way it sears into my skin. I bite my bottom lip, stifling the noises that threaten to escape. His breath hitches, his finger continuing its leisurely path, writing a confession against my skin.

As the final notes to the song fade away, so does his touch. I stay perched on the counter, trying to reclaim whatever scraps of composure I can muster. Trying to calm my galloping heart.

James moves to a stool, placing distance between us.

Silence stretches. Both of us look at our feet instead of each other.

What do you say to the man you love but pushed away?

He's laid it all out, more than once.

And all I've done is whipsaw between fear and indecision.

I grab my phone and change the music. Not-so-innocently, I put on Tinashe's Christmas album. The familiar chords drift through the air, an instant throwback to a night years ago of stolen glances and undeniable connection. A night that led us to this moment.

"Any reason in particular you picked this album?" James asks.

"Nope."

I meet his gaze, daring him to call me out, to acknowledge any of this.

But he doesn't. He lets out a quiet laugh, shaking his head. The strain between us loosens. We slip back into something familiar, talking about my cases, his buildings, running, books, travel. The mundane details of our everyday lives act as a buffer against everything simmering below the surface.

This part has always been effortless. When we're alone, we can let the outside world fall away. We never run out of things to say, and when we do, the silence between us is comfortable.

One hour turns into two.

It's well past midnight—the hour when reckless decisions are made.

"Should we go to the sunroom? It's more comfortable than a hard countertop." His voice is rougher than before, suggesting he's reached his limit for aimless talk.

Without overthinking, without giving myself the chance to second-guess, I slide off the counter. My heels click against the hardwood as I lead the way.

The moment we step inside, the past rushes in. Neither of us speaks. The faux ease from downstairs slides away, leaving only what we've been hiding from. He silently closes the French doors, flips the lock, and leans against them, taking his own time.

I settle in a chair and turn toward the window, feigning distraction, but I feel him. Each step reflected in the window as he closes the distance. The only light comes from the Christmas tree, casting gentle shadows and sparks of color, wrapping us in a space that's only ours.

He spins my chair around.

And he's there.

On his knees.

I part my legs without thinking. He moves forward, closing the space I've wordlessly offered. His fingers skim along my cheek, and I arch into his touch like a cat seeking the warmth of the sun. A quiet, shuddering breath escapes him, and I draw it in, feeling it down to my toes.

He rests his forehead against mine as his hands drift lower, his thumbs pressing slow circles against my thighs. An ache ignites inside me, deepening with every stroke of his fingers. A small, helpless whimper escapes my lips. His eyes darken, fingers flexing against my skin.

We've never kissed. We've never crossed any physical line.

But emotionally?

We've plunged headlong, ignoring rules and expectations. We've blurred every boundary—family, commitment, loyalty, the lives we're bound to—until there's nothing clean left. We're both committed to others, tied, in theory, to separate futures.

And yet, here we are. On the precipice again.

"Do you still believe this is too much?" he asks, breaking the silence.

I don't want to run anymore. Tonight, I don't want to pretend. I want to fall.

"I dream of you." The confession tears from me. "I dream of your hands. Your fingers. Your mouth." My breath fractures on each word. "So much. It's embarrassing."

The admission hangs in the air, impossible to take back. His eyes darken to the deepest green—like the farthest corners of a forest, where you know danger awaits, but you keep going anyway.

"Do you touch yourself when you think of me?" His voice is rough, pained.

"Yes."

"Do you imagine it's me when your husband fucks you?"

"Yes."

No hesitation. No mercy for either of us.

His head falls back on a sound that's half groan, half prayer, exposing the vulnerable column of his throat. Time stretches thin as he absorbs what I've given him. This terrible, beautiful truth we can't unknow.

"Will you show me?" he leans in, lips brushing my ear. "Show me how you touch yourself."

The world narrows to this moment, this chair, this man kneeling before me. I squeeze my knees into his hips, the ache between my legs overriding all sense.

His hands find my ankles, slipping off each heel like unwrapping something precious. His eyes never leave mine, each touch a question I answer with a nod, each movement an appeal I meet with trust. We hold our breath as if a single exhale might wake us from this dream. Slowly, torturously, he draws my tights down, leaving trails of fire over my skin. He presses a kiss to the inside of each ankle, soft as an exhale, before his hands return to my knees.

A low groan punches the air as he takes in the sheer lace at my thighs. All restraint dissolves around us. My core clenches, and my chest vibrates with anticipation. He closes his eyes for one brief second; fingers twitching, aching to move. Instead, he keeps them on my knees, slowly inching them apart. My fingers find the heat between my legs, and I hum with pleasure.

"Are you wet?"

"Soaking." The word barely makes it past my throat.

When I touch myself, the sensation shoots through me. This rhythm I know by heart, this dance I've performed countless times with his name on my lips, his face behind my closed eyes. But now he's here. Watching. His hands grip my knees, knuckles white, battling the effort of staying still when everything in him wants to reach for me.

Our breathing—mine shallow, his ragged—is the only noise in the room.

I pick up the pace, hips rocking, building toward release. When I shatter, it's with his name caught between my teeth. Pleasure crashes over me, fast and relentless. James's grip tightens. A sharp breath drags from him. I bite my bottom lip, willing myself to stay quiet until the trembling stops. My head falls back. Jaw goes slack.

He catches my hand, brings it to his mouth, and tastes the pleasure coating each finger. His tongue traces their outlines with something approaching worship before he presses my palm to his chest, over the wild drumbeat of his heart.

"God, I've fucking missed you." He rests his forehead against mine.

"Me too." I exhale, and because my mind is fried, I ask without thinking, "Do you... think of me when you're... with her?"

"No." His face is serious, and my heart stops. "Because I haven't touched her in a year."

"You... what? Why?"

His fingers brush back a lock of hair. "You were always there. Forefront of my mind."

I close my eyes, overwhelmed by all of it. This confession. What just transpired. Jules's words from our call: he's heartbroken, going through the motions, only with her to not lose connection to me. It all circles and prods the walls that have been crumbling all night.

"It's been torture only hearing scraps from my mom."

"She's still arriving tomorrow?" I struggle to swallow the lump in my throat.

"Yeah, she is." His voice comes out weary, tinged with the crushing reality of this week. "I think she's more excited to see you than me."

"We both need some rest. People start arriving early, and it's already so late."

James reaches for me, reeling me back into his body, his fingers brushing back my hair, holding me at the base of my neck—unwilling to let me go.

"I promise I'm not running," I thread my fingers through the scruff of his beard, memorizing the feeling of him. "I've thought about us nonstop."

"I'm still here, Sydney. This—coming here—was the only way I could see you. You didn't answer any of my texts. I didn't know what else to do. I know how this looks, especially with... what's supposed to happen in a few days." His lips ghost over my neck, only a feather of touch below my ear. "But I don't feel any different than I did last year. I want to leave here with you. You. Me. Anna. That is the only outcome I want at the end of this week."

"Not a day's gone by that I haven't wished I'd heard you. That I'd listened, on New Year's."

James exhales a breath of relief, as though the air has been stuck in his chest for a year. He wraps his arms around me, pulling me close, processing my confession.

I *should* feel guilty.

He's supposed to marry Ivy in a few days. I'm still married to Mason, even if we haven't slept together in a year, we're still married. Pretty sure masturbating in front of another man crosses the vow to be *faithful*. I'm well beyond that. Infidelity started long ago, even if we've never kissed.

But the only thing I feel is contentment. Because he's here. And I'm finally listening.

"I'll see you in the morning." I slip down the hall and fall into my cold bed.

When I drift off, it's to dreams of green eyes, whispered confessions, and a love as clear and constant as moonlight. I sleep soundly until a sudden weight presses against me. Little hands creep toward my ribs. I wait for her to get close enough and strike. I flip Anna onto the bed and attack her with tickles. She shrieks with laughter, her tiny hands pushing at mine—joy in its purest form.

"Mama! Noooo!" she wails through her giggles.

Mason stands in the doorway, watching, his face carefully blank. He could be observing a piece of art or a basketball game for all I could tell. I don't know if he wants to join, or if he even knows how. He's never been able to surrender to these simple joys with Anna. Not the way she needs. Not the way she *deserves*.

"Sorry to wake you." He inclines his head politely and sets their bags down. "But it's getting late. People will be arriving soon. Have fun at the party?"

"I was up late... cleaning. The party was fine. You know how those things are."

He nods, but doesn't comment.

Anna snuggles into me, her soft curls tickling my skin, her pert little nose brushing my cheek. Every part of her wrapped around me, trusting completely.

The weight of the choice settles deep in my body.

Loving James, choosing him, has never been the question. The choice I have to make is letting go of the damage left behind by my parents, who chose their happiness over their child.

Facing my fears of repeating their mistakes.

That's what I've been battling since I saw those positive pregnancy tests.

Because if I leave Mason, I'll have to share Anna. I won't get every holiday. I won't be the one who tucks her in every night or wakes to her sleepy smile every morning. I won't always be there to kiss scraped knees or chase away bad dreams.

And that thought cuts me clean through.

I know what it means to grow up wondering if you were the reason someone left. And that fear—Anna feeling my loss, associating it with me leaving her father—is the kind of pain I have to be willing to risk. I press my lips to Anna's curls, hoping her steady breath might hold the answer.

TWENTY-EIGHT

"The Dickens Festival is this afternoon. Anyone planning to go?" I ask over a quiet breakfast.

Ivy doesn't look up, scowling from her corner of the table, her spoon clinking aggressively against her coffee cup. She's sullen, not the picture of bridal bliss from the day before. Her friends left early for a day of skiing. James sits beside her, but there's a stiffness in how he leans away.

We have kept a careful distance; the epitome of courteous and friendly. Nothing more than a hello as everyone sat down.

Still, from time to time, when my eyes skirt to that end of the table, I see him staring right back. He watches me as he sips his coffee, finds me when Anna and I laugh. Every time he looks, my stomach reacts, and I squirm at the memory of my fingers in his mouth.

"Sydney." Margaret brushes my arm.

I blink back to the table. My mother-in-law. Her warm eyes hold a hint of concern. "Sorry. What did you think about going to the festival?"

"I hadn't thought about it, with the wedding and everything," Margaret replies.

"If anyone wants to tag along, I'm planning to go."

I glance around the room, keeping my expression easy, pretending I don't care who says they'll come. But I know who I want to join. He won't, though, not until I tell him I'm in. All in. No more fucking around in. Jules catches me looking and smirks. She knows. Of course she does.

"Aunt Sydney, can we come with you?" Beck looks up from his phone.

I blink, momentarily caught off guard. It's hard to reconcile Beck and Leo as tweens, so far from the sticky-fingered, babbling toddlers they once were, now with the long, skinny legs of a colt, ready to burst and take off. Their worlds have expanded beyond their parents, filled now with screens and friends. Their conversations are quick, their attention split. Their needs are different. Jules says this stage is more about being present when they invite you in.

Anna, even in her small orbit, is beginning to show her independence. She has opinions, clear likes, and dislikes. She chooses who she trusts. One day, she'll step into her own life. And loving her will mean giving her space to grow, to fail, to rise. She won't need someone to hold her tight. She'll need someone who knows when to let her fly.

A mother who shows her how to take risks.

"You bet. Want to leave around eleven?" I smile at Beck and Leo.

They nod, already back to their digital worlds.

Anna slides a bite of pancake to Bell, who rewards her with a slobbery kiss, sending her squealing.

"Anna, don't feed the dog," Mason scolds. "It's not nice table manners."

"Hush, Mason. Anna can do what she wants," Gary scolds. "James, what project are you working on out West? Must have been pretty late when you got in last night if you missed all the bachelorette festivities."

Mason's eyes shift from me to James. I see the wheels turning, wondering if we saw each other. I do my best to keep heat from rising in my cheeks. Across the table, James clears his throat, his expression unreadable, though I'd bet his thoughts jump to the same place.

"I've got a few homes in the design phase outside of L.A.," he answers, gaze fixed on his coffee, not bothering to acknowledge the rest.

"Mom, do you think we could have chicken parmesan tonight for dinner? Since we all learned it is James's favorite." Ivy's voice slices through the room, sweet and sharp all at once:

The words land hard, and the silence that follows is palpable. The tone. The glance. Her eyes widen, as if she hears what she let slip. Her frustration has broken through the carefully painted veneer. She recovers fast, smile sliding back into place.

"I think it would be nice since your mom and Darrell arrive today. What time do they get in?"

James, unsure of the minefield, tentatively says, "I'm leaving soon to pick them up. Their flight lands at ten."

"Should I come with you? It'd be nice to meet your mom before everyone swarms her."

Jules lets out a short, dry laugh. The kind that stings.

"Something you want to say?" Ivy stiffens.

"I think you already know, Ives." Jules unapologetically doubles down.

And with that, she stands, gathering empty plates, her words ricocheting around the table.

"Jules, I need to speak with you. On the back deck. Now." Margaret's tone is firm.

It startles the table into silence, and we watch them walk off, bickering in whispers. The only thing I hear before the back deck door slams is Margaret saying, "Stay out of it. It's her choice." On the back deck, Jules's hands fly, continuing their argument.

With her head held high, Ivy pushes back from the table, giving no ounce of emotion other than her abrupt withdrawal.

Everyone's eyes stay on their plates.

"Uh oh!" Anna's cry breaks through as her juice tips over, spilling across the table.

"It's okay, baby," I say quickly, grabbing a towel and wiping the mess.

"You're right, it's not Anna's fault. Why can't you just give her a cup with a lid on it?" Mason presses, his tone as sharp as the glacial tint in his eyes.

"Mama." Anna lifts her arms, her eyes flashing to Mason, then back to me, almost like she hears the tone in his voice. "Mama, up."

James pushes back from the table, eyes hard and unyielding. "I've gotta go. Airport and such."

"Guys, remember, we're leaving at eleven." I take the escape.

***

It ends up being Anna, the twins, and me heading to the festival.

The boys mumble a goodbye before they dash to the hot chocolate stand and vintage game arcade. Jules has given them the green light to roam the quaint village together.

Anna walks beside me, mittened hand in mine, her little boots crunching over the snow as we make our way to the bookshop. The village is a winter fantasy land. Light poles are wrapped in evergreen garland, glass ornaments swaying gently in the crisp breeze, the air rich with the scent of chocolate and chestnuts. Last-minute holiday shoppers slip in and out of shops. Kids run, occasionally pelting each other with snowballs. Families wander, sipping hot chocolate.

The alluring combination of cinnamon, orange, cloves, and paper hits first as we walk into the bookshop.

Today, the train table is its own snowy miniature wonderland. Animal figurines gather in family clusters. Bear cubs with two moms, kittens with two dads, puppies with a single mom—some with full extended families, others with only adults and no little ones.

It's this simple display, built for little hands and make-believe, that brings everything into focus.

Families aren't made from blueprints and legal documents. They're built in the quiet, ordinary moments: who shows up, who loves without conditions. Family is who keeps choosing you, over and over, without ever needing to be asked.

I'm still standing there when I hear Anna's unmistakable cry of delight.

"Unca J!"

My head snaps up.

And there he is.

James stands inside the doorway, Vera beside him, Darrell next to her.

Vera's eyes soften the moment she sees me, wrapping me in a tight hug. Her sweater is soft against my cheek, carrying the faint scent of her smoky perfume. She holds me for a long moment, clinging to more than a greeting.

Her eyes shine with tears when she finally pulls back.

"When James mentioned this little festival, I *had* to see it for myself." Vera dabs at the tear slipping down her cheek.

She turns to Anna, half-hidden behind my legs in her boots, leggings, and the ballet tutu she insists on wearing everywhere, a shy smile at the corners of her lips. They always play this game.

"I see a beautiful ballerina, but where is Anna?" Vera looks around theatrically.

"I'm here, Miss Vera." Anna jumps forward, her little hands reaching high into the air.

Vera gasps, feigning surprise. "Oh my. You've grown so much since I last saw you!"

Anna twirls and runs straight to James. He crouches as if drawn by instinct, arms open, smile wide. She goes straight to him. No hesitation. A trust so implicit, so unwavering it stings—because to her, there's no question of right or wrong. She knows James will be there.

"You got her? I'm going to go find a book."

Weaving through the shelves, I don't see the books; I just need space. The twinkling lights guide me deeper into the shop, the soft hum of laughter and the rhythmic chug of the train following behind. My fingers trail along the spines, feeling the grooves and worn edges, the scuff of leather and cloth, the shiny hardcovers and soft paperbacks.

My hand falls still. Nestled between two glossy hardbacks is a familiar cover: *Little Women*. The same book Madame Rousseau once wrapped, tucking a piece of hope into my empty hands. The book I clutched that Christmas morning when no one else noticed I was there—my escape into the March family's messy, imperfect, fiercely loving world.

When I met the Wallises, I thought maybe I'd found my own version. A family to belong to, a place to feel wanted. But it wasn't real. Mason was never the warmth or freedom I dreamed of.

He's the safety of a cage.

I clutch the book to my chest, blinking back tears as my gaze wanders to the front of the shop. James sits with Anna curled against his chest, both of them lost in a book. His smile is wide and easy. Anna throws her arms in the air as they laugh together over the story. Nearby, Vera and Darrell lean in, their smiles warm with affection.

James glances up, as if he can feel me watching. "Hot chocolate next?"

I nod, because I can't speak. Because that image is the opposite of a cage. It's… everything.

"I actually want to check out the boutique next door," Vera says. "I'll be a minute. Darrell, want to come? You guys go ahead and we'll catch up."

James lifts Anna, settling her against his hip. His other hand finds the small of my back. Our eyes meet, and I see the same quiet decision in his gaze, mirroring my own. He wants to stretch this into eternity, too. We meander toward the hot chocolate stand where Scrooge, resplendent in full Dickensian garb, hands out steaming cups. The hot chocolate is legendary: rich, velvety, crowned with clouds of freshly whipped cream and delicate curls of chocolate that melt on your tongue.

"Bah! Humbug!" Scrooge bellows as we approach, his face contorting into a theatrical scowl that doesn't hide the mirth beneath. He hands us each a cup with a grand flourish, then pauses, studying us with eyes that twinkle.

"Now, don't forget what old Scrooge learned," he says. "There's nothing richer than time spent with the ones who make you feel at home. Merry Christmas to you all."

I nod my thanks. James's lips lift, pleased by the illusion Scrooge handed us. This small window into the family he promised we could be. I should ignore the flutter in my chest. I should.

But I'm so damned tired of the lie.

TWENTY-NINE

At Christmas Eve dinner, the conversation inevitably turns to the wedding.

I keep my expression pleasant, composed, though every cell in my body is screaming to run. I fix my gaze on my plate, sip my water, and nod at the right moments, while my mind spins with one impossible question: *How the hell do I do this?* I have three days to overcome somehow thirty-nine years of hurt, wrap up a life with Mason, and figure out how to rebuild everything without harming Anna in the process.

No version of this doesn't hurt.

But maybe that's what real choices look like. They're messy and painful, but necessary anyway.

"Syd, did you hear Ivy's question?" Mason lightly touches my arm.

"What did you ask?" I compartmentalize the deadline barreling toward me.

Ivy looks directly at me. "Have you and Mason picked out the reading you're doing together at the ceremony?"

"No, I haven't," I reply, a little too curt, judging by Jules's raised eyebrow. I soften my tone and continue, "I haven't found anything that feels... right."

James is seated between Vera and Darrell, carefully positioned away from Ivy. I didn't witness their introduction, but Vera's eyes soften as she watches Ivy—like someone watching a car crash, they're powerless to stop. James glances, his eyes saying exactly what I'm thinking. This is excruciating.

Anna sits beside me. Bell's tail thumps against my chair as she begs for another bite.

"You don't have any sisterly words of wisdom to share with me and James as we step into this chapter? As we become husband and wife." Ivy continues, faux-pleasant.

I bite the inside of my cheek, nodding, pretending to listen while my fingers tighten around the napkin in my lap. My stomach asks me if we can leave. But we can't. We've been trained to perform and endure. One wrong word, and I'll ruin dinner. Ruin this holiday for everyone.

Jules swoops in. "I read the perfect thing this morning. Let me grab my Kindle."

Whatever transpired between Margaret and Jules after breakfast is tucked away with all the inconvenient truths we look past. They're smiling and joking as if this morning didn't happen.

James chuckles, imagining the kind of material Jules considers *perfect*. Ivy shoots him a glance so sharp he stops and looks down at his plate.

"Oh no, you don't," Margaret cuts in. "I know exactly what kind of smut you read. Let's go with something more traditional. What about *When You Are Old* by William Yeats? It's a beautiful poem, perfect for two people to read together."

Ivy's already pulling out her phone. "Do you know it, Syd? Let me read it, and we can see if it works. James, Mason, you too. We should all be invested in this reading."

I feel James's eyes on me, but I don't look back. I grip the napkin in my lap as if it might restrain me from doing something I can't undo because I know the poem. I studied it in undergrad, and there is no fucking way I'm reading that.

The irony isn't lost on me.

I wrote a scathing critique of it, missing the connections and meanings I now understand. I was lost in the despair of my mother's death, how her loss shaped everything I believed and didn't believe about love. I'd scoffed at the idea of love enduring through age and regret, never guessing how deeply it would one day cut.

Anna's laughter cuts through the room as she throws another piece of chicken for Bell. Bell's paws pound across the floor to chase the food. All our eyes fall on her and we take a deep breath.

Until Ivy starts reading.

When you are old and grey and full of sleep,
And nodding by the fire, take down this book,
And slowly read, and dream of the soft look
Your eyes had once, and of their shadows deep;

My chair scrapes violently as I stand too fast. The legs catch. It crashes to the floor with a crack.

Forks pause mid-air. Every face turns toward me.

Jules doesn't miss a beat.

"That's perfect. Great choice, Mom. Syd, come help me with the pie in the kitchen?"

She doesn't wait for an answer. She rights my chair and pulls me out of the room, her grip firm but gentle. The moment we're alone, Jules hisses through clenched teeth. "How can you sit there and pretend any of this is okay?"

"How do I... how do I do this?" The worry folds my voice into a broken whisper.

Jules pulls me into a hug. "Anna will be okay. She's loved by so many people. But you also get to want something for yourself. You're allowed to choose this. And that isn't selfish. It isn't anything like what your parents did."

I meet her eyes, drawing strength from her certainty.

Before I can move, Mason steps in, his face tight.

"I don't know what's going on with you. That was embarrassing. It's a reading. Ivy and James are getting married. That doesn't matter to you, right?"

He holds my gaze as Jules grabs my hand. We stand locked in a tense triangle.

"Hey, Mason, I heard the Celtics are on. Why don't you kindly *fuck off* and let me finish talking to Syd?" Jules steps forward, amber eyes glaring, full of challenge.

"I need a moment alone with my wife." He grabs my arm, fingers digging in, enough to make a point.

I stare at his hand on my arm for one deliberate second. Meet his eyes. See if he remembers what I told him about touching me and shake him off.

"Syd, these dramatics are inappropriate. Get it together," he hisses.

I paste on a Barbie smile—perfect, plastic, empty—and carry in a few plates of pie. Let my rage simmer in the depths of my stomach.

Margaret scans the room: Mason and me. James and Ivy. She senses it. This isn't betrothal bliss or holiday cheer. It's a masquerade of strained smiles and fractured silence. And whatever she's thinking, her words from earlier make it clear. There's only so much intervening she's willing to do.

"Vera, that sweater is lovely," Margaret says. "Is it cashmere?"

"Thank you! I picked it up today at that charming little boutique in town. The one with the yellow door." Vera beams, smoothing her hand over the soft blue material.

"You stopped in town?" Ivy's fork stops halfway to her mouth.

"We decided to stop at the winter festival on the way back." James lifts his wine glass and takes a slow sip. "My mom wanted to see it in person after I told her so much about it."

"It was lovely," Vera adds, her eyes finding mine across the table.

"You should've seen James on Galaga," Beck beams. "He crushed the high score!"

A beat of silence follows, the glances around the table saying more than his words.

"You all hung out?" Ivy looks from me to James. Her voice is light, but the accusation beneath it is unmistakable—wanting one of us to confess. But to which crime?

"A quick bite at the arcade," Vera says breezily. "I needed to connect with Sydney about one of her shelter cases."

Margaret takes the opportunity to change the subject and jumps in. "How's that going, Sydney? Must be a big shift from corporate law."

I exhale, leaning into safer territory. This is something I can share freely and happily.

"It's been eye-opening. I've always been proud of my career. But volunteering, helping these women rebuild their lives, it's something I didn't know I needed."

The tension in my shoulders eases because this part of my life, at least, feels honest. I love this work. Representing these women? It's about helping people. It's not money or living up to someone else's expectations. It's all mine.

And it pisses Mason off.

Every weekend that Anna and I pack up to fly out to Rochester is a small act of defiance against Mason's world of power and prestige, and the last name I was born into. I look over to see him swallow down his thoughts, at least smart enough to know this isn't the crowd for his rather limited view of my pro bono work.

"That's sweet of you, Syd." Ivy's gaze is pointed. "I didn't realize you were so involved. How long has that been going on?"

"A while," is all I say with a smile.

"Maybe I can help with marketing after the wedding, Vera?" Ivy adds, swallowing all the worries and suspicions behind a smile.

"That would be lovely, Ivy," Vera replies, her voice warm. "Your mom showed me some photos you took. They are beautiful. Do you still get out with your camera?"

"No, I don't do that anymore."

"I hope my son hasn't had anything to do with that. I've always told the women in my life to keep something of their own. It took me too long to learn that myself." Vera's tone carries weight, her smile gentle but pointed.

"No, it's not him," Ivy says. "I...figured my time was better spent planning for the future instead of chasing some silly dream."

Vera's gaze sharpens. "Dreams are always worth chasing. You have such a beautiful gift."

"Not all of us can get everything we want, can we?" Ivy smiles tightly.

The words hit me like a physical blow. I try to hold my brittle smile, but something about Ivy's voice makes my stomach twist.

"Time for bed, Anna. Santa's waiting."

I carry her upstairs on autopilot, my body moving through the motions while my brain spins. I reach for flannel pajamas and try to lose myself in a book. But the words blur, my mind refusing to stop—everything I need to figure out, everything I need to say.

The mattress shifts. Mason sits on the edge.

"Syd, what's going on?" he asks, reaching over to tuck a loose strand of hair behind my ear. The tenderness throws me off. His eyes are a soft blue, his touch gentle.

"Nothing. Sorry about dinner. I haven't been sleeping well."

"You know, maybe…" His fingers trail up the length of my leg. "I could help distract you."

My body stiffens like a lock clicking shut.

"I'm sorry, Mase. I'm exhausted." I pat his hand, a firm boundary, and turn onto my side, willing him to let it go.

Because that? That isn't happening. Not tonight. Not ever again.

"Hey, will you talk to me? I'm here. I'm trying. Let me in," his voice gentles.

"Why are you doing this now? We've had plenty of time to talk about what happened. What's *been* happening. But you've shown no interest, hell, in years."

"I'm not used to… I don't know what you want. It's not like you've been a ray of sunshine this year. You've been… different since New Year's. What the hell happened?"

I stare wide-eyed at him. I didn't know he was aware enough to notice my mood, to see past my contrite smiles and one-word answers.

This sudden interest is no surprise. The pattern is familiar by now. It's not about me at all. It's about James. Mason feels him in the room, in my pulse, in the way my eyes drift across the table. And so, he reaches for me, staking his claim. This is the closest he's come to asking me to name what he suspects since that night on the deck last year.

"You mean besides you grabbing me? Treating me like property instead of your wife?"

"I've apologized for that night, Syd. Are you going to hold it over my head for the rest of our lives?"

"No, Mason." I half-laugh. "I'm not."

With that, I roll over. He exhales sharply. Within minutes, his breathing evens out into sleep.

And I lie beside him, staring at the wall, seeing James's pleading eyes from across the dinner table. The way they seemed to be asking: *Can we get the fuck out of here? Can we please stop this madness?*

THIRTY

The hours stretch on, each tick of the clock another chisel against my already fragile resolve.

By the time Christmas morning arrives, exhaustion has settled deep into my body. I hear Jules's boys in the hallway, their eager whispers turning into impatient whines: "Is it time yet? Can we go down now?"

They may be almost eleven, but Christmas is still their favorite holiday. And it starts early.

I turn to Anna, curled against me, soft and warm in sleep. "Merry Christmas, Bug." I kiss her temple and gently rouse her. She blinks up at me sleepily before breaking into a slow, sweet smile, her little arms wrapping around my neck.

Downstairs, the room is alive with the murmur of morning. Margaret and Vera huddle near the kitchen, sharing soft conversation over a plate of cinnamon rolls. Tom and Jules try to keep their twins from combusting with excitement. Gary and Darrell observe it all from the sidelines. James stands near the counter, coffee in hand, eyes distant as he stares toward the mountains.

"Good morning, Bug," Margaret greets warmly, kissing Anna's cheek. "Where's Mason?"

"Sleeping." I shrug, setting Anna down. "Said it wasn't worth getting up since she won't remember it."

Margaret's lips press into a thin line. She hasn't said anything outright, hasn't pried, but she sees the cracks. Though she doesn't ask questions, her silent reproach is unmistakable, but she smiles and lets it go. Again.

Before she can ask something I can't lie about, I gain some distance as James crosses the room with two mugs in hand.

"Merry Christmas," he says, passing me one.

Curling my hands around the warm ceramic, I try to keep my face blank so no one sees how much this simple gesture undoes me.

He's devastating this morning. A forest green sweater clings just enough to hint at the strength beneath. The color sharpens his eyes to something wild and vivid. His hair's tousled from sleep. And those black sweatpants? Absolutely criminal.

I bite the inside of my cheek, trying to hide my entirely inappropriate reaction. Especially here, in my in-laws' living room. But his gaze drops, nostrils flaring as he takes me in.

Jules claps her hands. I stumble back.

"Alright, fam. Coffee's poured, and presents were delivered. Let's do this," she announces.

Wrapping paper flies, laughter rings. Anna, unsure at first, quickly catches on. She might be two, but the moment she sees her cousins tearing into their gifts, she understands—then she owns it. She rips open her presents with unrestrained glee, shrieking in delight at every new treasure. She races over after each gift, pressing them eagerly into my hands, into James's, demanding our full attention.

"Look, Momma! Look, Unca J!"

And we do. We marvel. We laugh. We admire each toy with exaggerated wonder, our delight matching hers beat for beat. For a little while, nothing exists outside of her joy. We lean into it, pretend it's the three of us.

If the others notice, they don't say a word.

Clutching a new book in her small hands, Anna walks straight to James, crawling up beside him. She hands him the book and leans back against his chest. He stills, looks from her to me, and takes a slow, deep breath, steadying himself to absorb this little gift. He opens the book and begins to read, bringing to life the tale of a girl and her unicorn.

I tug the collar of my turtleneck up over my mouth, burying my face in the fabric as tears threaten to spill—the sheer perfection of this moment.

When I look up, Ivy is standing at the bottom of the stairs. I catch her wiping a tear along with the worry on her face. In the next breath, she smooths her expression into something bright and polished. In that high sing-song voice she wears like armor, she says, "Merry Christmas, everyone."

***

ONCE ANNA SUCCUMBS TO the morning's excitement and drifts into a nap, I head to the sunroom to gather myself for the night ahead.

But raised voices stop me as I near.

"Ivy, will you wake the fuck up? This is not what getting married should be," Jules snaps.

"I need to get him to the altar. Once we're married, everything will be better."

"Do you hear yourself right now? Who are you? When was the last time you picked up your camera? Went surfing?"

"Don't start with me. This is what grown-ups do. You get a real job. You meet someone. You get married. You move to the suburbs. He's a good man. I'd be insane not to marry him."

"You're so young. Don't do this. Don't settle. You deserve someone who aches when you're not around, who makes you feel cherished and understood. Loved for being you."

"I'm not stupid. I know he had a crush on Sydney. Maybe he still does. I mean I get it. She's beautiful, accomplished, and smart." Ivy's voice wavers. "But he's marrying me."

"No." Jules's firm voice cuts in. "You don't settle for being someone's second choice. You *deserve* to be someone's first choice."

"I. Am. His. Only. Choice. She's not a possibility with a husband and child. I'm the one who's here."

"I'm not going to bring this up again, so please hear me." Jules pauses, waiting for Ivy look up. "Marriage is hard. You have to choose each other every day. What Mom and Dad have? That's not magic. That's work. Honesty. Respect. Friendship. And it starts with not ignoring red flags and hoping they'll disappear."

A crack in Ivy's voice.

"I need this to happen. It's all I have."

Unable to breathe in the suffocating stillness, I take the stairs two at a time, desperate for fresh air.

I know she's scared. But how can she so blatantly overlook all of this? I wish I could tell her the truth, revisit that conversation from the deck all those years ago, without being quite so polite. Tell her what it means to marry someone who looks good on paper, who checks all the boxes but never sees you. I want to be more than a sister-in-law. I want to be her mirror.

To stop her from making the mistake I've lived through.

Whatever I decide about my own marriage, Ivy deserves better than settling for someone who doesn't choose her every day.

Intent on losing myself in the quiet solitude of the woods, I grab my coat. As I reach for gloves, Vera joins me. Her tiny frame is bundled in a warm parka with James's forest green beanie pulled over the neat chignon she wears. There's a soft but serious expression on her face.

"Mind if I join you?"

For half a second, hesitation takes hold. Spending time with Vera has been one of the unexpected gifts of this past year; her wisdom and quiet strength have become a sanctuary. She's become something like a mother to me, though not in the way I once imagined mothers should be.

I used to picture Margaret as Marmee from *Little Women*—warm, selfless, steady. But neither Margaret nor Vera is Marmee, because motherhood is never that tidy. Margaret once gave me a bracelet, my name etched into its delicate curve, a gesture at the time I desperately needed. But she also looked away when I needed her to see. Instead of untying the knots, she helped Mason tie them tighter.

Vera has shown me another way. That strength isn't always in sacrifice. Sometimes it sits beside you in silence, letting the ache pass through without rushing to fix it. Other times, it walks right up and asks for the truth.

And this walk? It won't be casual. She's been holding back, but I can feel the shift. See it in her eyes. In the unyielding set of her mouth. She's not letting me off the hook.

Not this time.

We set off down the snow-covered trail behind the house. Our boots crunch over fresh powder, the woods silent except for the snap of a twig or a lone chickadee's call. As we walk, our breath forms delicate clouds that dissolve into the bitter air.

I let myself settle into the rhythm of the walk, hoping, maybe foolishly, that she'll let me hold onto the quiet. She takes a deep breath and asks the question I've been bracing for.

"Do you want to talk about what's troubling you?"

"If I say no, will it matter?"

"You're right. I'm going to say what I should have said months ago." She squeezes my hand firmly enough that I can't pull away. "I know my son better than anyone. And if there's one thing I can say with certainty, it's that he's never been good at hiding his feelings. You might be a stone wall, Sydney—but that man wears his heart on his sleeve."

I stay silent, preparing for the words I know are coming.

"Should I tell you how he came to stay with me after last New Year's? He was suffering and heartbroken, but he refused to talk about it. And yet, there he was. Engaged."

Tears spill down my cheeks, freezing in the cold air.

"Shall I tell you how often he mentions you, how often he asks about you? It wasn't until I saw you two together yesterday, until he brought up the festival on our drive from the airport. His face said everything he wouldn't say out loud. That's when it clicked."

I let my tears spill freely. Let her see how deeply she and her son have broken through all my defensive layers.

"My experience with my ex-husband taught me a painful truth: guilt is a heavy burden. Yes, I regret the years I stayed, the moments I should have left. And the way it ended... with James... that's a scar I'll carry forever. But life is about change. We make choices, sometimes the wrong ones, but we don't have to be chained to them."

She brings a gloved hand to my face, gently wiping away tears. "I understand how much heavier these choices are when you have a child. But choosing your happiness, Sydney, is not selfish. In fact, it's essential. You can build the life you want and still be an incredible mother. They're not mutually exclusive."

Her green eyes, a soft seafoam color, are filled with a depth that tells me she's lived all of it. She knows about the murkiness clouding what's right and wrong.

And maybe that's the answer.

That we don't always have to be right; we just need to be willing to feel what's real.

To live untethered from the illusion that life is easy, that choices are ever simple. That sometimes there isn't an answer without pain.

We stand in the snow, her words settling in deep.

"Thank you. I... I'm going to keep walking and think about what you said. Go back inside, you're freezing." I give her one last squeeze before continuing on my own.

As time and miles stretch on, I let Vera's words take root. They echo in the stillness, each one a gentle nudge toward the truth I've been circling for years. All this time, I've been asking the wrong question—fixating on what I might lose if I leave.

But this choice isn't about loss. It's about what we'll gain.

Because what we'll gain is far greater than what we have now. Anna's life will be filled with joy, with the kind of steady love James brings by being himself. He won't be a wound she has to learn to live around. He won't disappear or disappoint. He'll show up, again and again, with laughter and stories and arms always open. Anna has always recognized that in him. Loving him without apology, choosing him. It's been me holding us back.

She'll grow up knowing she's loved, even if I'm not always there. Because in our home, love won't be questioned or withheld.

She might be away from me at times.

But she'll know I'll always be ready to welcome her back.

I reach a frozen pond and study my reflection. The woman with bright cheeks and clarity in her eyes staring back isn't the same woman who spent years shrinking herself, folding into shapes to meet the expectations of others. This isn't the woman who's buried her desires.

No. She's done with all of that.

And there's no going back.

THIRTY-ONE

Fate appears to be conspiring against me.

In all our years of early mornings and late nights, James and I have never struggled to find time to talk. But now, it's as though the universe has decided we can't be trusted alone together.

Every time I find him, someone is there. We're never given a moment.

Waking up early for a run? Ivy's already lacing up her shoes, smiling brightly as she insists on joining. Staying up late, hoping for a chance encounter in the sunroom? She's there too, with fingers looped tightly through his arm, her face placid as she follows him into the room with a new book—*Dune,* of all things.

I just need five minutes. Even a text feels impossible under Ivy's constant surveillance, especially considering Mason's vindictive tendencies if he were to discover something in writing when I finally ask for our separation.

Every time James meets my eyes across the crowded room—beyond the chaotic swirl of family, beyond Ivy's grip, beyond final wedding preparations—his gaze holds a single, unmistakable question. The same one he's been asking for years: *Choose me.* He's still here, mechanically going through the motions of a wedding we both know is wrong and waiting for the one word that will end this whole charade: *yes.*

But it's the night before the wedding, and I'm out of fucking time.

There's no rehearsal dinner. No rehearsal. I don't know how that happened, but maybe Ivy realized making him look at the altar twice wasn't wise.

After our family dinner, I pull Jules aside.

"Can Anna sleep over with you tonight?" My voice is frantic, my hands twisting into each other, unable to stop fidgeting.

Her eyes go wide. She knows exactly what I'm about to do.

"Fuck yes!" She pulls me into a fierce hug. "I've got Anna and your cover. Go do the damn thing."

A line from our favorite Bachelorette and the final push I need to do the most reckless, and possibly bravest, thing of my life.

Ivy commands the dining room table, issuing final orders before the big day. With James tucked away at the hotel, she's fully absorbed in last-minute preparations, confident he's safely out of my reach. All eyes are on her. No one notices me slip away toward the basement.

My running gear waits where I left it a few hours ago, when my plan took form. Near the exit. My personal escape route. I strip off my jeans and sweater, pulling on my winter running gear with clumsy fingers. My zipper sticks, betraying the calm I'm pretending to feel.

I have my phone. My keys. And one plan: find James.

The resort isn't far. Just a few miles of road to where James, his mom, and Darrell moved earlier today. The distance slips away, my mind cycling through everything I need to tell him. Every truth I'm finally ready to ask for and give in return.

Words I've buried for years rise demanding to be spoken.

As the lodge comes into view at the base of the ski resort, a glowing beacon in the dark, I push myself even harder. I break into a sprint, breath ragged, heart hammering. The lobby glows with holiday warmth. Twinkling strands of light hug the thick wooden rafters, shiny red and green ribbons hang from wreaths. Guests move past, going about their evenings, even as something monumental—years in the making—is about to happen.

But I only see one person: the dark-haired man, at the bar, staring into a crystal tumbler of amber liquid.

His hair is disheveled. Dark circles shadow his eyes. Nothing about him is relaxed.

He looks up and sees me. A lifetime of emotion compresses into a single, searing glance. Desperation. Pleading. Love. His expression shifts from wrecked to hopeful in a heartbeat.

"You're here?" His eyes sweep over me, drinking me in. "Did you *run* here?"

I lift his glass from the bar, holding his gaze as I bring it to my lips. He watches my mouth close over the rim. The whiskey burns going down, but my lips quirk in a playful smirk.

"Well, I figured I could use the miles and, you know... happened to end up here."

"Sydney..." His voice is a choked whisper. "I don't know if I can take a joke right now. Why are you here?"

I set the glass down, pull off my mittens, and trace the line of his jaw. "Can we go somewhere to talk?"

He doesn't hesitate. Tossing a stack of bills on the counter, he takes my hand and leads me to the elevators. He doesn't let go—not as we walk, not while we wait, shoulder to shoulder with other couples. He's still holding on when we reach his room, when he opens the door, when he guides me to the small couch.

James closes his eyes for a moment, exhaling slowly through his nose. "Before I have a heart attack, can you please say it?" His voice is deeper than usual, rougher. "Tell me what this means."

"I'm sorry it's taken me so long to get here."

"What does that mean? I need you to be very specific." He drops to his knees, bringing himself to my eye level.

"James..." I whisper. "I'm here for *you*. For me. I don't want you to marry her."

With an exhale that sounds like relief, James pulls my hat off and cups my face with shaking hands.

"Say it again."

"Please, choose me."

His breath is soft against my hair, his heartbeat a steady rhythm against mine as he draws me closer. "Sydney, I've been yours for years. I've just been waiting for you to get here."

I close my eyes, soaking in the rise and fall of his chest, the scent of his skin, the sheer rightness of being here. His fingers slide up my back, into my hair, before moving back down, as he tucks his face into the crook of my neck. Our bodies settle into perfect understanding.

Soft laughter in the hallway, the distant ding of the elevator—the reality of our tangled lives. It all gradually filters back in. The clock on the wall reminds me that hours from now, he's supposed to marry someone else.

"James, I promise that I'm here. I won't run or push you away. I want you. I want everything with you. But we have to do this right. I have Anna to think about." I press back from his chest, fidgeting with the seam of my jacket.

"I know that. I do. But, Christ, Sydney. What are you saying?"

"I'm asking you to let me do this the right way. For Anna. For us. I need to end things with Mason amicably, and you need to untangle yourself from Ivy in a way that doesn't leave scorched earth behind."

His laugh cuts through the room, sharp and bitter, as he drags a hand over his face. "I think that ship has sailed. God, it's the night before the wedding."

"Let's not add fuel to the fire. We owe it to ourselves to do this right. No secrets. No sneaking around." My voice steadies as I continue. "I need time to stand on my own feet. To step away from Mason. To leave my job. I don't want to be a corporate lawyer anymore. I want to help women—every day, all day—with your mom." I draw in a shaky breath. "And I need to know I can do this myself. I don't want any more shields or life rafts."

"You're really here this time?" His fingers thread through mine again.

"I am."

"So I'm supposed to call off the wedding and let you walk away? Go back to D.C. with your husband, and wait for you to decide when you're ready?"

"Yes. That's exactly what I'm asking."

He pulls me closer until we're inches apart. I'm perched on the edge of the couch, and he's still kneeling between my legs.

"I'm so fucking tired." He scans my face, searching for anything that might make this easier. But there's nothing easy about it. Tenderly, he brushes his fingers against my cheek, then picks up his phone. "I ordered you an Uber. Please, take it back to the cabin. I need to know you're safe."

He stands to walk away, but I can't bear for it to end this way.

"James."

I reach forward and pull him back to me. In that pause, his breath catches. I surge in and capture his lips in a kiss I hope tells him everything my words haven't.

It isn't rushed or desperate, or full of unchecked hunger. It's everything we've said—the years of anguish, of love unspoken—pressed into a single, tender kiss. My fingers run through his hair, aching to grab hold, to pull him closer and never leave this room.

His hands land on my hips, gripping me firmly as if he's on the same page.

But he wrenches his mouth from mine, leaving me breathless, shaking. And for the first time, I don't know what I'm seeing in his eyes as they search mine, what he's trying to find. Reassurance, maybe. Conviction. But whatever he sees, or doesn't, he walks away. And I'm left in the silence, unsure if I've set us both free... or lost him for good.

THIRTY-TWO

The December sky blooms like a secret it can no longer keep.

As the sun edges above the horizon, pink light spills across the world. Everything feels suspended, as if the day itself is holding its breath. A sacred start to the day that feels alive with possibility.

With each passing minute, the silence grows louder.

An invisible band tightens around my chest, squeezing the air from my lungs. My hands shake as icy dread starts in my toes and spreads upward, seizing my entire body.

There's been no word. Ivy is already starting to get ready. The house buzzes as bridesmaids, hair stylists, and makeup artists begin arriving.

"Where'd you go last night? I couldn't find you." Mason heads straight toward me, where I'm still curled on the sectional, staring out the windows, dressed in my running clothes from the night before.

"I went for a long run."

"Can you get your shit together and act like my wife today?" He grabs my wrist.

"Let. Go. Of. Me."

"Syd, will you talk to me? What's going on?" Dr. Jekyll appears, his voice going all soft and gentle.

"Just drop it. I need more coffee," I say, walking off.

He doesn't follow. Maybe he thinks the wedding will fix everything. He probably thinks I'll go back to being compliant, accommodating Sydney. Or he's already calculating his next move.

Sorry, Mason. Your reckoning is coming. Wedding or not.

Ivy stands at the center of the kitchen, ethereal in her robe. The perfect picture of a bride about to step into the life she's meticulously planned. She leans against the counter, a satisfied curve to her lips.

"Morning, Syd."

"Good morning, Ivy." I keep my head down and go straight for the coffee pot.

"Lovely day for a wedding, isn't it?"

My hands shake as I pour coffee into my mug. I blink back the tears I've been holding in since James walked out of the room. *Oh God. Is he really going to marry her? Why hasn't he called it off yet?*

Before Ivy can dig the dagger in any further, the front door opens, and Darrell and Vera enter, carrying a large white box.

"Good morning," Vera calls cheerfully. "We brought pastries."

Footsteps thunder across the floor, and Anna barrels into me, wrapping around my legs. Jules scans the room, trying to piece together what she walked into. I shrug. I wish I knew. Margaret follows, greets Vera and Darrell, then hugs Ivy.

Jules strides to the speaker and clicks it on, breaking the quiet like a raised eyebrow.

"Good morning, wedding people! Thought I'd crank the vibe up to 'It's wedding day.' You're welcome." She smirks as the lyrics kick in.

Usher croons about losing control, being swept up in someone. Someone who's usually in control but suddenly finds themselves entangled beyond reason. She's the best and the worst.

Thanks for that, Jules.

While she steals everyone's attention with her over-the-top dance moves, Vera drifts over to me. She leans in, her voice low. "Go along with this."

I blink, but she's already crossing the room, slipping into conversation with Margaret and Ivy. I stand there, confused as I watch her continue chatting. She stops, hand half raised mid-conversation, then clutches her chest, her breath catching.

"Oh... my..." Vera whispers before crumpling to the ground.

"What's wrong?" Margaret drops beside her.

"My chest... it's... so tight," Vera gasps. "I... I can't breathe."

Jules and Tom rush forward, instincts kicking in. Their voices are calm but urgent. "What are you feeling? Is it radiating down your arm? Can you breathe? Mom, aspirin now!"

Margaret's already dialing 911 as she ransacks the cabinets.

At the center of the kitchen, Ivy stands frozen. She watches the action taking place in front of her with a detached calm. There's no worry or urgency in her eyes, only the fading of her smile.

Vera closes her eyes. "I don't know... it's so tight..."

Through the blur of movement, through the crowd pressing in around her, she darts a look right at me: *Go along with it.* I blink, stunned, and in complete admiration.

She's faking this whole thing.

My own acting skills kick in. "Darrell, call James. He'll want to meet you at the hospital."

The corner of his mouth twitches before reining it in and calling James. "Your mom collapsed. We've called an ambulance. I'll text you when we're on the way." A beat—James must say something. "Yes, I know. I'll tell her."

Darrell kneels beside Vera, still clutching her chest on the kitchen floor like she's halfway to the pearly gates, and whispers something I can't hear. Vera gives the faintest nod.

Oh my God. This is happening.

This is the plan they cooked up?

When the paramedics arrive, Darrell follows the gurney without a backward glance. This will be a costly trip to the ER. I'm still not clear why this was the best idea, but James must have talked to them after leaving me last night. Maybe he thought separating the wedding and the breakup would be easier on her?

Whatever the reason, I don't care. As long as it means James isn't getting married today.

Ivy watches the gurney rolling through the front door. Her mouth is tight, her eyes wet with tears. She doesn't move until Margaret guides her to the sectional in the living room.

"What does this mean?" her voice trembles.

"I think it means we wait." Margaret brushes Ivy's hair off her face. "We see if Vera's okay."

"But the wedding's supposed to start at noon... It's already eight. How can he go to the hospital and be back in time?"

Realization begins to settle on her face. Slow. Suffocating.

Margaret scans the room, searching for someone to say what she won't. Her eyes land on Jules.

"Ives." Jules moves cautiously toward her sister. "I think we have to assume he won't be back in time. We should start calling vendors and guests, talk to everyone upstairs getting dressed."

"NO!" Ivy screams. "We... we need to get married!" And the tears finally break through. She sobs uncontrollably into her hands. Through gasping breaths, she repeats, "We need to get married."

"I'm so sorry, love." Margaret pulls her close. "Right now, we need to focus on Vera and wait for news."

"Mama?" Anna wraps her arms around my legs.

"Aunt Ivy's sad. Let's go upstairs." I look into her wide, searching eyes and scoop her up, grabbing her a muffin and hustling us away.

I've made so many mistakes over the years, and now this—letting it get to this point, the morning of her wedding. While she might only be in love with the idea of him, these tears aren't fake. This is any bride's worst nightmare.

Anna and I retreat to the sunroom, curling up on the rug beside a basket of toys. She hums as she lines up animal figurines, the chaos from downstairs now muffled by distance and closed doors.

The sunroom, filled with years of memories, some painful, others beautiful, holds me like an old friend as I sprawl starfish on the floor and let it all wash over me. Surrounded by a child's innocent play, the aftermath of a canceled wedding, and the first glimmers of real possibility, I begin to see the path forward. Not an escape, but a journey toward something better. A future that is mine to claim. No more pretending. No more lies. No more desires buried. A life waiting to be lived in all its messy beauty.

"Mama, want to play?" Anna's soft voice breaks through the quiet.

"Yes, Bug. I want to play."

And so we play together, while the world rearranges itself.

***

A COLLECTIVE EXHALE MOVES through the room as Vera, James, and Darrell step inside the cabin. Vera waves off concern, assuring everyone she's fine. *Not a heart attack. Just stress. Exhaustion.* Relief ripples through the family in waves.

After everyone's had their turn, hugging and fussing, I step forward and wrap my arms around her tiny body, fierce in her love and protective of those she cares for. She whispers, "I didn't do this for him. I did it for you. Whatever you choose next, I believe in you."

A single tear falls as I meet James's eyes over his mother's shoulder. In that moment, the rest of the room falls away—the relieved chatter, the movement around us, everything. His gaze holds mine, speaking a language we've perfected over years of silence. He nods, so subtle that anyone else would miss it. But I catch it, and with it, the promise.

He'll be there when I'm ready.

"Thank you," I murmur and step back out of Vera's embrace.

Mason moves to my side, his hand finding the small of my back. Despite the way I recoil, he steps closer. My skin crawls beneath his palm, and I don't hide my discomfort. I step out of his reach and cross the room, putting distance between us because if I don't, I might not be able to resist saying something I can't take back. Things are already over, but now is not the time for that conversation.

Relief in the room is palpable, but short-lived.

Ivy's smile has returned. After a quick inquiry about Vera's health, she launches into forced chatter about rescheduling the wedding. Her voice is overly cheerful, too rehearsed, like she can manifest the day back into existence. But the way she keeps smoothing her dress with shaking hands betrays what her voice won't.

She's oblivious to the tension radiating from James. The pressure in him is visible, thick and vibrating, building toward the surface.

"Ivy."

His sharp voice cuts her off mid-sentence. A moment of panic flashes across his features—clamped mouth, wide eyes. This outburst, so uncharacteristic, catches everyone off guard, and the room stills. But I know. After the past few days, after the past few years, James is done. No more pretending. No more carefully constructed façades. As much as he hates hurting people, there is no more room for indirectness.

Even if this conversation was never meant to happen tonight, it's going to.

"Can we take a walk?"

Ivy's face crumples. But she grabs her jacket and drags herself out the door.

We all stay frozen, processing what we witnessed. The careful politeness that's held this family together for years is finally cracking open.

Margaret smooths her dress with trembling hands. Gary studies his whiskey as if it holds answers. Jules stares at the door they left through. Vera and Darrell shift uncomfortably.

Mason makes the first move. "We're leaving first thing in the morning."

I meet his gaze directly. "Do what you want. Anna and I will leave when I'm ready."

"I'm not dumb, Sydney." His hand reaches out, grasping my arm. His voice is low and threatening. "Don't think I've missed what's happening. I'm not going to let you tear our family apart."

"Mason, take your hand off me right now." I lower my voice, matching the venom in his.

My breath doesn't catch, my fingers don't tremble, because I'm done with letting him tell me what to do. We'll deal with this back in D.C.

"Good night, everyone," Vera calls, discreetly looking to exit before Ivy returns.

"Vera, can we talk about the shelter quickly?" I call after her, leaving Mason to stew.

She pauses and turns with a smile that's gentle but knowing. "Of course."

We walk toward the far wall. I'd rather speak in the sunroom or on the back deck, but there's no subtle way to slip off. And this won't take long.

"Today's been... a lot," I say, managing to share a small smile. "We don't have to get into details. But I'm starting my own family law practice. I want to give as much time as I can to the shelter." I lower my voice. "It's time I began living the life I want."

She doesn't speak, only pulls me into a hug. When she steps back, her eyes glisten. "Call me when you're ready."

"I've already sent my resignation letter. I'm not waiting to get started."

"Good. And remember this strength. Your worthiness. When you do the rest." Her eyes flick to Mason.

"I will. I know now what I deserve. And what Anna deserves."

"Take the time you need. Everything else will be there when you're ready." Her eyes hold mine, urging me to read between what she doesn't say.

Anna pulls at my sweater to be picked up. She leans her head against my shoulder. "Bye-bye, Miss Vera."

"I'll see you soon." Vera kisses Anna's cheek, then mine, and rejoins Darrell.

"Mama, I tired."

"Okay, Bug. Let's get you into PJs."

Once Anna drifts off in our quiet room, serenity settles like the first snow of winter. I lie beside her, watching the peaceful rise and fall of her breath, the smile still playing on her lips even in sleep. I trace the curve of her cheek, smoothing her hair back from her face.

While I've stumbled through these years, making choices that felt impossible and mistakes that felt inevitable, she's been my constant—the North Star I kept in focus when I couldn't see my own path. She's happy. She's loved. She has the childhood I dreamed of giving her—and somehow, despite everything, I kept that promise.

This next chapter, uncertain as it is, holds the promise of a new dawn.

We'll go home in the morning.

Not to what it was, but to something entirely our own.

2023

She found her song not in the silence after pain,
but in the harmony of all her broken and beautiful notes.

THIRTY-THREE

THE FAMILIAR WOODEN CABIN stands as I left it—stoic in the falling snow, unchanged by time—while everything in me has shifted. In the year since I last stood on this porch, I've dismantled my entire life and rebuilt it on my own terms. Brick by brick, I laid the foundation of the life I was meant to live.

It's taken me so long to reach this moment. Four years of wanting what I couldn't have, fighting what I shouldn't have denied, all while trying to be someone I was never meant to be. The woman who feared happiness, who believed she didn't deserve it—that woman's gone.

I told James that I needed to find myself before I could find us, and that's exactly what I've done.

Starting my own family practice meant stepping into a life that had been waiting for me. I still remember my first client, the moment her shoulders relaxed when she realized she wasn't alone. I've reclaimed friendships that withered during my marriage. Jules remains my cornerstone, but now she's surrounded by a constellation of other connections: running groups on Saturday mornings, book club every third Thursday. The brownstone I bought is filled with overstuffed chairs, thriving plants, and color bursting from every corner. It's the opposite of the sleek condo I shared with Mason.

So many times, my fingers hovered over James's name in my contacts, but I never touched it. Not because I didn't want to reach out, but because I needed to finish what I started.

And I didn't want to give Mason any fodder if he challenged my divorce proceedings or custody requests. I kept our communication cut off, hoping it would lessen the chance Mason would fight back. In fact, James and I have had no contact in a year, until two days ago when a text appeared out of the blue:

Skating Stud: *I'm at the cabin. Can you come on the 22nd?*

Now, two days later…I'm standing on the precipice of the life I've spent the last four years dreaming about. I asked him to wait. I hope his text means that he has. I take a deep breath, pushing down the stomach-curdling fear that he hasn't.

"Is Unca J here already?" Anna asks, bouncing on her toes.

"Should we go inside and see?" I keep my voice light despite the weight of what awaits.

Jules is the only Wallis who knows the whole story. I've been helping maintain the illusion, not for Mason's sake, but for Anna's. Every time Gary and Margaret visit, Anna and I play along like a happy family. I've been pressuring Mason to tell them the truth for months. Finally, he asked me to come for one last holiday, promising we'd tell the family in person.

I think he hopes this place might pull me back into his world. *This place is magical, but it's not miracle-working because that's never going to happen.*

Together, Anna and I walk into the cabin, ready to face whatever comes next. The quiet strikes me immediately. No kids racing down the hall, no laughter from the kitchen. Green garland wraps its way up the staircase, mistletoe dangles, and white twinkle lights frame the windows. Margaret's touch is everywhere, but she's nowhere to be seen.

Even Anna hesitates, staying close, feeling it too. A strange hush that doesn't belong here.

"Kind of eerie, huh?" a deep voice murmurs from behind—his voice. The sound of it, low and familiar, wraps around me before I even turn. Goosebumps ripple across my skin as the timbre sinks in. Rougher than I remember, maybe deeper. Or maybe it's that I've missed it for so long. I don't have to look to know he's smiling. "Feels like the setup to a thriller. A man, a woman, and a child enter a quiet wooden cabin."

"Unca J!" Anna shrieks and crashes into him.

I turn slowly, finally allowing myself to look at him. He's kneeling to catch Anna, his arms open wide, that dimple deepening as she launches herself at him. The sight hits me with a wave of certainty. While this year has been everything I needed, one thing is missing. Him.

"Hey, Bug," he says, scooping her up. His eyes lift to mine over Anna's head. "I missed you."

"Hi," I say simply, feeling strangely calm despite the storm in my chest.

"Hi." His voice is carefully neutral and utterly infuriating. "Can I help you carry your things upstairs?"

A question, not a statement or demand, and a reminder of how low my expectations had sunk, how carelessly Mason treated me. With James, I'll always have the choice.

"Thank you." I pass him one of the bags. "I've got the rest."

"Margaret and Gary are in Florida," he says, voice even despite the anxious way he keeps rubbing his beard. "But they'll be here tonight."

I look over at him as I ask, "Where's Ivy?"

"I don't know. Not sure if she knows I'm even here."

Before I can respond or ask any of the million questions I have, Anna jumps in. She begins chattering about snowmen and sledding and whether Santa knows she's here. James responds to each thought seriously, as if her concerns about reindeer navigation systems are the most important thing in the world.

"I'll make some coffee," he offers as we reach the doorway. "Can we talk?"

I meet his eyes and see the nerves behind his cool exterior. "Okay. I'll be down in a bit."

***

ANNA HAS LONG SINCE crashed for a nap, her tiny body curled beside me in peaceful stillness. I lie there, watching the snow fall faster than when we arrived, thick flakes swirling in the gray afternoon light.

The room has been redecorated since I was here a year ago. Cascading eucalyptus wallpaper in the lightest shade of green lines the walls. Replacing the large sleigh bed is a new sleek platform with a tufted headboard the same color as the walls. It's been moved, now placed to more easily gaze out the windows flanking the corner. A toddler bed sits opposite filled with colorful blankets and pillows.

I'm gathering my courage for the conversation waiting downstairs.

Vera's given me glimpses of his year, broad strokes and careful words. All I know is that he ended things with Ivy, and he's been focused on work. I calm my mutinous stomach, and I find him in the kitchen, leaning against the counter, his fingers drumming against the granite. His eyes meet mine, but instead of his lopsided grin, I'm met with hard lines.

He pushes off from the counter and reaches for the coffee pot. "She's asleep?" he asks, offering me a mug.

"She was exhausted from the early flight."

We stand in awkward silence, a year's worth of distance pressing against us.

"Ivy and I aren't together," he finally says, setting his mug down. "I thought my mom or Jules would've told you."

"They did. But I'm confused. Why are you here?"

"Gary called me a few days ago. They were having a hot tub put in, and something happened. They were in Florida and needed someone they trusted to check out if the foundation was damaged. Couldn't find anyone local who could do it. Called me in a panic."

"Oh." I pause. Not sure I want to ask my next question, but I gulp down my fears and ask anyway. "Did you know I was coming when Gary called you?"

"Mom's told me bits and pieces about what's going on with Mason and you. She said you were coming here for one last Christmas."

"Yes. That's why I'm here. To tell the family, Mason and I are over."

"Right." His voice is carefully neutral again. "And I suppose you'll head back to D.C. after."

I nod, uncertain where this is going.

"So this is... closure for you? Tying up loose ends?" The edge in his voice sharpens. "Because it's been a year, Sydney. With no word from you. Not even a text."

"I was doing exactly what I said I needed to do."

"And did you?"

"I think we should talk after I've had a chance to collect my thoughts." I set my mug down, feeling my throat constrict, nails biting into my palms.

"Sure." Disappointment flashes in his eyes. "Take your time. It's not like we haven't had plenty of that already."

"That's not fair."

"None of this has been fair." He runs a hand through his hair and looks out toward the mountains, pausing before pinning me in place with a flash of eyes darkened by pain. "You asked for time, I gave it to you. But I didn't think that meant complete silence."

I walk away to gather myself. But I stop before I reach the doorway. This is what I would do before. Run. Escape. Deflect. That's not who I am anymore.

When I turn back around, his eyes lock onto mine. I step forward until I'm inches in front of him and reach up to run my fingers along his tense jaw.

"I'm sorry. I don't need a minute to collect myself. I'm just... nervous."

His body softens hearing those words. I feel the tension drain from him as he finally breathes, releasing air he'd been holding. His hands span my waist as he sets me on the countertop and steps between my dangling legs.

"James," I start, but his head dips, and a strangled noise escapes me as his nose brushes the crook of my neck, his breath warm against my skin, sending a shudder through me. He tentatively presses his lips to my skin. A deep groan rumbles from his chest, reverberating through my entire body.

"I'm sorry I didn't reach out," spills out of me. "I was worried what Mason would do if he learned of this. I didn't want to give him anything more to hold up the divorce or try to change our custody agreement. The family doesn't know about any of it. Only Jules."

James inhales deeply and exhales even slower. He cups my face in his palm. And for the first time since I got that text from him, I take a long, filling breath.

"So you came here because Gary needed help?" I ask, trying to understand.

"That was my way in. My mom told me you were spending Christmas here. I had a suite reserved at the resort before Gary called me. I was coming regardless. I was tired of waiting for your call." He smiles slyly and kisses my temple. "I'm sorry if you weren't ready. I know this makes me a selfish prick showing up here."

"Don't. I needed the push. I can't let him dictate my life forever." I lift a hand to cup his face, my fingers brushing over the rough scrape of stubble. "And not calling or the time I asked for, it was never about you. You've always given me everything—patience, understanding, space. I... I want to be with you, James."

His face glistens with tears that catch the afternoon light, turning gold against his skin. The sight squeezes something in my chest. He's seen me cry and break more times than I can count, but now this strong, sure man is allowing himself to be vulnerable with me. I wipe a tear from the corner of his eye and breathe in his familiar scent.

"I'm sorry, I just—" He sniffles. "I wasn't sure I'd ever hear those words again."

"So does that mean you also want to be with me?"

"Yes. God. Yes." His words are breathless, edged in desperation.

He slides a hand into my hair at the base of my neck and tips my head back, brushing his lips against mine. For a heartbeat, there is only the warmth of his mouth, the press of his body as our lips meet, soft and tentative at first. A deep rumble emanates from his chest, and my nails rake against his scalp. I tilt my head and dive in deeper, touching my tongue to his. Gooseflesh erupts over my skin, and I revel in his touch, his lips. The spark that's always been there, burning between us from day one, ignites my blood.

Our kisses are languid—bitter coffee on my lips and the aching promise of something more. No teeth clash, neither of us fumble. It's as natural as everything else between us. And we stay there, learning each other's mouths, the feel of our bodies. I moan, unable to help myself, and it seems to be his undoing. His fingers twist tendrils of my hair between his fingers, angling my head so he can better taste me.

"Mama!" The monitor crackles to life.

I pull away, panting and trying to regain control. James watches me, breathing hard, eyes glazed.

"Okay." I force myself to step back, the air still crackling with heat. "Let me go get Anna, and we can finish talking about what's next."

With my heart hammering against my ribs, I head upstairs. I know what I need to do. I've spent too long hesitating at the edge of happiness. I won't make that mistake again.

***

BY THE TIME ANNA and I make our way downstairs, the rich aroma of something savory greets us. James stands at the stove, stirring a pot, his broad shoulders relaxed.

An avalanche of affection rolls through me. In mere moments I expect it to knock me on my ass with its totality. I love this man, all of him: the fierce and the gentle, the challenger and the soft landing. The same way he loves all of me. He isn't afraid when I push back. He never flinches at the sharp parts of me or tries to mold me into someone I'm not.

Anna doesn't hesitate. She runs straight to him, her giggles ringing as she throws her little arms around his legs. He scoops her up, spins her once, and settles her on his hip, one arm holding her steady while the other stirs whatever smells so delicious.

"I've got mixed news," he says, pausing, his attention caught by my exposed shoulder where the sweater has slipped.

I swallow, forcing a breath so deep it scrapes the bottom of my feet.

"The good news," he continues, "is that outside is a winter wonderland, and we're building a snowman tomorrow." His lips quirk up, tickling Anna. But his eyes remain steady on mine, gauging my reaction. "I heard from Gary. Their flight into Burlington was canceled. They asked me to stay until they get back. They'll text Ivy to let her know. She's supposed to arrive tomorrow." He lets that sit, then quietly asks, "Do you know if anyone else is arriving tonight?"

I let out a long exhale, looking around the quiet cabin, the fire crackling in the hearth, the snow falling outside, and Anna giggling in his arms. The world has conspired to strip everything away, to leave this.

Us.

It's me, James, and Anna.

I watch the snow piling high on the deck, silently thanking the universe for giving us this moment in time—a chance to get it right.

"Maybe Jules and Tom. But with the snow, I'd bet they'll wait." I meet his eyes, letting him see that the idea of being alone doesn't scare me in the slightest. "What are you making?"

His mouth curls at the edges, pleased by my reaction. "I know how much Anna loves spaghetti. So I'm making a Bolognese sauce and fresh pasta. Want to help me?"

"You're making it from scratch?" I raise a brow, eyeing the flour and eggs on the counter.

"Of course. I wouldn't be a very good Italian son if I didn't." The smile on his lips widens, and it's all I can concentrate on. "It's not too hard. I'll show you."

Anna wriggles out of his hold and runs off to grab toys. She assembles them in the family room, lost in her own little world, leaving us alone in the kitchen.

"Alright, Maestro. Teach me your pasta ways." I press play on a Christmas playlist, soft holiday music filling the space, blending with the scent of simmering tomatoes and garlic.

James steps behind me, his warm breath against my ear. "First...we need to put this in a ponytail." He pauses to see if I'll step away, but I don't. There's a slight tremor in his hand as it trails up my exposed shoulder. A sharp intake of breath as he slides his fingers into my hair. His touch is soft as he works his way from the ends to the roots. This moment so different from the bathroom when he pulled my hair back to avoid vomit landing in it.

Then, I resisted. Refused to acknowledge the effect he had on me. This time, I close my eyes and feel every brush, every touch.

When he finally gathers it all at the crown of my head, he tugs, just enough to send a wave of awareness through my entire body. I arch instinctively as a delicious ache forms. This dangerous new freedom, this space we've never had before. His hands land on my shoulders, an exhale shudders from his pursed lips, and he steps back.

"Making pasta is all about feel. Start by making a well in the center," he instructs, temptation in every syllable.

Trying to shake off the sensation of his fingers in my hair, I adopt an exaggerated English accent, channeling my best Gordon Ramsay: "Yes, make a well. Well done. That's right." I laugh, hoping to break the seriousness in his face, to make him smile, to bring him back into the ease we've always shared.

But there's a new tension. Not the one of the past years when we wanted to touch, but one that screams: *What are you waiting for?*

"Now, slowly add the eggs. One at a time."

"Yes, My Lord," I say, softer this time, trading Gordon Ramsay mockery for the demure purr of a medieval princess. "Am I doing this right?"

The space between us vanishes as his chest presses against my back. "I thought you once said I'd never be cast as an English aristocrat in your story?" He reaches around caging me in, guiding our hands to knead the dough.

The smile slips from my lips as the heat returns, sharp and immediate.

"That's it," he whispers, his breath caressing the shell of my ear. "Don't be afraid to get your hands dirty."

His warmth radiates over me, and I turn lifting my flour-dusted hands to the hard lines of his chest. His lips part as my fingers drift lower, down his stomach, feeling every tense muscle along the way. When I pause above his waistband, his breath hitches.

"I've never been one to shy away from getting dirty."

"I have no doubt about that." A low chuckle vibrates through him, the sound shooting straight through my fingertips. His nose nuzzles into my neck, breathing me in with the desperation of years of need. "You always smell so damn good. What's that scent? It's been driving me crazy for years."

"It's an essential oil. Combination of sandalwood and vanilla." My voice comes out husky.

Who knew making pasta could turn into such foreplay?

He places his hands on my waist, then steps away. We both inhale sharply. His restraint, always so careful, is cracking. I remember those moments in the sunroom last year, his knuckles white and breathing ragged taking in the sight of me unraveling. I want to know what happens when that restraint finally breaks.

"We're almost done. Now we need to roll the dough out and cut it." He sucks in a breath.

"Margaret has a pasta attachment on her mixer. Wouldn't that make it quicker?"

James leans back against the counter, all casual ease, trying not to betray his fracturing control.

"Quicker isn't always better," he says, his voice low, gravelly. "I like to feel it in my hands. Take my time. Make sure every inch gets the attention it deserves." He pauses. "Sometimes, slower makes it all the sweeter."

His pupils are blown wide, eyes so dark they look black, and my knees nearly give out. I could drown in that stare as deep, sensitive parts of me tighten and throb. We've definitely taken our sweet, fucking time.

"Mama, phone!" Anna yells, wandering in with my buzzing cell.

"Oh—thanks, Bug." I cough, still lust-hazed. I take a few steps towards the foyer. "Jules, where are you guys?"

"We're stuck in New York. The snow's insane. Tom doesn't want to risk driving today," she explains, but her voice softens. "You sound... tense."

"I'm good. Anna and I got to the cabin earlier. Did you know your dad asked James to come here to check out a problem with their new hot tub?"

"No. No, I did not." Even quieter, she asks, "Ivy isn't there, is she?"

"Nope. Neither are your parents. Their flight was canceled because of the storm." I slip further away. "We're making pasta. I'll put Anna to bed. Then...Is this horrible of me?"

She half laughs. "You're single. He's single. What's stopping you?"

"You don't think it's in bad taste? You know, here?" I ask, heart thudding as I try to picture the next twenty-four hours.

"I'm the last person to ask if you want someone to talk you out of it."

"You're such a bad influence. See you tomorrow."

"Wait—Syd?" She quickly adds: "Hope you packed some cute underwear."

And hangs up, leaving me sputtering with indignation.

Cute underwear? Yeah, no.

But I look up and see him staring at me. Well... maybe on second thought.

THIRTY-FOUR

ANNA NESTLES BETWEEN US on the couch to watch her favorite Christmas movie. Little Cindy Lou Who sleds down the hill, desperately trying to deliver her letter to Santa. The dog, Max, licks her face after her epic crash. She watches with wide-eyed wonder until her eyelids begin to droop.

"Mama, skating tomorrow?" she asks dreamily.

"Of course, Bug, if the rink's open." I reach for her, but James is already moving.

"I've got her."

He lifts her, her small body folding into his broad frame, and tucks her head into the curve of his shoulder. The same way he held her all those years ago, caring for her as an infant.

He carries her up the stairs and lays her in bed. She curls around her ladybug and her sleepy voice drifts out: "Will you sing me Twinka, Twinka, Unca J?"

I turn away, fighting the swell of emotion tightening my throat.

It was the end of a beautiful day. One of those days in D.C. where winter receded and spring burst forth even in January. It was two weeks after we left the cabin. Anna and I had spent the entire day outside. At bedtime, Mason stood in the doorway, watching. She had looked up at him, hopeful. "Dada, sing Twinka, Twinka?"

He mumbled something about being tired and walked out.

When I looked at Anna, her eyes quivered in tears, but I saw her swallow them down instead of letting them fall. So reminiscent of how I responded to my parents' dismissals.

It was a small thing, but it was the moment I knew. I just needed it to be done.

That was the night I told Mason we were separating.

It hadn't been easy. The conversation had unraveled into anger, blame, and hurt. While at times he plays the part of respecting my wishes, he still asks when I'm coming home. I don't think he realizes this is permanent, even though the divorce papers have been filed and custody agreements are in place. He clings to the delusional hope that I'll "come to my senses."

Now, standing in the doorway, listening to James's deep voice crooning the lullaby while he tucks the blanket over Anna, a wave of longing sweeps through me. This is what it should have always been.

"So, what should we do now?" He walks over, monitor in hand, a smirk playing at the edges of his lips.

We're alone. Anna's asleep. This night is ours.

"We could read. The sunroom is lovely this time of night. I have a new book I've been dying to crack open." I tease, grabbing his hand and interlacing our fingers.

"Hmmm, interesting idea. I had something else in mind." His grin widens, that devastating dimple deepening. "We could test out the new hot tub."

"Let me think. That's a hard choice. I'd say hot tub, but I don't have a swimsuit with me."

"That's no problem." His voice lowers to a pitch that has the hairs rising on the back of my neck. "I'm sure you have a pair of shorts and a sports bra. Why don't you get changed, and I'll make sure it's set."

He winks and walks off towards the basement. If I weren't so turned on, I'd laugh. Instead, I hurry back to my room and tear through my suitcase. I went shopping after I got the text from him, securing a few new items, just in case.

I could play it safe. Wear something conservative. Practical as he suggested. Or I could go...a different route. See how far I can push before his restraint breaks.

Yep. I want to see an unleashed James. The one that's done holding back.

***

New French doors open behind the pool table onto the newly constructed patio.

The hot tub isn't your typical plop-it-down-on-the-ground model. They installed it in the ground and laid a stone patio across the entire length of the basement. But it's the rest that stops me in my tracks. A gorgeous wooden trellis spans the ceiling and sides, with vines and garden lights twined throughout. There are pots filled with trees separating the hot tub from the view of the woods.

James stands in the center. Black swim trunks. Soft instrumental music playing.

"What do you think? Since everything was fine with the foundation, I needed something to keep me around for a few days. So I came up with the trellis and plants. I thought Margaret would appreciate it." His eyes narrow and darken, seeing my eyes travel the length of his body. My not-so-discreet ogling. He stands there and lets me get my fill.

I take my time, appreciating every ripple of muscle. The dark hair that trails down to his waistband. His legs are sculpted from thousands of miles. Finally meeting his eyes, I smile, feeling the blush on my cheeks. He hits me with that cocky smirk. I exhale shakily, steadying my nerves.

"This is amazing. I can't believe you made this. Since when do architects do the actual building?" I cinch the tie on my robe, overwhelmed about the idea of dropping it—and showing him my forty-year-old body, with all his perfection on display.

"I know how to use a saw. I enjoy the building part. Picked up a thing or two kicking around construction sites." He takes a step closer. "Are we going to stand here all night talking about the woodwork or are you going to drop that robe and get into the water?"

My pulse stutters, my heart thrashing against my chest. I turn away, trying to gather some of the courage I had upstairs when this idea seemed wise.

"It's not fair how handsome you are. You know I've had a kid and things aren't…"

He's standing in front of me before I can finish the thought. "Don't do that. I've imagined this more times than I care to admit. Is it okay if I undo this tie?"

I nod and wrap my shaking hands behind my back. He slowly undoes the knot, and the robe falls open an inch, not enough to see anything. His hands tremble, reaching for the fabric on my shoulders.

He lets out a muffled groan and backs up a few steps. His ribs expand with each slow exhale as he stares, drinking me in. The flare in his eyes is exactly what I need.

I let the robe fall to the ground. I stand before him. Sheer black bra. Matching thong.

There might be fabric separating his eyes from my body, but everything is visible.

A pin drop would've sounded like a scream in the charged silence.

After a long moment, he takes a deep breath and closes the distance between us. His thumb traces the curve of my bottom lip, a delicious humming noise rumbling from the back of his throat.

I lift my chin, and he leans in. For a second, a sweet prelude—our mouths ghost over each other and we pause, breathing in this mind-shattering tipping point we've dreamed of for years.

Our lips meet in a kiss that's anything but tentative.

It's achingly sweet—not soft, but slow and deliberate. His knuckles trace along my cheek, sending a shiver down my spine. I press closer, aching to be folded into him.

One hand cups the nape of his neck as my lips part, my head tilting to deepen the kiss. He lets out a groan, and fire ignites in my blood. I pour into it every ache, every unspoken longing I've buried. All that exists is the heat of his body pressed to mine, the taste of him on my tongue, mingling with the woodsy scent of his cologne mixed with the bitter winter air.

Everything I want is here with me—Anna is tucked into bed upstairs, and James is kissing me in this little Eden he created.

When his hands find their way into my hair, he pulls back, breathless and shaken. "God, I've missed you."

"Me too." I kiss his dimple, his cheekbones, his temple, his mouth. "I know I've messed this up so many times. But I'm here now. Fully. Completely."

I cradle his face in my hands, memorizing the texture of his rough stubble and sharp jaw. I've imagined touching them a thousand times, searching for the words to tell him the depth of my feelings. To give him the words he's so freely given to me over the years.

"James, when I look at you, it feels like I'm finally breathing. You made me believe there was more to life than enduring it."

He claims my mouth again. Goosebumps line my arms, and a shiver runs up my spine from his effect on me. From the bitter air.

"Come on, let's get in the water. You must be freezing." Without waiting, he reaches down, wraps his massive hands around my goose-pimpled backside, and my legs cinch around his waist. He carries me into the water, his mouth never leaving mine.

A whimper escapes at the assault of hot water combined with the hardness of him pressing against me. James tears his mouth away and floats to the far side of the hot tub. My chest heaves, taking in the hazy, dazed look in his hooded eyes.

"Wanna tell me what happened? Why are you all the way over there, and I'm over here?" The urgent edge to my voice has the corners of his mouth curling up.

"I thought you wanted to read tonight. Did you bring your book out with you?" he asks, his voice rough.

"I see how it is. Here I was thinking you might have something else on your mind."

"Oh, I have a lot of things going through my mind." He smirks and spreads his arms on the outside of the tub. "But I'm not going to do any of them to you—not here, not in this hot tub, not in this house."

"What?" I scoff indignantly.

"I haven't waited four years to have a quickie. I need a bed and a lot of time."

"You can't be very comfortable. Unless that was a hammer in your trunks." I squeeze my legs together, trying to ease the ache, as I take in this man I've loved for so long, telling me he's still willing to wait. He doesn't want to rush.

"I am extremely uncomfortable. But I'm used to it. I've had years of managing being around you without being able to touch you."

I lift my hips and sit on the edge of the hot tub, feeling the cool against my very exposed and very aroused skin. I shiver with anticipation, watching his eyes follow the beads of water trailing down my throat, between my breasts, along my stomach.

"I'm very uncomfortable, too." I bring a single finger to my knee and start to inch it up. "And I won't sleep well feeling like this."

James takes the bait and is before me in an instant, sloshing water over the sides. He fits his body between my legs, pushing my knees further apart. "What are you going to do about it?"

"If no one wants to help me, I'll have to take care of myself." My finger reaches the apex between my legs and swipes over the fabric.

He surges in and kisses me. I slip my hands around his waist and press my body more fully into his. He delves in with his tongue, and I meet him with mine. Heat races through me as our hips align.

I drag my nose along the edge of his jaw, relishing the bristle of whiskers against my heated skin. I trace every ridge of muscle, following the V that leads tantalizingly down to the waistband of his swim trunks. His skin is warm beneath my fingertips, scattered with freckles like points on a map I intend to visit. I feel him everywhere—every hard plane of muscle, every warm breath against my skin.

It's a dizzying assault on my senses.

He stays focused, sucking, nipping, and licking until I'm panting. I pull his mouth back to mine and kiss him long and slow, like the slide of his tongue against mine is the only thing that exists. I wrap my legs around him, erasing any remaining distance.

"Sydney..." he groans.

Hearing my name, both prayer and promise, lights every nerve. With nothing but the press of his body, the heat of his tongue, the sound of my name tumbling from his mouth, I shatter.

As the tremors roll through me, I moan, relishing every tremor. James watches, committing each sound and every roll of my hips to memory. I pull him tighter and keep the pace of our hips rolling. His fingers dig into my hips, his breath shortens, and with a deep, guttural noise that is the sexiest thing I've ever heard, he stills and pulses against me.

When I'm able to catch my breath, I run my hand through his hair and pull his head back.

"I'm looking forward to doing that without these pesky layers between us."

"You're going to be the death of me." He laughs, loud and free. "Here I am, trying to be noble. Make sure you know I don't only want you for sex."

"Dude. If you just wanted me for sex, I think the last four years were overkill." I smirk and lean in to kiss the corner of his mouth.

He smiles, slow and sexy. His dimple begs to be touched.

"Will you stay with me tonight?" he asks, leaning in to claim my mouth again.

"I'll stay as long as you'll have me." The words tumble out. I mean exactly what I say. This promise hangs between us like the first brave green shoot after a long winter.

"We're wearing pajamas, though. Maybe a snowsuit." He laughs and swats my ass, then steps out of the hot tub and holds up my robe for me.

***

WAKING TO THE SUN streaming through the wide windows and a warm body wrapped around me, I sigh contentedly. We fell asleep on the sectional watching a movie and stayed curled into each other all night. True to his word, we're both bundled in sweats. I burrow deeper against him, his chest rising and falling with each breath, his clean, masculine scent making my toes curl. The morning light turns the cabin golden and dreamlike, but James's solid warmth against me is deliciously real.

I lift my head from his chest and find him already awake. I rub the tip of my nose against his. "Good morning."

He lifts his head to find my mouth, and we kiss for a long, sweet moment. His heat wraps around me, and I imagine never leaving this cocoon of perfection. He tastes like sleep and promise and happiness. But then he groans and rolls off me.

"What are you doing?"

"I'm not making out with you on that sectional." He looks away, and I realize he's thinking about that morning I saw him and Ivy.

"James," my voice softens, "what if we replace those memories with ones of our own?"

He leans down, reconsidering, slides his hands to my waist, wraps my legs around him, and carries me to the kitchen.

"You can't pick me up like that!" I squeal, protesting half-heartedly, trying to squirm out of his arms.

"Just trying to be efficient. I've got longer legs, and it gets us here faster." He sets me on the counter and kisses a tender spot on my neck I never knew existed. Against my skin, he murmurs, "Do you ever think about that night here last year? Then afterward... in the sunroom?"

"Hmm... nooo, I have no idea what you're talking about." I thread my fingers through his thick hair, pulling to see what sound he'll make. It doesn't disappoint.

"That smart fucking mouth." He nips my bottom lip, eliciting a delicious moan from me.

"You love my smart mouth."

"You're right. I do." He flashes that lethal smile, dimple and all. His hands tangle in my hair, one cupping the base of my neck, and then our mouths crash together—hot, hard, and completely out of control.

"I've used the memory of that night more times than I'll ever admit. I remember exactly how much I wanted your lips on me. How badly I needed your touch instead of my own."

"Your taste..." He groans against my mouth as his hips rock forward. I gasp and pull him closer, ready to lose myself in everything he's offering.

"Mama!" Anna's excited voice bursts over the monitor.

Laughing at her perfectly timed interruption, I run my fingers through his scruff. "Life with a three-year-old. Are you up for it?"

"I'm more than ready," he rasps, and his lips find mine in a final, soul-stealing kiss—a kiss that promises more and seals a future neither of us could have imagined. "Besides, I've been practicing my *Frozen* songs for years. I think I'm ready for the big leagues."

"Okay, Mr. Big Leagues. Will you finish the coffee?"

THIRTY-FIVE

"Unca J made pancakes!" Anna tugs me to the island. "My fav'rits!"

I settle her onto a stool, her little legs swinging excitedly, surveying the spread before her. A stack of fluffy pancakes, a bowl of fresh berries, and a container of orange juice wait for her to devour. The scent of vanilla and butter fills the kitchen. I turn to grab my coffee, only to be met with a steaming mug.

"Here you go." Oat milk froths around the rim, perfect as always.

"Careful, I might never let you return to Boston."

His eyes pin me in place. "I hope not."

We stare at each other, a silent agreement passing between us: we're not going to take this slow.

"Snowman, Mama?" Anna asks between bites of pancake, syrup dripping down her chin.

"Of course, Bug. That sounds like fun." I force a shiver, half for her amusement, half to shake off the lingering arousal. "We'll have to bundle up, though. Looks freezing out there."

Anna turns her hopeful gaze to James, clutching her fork with syrup-sticky fingers. "Unca J, play in snow too?"

Her voice is so full of trust, of certainty that he'll say yes.

"That is the best idea ever, Anna-Bug." James wraps an arm around us both.

I sink into it, let myself feel the solid warmth of him, his hand resting on my hip, Anna beaming between us. The three of us here, at last. Not stolen moments or careful distances, but simply a lovely morning. The ordinary magic of pancakes, snow plans, and sticky little hands.

"I heard from Gary while you were showering. They can't get in until tomorrow. He wanted to check in and make sure everything was good."

I nod, sensing there's more.

Quieter, more measured, he adds, "He said Ivy is arriving later today, assuming her flight isn't canceled. She knows I'm here."

"Mason's supposed to fly in this afternoon too. But let's not let them ruin this morning. Jules texted and they're waiting until tomorrow; Tom got called into an emergency at the hospital." I drain my coffee as their eager expressions lock on me. "I think it's snowman time. What do you guys say?"

With Anna distracted, I tug James around the corner. Three-year-olds aren't known for their discretion, and I don't want to risk a moment she might repeat to the wrong person. I kiss him hard, hungry and grateful, tinged with desperation, knowing that soon this perfect bubble will pop. But I need this kiss. And I need this morning, this sliver of peace, before we face everyone else.

"Thank you," I whisper against his lips.

"For what?" His mouth travels over my jaw, down my neck, finding a spot that snatches the air from my lungs.

"For making pancakes. For wanting to build snowmen. For being here."

He pulls back, hands bracketing my face. "There's nowhere I'd rather be."

And I believe him.

With full bellies, we pile on layers to face the frigid cold and a little girl's dream of a snowman. The winter air nips at our cheeks as we step out onto the snow-covered world. A thick blanket of white stretches as far as the eye can see, sparkling under the bright morning sun. Anna, bundled in her puffy pink snowsuit, squeals with delight, her tiny mittens reaching for the fluffy snowflakes that continue to fall.

"Mama! Make a snowman!"

"Let's make a whole snowman family." James grins, quirking a brow.

"A family? Like us?" Anna asks.

The words hang in the frozen air, simple and profound all at once. My heart, like the Grinch's, grows three times its size.

"Exactly like us," James says, his eyes finding mine over Anna's head.

We set to work, rolling the snow into balls of varying sizes. She darts between us, her tiny hands helping to pat the snow into shape, leaving miniature handprints everywhere. James lifts her to place the carrot nose in each snowman, showing her how to use twigs for arms and pebbles for the eyes and mouth. His patience is endless as she adjusts each twig to her satisfaction.

Anna steps back to admire our handiwork.

"Look, Mama!" she exclaims, pointing to the three snowmen standing proudly in the snow. "It's me, and you, and Unca J!"

The casual statement, something Anna cheerfully shares without understanding its weight, takes my breath away. She sees it so clearly—what we are, what we've always been under all the pretense and waiting. Whatever happens next, whatever complications walk through that cabin door, I know this is us. Forever.

With Anna in my arms, James envelops us, blocking the bitter wind and warming us in his embrace. His lips brush against my hair, whispering, "This feels like home."

"Because it is," I say.

After hours of play, we make our way inside for a quick lunch before tucking Anna in for her nap. She falls asleep, clutching her ladybug, her little face peaceful and rosy from the cold.

The soft strains of Tinashe draw me down the hall, the familiar melody calling me toward the sunroom. It's where laughter and secrets curled into the corners, forbidden but undeniable. Where we found love in small, fleeting moments.

He stands at the windows, his silhouette a dark outline against the snow-covered landscape. He's changed into a soft gray t-shirt and faded jeans, hair tousled. I wrap my arms around his waist and press my nose into the fabric.

He doesn't move, doesn't speak. His hand comes up to cover mine against his stomach. I close my eyes and let myself enjoy this simple comfort.

"Dance with me?" Still holding my hand, he spins around and guides me into a slow, intimate sway. The music surrounds us, its rhythm a heartbeat in the quiet house.

We stay tangled in the moment, kissing and whispering sweet nothings, getting lost in the freedom of being able to touch without the risk of someone coming in. There were so many broken moments, interruptions pulling us back. But now, in this sacred space, we can just be.

But I can't shake the knot in my stomach, the certainty that the outside world is going to invade soon. Neither of us has heard from Ivy or Mason. Their flights should have landed by now.

I pull back, making sure he's looking straight at me. "I know I told you I moved out. But I filed for divorce. In case that wasn't clear."

Pinching his eyes shut briefly, James's chest expands on a deep breath. His lips claim mine, firm and demanding, a groan rumbling from his chest that sinks into my skin and rattles through my bones. He's pure heat and need against my tongue, something I'll never get enough of. His grip tightens, pulling me closer until there is nothing between us but breath and desperation, the music forgotten as we sway without rhythm, lost in each other.

"Hold on." I push back, gasping for air. "Are you going to stay after Gary and Margaret arrive?"

"I don't know." He sighs and runs a hand through his hair. "Guess I'll see how it goes. If Ivy is cool or not. How Mason reacts to my being here. He's not my biggest fan."

His face falls, realizing the distance we'll need to keep once everyone else arrives. My chest aches at the thought of pretending again.

"What happened after the wedding? When you and Ivy went for the walk?"

"I never intended for it to happen that way," his voice softens. "I just... couldn't let her keep going on like she was. I told her I didn't want to reschedule and that we needed space. She begged me not to break up with her that night. So I left. She wouldn't listen. A few weeks later, back in Boston, I made it official."

"How did she take it?"

"Not well. She still calls, texts regularly. I don't think she wants to believe it's really over."

"This is going to be so awkward when they get here."

He kisses me softly. "How is Mason handling everything?"

"As you'd expect. We just need to get through the next few days as best we can." I link our fingers, holding tight to the rough warmth of his palm.

"Okay. Once everyone else is here..." his grin fades. "I'll keep my hands to myself."

I see his hesitation, and instead of answering with words, I melt into him. Our lips devour each other. A soft whimper escapes my throat as his hands skim lower, pulling me flush against the hard lines of his body. He holds me like he's pressing me into memory, so I'll still be with him when we have to pretend we're something less. And he's leaving something of himself behind for me to remember. He steals the breath from my lungs, and I let him.

Tires crunch against packed snow. We freeze, breathing raggedly. My chest tightens. His hands cup my face.

"It's okay. We'll be okay." James doesn't promise me easy or feed me false hope. He stands there, solid and sure, offering something far more powerful than words. His presence. His strength. The unwavering truth that I'm not alone.

"Together," I whisper.

It's more than an agreement. It's a quiet promise to him and to myself.

But a surprised laugh slips out.

"You might want to... take care of that before we head downstairs." I lift a brow, nodding toward the very obvious evidence of his arousal.

His smirk is slow, shameless. Unbothered. He pulls me close one more time, his palms warm against my skin, his lips brushing mine one last time. He dips his mouth to my ear and murmurs, "Yeah... pretty sure what's waiting for us will take care of it."

And with one last look—dark, amused, and far too confident—he grabs my hand... and leads us toward the stairs.

THIRTY-SIX

THE FRONT DOOR SWINGS open, and a gust of cold air whirls through the house. Voices cut through the quiet. Mason. Ivy. They must've shared a ride from the airport.

"Hello? Syd?" Mason calls out, his voice carrying that tone I know so well. Expecting. Entitled.

The moment Mason sees James walking beside me, his face goes rigid. "What the hell are you doing here?"

Ivy steps forward and pastes on a bright smile.

"Dad invited James. He was worried about some house project and needed someone he trusted to check it out." She smiles, soft and inviting. "And of course Dad thought of James."

"Why are you still here? If everything is fine." Mason's anger coils tighter.

"Gary wanted me to stick around until he got back. Their flight was canceled, and they can't get in until tomorrow." James folds his arms across his chest, meeting Mason's eyes.

"And when did you arrive, Syd?" Mason's careful tone tries to hide what's behind those words.

"Anna and I got in yesterday," I reply with the basic facts because I don't owe him anything more.

"James," Ivy's voice purrs. "Would you mind helping me with my bags?"

He drops his gaze as though he needs a moment to collect himself. When his eyes lift, I see the shift—the contrite smile. The pleasantness meant to convey friendship, a boundary. "Sure. After we eat." He heads to the kitchen without looking back.

I clutch at the pieces of him still fresh on my skin, trying to hold onto what we had in the sunroom, but we both know the rules. The dance. The careful distance. Everything we've promised is now neatly folded beneath polite smiles and measured words.

Ivy stands there for half a second, processing the way he politely distances himself—despite the years they spent together, despite the engagement—before she follows him into the kitchen. I can't make out the quiet murmuring that follows.

"Is Anna napping?" Mason grabs his bag, tone softening.

"Yeah. She should be up soon."

He hesitates, searching for words he's never been good at finding. "Can we talk later?"

"Yes, after she's asleep tonight," I nod, and he walks off toward the guest room. A long, slow exhale finally escapes me, but the quiet doesn't last long.

Ivy's voice shatters my solitude, loud and so un-Ivy-like: "James, I'm only asking for another chance. We were so good together. We can be that again."

I take a few steps closer when I hear James's deep timbre. He isn't harsh, but there's finality in his tone. "I didn't come here for that, Ivy. I don't want to hurt you again, but we're not getting back together. You are great. Beautiful. Kind. And someone's going to be lucky to fall in love with you. But it's not me."

"Why not? What's wrong with me?" Ivy takes slow, gasping breaths.

"There's nothing wrong with you," he says gently. "That's the truth. The problem was never you."

I hear her breathing, shaky, uneven. The kind of breath you take when the ground beneath you has started to shift.

James waits, giving her a minute. When he speaks next, it's quieter. Regret coats every word. "I made a lot of mistakes when we were together. But the worst of them was letting things go on when I already knew. I should have been honest a long time ago."

"I don't understand. We were supposed to get married." Her voice is soft, broken. "This isn't the first time we've broken up and gotten back together. After that first Christmas here, we barely spoke for months, then came back from it. Why not now?"

James exhales. Loudly. I imagine he's running his hands through his hair in that pause.

"This isn't like that, Ivy. I never told you the full truth about why my parents separated. My dad hurt my mom. Not just emotionally. It was... more than that... and I vowed to never be like him. But by dragging this out, by not being honest with you sooner, I hurt you anyway."

He pauses again, swallowing hard. Ivy's quiet cries pick up.

"I'm sorry, Ivy. You didn't deserve any of this."

I step away, not wanting to hear any more. His painful words and her devastation after all this time pull at my chest. Guilt knots there. The damage left in our wake. The hurt. The fallout. And the family I've loved for so long is caught in the crosshairs.

Wetness slides down my cheek, and I search outside through the setting sun. Two birds cut across the orange sky, wings steady despite the wind, flying toward something I can't see but somehow trust is there. Together they're going where they're meant to be.

Before long, Ivy escapes from the kitchen, face in her hands, and runs up the stairs.

I walk into the kitchen where James is leaning against the countertop, rubbing his jaw. When he sees me, he gives me a sad, quick smile. I want to go over and comfort him, but I know I can't. Not right now. Instead of wrapping my arms around him, I open my phone and select a song. The soft, familiar notes hum through the speakers.

John Legend's voice, warm and soulful, fills the quiet.

James's eyes pin me in place, and I sink against the fridge, never looking away. As we've done so many times when words failed or too many eyes were watching, the lyrics say everything.

"Thank you," he mouths.

I nod, fold my hands over my heart, and let the words carry our vows to each other. Because *All of Me* is ready for more.

"What do you think about ordering pizza?" His tone is soft, still caught in Ivy's pain. He opens the drawer where Margaret keeps the takeout menus. "Pretty sure we're headed into the most awkward dinner of our lives."

And somehow, I laugh. The tension slips from my shoulders.

I shake my head, smiling at this beautiful man I get to call mine. I reach for the menu, our fingers brushing briefly. "We'll need wine. A lot of it."

"Already on it." He pulls a bottle of Pinot Noir from the rack. "I have a feeling this is going to be a long night."

***

LATER, AFTER I TUCK Anna into bed, I curl up beside her, listening to the rise and fall of her breath, steadying myself for the conversation ahead. Her voice whispers through the dark. "Mama, I loved today. Will Unca J play again?"

The innocent question hits with a gentle ache. Tomorrow. The day after. Every day, if I have my way.

"Yes, Bug. I think he will." I brush a curl from her cheek and slip out to find Mason.

It's time to finish this once and for all.

He's on the back deck, hunched over the fire pit with a glass of whiskey, his gaze lost in the flames. He's resisted more than I expected. I knew he'd push back, but not this hard, not for this long. The late-night texts and pleas to try again. Dinners to talk things through. Contesting the divorce. Even showing up for Anna in ways he never had before—taking her on fun outings, giving her his time when they were together. He's now decided parenting is worth showing up for, or maybe he's trying a new manipulation tactic.

I sit down beside him, wrapping my arms around myself, and tilt my head to the stars scattered across the onyx sky.

"It's beautiful out here. I always forget how quiet this place is compared to D.C." Mason's voice barely carries over the crackle of the fire.

"That's always been the appeal," I say, though the quiet here was only another space filled with silence between us. But no amount of beauty can disguise the truth. This place—home to so many holidays, the place where I fell in love with his family and with someone else—isn't where I belong anymore.

"Mason, I think we need to talk about the future."

The fire cracks loudly, a sharp punctuation in the cold air.

"Is this when you tell me you're moving home?" His words sound hopeful, but when I look over at him, he knows what's coming.

"No. We aren't getting back together."

"Do I get a say in this? In my own marriage?"

"Please don't do this. Just sign the divorce papers. We haven't been good for a long time. I know you've felt it too."

"Syd, we promised forever." He inhales deeply and exhales even slower. But no amount of breathing hides the edge in his voice.

"We've had this conversation so many times. We've changed. And I can't ignore that anymore." My own voice sharpens. I hope he hears the conviction and stops.

"I can do better. I *will*."

"You deserve better, too. I'm not in love with you. I wouldn't trade our years together or Anna for anything. But we both deserve better than this."

My thumb brushes over my bare ring finger. Instead of feeling empty, it feels whole.

"So this is it?" His eyes shine with unshed tears. Tears I've never seen from him.

"We have Anna," I speak in a tone you'd use when trying not to provoke a wild animal. "I hope we can be good co-parents. She deserves that. We can give her a steady, loving life even if we aren't together."

We sit side by side, staring out at the night, two people who once promised forever, now facing the quiet of an ending.

"Can we tell your family tomorrow, once everyone's here?" I ask.

"Are you with *him*?" His eyes narrow.

"This isn't about anyone else, Mason." I pause, making sure he's hearing the truth I'm giving him. "It's about me. About what I need for myself."

Mason stares at me. His jaw tightens. Whatever vulnerability cracked through earlier slams shut. Without a word, he walks inside.

A weight lifts from my chest, and a lightness I hadn't realized I'd been missing takes its place. It's like I've been carrying the burden of a thousand unspoken words, and finally they're out.

Stars gleam above the mountaintops. I stay outside long after my fingers go numb, my nose running from the cold. I stare at the stars, no longer needing them to guide me or make wishes upon them. This time, the stars don't have to tell me who I am.

THIrTY-seven

When morning finally breaks, pale and cold, I move through the house like someone surfacing from deep water, taking her first real breath after years of barely breathing.

Despite my lack of sleep, I feel renewed and refreshed. The rich aroma of coffee fills the air, and I breathe it in deeply, feeling, for the first time, truly free. No longer tied to a past defined by hurt, I look ahead to the future waiting for me.

Ivy appears in the doorway, her hair wild and sleep-mussed. She wears wide-legged sleep pants and a wrinkled, self-cropped college T-shirt. She settles onto a stool at the island, cradling her coffee cup.

"I'm sure you heard my fight with James last night. He told me we're over." Her gaze settles on me, more searching than accusatory. "I feel so lost. I don't even know what I want anymore. I'm thirty-two and asking the questions of a teenager." She pauses, and behind the heartbreak and questions, there's a spark of life that's been missing. "You seem different. More sure of yourself. How did you find your way?"

"Mama!" Anna's sweet voice sings through the baby monitor.

"I've got to get Anna." I stand, but stop before I leave the kitchen. "The questions you're asking are the right ones. They're the ones it took me too long to be brave enough to ask."

Ivy's breath stutters, and tears gather at the corners of her eyes.

"The thing is..." I hesitate, aware of how hollow this might sound soon. "I was trying to meet expectations that were more about what I thought I should want than what I actually needed."

"What's changed, though?" Ivy asks.

"Me. I've changed." I let that settle before I continue. "I started choosing myself."

"Moooooommmmmaaa!" Anna's voice rockets through the monitor again.

"I'll see you later." This time I hustle out.

With the speaker pressed to my ear, I listen to Anna's laughter and the creak of the bed as she bounces. James's deep voice wishes her good morning. He must have heard her through the open door and come to check. I listen to their little conversation, and when I peek through the doorway, Anna's wrapped around him, face buried in his shoulder.

"Hi Mama!" Anna exclaims when she spots me.

"Good morning, Bug," I say, kissing her head. As I straighten, his lips brush against mine, brief and tender.

"Breakfast, Mama?" Anna asks, already focused on pancakes and syrup.

She's blissfully unaware of the tension swirling around her. Last night, we ate pizza on the couch and watched a movie. She thought it was the best thing ever. Her focus stayed on *Frozen* while the rest of us barely ate, sipping our wine.

James lowers her to the floor, and she dashes toward the stairs. Before I can follow, he catches my hand, pulling me close.

"Mason and I talked last night," I say. "We're telling the family tonight."

"Once Gary and Margaret arrive, I'll take off. I don't want to hurt Ivy any more than I have. She was pretty upset last night." He squeezes my waist, and I can hear the exhaustion in his voice as he says, "I'm ready for all this to be over."

I lean back into his body for another second. "As long as things don't go too badly tonight, I should stay through tomorrow. Give Anna one last Christmas with me and Mason both there. Maybe we can meet at the resort?"

"I'm not leaving here without you. That's the only thing I know for certain." He quickly kisses me.

"Pancakes?" Anna reappears in the doorway, her face lighting up as she sees us standing close and whispering. She steps between us, grabbing each of our hands.

"Yeah, love. Let's make pancakes."

Over the next several hours, the house fills with the familiar chaos of a family reunion. The high-pitched squeals of children mingle with the low hum of adult conversation as new arrivals catch up, easing some of the earlier tension. And for a while, the air feels normal.

James shows Gary and Margaret the extras he constructed around the hot tub. Margaret comes upstairs with tears in her eyes, asking us all to see.

She leads the way, with Jules, Tom, Ivy, and me following closely. James trails behind, hands shoved in his jeans, and chin tilted down. When she throws open the doors, her arms lift, unveiling the masterpiece.

"Wow, this is incredible." Jules scans the setting, then cuts her eyes to me. "I bet it's very romantic at night."

I swallow hard, fighting the heat rising in my cheeks, and turn to examine the wood work.

"I can't thank you enough, James. Gary was beside himself when the construction crew called. And I can't believe what you created here." Margaret looks to Ivy, a silent question in her eyes, before turning back to James. "Will you stay with us for Christmas? It's the least we can do. Right, Ivy?"

"This is incredible, James. And please stay." Ivy leans against the doorframe and says, "Someone said something wise to me today. And it's time I move on. I won't make it awkward."

She keeps her head high and shoulders squared. She might not be truly over it, but I see that she'll be okay.

Tom grabs James and starts asking him questions about the construction, while Margaret and Ivy wander inside whispering to each other. Jules comes up next to me.

"When are you and Mason telling everyone?" she asks, keeping her voice low.

"Maybe before dinner? I didn't actually ask him when he wanted to do it, beyond agreeing on today. I haven't seen him all day. I think he went skiing."

"And do you want to tell me about how amazing the hot tub is?" Jules grins and pulls me away from the men. "Come on. You can't tell me you guys didn't test this out the other night."

I look over to James. His head tilts, half listening to Tom, half listening to us. When our eyes lock, heat floods my body.

"Let's just say it exceeded all expectations."

"Well, well, well. Someone finally got their Christmas miracle. And it came with excellent... construction skills."

A laugh bursts out of me—that loud, ungraceful snort. My hand flies to cover my mouth as I look over at James. He's standing there grinning. I'm grateful it's only Jules and Tom here because the way he's looking at me right now, there's no hiding the love in his eyes.

"This right here is what I've always wished for you. Him grinning like a fool because you made that awful noise, you blushing because he's grinning. Someone who thinks your weirdness is wonderful." Jules kisses my cheek. "I love you."

My throat tightens as I blink back the wetness. Finally tearing my gaze away, I clear my throat.

"Come on. We need some wine before you make me cry. And help me figure out what to say when Mason and I tell everyone." I pull her away from the men and into the cabin.

***

As the sun dips lower, painting outside in shades of rose and amber, I stare at the untouched landscape, the snow glowing in the last wash of daylight, serene and undisturbed. Everything I wish I could feel. This conversation with the family can't come soon enough.

"Oh, Anna," Beck calls, glancing up from his phone, something mischievous crossing his face. "I heard the tickle monster's on his way. You'd better run. Attack!"

Anna's shriek pierces the quiet, followed by a stampede of little feet as the kids tear through the room in a chaotic game. Their laughter fills the space, bright and careless, as they weave between furniture and adults like water around stones. Within moments, the room empties of children, their game spilling into the basement, leaving a sudden, heavy quiet in their wake.

It's the kind of quiet that feels expectant.

Mason approaches me, his footsteps heavy as if moving slowly enough can stop what's coming. He holds out a glass of wine, an oddly formal gesture.

"Are you sure about this, Syd?" he asks, his voice matching the lost look in his eyes. "What about counseling? We never tried that."

"Please don't. I'm not changing my mind."

"I could tell something shifted a few years ago. But every time I tried to figure out how to fix it, I came up empty-handed. I didn't know what broke us."

"We've had this conversation plenty of times. We... grew apart. We met at twenty-six. We're forty now. People change."

I draw in a long breath, trying to quell my simmering rage—keep this amicable as I've been doing the whole year. I see the others keeping their distance, pretending they aren't watching.

"Think about Anna. Don't we owe it to her to try harder?"

"How dare you?" The words fly out before I can stop them, my voice loud and unrestrained. "You think I haven't thought about Anna? You think I haven't spent every goddamn night agonizing over this for years?"

I step back, my breath coming faster. The room has gone silent. The family stands there, eyes wide, conversations forgotten. James's gaze locks onto mine, fierce and unwavering.

"I've tried being nice, Mason, but the truth is, I need more. I want a partner who fights for me, who challenges me, who actually sees me. I would rather be alone than stay with someone who isn't fully there or looks at me like I belong to him."

Mason pales. The fire crackles. No one speaks.

"I'm sorry you're finding out this way," I say, my eyes sweeping across the others. "I moved out months ago and we're getting divorced."

As the finality of my words settles over the room, I meet each set of eyes. Jules raises her wine glass. She's been waiting for me to let loose on him for years. Ivy stands in the doorway of the kitchen. Her expression is harder to read, a complex mix of shock and realization. The unsaid parts of our conversation earlier now make sense to her. The fight I mentioned wasn't philosophical. It was real, and this is the change.

Before the silence threatens to suffocate us, the kids thunder back in. Anna leads the charge, cheeks flushed, eyes bright. She throws herself into my arms.

Life doesn't pause for change. It keeps going. And we must move with it.

Margaret is the first to act. She crosses the room with quiet purpose and pulls me into a firm hug. She holds me tight, her embrace the same as it was that first Christmas. "I still love you, Sydney."

She walks to Mason and guides him toward the back deck, away from the audience. He resists, staying rigid, but when his face crumples, he lets her lead him away.

Some things have to break before they can heal.

***

Dinner is a quiet, fractured affair.

People drift in and out of the kitchen, making plates and retreating to different corners of the cabin. By the time I help Anna with her bath and tuck her into bed, the house has settled into an uneasy peace. James's voice drifts from the sunroom, talking with Tom. It's the sound of him staying, proving again that he won't run when things get sticky or uncomfortable.

Tomorrow is Christmas, and I need to make sure it's special.

Margaret stands in the kitchen, working on her cinnamon rolls. When she sees me, her smile carries the weight of everything we've shared. Our moments that span over a decade, beginning with that first Christmas, making cinnamon rolls together. Her guidance during those months before Anna was born. Her care after that first Christmas with Anna, when it was hard to ignore Mason's lack of help. Our relationship will change too, maybe for the better.

"I can leave if you think that's better," I offer, stepping inside.

"No, please don't do that, Sydney. Let's have one last Christmas together as a family, and after that, you can figure out where you're headed." Margaret keeps kneading the dough, her gaze holding more understanding than sadness.

"Mind if I help?"

"Of course, dear." She hands me the familiar checkered apron.

We work in silence, our movements practiced and easy, a rhythm we've perfected over the years. Flour dusts the counter like fresh snow, and the dough yields beneath our hands—soft and pliable, forgiving in a way words aren't.

Once the rolls are nestled to rise, she pours wine and gestures toward the armchairs by the fireplace.

"I'm sorry if I missed how unhappy you've been." She reaches across, gently squeezing my hand.

"Please don't. You taught me what to expect from a partner, what love should be. Seeing you and Gary it helped me realize what was missing. What has always been missing." I wrap my hand around hers. "I never wanted you to find out like that."

"I know, dear. Relationships don't end in a vacuum. Everyone plays their part." She squeezes my hand with the strength of a woman who knows the challenges of life and love. We sit together sipping our wine, watching the flames play across the burning logs.

When James walks downstairs to the kitchen, I catch her watching me from the corner of her eye.

"I want you to be happy. You deserve someone who sees you the way you described. Don't settle for less than that. Love is always worth fighting for, even if it's complicated." She touches my shoulder lightly. "Goodnight, Sydney."

I'm grateful for this woman. Margaret could have blamed me and chosen sides. Instead, she treated me with the same kindness she always has. She might not be Marmee, but that's okay because real is better.

There's one more person I need to see before I can think about sleeping.

I find Jules sitting by the fire pit outside. She's curled in an oversized chair, Kindle in hand, her face lit by its soft glow.

"Well, that was a shit show," I half-laugh, sinking into the chair beside her.

"He had it coming." She pulls me into a massive hug, her arms squeezing every ounce of tension out of me. "And I'm so damn happy for you." She leans back, eyes twinkling in the firelight. "Are you going to spill about your twenty-four hours?"

"Hmm," I laugh, my voice deliberately playful. "It was... eventful." But when I glance toward the living room window, my smile fades. Ivy walks into the family room and curls up on the sectional. "I think we all need some breathing room after today."

Jules follows my gaze, her expression softening. "I spoke to her earlier. She'll be fine. She actually cracked a joke," Jules says, squeezing my hand. "Speaking of finding yourself... have you read *Happy Place* by Emily Henry? It's about this couple. They're in love, but they fall apart. They don't talk. She's stuck in people-pleasing mode... until they're forced to spend a week together and she finally has to figure her shit out."

"Let me guess. She chooses the guy?"

"More importantly, she chooses herself. The guy's just a hot bonus."

I laugh, and it sounds like something breaking open. "I'm going to miss these fire-pit conversations with you the most."

"You're stuck with me, and my romance novels, for life," Jules says, bumping my shoulder with hers.

"Maybe James and I can find a place up here. Something tucked into the woods so we're close by."

Jules's eyes widen, seeing the dream I'm already forming. "Tom and I'll be your first guests. The boys aren't giving up their favorite video game partner anyway."

"I love you."

"You too, babe." Jules hugs me once more.

THIRTY-EIGHT

As I head upstairs to get ready for bed, my phone pings.

Skating Stud: *Can I come say good night?*

Me: *Yes please.*

Less than three minutes later, the door clicks open and James slips inside.

"I couldn't sleep without seeing you first," he says, cupping my chin. "You were fucking magnificent tonight."

He leans down and claims my mouth—slow, deep, certain. A deep purr starts in my throat and works its way down to my toes. His hands slide down until he reaches the hem of my sleep shirt. My legs shake, waiting for his fingers to continue their descent. Instead, he pulls back. His eyes are hazy, darkening as he takes in my pajamas. A long button-up sleep shirt riding up just enough to reveal a hint of black boy shorts beneath.

"This is what you sleep in?" A note of pleading is in his voice.

"My old sleep shirt. Not exactly my greatest seductive effort." I laugh. "But this is me. Messy bun. Unshaved legs. I'm not glamorous. I don't wear silk negligees to bed. I hate doing the dishes. I drink way too much coffee and not enough water."

Before I can keep rambling, he lifts me in one fluid motion, my legs wrapping around his waist as he carries me into the bathroom—putting space between us and the sleeping toddler.

"I don't want glamorous. I want you. Exactly like this."

The door clicks shut behind us, and he sets me on the edge of the vanity, fingers working the top buttons of my sleep shirt, popping them open one by one until it slips off my shoulder. His mouth finds that sensitive spot beneath my ear, before trailing to my bra strap and tugging it down.

My breast stays mostly hidden, still cradled in the sensible black cup. He leans down and sucks my breast into his mouth, bra and all.

"Oh fuck," I moan, head hitting the mirror as his mouth works over the fabric, stubble grazing my skin. My back arches, and I suck in air like I'm about to dive and never surface.

"I've been thinking about this since that damn night in the sunroom. I couldn't get the look on your face out of my head. That rubber band... I nearly lost it. Was this the same shirt?" he asks, his mouth still against my skin.

"Hmmm. Might be." I nod, distracted by the need overtaking me. "You remember the night by the fire pit that first year?"

"You mean the night you called bullshit on my whole poetic music metaphors?" He presses a kiss to my collarbone while his fingers rebutton my top.

"I dreamed of you that night. I already had a feeling I might be pregnant. But when I fell asleep, I dreamed about the baby, and the man looking down at us had the most intense green eyes." I press my lips to his, sealing the confession with a kiss.

With more restraint than I can fathom, he says, "We've waited four years. I think we can wait for somewhere more romantic than a bathroom."

But my body disagrees.

My legs lock around his waist, pulling him closer. I rock my hips, desperate for friction, until a low, feral growl rumbles from his chest, and I'm pressed against the door.

"You're playing dirty," he rasps, easing my feet to the floor.

His mouth trails down my neck as his fingers make quick work of my sleep shirt and bra, leaving me in nothing but my underwear. Unshaved legs and messy hair no longer matter. All that matters is the look on his face, complete and total reverence. I grasp the back of his shirt between his shoulder blades, and pull it over his head. My nails dig into the thick muscle.

"You are... everything," he breathes.

I moan as he kisses lower, worshipping his way down. He drops to his knees, hands sliding down my waist, pausing at my hips.

"You know how long I've dreamed of this?"

"Tell me," I whisper, trembling.

"Since the night you called me out by the fire pit," he confesses, with a sinful grin. He traces the seams of my underwear, fingers brushing my wetness. "I wanted to drop to my knees right then, to make you scream my name so loud that the entire forest would know I belonged to you. And you to me."

He hooks his fingers under the waistband and slides them down, inch by inch. Taking his time to look at me before dipping his head to drag his tongue through my folds. His eyes close, savoring the moment. Mine never leave him.

"Oh, and Sydney..." He lifts one of my legs over his shoulder, letting anticipation build. "Remember there's a toddler on the other side of the door."

What follows is exquisite torture. Him bringing me to the edge only to pull back, ignoring my pleas, and maintaining a leisurely pace. He takes his time learning what drives me insane, four years of wanting condensed into every kiss, every touch. When I finally feel a thick, rough finger slip inside me, my body careens over the edge.

I cry out his name before biting my lip as waves of pleasure roll through me, each one coaxed carefully by his attentive touch. Bringing me pleasure isn't a step toward his own release; it's an act of devotion in itself. And I immediately want him to feel the same way.

Kneeling to meet him, I rake my fingers through his hair, tugging gently to bring his mouth to meet mine, tasting the evidence of my pleasure on his lips. My hand runs down his chest and finds its way beneath his waistband, the smooth, hot skin and firm weight of him in my palm. His breath catches. A sharp, breathless sound that sends a pulse of satisfaction through me. I stroke him slowly at first, savoring the heat, every noise he makes as I tighten my grip and learn what he likes.

"Darling," he grits out, voice frayed and wrecked. "Keep that up, and I'm going to lose it all over your hand."

"That's the idea, my dear." I stroke him harder.

And when he does, it's not a moan but a rupture, pulled from the hollow of his gut. His eyes are still dazed as he pulls me tight against him, his fingers finding their way back between my thighs.

"James…" I trail off, utterly consumed as he tips me into another release.

We collapse on the bathroom floor, tangled and shaking, foreheads pressed together, breath coming in uneven bursts. The stone floor is unforgiving against our knees, but neither of us cares.

"I'll never get enough of you," he murmurs, a slow, satisfied smile curving his lips.

"Good, because I'm not going anywhere."

"I love you. I've loved you for so long, I can't remember what it felt like not to."

A tear slips down my cheek, and his thumb is already there, brushing it away.

"I love you too," I whisper, saying the words out loud for the first time, every syllable a release of all the feelings I've swallowed for too long.

"Say it again."

I press my hands flat over his heart. "I love you, James Navarro."

We stay there, foreheads resting together, suspended in this moment—not a fantasy anymore, just us, finally saying everything.

He slowly pulls away and begins redressing me, smiling as he holds my underwear out for me to step into. He lifts my sleep shirt over my arms and shoulders, rebuttoning it with soft kisses between each button—navel, ribs, between my breasts, collarbone, mouth. I clean him up with a warm cloth. He groans, presses a kiss to my shoulder, and wraps me in his arms.

Anna's soft breathing from her cot fills the quiet space as we sneak out of the bathroom. James stands in the darkness, struggling to pull himself away. I decide for both of us, my fingers finding his.

"Stay."

It's reckless, but I'm so damn tired of being without him. I feel him wrestling with the same conflicted thoughts, his fingers tightening around mine, wavering between what we should do and what we both want. He slips under the sheets and pulls me flush against his chest. His warmth seeps into my skin as I tuck myself into the curve of his body.

"I'll set an alarm. We'll wake before anyone notices." I kiss him one last time and snuggle deeper into his arms.

Another breath leaves him, slower now, softer. His arms tighten around me, and his lips brush the crown of my head. My heart thuds with the quiet, terrifying certainty of it all. And when sleep finally comes, it's deep. Undisturbed. Dreamless in the best way.

THIRTY-NINE

The soft chime of my alarm stirs me in the blue-gray hush of early morning.

Warmth cocoons me on both sides—Anna's tiny body curled against my front, and behind me, the solid weight of James. His breath warms the back of my neck as I turn to find him already awake, green eyes drowsy and soft, moving from my face to Anna's.

"Merry Christmas." His lips brush mine in a gentle morning kiss.

I lean into him, savoring the quiet perfection of this moment while reality waits beyond the door. We trade whispered plans about sneaking him out, our stifled laughter making us feel like teenagers breaking curfew. In the bathroom, our kiss deepens. His hands thread through my hair until I reluctantly pull away.

"One more day. Then no more hiding," I say, peppering kisses along his jaw.

"I'm going to reserve a room at the resort for a few nights. Okay?"

I kiss him for confirmation, long and slow, knowing this will be our last for the day. "I love you."

"God, I'm never going to get over hearing that. I love you, too." He groans and wrenches his mouth away. "But I should go; others will be up soon."

With Anna still sleeping, we tiptoe across the room, and I crack the door open to an empty hallway. With a quick nod, James slips out, barefoot and silent. His fingers brush mine, a final tether, before he goes to shower and change into clean clothes.

The moment I enter the living room, my bliss evaporates. Mason sits rigidly, his face tight, focused on the mug in his hands. Ivy chats leisurely with Jules and Tom. Of all years, they decide to show up. At least Anna will get one Christmas with us all together.

I hide in the kitchen until Anna's excited voice breaks through.

"Did Santa come?"

This year, Santa's magic is real, and each present under the tree is a marvel waiting to be discovered.

"Merry Christmas, Bug." I sweep over to the staircase and gather her into my arms. "We have to wait for Beck and Leo, but you can peek at everything under the tree."

I click on some cheerful holiday music. Anna giggles and twirls, her excitement spilling over as she takes in the stacks of presents adorned with ribbons and bows.

"Mama, where are mine?" she asks, bouncing from box to box.

"Remember what the letter A looks like?" I ask, pointing to the tag. "A is for Anna. Look for those."

I leave her to take inventory and escape back into the kitchen to settle my nerves with more coffee.

Gradually, the others filter in. Margaret and Gary settle on each side of Mason, careful buffers as his glower only grows. James joins, fills his mug, and takes a corner seat, trying not to draw attention.

Anna flutters among the adults, excitedly bouncing and sharing her thoughts on all things Christmas. Mason, caught in his own world, gives her a forced smile—but it doesn't take long for her to sense his detachment and half-hearted responses.

"Unca J, can I sit on your lap?" She pivots, knowing where she can turn.

"Of course, Bug." He sets down his mug as she melts against him. She delivers her Santa report. Cookies are gone, carrots too. He listens with rapt attention.

Once Leo and Beck join the mix, Christmas chaos erupts. Presents fly open in a flurry of paper, and joy briefly lifts the tension.

But the ease of past years doesn't return.

Even as James and I keep our distance, the truth hums, impossible to ignore. We aren't doing anything inappropriate, but what's between us is unmistakable. Every time Anna calls him "Unca J," every shared smile over her head, every instinctive reach toward each other that we catch mid-motion, it's all evidence building a case we can't deny.

I feel Ivy tracking every glance, cataloging every unguarded moment of familiarity. There's something different in her expression—it's quieter, more contemplative. It's not animosity or judgment, rather a careful, neutral set to her face as if she's seeing what was always missing between them.

Mason grips his coffee mug tightly to the point his knuckles have gone white. When Anna moved to James after his disinterest, he immediately saw it for what it was. His face darkened in that possessive way I've seen before. His anger simmers, his face hard as granite, even as he sits amongst the joy of the kids opening their gifts.

Anna rushes over, her cheeks still pink with excitement. "You and Unca J and me p'ay in snow again?"

My heart hammers so loudly I'm sure everyone can hear it.

"Yeah, baby," I say, and she runs off upstairs.

I keep my eyes on Anna's retreating form, deliberately not looking at James. I reach for my coffee, focusing on the warmth of the mug in my hands rather than the weight of attention in the room.

Ivy sets down her coffee mug with a small clink and leans back. She considers me and James.

"You guys are in love, right? That's the thing we've all been watching happen."

The energy in the room shifts instantly. Gone is the forced Christmas warmth. There is no more pretending this is a normal family holiday. I close my eyes for a brief second, steadying myself. When I open them, I'm clear-eyed.

"Yes. We're in love."

I don't rush to justify or offer explanations. I meet each of their eyes without flinching.

"I won't apologize for finding happiness, and I hope someday you'll understand. But I'm not going to answer any questions. The details won't change anything."

We've all been dancing around this truth for years, and now we're standing in the ruins of all the deception. We all played a part in getting to this moment, even if James and I get cast as the villains.

I scan the room—every twinkling light, every lovingly placed ornament, the warmth radiating from every corner of this home. The family I once thought could fill the emptiness of my childhood. But only I was able to fill that space.

Some relationships will be irrevocably changed. Some will never heal.

And others, the ones that matter, will still be there. Choosing to remain family—the one we want rather than the one bound by contracts and titles.

A silent conversation passes between James and me as we both stand and walk to gather our things. Mason stomps behind us. "Wait."

James grabs my hand, linking our fingers. But I stand tall, chin high. I'm not going to cower in front of Mason ever again.

"I don't want all the details, but you owe me enough courtesy to tell me when this started." Mason gestures toward our joined hands.

James opens his mouth to respond, but Mason cuts him off with a sharp swipe of his hand. "Not from you." His tone drops to something lethal. "I don't want to hear a goddamned word from you. Because no matter what's been going on between you two, you lied to and led on my little sister for years."

The truth lands hard, but there's nothing we can say to rewrite our timeline. We made mistakes, and there's no way to soften the reality of what we've done. His eyes drop to his feet as guilt washes over his features.

I squeeze his hand, and when his eyes meet mine, I squeeze again. We're in this together.

"Mason, don't act like you've had my best interest in mind." Ivy walks towards us, chin raised, her fuzzy pink slippers making soft patters against the oak floors. "You knew this was happening as much as I did. We both ignored it. Instead of yelling at them, maybe you need to take a good, hard look in the mirror."

All four of us stand there for what could be a second. Or a minute. Until Ivy walks away.

Mason stares after her, her words clearly hitting home. But instead of self-reflection, his face twists with something uglier. The need to lash out and make someone hurt as much as he does.

"Did you fuck him here? Fuck him in the room we used to share?" Mason's shout echoes off the walls, filling every corner.

The room freezes, and no one can deny seeing the ugliness he usually hides.

James shifts beside me, his body tensing, but he remains silent, understanding this isn't his battle to fight. This is mine to handle. Not because I need to, but because I want to.

"No, Mason," I say, keeping my voice even. "We didn't fuck here."

His nostrils flare, shoulders rising and falling with each breath. But I'm not done. If he wants honesty, I'll give it to him.

"You want the truth? Pretty much every time in the four years since I met him, when you kissed me, when you touched me, I imagined it was James."

My chest heaves as I try to drag air into my lungs. James runs a hand along my back, reminding me he's right there. Mason's mouth tightens into a thin, bloodless line, and I see our audience wince like someone wiped out on the ski slopes.

"Does that make you feel better?" I ask with bitter sarcasm. "Would it be easier if this were about sex? If I were just some cheating wife looking for a thrill? Because that would be simple, right? But life isn't simple."

"Jesus. You had me thinking I was going crazy. That it was all in my head." Mason's voice moderates, realizing the family is near. "At least I know right from wrong. I didn't cheat."

With that, my restraint detonates.

"Right, what was it you said? *Want me to fuck you here so he can watch? Bend you over the railing?* Just the casual threat of sexual assault on the deck." I pause, watching his face absorb every word. "Or how about the years you spent cutting me down, trying to keep me small and compliant? I can give you those examples too, if you can't remember?"

James takes my hand, uncurling my clenched fingers, and links them with his, pulling me to face him. His face is rigid, barely containing his fury. His nostrils flare as his eyes search mine, and I see the guilt. He's blaming himself for not knowing, not stopping it. The boy who once stepped in to protect his mom wasn't there to protect me, and it's tearing him apart.

I squeeze his hand, a silent assurance that I'm okay. There's freedom in finally telling the truth, in no longer carrying this burden alone.

A gasp, possibly from Margaret, fills the stifled air. Everyone is staring. They heard every word. Jules turns to her mom, who is wiping her eyes, and she guides them out.

"So go ahead and blame me. Because the truth is, we never should have gotten married. Not when I knew I loved your family more than you." I continue, my tone shifting to something calmer. "When you're ready to talk like adults and co-parents, let me know. Anna needs both of us."

Mason swallows hard, his Adam's apple bobbing visibly, and he finally has the decency to look ashamed. I take the stairs one at a time, James's hand still in mine, past the Christmas garland and pine-scented air that used to smell like belonging. Now it only makes me ready to leave. I'm packing for the last time, not just clothes, but the life I've outgrown.

The weight of the past, the guilt, the need to hide, all of it falls away. The future is waiting, and for the first time in four years, I'm walking toward it without looking back.

FOrty

We escape to the resort, grateful to find an open suite, and spend the day ice skating, eating cookies, watching Christmas movies, and ordering room service.

It's an unconventional Christmas, but Anna is unbothered by the change. She happily accepted our departure from the cabin, more focused on the promise of hot chocolate and playing in the snow than on leaving her dad behind. She's spent the day playing with James and me, a grin never leaving her face. We haven't had a chance to talk about everything that happened earlier, but there will be time for that. Today has been a glimpse of the future we fought for, the one we refused to give up on.

But tonight is for us.

After settling Anna onto the pullout couch, we retreat to our room.

I slip into the bathroom, pulse quickening, savoring the build-up. I remove my purchase from its tissue, a red lace confection that makes me blush even as I imagine his reaction. My fingers trace the delicate fabric before I slide it over my skin. I take my time with every detail—soft waves framing my face, dabs of my favorite essential oil, freshly shaved and moisturized skin.

When I open the bedroom door, I freeze.

Dozens of candles flicker across every surface. Reflected in the windows, their glow turns the ordinary suite ethereal. And there, at the foot of the bed, sits James, his chest bare above black sleep pants.

"Where did you find that?" he asks, leaning forward, voice dropping into a low growl.

I let my fingers drift to the hem of the sheer lace, teasing it up enough to reveal the matching thong beneath.

"Oh, this?" I ask sweetly. "Do you like it?"

A muscle ticks in his jaw as he exhales sharply through his nose.

"I found it downstairs in the boutique when I wandered off earlier," I smirk, savoring the way his eyes darken. When I purchased it, I'd imagined his boyish blush, maybe a nervous laugh. But there's nothing boyish or hesitant about him.

He rises from the bed, closing the distance one deliberate step at a time.

"How did you do all this?" I ask, taking in the glowing room.

"The resort was very accommodating when I asked for every candle they could find." His gaze roams my every curve. "But now that I see you... I didn't get nearly enough."

His lips claim mine, tender and gentle, unhurried. There is no rush to cross this final barrier. But when I reach up to cup his face, he pulls away, breathing labored and his gaze drops to his feet.

"What is it?" I whisper, reaching for him, closing the distance.

"I... did the Mason thing happen on the deck before New Year's Eve that year?" His breath shakes against my palm.

"Yeah, but he didn't touch me, and he hasn't touched me since. It's why I walked away from the stairs so abruptly. I didn't want him to catch us and get angry again."

"Fuck." He blows out a sharp breath. "I'm so sorry. I should have realized something had happened. I saw how upset you were at breakfast that morning—this was after we spent the day together, wasn't it?"

"Don't. You didn't do this, and I handled it." I wrap my hands around his body, pulling myself closer.

"You shouldn't have had to handle that alone. That's not nothing."

"It's over now. He's not here. It's just us. Don't let it ruin tonight."

"What he threatened... that's not something you move past in a single conversation." He exhales slowly, his thumb brushing along my collarbone.

"James, it happened almost two years ago. I've processed it. Gone to therapy. I'm okay. I'm not brushing past it or ignoring the severity of it." I meet his eyes.

He studies my face for a long moment, then slowly pulls me closer, resting his forehead against mine. "I... fuck, we've wasted so much time."

"Then let's not waste a minute more."

His lips crash into mine. A hard, desperate kiss that steals the air from my lungs and makes every moment of waiting worth it.

"I love you," he breathes against my mouth.

My heart aches for everything we lost, all the moments we were forced to bury. But none of it matters now. I kiss him back, pouring years of longing, regret, and love into every touch.

He pulls back, eyes dark and pleading. "Say it."

A slow smile curves my lips. He watches it like it holds every answer he's ever wanted.

"I want to hear you say it," he repeats, his voice hoarse.

I cup his face, feeling the slight tremble in his jaw. "I love you. Today. Tomorrow. I don't know what the future holds, but I promise to show up and keep choosing you."

A tortured sound escapes him as he lifts me, my legs wrapping around his waist, and he sits with me straddling his lap, breathing deep. My hands bury themselves in the dark waves at his nape, guiding him closer as his mouth meets mine. A kiss that offers everything and asks for nothing.

With one finger, he slips the first strap off my shoulder. He presses his lips between my breasts before gently sliding the other strap down my arm. I lift my hips, easing the slip and thong away. And I let him see me. Not the woman trying to be perfect, not the mother burying her desires. Just me. His fingers trace my curves as his eyes study every inch of my body.

"I used to lie in bed dreaming of these freckles," he whispers, kissing the scattering of brown dots on my collarbone, trailing down my chest. "Fantasizing how far they traveled down."

His tongue follows their path. I groan when he finds the tender skin of my breast.

"I've waited a long time for this." His mouth claims mine again. "But now I'm yours and I'm never letting you go."

"We're ours."

There's no urgency, only a slow undoing. The candlelight flickers around us as we strip away years of distance, moment by moment.

When I slide his pants from his hips and stretch my body over his, we both let out shaky breaths. Skin to skin, nothing separating us. The heavy, hard length of him rests between my thighs as I slowly move against him, my warmth seeking his fullness.

"Sydney," he groans, eyes heavy-lidded. "You keep doing that, I'm going to last maybe ten seconds. Let me love you first."

"Show me what you've got."

And he does.

His mouth worships every part of me, slow and unrelenting, learning exactly how to make me shatter—with his tongue, his fingers, his unrelenting devotion. He brings me to the edge again and again until I'm trembling and sated. Sparks dance beneath my skin. Flaring and fading, firefly-bright. He crawls up my body, kissing me through the tremors and groaning like the sound of me unraveling is his favorite thing.

I flip us in one swift movement. My tongue takes a slow journey down his body, memorizing him the way he did me. James's fingers roam across every inch of skin he can reach, my name spilling from his lips between groans when words fail him.

"Darling," he rasps, "I'm holding on by one tiny thread of control."

"I've always wondered how far I could push you before that restraint finally snapped."

He groans, his hands tightening on my hips. "This... is my breaking point."

Slowly, I lower onto him, inch by inch. I feel every place where we become one, the exquisite stretch of my body accommodating him. A gasp spills from my lips.

"I may have overestimated those ten seconds. You feel—" He groans, voice wrecked.

"Save the grand declarations for after. I need you to move."

But he doesn't. His hand slips between us, rubbing me with firm, steady pressure. Each stroke winds me closer to the edge, until pleasure fractures through me in waves I can't contain. Then his control finally breaks. With a guttural groan, he thrusts up into me, burying himself deep. He presses his face in my neck, groaning a breathless, *"holy shit,"* as he follows me over the edge.

Tangled in sheets that smell of candle wax, sweat, and us—we stare. Breathe. A tear slips free. I trace his dimple with my fingertip as he wipes it away.

"I don't think a hundred years together would be enough." I sigh and relax into his arms.

"Hmmm. This Sydney, all sweet and cuddly, is new. Where did your claws go?" He pulls me close, my back to his chest, his hands gliding down my stomach.

"Multiple orgasms will do that." I laugh, then reach an arm around him, digging my nails into his back. "Want my claws to come out?"

"We may be forty, but I hope you're not planning on getting much sleep tonight."

"Hmmm. Anna will probably come looking for us eventually," I murmur, distracted by the path of his fingers.

"Will it be okay if I'm here? In bed with you?" He nips my ear and presses against me, already half-hard.

"Yes, love. We'll explain it if she asks. But she didn't seem to be troubled today." I turn to face him, needing to see his eyes for this moment. "I know technically we've only been together for a few days... I don't want to scare you. But I can't spend any more time apart. I don't know what that means with you in Boston and me in D.C. until everything is finalized."

"Sydney, I don't give a damn if it's been three days or three decades. I'm not going anywhere. I'll come to you. I can work remotely, and we can figure out the details from there. Together."

I kiss his temple, his dimple, down to his neck.

"I've spent my whole life waiting to feel like I was enough for someone to love. I didn't think I could trust anyone to be there when I turned around."

"Turn around all you want," he says, brushing a strand of hair from my face. "I'll still be here."

He closes his mouth over mine, and we don't talk for a while.

When exhaustion claims us, he slips his T-shirt over my head and pulls on sleep pants. I drift off into a deep, completely satisfied sleep, his heartbeat steady beneath my ear, our arms and limbs tangled together.

Sunlight reflects off the snow-covered tree tops, waking me to the stir of a small body nestled at my front, and solid warmth pressed to my back. Anna joined us as I predicted. James drapes his arm over us. I sigh with contentment, and Anna snuggles deeper into the warmth until realization hits.

She shoots up, eyes wide. "Is Unca J gonna live with us?"

The question is so straightforward in the way only children can be.

"Would that be okay with you if he did?"

"Yes! This is the best!" she squeals, bouncing on the bed, her nightgown twirling with her.

He chuckles, his voice thick with sleep as he presses a kiss to the back of my neck. Anna jumps between us, laughing and demanding attention. James leans over and tickles her until she's wriggling like a fish out of water. The sound of her giggles is a perfect soundtrack to this new beginning.

She escapes his grasp, bouncing across the bed. Life with a three-year-old leaves no room for mornings spent tangled in sheets. Anna, fully awake and ready to conquer the day, has no patience for her lovestruck mama and Unca J.

James tosses me some leggings from the floor, and I slip them on. "Come on, Bug. Let's get some breakfast."

I start the coffee and place a quick order for room service. Through the open bedroom door, I admire James sprawled in bed, one hand scrubbing his face, the other reaching for the spot still warm from my body. He catches my eye and gives me a slow, sleepy smile.

Anna starts jumping on the pullout bed. Laughing and throwing her toys in the air, she twirls in delight. I watch her joy and smile. I should tell her to stop, but seeing her this free, I don't want to clip her wings or ask her to be quieter or smaller. I want her to live big—even if that means jumping on the furniture.

"Who's making all that racket?" James stands in the doorway of the room, a scowl on his face.

Anna freezes. I study his expression and catch the mirth in his eyes, the mock sternness.

"I heard the tickle monster's on his way to make sure she yells even louder!" And the grin finally breaks as he runs toward her, tickling her belly. She squeals with delight, thrashing. He looks over at me with a smile a mile wide.

"I heard Mama wants to be tickled, Bug. Let's get her."

"Oh, no, you don't." I step away, but he's already there, throwing me over his shoulder and adding me to the pile on the bed. They both attack me, and I gasp between fits of laughter. It's not long before that damn snort escapes.

"I love that sound." He smiles, and the tickling finally relents. We lie there tangled together, breathing in our new reality.

"What should we do today?" I look between their expectant faces.

Anna tilts her head and says, "Cookies!"

I laugh. A light, carefree sound I barely recognize as my own. Of course, she wants a cookie. Because for her, life is simple. She has what I never did. A childhood wrapped in love and warmth, in comfort and safety, and yes, in cookies. The childhood I've dreamed of giving her.

The three of us lie there, hand in hand, bathed in the soft glow of the morning sun. Our family—not perfect or conventional—but ours. The one we found and fought for. The one we'll claim every day for the rest of our lives.

Through laughter and tears, joy and sorrow, we'll build something real.

Something beautifully messy.

Just like us.

2024: EPILOGUE

James's Perspective

We're here again, pulling into the Wallis family cabin driveway, greeted by the snow-covered peaks and ice sparkling between the logs.

Only this time, the right woman is beside me.

I bring Sydney's hand to my lips, pressing a kiss to her warm skin as I take her in. She's breathtaking—the way her brown hair grazes her chin, cut shorter like that New Year's, the soft lines at the corners of her eyes she complains about, but I adore. The full lips I can never resist. I promised always to worship her, and it's a promise I plan to keep.

This place witnessed our love—the stolen glances, the heartbreaks, and finally, the year that changed everything.

If it hadn't been for these walls, for what we fought through, I don't know if we'd be here. If I'd walked away, made the easy choice, I'm certain we'd both be miserable.

Instead, we're here. Together.

There's a weariness in Sydney's face, waves of anxiety rolling off her with every finger tap against her thigh, each slow, exaggerated breath. We're dropping Anna off to spend Christmas with her dad and his family. It's the first Christmas they won't be together.

"Ready?" I ask, tucking a strand of hair behind her ear.

"Sitting here won't make it any easier." She swipes a tear from the corner of her eye. "You ready, Bug?"

I reach back to unbuckle Anna and give her a high five. "Merry Christmas, kiddo. We'll see you in two days. Get ready for more presents and ice skating!"

"Will we go back home then?" Instead of high-fiving, she grabs my hand and squeezes. Her big eyes, so similar to her mom's, are glassy with unshed tears.

This kid is a champ, navigating her changing world with more resilience than any four-year-old should ever need.

"Yeah, Bug, we'll go home then."

She climbs into the front of the car, wraps her arms around me, and says, "Love you, Daddy J."

I squeeze her back. It never gets old hearing her call me that. She might not be mine by blood, but I love this little girl with everything I have.

After leaving Vermont, we didn't waste time. I relocated to D.C. while Sydney and Mason finalized the divorce. Once that was settled, we realized city life didn't suit us, and we moved close to my mom in the suburbs of Rochester. Quiet streets and open fields, trails for running, space for Anna to play—everything that felt right for us.

Sydney expanded her family law practice and continued working with domestic violence survivors alongside my mom. I work remotely now, traveling only when necessary.

We've settled into a fragile but peaceful co-parenting rhythm with Mason. Anna spends one weekend a month in D.C., and she loves her time with him. He might never be my favorite person, but he's shown up for Anna this year.

I wrap one arm around Anna and the other around Sydney, pulling them in for a tight hug. "We'll be okay," I reassure them both. "You have fun with your dad and everyone here, Bug. And we'll be back before you know it. We're staying down the road so your dad will call if you need anything."

"Is Santa going to bring me a cat?" Anna's teary eyes go wide and hopeful.

"Ha, good one, kid. No cats." They both love to tease me about my dislike of cats. "Didn't you ask Santa for a dog?"

"She sure did." Sydney smiles. "You'll get presents here from Santa tomorrow, and he'll deliver some to our house. Those you can open when we get back. Nana Vera promised to check and make sure a puppy wasn't locked in a box under the tree."

"Okay, Mama. Two days until you get me?" Anna slides over to Sydney's lap.

"Two days." Sydney kisses the top of Anna's head. She wipes her eyes and says, "Come on. Let's go say hi to everyone."

They get out of the car and walk toward the waiting arms of her dad and grandparents.

Anna, always our little ray of light, turns back, her curls bouncing as she runs straight into Sydney's arms for one more hug. Sydney holds her tight, whispering into her ear before letting go. Anna puts a hand over her eyes, warding off the sun, and waves to me before skipping into the cabin.

A tumble of curls hurtles down the stairs and tackles Sydney in a massive hug. Jules is the one person who truly understands the complicated, messy choices and who has supported her every step of the way. They laugh and chat their way to the car. Jules salutes me and hustles back inside.

Sydney's eyes are red-rimmed, and her mouth trembles. But she doesn't hide her pain. She lets me see the highs and lows. No longer swallowing it down, she knows I won't run when things get hard.

"Let's go to the resort," she says, leaning over the center console to press a kiss to my lips.

I thread my fingers through hers and steer us toward the village.

Her face lights up as she figures out where we're going. "Have I told you how much I love you today?"

"Doesn't hurt to say it again," I smirk, and she leans in to kiss the corner of my mouth, her lips finding my dimple.

"I'll show you properly how much I love you once we check in at the resort."

And with a wink, she pulls me in through the bookstore doorway.

The store has been transformed into another holiday wonderland. A castle rises from the center of the train table, surrounded by tiny figurines. Elves and fairies, dwarves and knights, are all poised for adventure. It's whimsical and absurd, and absolutely perfect.

"We'll bring her here before we leave," she says, swiping at her eyes. "Anna will love this."

I live for the days when I can get under her skin and make her eyes flash that thin gold ring. That's when I know her claws are about to come out. But being the person she turns to for comfort? I hold her face in my hands and let my thumbs wipe away her tears.

"Did you ask Santa for books, or can we pick out some ourselves?" I joke, wrapping her in my arms.

"Careful, or you might find Mr. Whiskers sitting under the tree instead of the puppy." She flicks my nose and wanders off.

She passes the rows of books, fingers tracing spines, eyes scanning titles, and I can tell her mind is somewhere else. I grab a few books she'll love. I can't help it; learning her taste in stories was the first language we ever spoke fluently.

At the register, she looks around, eyes wide, and says, "That's it?"

"What do you mean?" I play dumb, though I have a good idea. She's not subtle when she's holding her breath, waiting for something.

"Are we leaving now?" She scans the shop again, her gaze darting from the train table to the counter.

"Did you want to grab something for Anna?"

"No...No, I'm fine," she stammers, already turning toward the door.

"Sydney, did you think I was going to propose?" I ask, holding back a Cheshire grin.

She shrugs, eyes dropping to her boots. "The thought crossed my mind."

I tuck a finger under her chin, tilting her face to mine. "I thought about it," I confess. "But I knew you'd see it coming. And I want to surprise you. Catch you off guard. Keep you guessing."

"You're impossible."

And I kiss her right there, slow and sure, in the middle of the shop, where anyone can see. No more hiding. No more pretending. I'll never tire of this, loving her out loud.

"We could skip the whole wedding circus, you know. Just go to the courthouse when we get back. I'd marry you anywhere."

"Funny you should say that. Should I return this?" I reach into my coat pocket and pull out a small velvet box.

Her eyes go wide as I lower to my knees, not the traditional one-knee pose, but fully down, both knees to the ground, a man in reverence, offering everything I have. Not because I think I need to, but because I want to. Her breath catches, her hands trembling at her sides as I hold out the box.

"Sydney," I begin, my throat tight, "our road to this moment wasn't smooth. Hell, sometimes we drove straight off a cliff. But even in the mess, even when we were standing on opposite sides of everything, I knew. I knew we were meant to find our way here. To each other."

I pause because I want her to see it, the truth in my face, the years in my voice.

"I know you don't believe in fairy tales, but I promise you this: I will be here with you for every dark and twisty day. For every laugh, every fight, every impossible moment life throws our way. I want all of it."

A tear falls down my cheek, but I don't wipe it away. I take a breath before asking, "Will you marry me?"

For a heartbeat, she doesn't move. Tears fall from her eyes, and she drops to her knees. She kisses me the way a woman kisses a man when every wall has crumbled, when every mask has been stripped away, and there is nothing left but love and truth and the courage to start again.

"I can't believe you fucking did that," she laughs, her forehead pressed to mine.

"Is that a yes? I need the words."

She pulls back, her eyes shining with tears and mischief and joy. "Yes, James Navarro. I will marry you."

We collapse into each other, laughing and crying, still kneeling in the middle of the store while customers cheer and clap around us.

She reaches into her pocket, pulling out a small square box. "I was going to wait until tomorrow to give you this. But since we're doing public surprises now..."

There's something in her expression that has me holding my breath. Her fingers linger, trembling just slightly, as she passes me the box.

I untie the ribbon, my hands not as steady as they should be, and I lift the lid. Inside is a sonogram picture.

Our baby.

Sydney's voice is soft, but her smile is wide and glowing. "You know how I wasn't feeling great last week? I went to the doctor and... ta-da!" She throws her hands up, a playful, triumphant gesture that makes me laugh through the sting of tears.

I hardly notice the people around us. The cheering fades into white noise.

All I see is her. All I feel is this.

I pull her close, holding her as if she's the only thing keeping me upright. Maybe she is. Maybe she always has been.

"Are you serious?" My voice cracks.

"Well," she shrugs, "we have all that space at home. All those bedrooms. Gotta do something with them."

I laugh, loud and full and so damn happy I don't even know what to do with it all. We weren't trying, but we weren't careful either—and at our age, the odds were long.

Brushing my lips to her ear, I whisper, "I fucking love you."

In the middle of the bookstore, surrounded by stories and strangers and the smell of paper, I feel the weight of the past dissolve into nothing. Every choice we made, every heartbreak, every fight, every lonely night, led us here.

To this.

To our family and the kind of love you fight for. The kind that doesn't flinch when everything burns and holds each other closer despite the scars.

The best parts of our story are only beginning.

PLAYLIST

Music weaves through the narrative as a means of exploring connection, allowing lyrics to communicate feelings that the characters struggle to express directly.

Here are the songs that help tell the story within these pages.

Woman - Kesha

Speak to Me - Ari Lennox

Good as Hell - Lizzo

God Rest Ye Merry Gentlemen - Tinashe

Delicate - Taylor Swift

Partition - Beyonce

Buttons - The Pussycat Dolls

Dancewithme - Maxwell

Tennessee Whiskey - Chris Stapleton

Flow - Sade

Boss Bitch - Doja Cat

Make You Feel - Janelle Monáe

Needed Me - Rihanna

Caught Up - Usher

All of Me - John Legend

ReaDer QuesTIons

1. How do Sydney's choices evolve across the five Christmases?

2. Do you believe Sydney and James's connection is inevitable or a product of circumstance?

3. In what ways does motherhood reshape Sydney's understanding of love, sacrifice, and self-worth?

4. How does the theme of being *seen* play out differently through Sydney's relationships with Mason, James, and Jules?

5. What role do Margaret and Vera play in Sydney's healing from her childhood neglect and mother's suicide?

6. How does the cabin function as both sanctuary and pressure cooker?

7. Do you believe the family ignored what was happening between James and Sydney or did they truly not see the tension building?

8. If Jules's support had been more tepid, would Sydney have made different choices?

9. What clues does the text provide about Ivy's level of awareness regarding

James and Sydney's connection? How do you explain her actions and responses?

10. How do you interpret Mason's escalating attempts to control Sydney? Do you see him as someone fighting for his family or someone who views Sydney as his possession?

11. How do loyalty and silence function within the Wallis family dynamic?

12. What role did gender expectations play in how each character navigated desire, responsibility, and truth?

13. How do the gaps between Christmases function in the story? What happens in the time we don't see?

14. Sydney calls herself the villain at one point. Do you agree with her assessment? Is there a clear villain?

want to read more?

For a bonus day with Sydney and James set a few years in the future,
grab *Beautifully Here*, a free novella,
by visiting www.noelleeverly.com
or subscribing to my newsletter here (ebook).

***

Ready to find out what happened at the cabin after Sydney and James left?
Turn the page to read Chapter One of *Wildly Ivy*.

WILDLY IVY

Chapter 1

My ex-fiancé walks out the front door holding hands with my sister-in-law.

He was the man I had imagined sharing a fairy-tale-perfect future with. The future that, since I was a little girl, the world told me adulthood looked like. Marriage. Babies. The house in the suburbs.

I should be in tears, right? But my eyes are dry.

Maybe that future wasn't what I wanted after all.

As the door shuts, a gust of cold wind whips through the room, jangling the Christmas tree ornaments, threatening to send them crashing to the ground—wistful angels crocheted by tiny fingers and glass ornaments filled with holiday ribbons from long ago. Remnants of when life was simple, when solutions to problems were easy.

Nothing is simple now.

What started like so many recent Christmas mornings, with awkward glances and everyone pretending not to notice the thing burning between James and Sydney, finally exploded.

My question—

Sydney's confirmation—

Mason's confrontation—

My parents huddle around Mason, speaking in hushed, serious tones. Tom has pulled Jules into a corner, wrapping his arms around her as she wavers between anger and tears, ready to tear into Mason the minute my parents release him. Sydney is her closest friend. And she didn't hold back, revealing the truly horrid way Mason had been treating her.

I stand apart from it all, watching my family fracture in real time. Everyone choosing sides, processing shock, dealing with their own guilt about what they missed.

A laugh escapes me before I swallow it down. This is so absurd. The whole spectacle. Really, I'm so damn tired of swallowing down my thoughts and feelings.

Years of private tears and silent assumptions led to the moment when I couldn't keep it in any longer. I had been watching them fall in love. And this morning, I asked. Breaking the unwritten rule that we somehow all agreed to follow. Don't name it. Don't ask the question you don't want the answer to.

Ignoring it meant our worlds wouldn't be rocked. We wouldn't have to address the real issues.

"Ivy..." Jules's voice comes out soft, cautious. It makes my skin crawl. She walks toward me now. "You don't have to do this. You're allowed to be upset."

I tilt my head, raise an eyebrow. "Jules, it's not like you to pull your punches. Don't handle me with kid gloves. I'm fine."

Looking around, I realize everyone expected me to break, to dissolve into mascara-streaked tears. Possibly reenact my breakdown after the cancelled wedding. It wasn't my finest moment. But honestly?

This morning, I watched Sydney—a woman that I've admired and been in awe of since I first met her—look us each in the eye, even her husband, and basically say: *Fuck it, I'm done living someone else's life.*

Maybe it's time I did the same.

"This is your fault," Mason says, pointing at me. "You couldn't just leave it alone."

"Fuck off, Mason. I can't deal with you right now," Jules says, stepping in front of me. Her face is set in stone.

"Of course you're defending them. Your perfect little bestie gets to blow up my family and walk away while I'm the villain." His voice cracks slightly on the last word.

"Mason, you need to stop right now. Our conversation is not over and this isn't helping." Dad wraps a hand around Mason's shoulder. "Let's go to the basement."

Mason finally has the sense to drop his eyes to the floor and follow Dad.

"I'm going to take Beck and Leo to the skating rink for a while." Tom kisses Jules on the cheek. "You okay?"

She nods and turns the full force of her gaze on me. Jules, ten years older, cast herself as my third parent the moment I was born. My actual parents, who spent most of my childhood in full-on "bonus round" parenting mode, were softer, more indulgent. For years, I was the center of attention by default, not because I demanded it, but because I was the last one left at home.

Jules exchanges a look with our mom, the kind that makes me feel about seven years old. My sister, half chaos master and half family therapist, walks to the kitchen and comes back with the coffee pot and bottles of whiskey and Baileys.

"Enough bullshit," she says, then sets to work refilling our mugs with something strong enough to have this out. "You don't have to pretend to be *fine*. I'm so sick of that word."

"No." My voice comes out steady. "What's hitting me isn't them. It's me. Why did I stay when I *knew*, when I felt it every time he looked at her?"

"There's no guidebook for this, honey. No right or wrong way to figure out what comes next. Whatever you decide, we're here." Mom reaches forward to grab my hand.

I let out a slow breath, my voice quieter now. "I kept thinking... if I could just be more polished. The kind of woman I thought he wanted, then maybe he'd look at me the way Dad looks at you, Mom. Or the way Tom looks at you, Jules. I wanted that kind of love so badly. I thought that was what I needed to make life start."

They both start to speak, but I lift a hand, stopping them.

"Wait, let me just get this out." Because now that I've started, the truth won't let go. "I ignored every instinct screaming that something was wrong. I twisted myself into someone I wasn't. And for the past year, I've just been stuck. That's what I can't forgive. Not him. Me."

Jules leans in, her voice fierce and sure. "Listen to me. The real Ivy, the one who laughs like a hyena and creates dirty Christmas carols, is way more lovable than the Stepford act you put on the last few years. I miss her too."

"God, and it wasn't like he asked me to do it. It was all me. Like I couldn't accept he would be with me, the real me."

"Life isn't about not making mistakes. It's about learning from them." Jules arches an eyebrow, taunting me to contradict her.

"Well, this was one big fucking mistake." I throw my hands in the air, then catch the look on my mom's face. "Sorry, Mom. But I think this deserves a 'fucking' attached to it."

"I don't want to sound callous, but you're handling this surprisingly well. Do you think you didn't really love him?" Mom asks, tilting her head to really look at me.

"I think... I loved the idea of him."

Mom squeezes my hand, there's no judgment in her eyes, just understanding. "At least now you'll know the difference when real love comes along."

"No love for me. I need... a break from relationships. Maybe just have some fun for a bit. Get out of Boston. Be on my own."

"Ives, I'm here for whatever you want. If it wasn't Christmas, I'd offer to take you down to the tavern for a night out, but if you want to get drunk, I'm here for it. We have plenty of booze," Jules says. "If you need to scream, ugly-cry, throw a fucking ham at the wall, I'm all in. Just tell me what you need."

A laugh barks out, loud and uncontrolled. "Tempting, but I have a better idea." I grab the remote from the sectional and pull up HBO. "How about an Eras Tour singalong marathon? I could use some Taylor energy right now."

"Fuck. Yes!" Jules pumps her fist into the air, like we've just declared war.

"You girls have fun. My old bones won't be able to keep up and I need to finish talking with your brother." Mom pulls me into a tight hug, then heads toward the basement, carrying the weight of everything in her slow, careful steps.

Never one to let a moment simmer too long, Jules snatches a champagne bottle from the fridge and pops it with theatrical flair. The cork ricochets off a cabinet. "This one's for Ivy Fucking Wallis, officially stepping into her Reputation Era."

After several Eras and a lot of questionable choreography, I spin dramatically, my throw blanket billowing around me like a witch's cloak. "You know what? Taylor is officially my spirit guide. This whole tour? It's the ultimate fuck-you anthem to every man who ever underestimated her. Fuck you, *Joe*. Fuck you, *James*. Fuck you, to the man!"

"Ohhh yeah," Jules cackles. "And don't forget her best revenge, finding herself a football stallion. Maybe you need your own NFL rebound?"

"Right. Like there's some emotionally evolved football player just waiting for me."

Jules clinks her glass against mine. "Babe, we're manifesting. You never know."

I fling my arms upward, half-drunk and fully outraged. "Two years, Jules. It's been two years since anyone's touched me *below the neck*. I'm basically a nun. Who stays engaged to a man who won't touch her? God, I'm so pathetic."

"Forget him, Ives. You need to clear out the cobwebs ASAP. Book a vacation with a side of dick delivery service."

"Do they list that in the amenities? 'Ocean view, bottomless mimosas, complimentary penis'?"

Jules pounds her fist on the cushion, laughing so hard she's wheezing. "Five stars, would highly recommend!"

Before I can second-guess my liquid courage, I grab my phone. Outside, snow gently blankets the cabin, but on my screen, another world unfolds: one filled with turquoise water, sun-drenched beaches, and infinity pools practically begging for me.

The Book Now button flashes red, daring me to hesitate. For a moment, I do.

Jules leans over my shoulder, whispering encouragement like the bad-influence fairy godmother she's always been. "Do it. For the cobwebs. For yourself."

I slam my finger down. "I'm going to Cabo!"

The earliest availability is ten days away, an eternity and a heartbeat all at once. Cabo isn't just a vacation. It's a siren call. A pull I can't name, toward a version of me I haven't met yet. It's time to burn the perfect-Ivy playbook and finally step into the daylight.

ACKNOWLEDGEMENTS

Wow. My first novel. One night last winter, I woke with a sudden question: what happens when your inner life looks drastically different than the one you're living out loud? The story of Sydney came out in a flurry of 3 AM writing as the world of the cabin, Wallises, and James slowly emerged, fueled by coffee and a desire to tell a story that doesn't fit in a neat box.

I couldn't have brought this story to life without an amazing team.

My husband and kids, first and foremost. Thank you for your endless patience and understanding when I said "I just need five more minutes" for the tenth time that day.

My parents who never tried to clip my wings even when it led me hundreds of miles away.

My beta readers: Chelsea, Kolbe, Mary Beth, Nicole, Crystal, Mira, Kelsey, Sheila and Nora. Thank you for the time spent reading and answering my incessant questions. Your ruthless feedback, including Kindle throws, made this story better.

Kim, you're an editing goddess. Your editorial vision shaped this story in ways I couldn't have imagined. Thank you for seeing what it could become and pushing me to tell every messy, necessary part. I would be lost without you.

Mindy, your early developmental edits were critical. Thank you for being Ivy's first advocate. The story is so much better for it.

Raina, thank you for helping me bring the vision of the cover to life. It's gorgeous!

And dear readers, if you've made it this far, THANK YOU! I hope you stick around because we'll see all of these characters again.

ABOUT THE AUTHOR

Noelle Everly is an American author writing stories about strong heroines navigating life's complexities and the compelling partners who challenge them. *Beautifully Messy* is her debut novel, the first in the Wallis Sisters series—exploring the messy reality of choosing yourself even while falling in love.

A voracious reader since childhood, she once set a goal to read three hundred books during fifth grade, Noelle brings her lifelong love of storytelling to contemporary women's fiction. She lives outside Rochester, New York with her husband, two children, and their pets. Noelle can often be found with a hot cup of coffee and a good book, or running along beautiful trails.